PRAISE FOR DIANN THORNLEY
AND *GANWOLD'S CHILD*

"A very good first novel. In most ways, it seems to fall within that SF subgenre that can only be called military bildungsroman in which a youngster plunges into a demanding military environment and is forced to find out just how good he is. Thornley subverts and transforms that subgenre at every turn.

"But the strength of the book is in Thornley's focus on the the alien society and and the way that it caused Tristan to see the world differently from other humans—even as he also sees the world differently from the ganan. The ganan friend who accompanies him on his journey is a constant source of strength and self-control for him; and yet he is also something of an albatross, keeping Tristan from fully assimilating to human culture.

"As for the military speak, the fact is that unlike most writers who toss that stuff in for fake authenticity, Thornley was career military and she uses that language because that's the way military people express their military ideas economically. This novel is exemplary for showing how the effective military mind really works—you'll find no romantic military nonsense here."

—Orson Scott Card, *The Magazine of Fantasy & Science Fiction*

"Thornley's first novel begins a military SF series set in a far future universe of alien slavers and bold fighting men and women.... The author's skill in bringing space combat to life provides strong focus.... Well-written."

—*Library Journal*

"Thornley's highly respectable debut inaugurates yet another saga laid in a future universe, The Unified Worlds.... Plenty of action ... and wit. Good, solid action SF."

—*Booklist*

GANWOLD'S CHILD

DIANN THORNLEY

A TOM DOHERTY ASSOCIATES BOOK
NEW YORK

This is a work of fiction. All the characters and events portrayed in this book are fictitious, and any resemblance to real people or events is purely coincidental.

GANWOLD'S CHILD

Copyright © 1995 by Diann Thornley

All rights reserved, including the right to reproduce this book, or portions thereof, in any form.

A Tor Book
Published by Tom Doherty Associates, Inc.
175 Fifth Avenue
New York, NY 10010

Tor Books on the World Wide Web:
http://www.tor.com

Tor® is a registered trademark of Tom Doherty Associates, Inc.

ISBN: 0-812-55095-1
Library of Congress Card Catalog Number: 95-5213

First edition: May 1995
First mass market edition: June 1996

Printed in the United States of America

0 9 8 7 6 5 4 3 2

For my parents,
Ray and Joy Thornley,
and all of my siblings,
for having to endure
my overactive imagination.

ACKNOWLEDGMENTS

Over the years it took me to write this book, many people in many areas contributed in one way or another to its completion. However, I owe particular thanks to First Lieutenant John T. Curtis, Captain Bradley K. Jones, Captain Dan Bartlett, Captain Daniel Smith, Lieutenant Colonel Dave Madden, Lieutenant Colonel Max D. Remley, and Colonel Mike Self (Reserve), my fellow officers in the U.S. Air Force; and Lieutenant Commander Warren Jederberg and HM3 Tim Moore, U.S. Navy, for all of their constructive criticism and technical assistance; to Elizabeth "Liz" Moosman, R.N., for her expertise and coaching on the medical aspects; and to my longtime friends and fellow writers, Marcha Fox, Mark Rhodes, and M. Shayne Bell, for their long-distance encouragement and moral support.

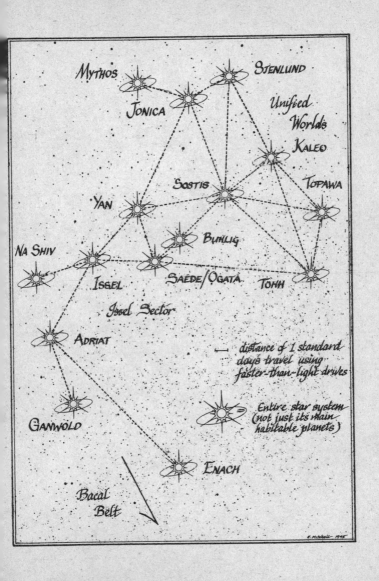

MYTHOS

STENLUND

JONICA

Unified
Worlds

KALEO

SOSTIS

TOPAWA

YAN

BUHLIG

NA SHIV

ISSEL

SAEDE/OGATA

TOHH

Issel Sector

ADRIAT

— distance of 1 standard
days travel using
faster-than-light drives

Entire star system
(not just its main
habitable planets)

GANWOLD

ENACH

Bacal
Belt

E. Mitchell 1995

PROLOGUE

Darcie didn't expect to live.

With the hand she could move enough to reach them, she tore the unit and command patches from her uniform shirt—left only her nametag, rank, and flight surgeon's insignia. She drew out the chain from around her neck, yanked off the two crystal pendants hanging with her ID tags, shoved them into the corner behind her.

"Mama?" The child stirred on her lap, trying to push himself back. "Why are—"

She put a finger to his lips, her other hand cupping his head to prevent its bumping the metal bulkhead. "Hush, Tris."

She could barely whisper. She sat on the bottom of a locker meant only for a pressure suit—one of four lockers in the maintenance compartment—with the toddler held snug between her body and her drawn-up knees.

Outside noises reached her: the roar of engines crescendoing toward thrust into lightskip—the fourth attempt.

She braced her head back in the corner behind the pressure suit, hugged Tristan to her breast and locked her teeth.

Clumsy masuki! she thought. *They won't have a catch left if they strain the transport to disintegration first!*

Lightskip warning horns screamed through the corridor outside the maintenance compartment; the vessel shook, groaned. In the turbulence, the child threw up.

Darcie swallowed against her own nausea at the sour smell of it. Wiped his mouth and the front of her uniform. "Don't cry, little soldier," she whispered. "Here now, hold on to me."

The horns wound down as they had before and she relaxed her brace against the plasmic sensation of entering lightskip.

She waited what seemed hours in the hot darkness. Her legs grew cramped, then numb from their position and the toddler's weight on them. She tried to shift a little, to ease them, and pain arced up her back.

Her thoughts tumbled over each other without any order. She thought of Lujan, her mate, waiting for them at their destination. Thought of the way he had kissed her good-bye months ago on Topawa.

The locker was growing hotter, almost stifling, despite the slits in its door. She wondered, in an oddly detached way, how long it would take for her and Tristan to smother. Wondered what Lujan would do when he learned they were dead.

Her reverie was shattered by the tremor of explosions. *Shooting?* she wondered. She heard the transport's minimal weaponry reply, and then footfalls: running, thudding up and down the corridor beyond her hiding place.

There was another hour's lull before the craft rocked at the impact of electromagnets, shuddered in the whine of winch cables. She started at volleys of light arms' fire and bootfalls ringing through the passages. Armored bootfalls this time, not scuffing masuk footsteps.

Catching her lower lip in her teeth, she began to stroke the child's hair.

The maintenance compartment's door slammed open.

Voices reached her—two or three of them, only meters away—but their words, modulated by their helmets' electronics, weren't understandable. Boots trod the circumference of the maintenance compartment. Over her pulse in her ears, she detected an oscillating hum.

She pressed a hand tight over Tristan's mouth and bit off a groan: she had used lifeform sensors before; the locker wasn't constructed to jam them.

The hum shot up to a sharp whine; the boots stopped outside her enclosure. She heard an order—

—and then banging. Metal clashing on metal until she thought her head would split and Tristan's sudden wail would be drowned in its clamor. When the locker door tore away, she stared up at three armored shapes silhouetted against the dull light.

Dominion legionnaires.

The nearest one shoved aside the pressure suit, seized her by the wrist and hauled her to her feet. She staggered, numb legs nearly buckling, and almost lost her hold on her child. From behind tinted helmet visors the other two soldiers let their gazes roam her body.

Darcie jerked her wrist from her captor's gauntlet and wrapped both arms around Tristan. "This is illegal, you know! It's been a month since the hostilities ended at Enach, and the talks are—"

"I don't think so," said the squad leader. "Where've you been for the last few years?"

She glared at him. Forced herself not to let her breath catch when one soldier stooped to search the locker. Straightening, he handed something to his sergeant. "Look at these."

The crystal hologram pendants. Her joining portrait and a picture of Lujan and Tristan.

The sergeant held them up to the light and she saw his eyes widen behind his visor. "Yeah, I thought the nametag looked familiar," he said. "The colonel will probably promote us for this!" He tucked the holodiscs into his utility belt and reached for her arm. "It's my duty to inform you, Lieutenant Dartmuth, that at no time in the last nine years has the Sector General recognized the governments of the Unified Worlds. He sealed the Accords under duress, so we're not breaking a legitimate treaty."

She evaded his hand. "Nine years? Surely you can lie better than—"

She cut herself off when she remembered the futile attempts to make lightskip. The masuk slavers must have succeeded at entering a time track, whether or not they had crossed space. She questioned the legionnaire with her look.

"The Enach Accords weren't ratified as easily as the Unified Worlds had hoped," he said. "They didn't fail as completely as Sector General Renier had hoped, either. You may be able to make that up to him."

"Renier?" Darcie stiffened. "Sector General?"

The squad leader smiled. "I wonder what kind of plea bargain the Unified Worlds might be willing to make in exchange for you."

"It won't work, you know."

"We'll see." His smile turned grim. "Move." He shoved her shoulder, indicating the corridor. "Maybe the war isn't over yet."

She yielded, her thoughts racing ahead. The transport had a cross-corridor aft of the bridge that had an emergency shield door. . . .

Hugging the child to her body, one hand rubbing up and down his back in reassurance, she set her teeth. One soldier strode before her, two behind. There were no restraints, no firearms ready to hand; they appeared to trust her feigned submission. But a glance back showed one soldier's hand resting on the hilt of a boarding knife—one of a dozen strapped naked about his hips like armor's tasses made of steel teeth. Boarding knives could be used as throwing weapons, she knew.

Several members of the crew lay in the corridor. She recognized Rahb Heike, the ship's captain, and recoiled. He lay facedown in his own blood. Masuk work.

A hand pushed at her back when she paused. She stumbled, stepping in Heike's blood as she caught her balance, and moved around another bloodied body. Lieutenant Baraq. He also had died before the legionnaires arrived. She swallowed dryness and turned her head away.

She felt brief satisfaction at spotting several masuki sprawled in the corridor. The Unified soldiers had died fighting. But the ship was too empty, of both military personnel and civilians.

Light from the intersecting corridor spread a square across the concourse deck ahead. She shifted Tristan to her left arm and curled her right fist, keeping her head lowered.

Ten paces . . .

She lunged left into the cross-corridor, her right fist punching the manual trigger on its bulkhead. The shield door dropped behind her with a *whoosh* that was lost in a crunch and her pursuer's garbled scream. She pressed Tristan's face to her shoulder and forced herself not to look back.

The cross-passage opened on one parallel to the corridor she had sealed. It led to the lifepods—if they hadn't already been jettisoned.

She pressed herself to the bulkhead to listen for pursuers and to peer into the corridor. It was empty, up and down, except for the smoke-obscured shapes of bodies on the deck. She tried to set the child on his feet, to rest her arm, but he clung to her, wide-eyed with confusion and the recognition of her fear. Darcie smoothed his hair, kissed his forehead. "Come on, then, little soldier," she said, collecting him again, and slipped into the passage.

Smoke from screen grenades stung her eyes, making them run and blurring her vision. She stumbled over a body and paused, panting. It was one of the surface troopers, a young man she didn't recognize. Flung beyond his hand lay an energy pistol. She stooped to snatch it up when bootfalls echoed up the corridor behind her, and glanced at the power cell in its grip. Its light still burned.

Five or six armored figures emerged through the haze. She leveled the E-gun, squeezed the trigger. Its bolt seared off the bulkhead into the knot of oncoming men. A cry rang back to her as one of them crumpled; another, too close to avoid, sprawled over him as the rest sprang for cover. Darcie turned for the lift.

It was jammed. The door stood half-open, the platform suspended between decks. She glanced over her shoulder. Two armored shapes were still closing on her, steel glinting in their hands. One drew his arm back, balancing blade and haft for the throw. She lifted the pistol.

Her shot went wide but her foes cowed, weapons still poised. Her hand was too small for the firearm's grip and weight, and the other one ached from carrying the child, but she fired until the power light began to dim. With her back to the bulkhead, she sidled toward the door to the emergency ladder. Its portal yielded to her shoulder's pressure and she ducked into darkness, onto a clanging platform at the top of a spiraling stair. A shot through the door mechanism sealed her off from the legionnaires.

She stood still for several moments, panting and letting her eyes adjust to the dark. The toddler's weight shot fire through her arm. She tried to put him down and fumbled the pistol, almost dropping it.

Her breath caught when she heard a scraping sound below her, several meters away. She stiffened, listening.

Nothing.

Nothing but her heartbeat, and Tristan sniffling on her shoulder.

Nothing but darkness, and the lifepods only meters away. . . .

Finger on the pistol trigger, she stretched out a foot, probing for the platform's edge and the first step. There would be twelve. She picked her way slowly, leaning on the rail, eyes and ears and weapon searching the blackness.

Three . . . four . . . five . . .

She nearly missed a step when pounding began at the door above.

Eight . . . nine . . . ten . . .

Something tall and odorous clamped long fingernails into her shoulders, dragging her off the step and against its hirsute torso. A masuk slaver. She didn't scream; even the gasp died when she felt steel pressed to her throat. The masuk snarled a command at her, but the child's crying made it inaudible. Darcie didn't struggle. She only had to twist her weapon hand a fraction, only had to squeeze the trigger once.

Her captor's blade grazed the side of her neck and clattered unseen to the deck as he lurched backward. Steadying herself, she felt a warm trickle roll down the base of her throat and into the neck of her uniform shirt.

It's not serious, she told herself. *He missed the carotid and jugular. It'll stop. Ignore it; it'll stop!*

She stepped around the corpse, reached the first lifepod bay. A red light glowed above its sealed entry hatch: it had been jettisoned.

Red lights burned over the second and third and fourth bays also.

"No!" she whispered. "He couldn't have launched them all yet!"

A green ready light beckoned above the fifth. She dropped the pistol, set Tristan on his feet. He reached up to her, sobbing for the security of her arms, but she ignored him. Her hands shook, muscles refusing to obey when she tried to grip the hatch handle; she tugged several times before it turned and the hatch shot open.

The entry lock was low enough that she had to duck. She retrieved the pistol, took the child by the hand and guided him ahead of her. "Come now, Tris. I'm right here behind you."

Inside, she pulled the hatch closed. Heard the cover suck into its seal and its three bolts slam into place.

Sinking into the nearest passenger seat, she gathered the toddler onto her lap and didn't move for several minutes. She just sat until the adrenaline receded and her quivering gave way to limpness. She stroked Tristan's hair and let him sniffle out his trauma on her breast.

When he relaxed, she rose stiffly, still cradling him, and moved forward to the control console.

It was simple: a trio of screens and an ignition switch. Two lines glowed on the center screen:

ALL ESCAPE VEHICLE SYSTEMS ARE AUTOMATED.
TO LAUNCH, PULL IGNITION SWITCH.

Darcie placed the child in the seat beside hers.

"Hold me, Mama!" he begged, stretching up his arms to her.

She shook her head. "You're quite safe there," she said as she closed the acceleration bars about him. "Just sit still for a bit."

Secured in the command chair, she steadied herself with a few deep breaths, recalling flying tours with Lujan, and reached for the ignition switch.

"Mama?" said Tristan.

She patted him. "Sit tight, little one. We're going now."

There was a tremor when she threw the switch, a roar as rockets fired and sudden acceleration shoved her back into the contoured chair. Then the thunder fell behind, the swoon passed, the pressure lifted. Darcie opened her eyes and glanced down at Tristan.

She smiled at his expression. "It's all right now, Tris," she said. "We've escaped!"

She looked forward, and her breath caught.

Before the viewpanes, a half-shadowed world hung in an unfamiliar starfield.

"My word, what's this?" she said.

She eyed the navigation screen at her right.

Data appeared line by line down its right margin. Green characters and graphics displayed the coordinates of the mothership when the pod had been launched, the pod's present velocity and trajectory, the distance to and characteristics of its projected landing site.

"Korot system," she said, half-aloud. "The masuki did cross more than time, then—and small wonder we were boarded! We're practically orbiting Korot's only inhabitable planet, and it's full of Dominion agricolonies!"

Her gaze rested on the emergency locator transponder. Slipped back to the nav screen. "A nine-year timeskip," she said. She pressed her face into her hands, kneading forehead and temples with her fingertips. "Nine years! We're legally lost by now! And the legionnaires are tracking us, most likely."

In another moment she drew the energy pistol from the stowage bin under the command chair.

She fingered the transponder's case for the catches, fumbled it open to bare its microcircuitry. Taking the pistol by the barrel, she smashed its handgrip over and over into gauzy components. Sparks leaped at her fingers; a bitter tendril of smoke coiled out.

Beside her, Tristan said, "Mama! You broke it!"

"Yes, I did," she said. "Now the legionnaires won't be able to follow us."

Not so easily, at least.

When Tristan fell asleep, Darcie inventoried the lifepod's equipage. Releasing her acceleration bars, she pushed herself from the seat and maneuvered in zero g. In overhead compartments and beneath the seats she found lightweight thermal blankets, water containers and food packets, a medical case, a large-display survival manual, and tools. There were enough supplies to support ten adults for about ten days.

She paused once, orienting herself to look out beyond the cockpit. Korot's inhabitable world, all beige and blue, filled the viewpanes. Ganwold. The nav screen showed the lifepod almost half a million kilometers from the planet. At its present velocity, the pod would begin its landing cycle in approximately twenty-eight standard hours and touch down near the equator about an hour after that.

Darcie awoke in dimness when the beeping started. She turned her head and saw an amber light blinking for her attention. There was a message on the center screen:

APPROACHING LANDING ORBIT.
PUT ON G-PANTS.

She took two pairs from stowage under the seats and pulled on her own before dressing the child. The pants dwarfed him, but she cinched the waistband snug enough to serve the purpose.

"It's too big!" Tristan said, kicking feet lost in the legs.

"It won't be when we begin to land," Darcie said. "It'll puff up like a bubble and squeeze you so that you won't faint."

"What's 'faint,' Mama?"

She smiled, securing his acceleration bars. "It's when you get very dizzy and fall asleep for a bit."

A new message flashed on the screen:

ALL LANDING SYSTEMS GO.
PLEASE REMAIN SECURED IN SEATS UNTIL
LANDING CYCLE IS COMPLETED.

And the braking rockets fired.

Bracing herself in the chair, Darcie felt the initial deceleration, a mounting pressure from beneath. The nav screen's graphics vanished and were replaced by digital readouts: altitude, speed, and time until touchdown. She watched the numerals change, watched velocity drop from seventeen thousand kilometers an hour to fifteen, twelve, ten, eight . . .

The roar of the brake rockets crescendoed as the pod passed through the outer atmosphere and into denser layers. The elements tried to embrace the craft, screamed at its heat, and shook it.

"Mama, hold me?" The toddler tried to reach out to her, his blue eyes very round.

"Not just now, Tris. You're safer where you are." Darcie slid out a hand for him to grip and said, "Look at the panes. Watch now."

They were shaded with the faint red of heat made visible, and they brightened, paling through pink to orange-red and finally white. Like riding the tide of a dawn, she thought with a sense of awe that something beautiful could come from this horror.

Twenty-five minutes from touchdown, directional thrusters fired. The pod oriented itself for landing, decelerating still more. Tristan whimpered with motion sickness, and Darcie, caressing his sweaty face, put back her own head, eyes closed, and breathed deeply.

She felt momentum ebbing under the rockets' roar. The digital clock indicated twenty-one minutes until touchdown. The pod pierced a bank of clouds like a pebble dropped into a pond.

Eighteen minutes.

Twelve . . .

A pattern of blue lights on the left screen showed activation of landing gear; Darcie heard subtle clunks and pneumatic wheezes as the gear locked. Beyond the cockpit's viewpanes, the mantle of vapor was half-lit by the aureole glow of the pod's reentry heat.

Nine minutes.

Five minutes.

Two . . .

Darcie felt the final scream of thrusters like a storm shaking the craft, felt a jolt and a settling before the thunder died and left her in silence. It was a moment before she realized that the lifepod had landed.

Environmental sensors fed data to her left screen: atmospheric content and pressure, temperature, gravity, wind direction and velocity. All suitable for human habitation. Darcie released her breath and turned her gaze on the dark beyond the viewpanes. "Nighttime," she said, and shoved herself out of the command chair. Her body's sudden weight surprised her. "Come now, Tris. Let's get you out of those trousers and go before the legionnaires come looking for us."

She was gathering supplies into a duffle when something on the console beeped. She turned around.

A message blinked across the left screen:

LIFEFORMS APPROACHING VEHICLE.
DISTANCE APPROX 100 METERS.

"Legionnaires already?" She moved to the console, switched on the visual monitor.

The five images on the screen were quadrupeds. Almost a meter high at the shoulder, she estimated, with eyes like embers and a slinking gait. Canine hunters. Jous, the computer library called them.

She bit her lower lip.

"Mama?" said Tristan.

"There aren't any legionnaires," she said. "Not yet. We're better off to stay here until morning."

Grating noises intruded on her slumber. Lying across the front row of seats, Darcie opened her eyes but didn't move. She listened as the scraping sounds persisted, noticed how predawn light filtering through the forward viewpanes muted the control console's screens—and realized in another moment that its warning beeper was sounding again.

The grating came from the hatch. She knew it could be tripped from outside for rescue purposes.

"They've found us," she whispered. Her mouth was dry.

When the first bolt depressurized and thunked back, she turned onto her belly and reached under the command chair for the E-gun. Her fingers closed around its grip; her thumb slipped off its safety.

Staying behind the chair's back, she watched the hatch. Braced the pistol on the arm when the second bolt shot back. She felt Tristan stir beside her. When he yawned and tried to sit up under the blanket, she stayed him with her free hand.

She locked her teeth as the third bolt hissed and thunked. She adjusted her grip on the sidearm—and recoiled from the flood of early sunlight as the hatch fell open.

The two shapes silhouetted in its opening wore no legionnaires' armor. Except for leather leg-wrappings and loincloths, they wore nothing but their own velvet pelts. And when the nearest one glimpsed Darcie, he ducked his shaggy head to touch his brow. "*Yung Jwei!*" he said, gazing first at her and then at her child. "*Yung Jwei!*"

ONE

Tristan spread dust around his eyes and across his cheekbones, smeared it in streaks over his chest and shoulders until, in the moonlight, his skin appeared to bear the dark stripes which were natural to his companion. He glanced up. Pulou gave him an approving look and held out his knife. Tristan took it in his teeth and followed him, staying low in the long grass.

Peimus clustered in the clearing, bulls on the outer edge of the herd: blocky shadows on stumpy legs, hoofs stamping and tails twitching, heads tossing forward-curled horns.

Crouched beside Pulou, Tristan pointed at one bull a little apart from the others. Pulou grinned, a flash of fangs around his own knife blade, and ducked away into the dark. When the grass stopped rippling, Tristan squinted at his quarry, measuring the distance, and went to his belly.

He could smell the peimu's muskiness, hear its whuffing breath and the stamp of its cloven feet before he could see it. He raised his head just enough to feel the breeze in his face, to be sure that it hadn't changed direction. Almost within reach of the bull's left shoulder, he gathered himself into a crouch, muscles taut. He tongued his knife blade, waiting.

Something rustled beyond the bull. Its head went up, turned away, its ears alert.

Tristan sprang from cover in its blind spot, seizing its horns. The peimu snorted, trying to toss its head, but Tristan braced his feet and wrenched the near horn down, the far one up, twisting its neck. The bull's hoofs flipped out from beneath it, flailing the air; its shoulder struck the youth's hip as it went down, landing hard on its side. Tristan pressed a knee to its shoulder, pinning it, and said, "Pulou!"

The peimu only bellowed once, kicking, when Pulou cut its throat.

The rest of the herd fled into the trees. Still pinning the dying bull, Tristan watched them go: ambling and awkward, tails in the air, leaving three carcasses in the clearing. The other hunters, slim shadows in the moonlight, were already gutting their kills, groping with clawed hands through the entrails to find the choicest parts, the liver and heart.

Minutes later they were gathered around a small fire, eight figures squatting shoulder-to-shoulder, licking blood from their fingers and turning tidbits skewered on knife points over the coals. No one spoke, but Tristan read contentment in the others' faces, in the muffled growls that rumbled from their throats as they tore at their meat. He bit off a mouthful of nearly raw liver from the chunk on his knife. Hot juice dribbled down his chin. He swiped it away with the back of his hand and closed his eyes, savoring his own contentment as much as the flavor of the meat.

Bellies full, they lolled in the grass, and Miru, the youngest, said, "It's good to be chosen, Haruo?"

By the ebbing emberlight, Tristan saw how Haruo stopped tonguing the half-healed scar at the corner of his mouth. Saw how he settled back in the grass and ran a fin-

ger down the white laceration beside his nose. He smiled a
them all. "Yes, it's good."

"You bite her, too?" Miru asked.

"No!" Haruo looked briefly shocked. Then he smiled
again. "But she *is* with young!"

The others grinned, fangs reflecting moonlight.

Next to Haruo, Faral said, "You aren't chosen, Miru, because you don't bring back peimus. You scare them away!"

The youngster swatted at Faral, missed when he
ducked, and the others grinned again.

"Malwi," someone addressed Miru's older brother,
"you need new hunt partner, or your mother puts both of
you out in rain!"

"Maybe you get more peimus, Malwi, if you hunt by
yourself!" someone else put in, and the proverbial impossi-
bility of that provoked another round of grins.

"Tristan is good hunter," said Pulou.

Tristan felt the others' attention turn to him; he smiled
and made a negating gesture.

"Him?" said Haruo, wrinkling his nose. "Mothers don't
want flat-teeth!"

Everyone eyed Haruo, and Tristan saw two or three of
them cock their heads in puzzlement before Pulou said,
"Shiga wants him, but she's of same clan."

"Shiga?" Tristan stared at Pulou. "Your sister? But she's
almost my sister, too!"

"Melu wants you," said Miru. "You bring back many
peimus, and you're tall. She wonders how many children
you can give her."

Tristan cuffed him lightly and laughed off his embarrassment. "She chooses me and she finds out!"

"In my mother's clan," said Haruo, "no one wants flat-
teeth. They scare away peimus and claw up soil."

The silence that followed echoed with a challenge. Tristan met Haruo's gaze over the bed of coals, curled his hands

like claws, and showed his teeth. He felt the others watching him, saw anticipation in their yellow eyes. But Pulou abruptly nudged him and rose to his feet. "We start home," he said, stretching. "Long way to go, and morning comes."

The others rose, too, reluctantly. Pushed soil over the embers with leather-shod feet and wiped their flint blades clean on the grass.

Tristan stayed quiet, scowling to himself as he lashed the peimu's back legs to the carrying pole. He glanced up only when Pulou pressed a shoulder to his own.

"Turn your back, little brother. Ignore it," Pulou said.

"Why?" Tristan said. "I *am* flat-tooth."

"Outside," said Pulou, "not inside."

Tristan didn't answer. He took the rear position when they shouldered the pole and furrowed his brow as they started out.

It wasn't the first time a gan companion had commented that he was different. He remembered how, when he was a child, adult ganan had fingered his tawny hair and stroked his pale skin, and gan children had asked him if he saw things in different colors than they did because his eyes were blue, not amber. But their curiosity had made him a desired playmate; they had begged him to join in their games.

When, by the age of fourteen he'd outgrown even his older hunting companions, he'd begun to notice how the young females stared after him, and how they teased him with their looks and with their smiles. That had embarrassed him at first, but it hadn't left him feeling angry or hurt as Haruo's scorn had. No one had ever implied before that there was anything bad about being a flat-tooth. He spent most of the journey back to camp watching Haruo and wondering at the reasons for his animosity.

* * *

Darcie was awake when Tristan ducked into their lodge. She looked pale even in the firelight, he thought, but she was sitting up, weaving her faded hair into a waist-length braid with thin fingers.

"Mum!" he said in the Standard she had taught him, and dropped down before her, touching his brow. "Are you feeling better?"

"For the moment," she said. Her voice rasped; she cleared her throat. With one finger she drew a clean line through the dust on his upper arm. "You look as if you've traveled a long way."

"Five nights," Tristan said. "We had to go that far to find a herd, but we had a good hunt. There's a peimu outside, gutted but not skinned yet." He offered her his game bag with a smile. "I brought you some lomo eggs, too."

"New ones?" Darcie reached into the bag and withdrew a ball of leaves. Unrolling the improvised wrapping, she revealed a tan oval peppered with brown. She touched the rough shell—recently laid—and smiled back. "If you'll bring in some water, we'll boil these up straightaway."

He felt her watching him as he pulled hot stones from the firepit with wooden tongs and dropped them into the gut cooking pot and then put the eggs in one by one. Watching as he pushed an old scrap of leather into the skin water bucket and used it to scrub his face and chest and shoulders. Watching him as if there was something she needed to tell him and didn't quite know how to say it.

He swallowed when he finally met her gaze across the flickering dimness. "It's . . . getting worse, isn't it?" he asked.

"Yes," she said, and muffled a cough.

They both knew how it would end. They had seen it often enough in her gan patients, from whom she had contracted it.

Tristan felt suddenly weak. "How long—?" he asked. He couldn't finish the question.

"I don't know, Tris. . . . Seven or eight months, most likely."

Seven or eight months! He bit his lip. Stared at the soil floor between his knees for a long while, fighting back the pain of the loss that was to come. At last he rose, pushed aside the doorflap, and went out.

The sun had risen; it would grow hot before long. The camp was quiet but for a baby's cry from a nearby lodge and insects buzzing around the peimu carcasses hung from tree limbs to cure. Tristan padded among the squatly dome shelters toward the hill that rose beyond, and climbed to the top.

There were no graves here, just the ashes of the pyre.

He had seen his only cremation when he was four. Curious, he had crouched at the front of the circle among the gan children, had seen the old matriarch with her face painted white drive her knife into the body on the pyre. He knew now that she was setting the soul free to return to *Tsaan Jwei*, the Life-Taker, but at the time he thought she'd actually killed the old man.

A wavering moan had jerked his attention away from her. The people who brought the torches began it, and as they thrust fire among the wood, others took it up. He had stood there sobbing—unable to look away from the flames that licked and charred the body, oblivious of the ganan swaying and keening around him—until his mother caught him by the arm and took him back to their own shelter.

He'd awakened with nightmares of the pyre for several sleeps afterward.

The next time there was a cremation, he'd hidden in the back of the lodge until it was over. Now he left camp entirely, on the pretext of hunting.

Tristan prodded powdered ash into tiny swirls on the morning breeze, blackening his moccasin toe, and shot a dismal look over his shoulder when he heard someone approaching behind him.

Pulou stopped, settling into a squat and blinking in the daylight. "Little brother?"

"I think," said Tristan. He shuddered. Fourteen years hadn't faded his memories of the pyre.

"To think," Pulou said, "is good for to learn but not to be sad."

"My mother is ill, Pulou. She gets worse."

"That is way of life," the gan said behind him. "*Yung Jwei* gives it and *Tsaan Jwei* takes it."

"Gan way," said Tristan. "My mother isn't gan." He used the personal honorific form of "mother." "She gets well if she's at her home."

"You know how?" Pulou asked.

"She tells me about it," Tristan said. "Her people have good medicines. Their lodges are tall as mountains, and they have things that fly." Squinting at the misted horizon, he added, "She tells me about my father, too."

"Father?" Pulou asked, wrinkling his nose.

"She tells me flat-teeth aren't like ganan," said Tristan. "They choose once, not every time they come in season. Both choose, and they stay together like hunt partners. She says my father is . . . *Spherzah*."

Pulou blinked with puzzlement.

"He's—" Tristan furrowed his brow, thinking. He didn't fully understand it himself, except that his mother had made it sound important and heroic. He drew on the only comparison he could think of: "He's like *Yung Jwei*'s Chosen Hunters in clan tales. He's strong and good, and he helps people."

Pulou studied him for a moment, head cocked. "Maybe he can help your mother."

Tristan blinked at that. Fixed a startled look on his companion. "Yes!" he said then. "Yes! We bring him to her and he can help!"

* * *

"Haruo!" Tristan said at the doorflap. "Haruo!"

He heard stirring inside, a noisy yawn, and then nothing more.

"Haruo!" he said again.

Pulou nudged his arm. "It's daytime, little brother. They sleep."

But a hand pushed the doorflap aside and Haruo's mate, all maternal belly and sagging breasts, stared at them from its shadow.

Already squatting, Tristan and Pulou hunched lower still, ducking their heads and touching their brows. "Peace in you, mother," Tristan said, using the common word for all mature females. "It's needed, why I talk to Haruo."

She said nothing, just let the doorflap fall.

In another minute a different hand shoved the cover aside, a large hand with peimu blood still under the long hunters' nails. Haruo squinted in the sunlight, blinking several times before he recognized Tristan. "Flat-tooth!" he said then, showing his pointed ones. "Night-sleeper!"

"Haruo," said Tristan, "flat-teeth are where?"

"Why? You go back to them?"

Beside Tristan, Pulou flexed his hand.

Haruo glanced at him, then back to Tristan. He came out fully, pulling the doorflap closed, and dropped to his heels facing them. "Why?" he said again.

Tristan said, "I need to know for my mother." He used the personal honorific this time, and Haruo raised what would've been an eyebrow, if ganan had any.

"That way," he said, pointing toward the northwest. "Cross flat land with bright twin stars on this side." He touched his right shoulder. "There are hills. Follow little river up to where it comes from ground, where my mother's clan is. On other side is big valley with big river. Flat-teeth are by river on near side, in lodges that don't move."

"They have . . . things that fly?" Tristan asked.

He felt Pulou staring at him; but Haruo said, "Yes. In white nests like this." He made a bowl with both hands. "They make fire and noise when they fly. They scare peimus away."

The humans had spacecraft, then; that was important. Tristan asked, "How many nights to go there?"

Haruo wrinkled his brow, counted on his fingers. "Three hands."

Tristan nodded his thanks and glanced sideways at Pulou. "At night," he said.

The embers were barely enough to see by. Tristan moved quietly about the lodge, poking through baskets and skin bags at one side for dried meat and roots and nuts, groping among articles hung from roof poles to find a canteen made of peimu gut. His hands closed on an object swathed in scraps of leather. He knew what it was. He untied it from the rafter and unfolded the covering.

The chain spilled out first, between his fingers, and its metallic discs clattered on the dirt floor. Tristan planted a foot on them, twisting around to see if the noise had awakened his mother.

She stirred. He waited, motionless, until her breathing steadied, audible but even.

The larger object was heavy in his hand. The embers cast a bloody gleam along its barrel and grip. Tristan turned it over, eyeing its mechanisms. "E-gun," he whispered. He put it into his game bag with the food and crouched to gather up the chain. He squinted at the characters pressed into its ID tags:

DARTMUTH, DARCIE
5066-8-0529
ADRIAT, FLT SURGEON

She had taught him characters when he was small, reciting the sounds of the shapes as she guided his finger across a patch of smoothed sand. Writing words and then sentences had been a game between them—until he'd grown big enough to learn to hunt. He hadn't had much use for it since then.

He remembered, though. Dropping the chain into his bag, too, he studied the form in the bed furs for several moments.

A myriad of fears and feelings tumbled through his mind: Fear that if he left, he would return to find that she'd died in his absence. Urgency to go, to bring help to her. Guilt, for not telling her of his intentions.

He needed to tell her, somehow, so she wouldn't be left to wonder about him. He took his knife from his belt and, using its point, scratched words into the hard soil of the lodge floor:

Mum, I go to find my father to help you. I will come back soon. Tristan.

He sighed, slipping the knife back into his belt, and crawled outside.

Night had settled over the camp, stirring the ganan to activity. The midsummer evening breeze in Tristan's face was a breath of cool after the day's harsh sunlight. Game bag in hand, he moved to the next shelter and squatted down at its entry. "Pulou!" he called.

His companion pushed the doorflap aside and motioned him to enter. He ducked inside, scanned the circle of faces around the fire, touched his forehead in respect to Pulou's mother.

Her face and throat bore the scars of many matings and her streaked mane had thinned and whitened, but the infant at her breast was the symbol of her authority. She was the *jwa'nan*, the clan matriarch, the mother of her people.

She said, "You go away, almost-son."

"Yes." Tristan bowed his head to her. "I hunt for my father."

The *jwa'nan* studied him, unblinking. "Why do you need your father? My children don't even know their own fathers."

"I don't need him," Tristan said. "My mother does. He knows how to help her sickness."

"Ah! You go in *jwa'lai*, in duty to her."

"Yes, mother." He used the word for her title.

"It's good," she said. "Your mother is like *Yung Jwei* to you, your life-giver. She gives you life, you give her your duty."

"Yes," said Tristan.

"But hunter who goes alone brings back no peimu."

Beside Tristan, Pulou said, "We hunt together, Mother."

The *jwa'nan* nodded approval. "Good. You come home with almost-son's father." Shifting her infant, she reached out to brush each of their foreheads with the backs of her fingers in a sort of benediction. "Good hunt."

Tristan met her gaze cautiously. Her own kind held her latent savagery in dread respect, but she had shown sympathy to a pair of stripeless, clawless strangers. "Peace in you, mother," he said, and crawled backward from the lodge.

Pulou emerged beside him, rose in a fluid motion. He beckoned to Tristan. Like shadows they melted into the dark beyond the clustered shelters. But Tristan couldn't keep himself from glancing back once at his mother's lodge.

Though twice Tristan's eighteen years, Pulou stood only to the human youth's shoulder. He took the lead, scanning the terrain with pupils so wide their irises seemed nonexistent.

Unable to distinguish obstacles in the moonlessness as

easily as the gan could, Tristan watched Pulou place his feet, watched his hand for warning signals, and followed.

They skirted the knoll of the pyre and entered a gully which led onto open plain. It carried no water this late in the season, and the scrubby trees hemming it rustled in the breeze. Tristan stirred them no more than Pulou did.

They left the ravine and trees as the first moon edged above the horizon, illuminating untouched kilometers of prairie.

When Pulou glanced at him, Tristan looked skyward for the twin stars, turned his right shoulder to them, indicated the direction with a nod. Pulou moved off and Tristan matched his pace, a jog that crossed great distances with little effort.

Face and shoulders streaked with dust, Tristan crept to the ridge's crest and settled flat on his belly. Early morning sunlight slanted over his shoulder, casting detail into minute clarity. He studied the valley below as if looking for game, blinked at the flash of sun on a ribbon of water. Shielding his eyes with one hand, he spotted the human camp where Haruo had said it would be. He put his hand back, motioning Pulou to join him.

Ten times the size of most gan camps, he guessed, the human one was made of square lodges in rows, a brown patch in the midst of endless undulating green. Beyond the lodges were larger buildings, and beyond those, a cluster of white bowls with walls higher than the lodges: nests for things that flew. They were guarded by things that looked like squatty animals with long necks. The necks moved up and down and swayed from side to side, lifting, moving, and setting down burdens hung from ropes. Their creaking carried on the breeze like the calls of frogs on a spring evening.

Tristan studied it all for several minutes, and the uneasi-

ness he'd felt on the night of their departure from camp settled over him once more. But this time it wasn't an anxiety
for his mother. Eyeing the square lodges, he remembered
what Haruo had said about flat-teeth. Remembered the
derision in his tone, and wondered again what had caused
it. Wondered if it had anything to do with the things his
mother had told him from the time he was a child—the real
reason he hadn't told her where he was going. His stomach
tightened under his ribs. "Flat-teeth," he said finally, in a
tone like Haruo's.

"Funny to hear you say it that way," said Pulou.

Tristan didn't smile—he couldn't—and Pulou said,
"Your father isn't here."

"No," Tristan said. "I know that."

Pulou cocked his head. "He's where?"

"There." Tristan indicated the sky. "Where my mother
and I fall from when I'm little."

"You fall in big, shiny egg," Pulou said. "Pelan and I
find you in it."

"Yes. We go back in one, too." Tristan pointed. "Flat-
teeth have them in those white nests."

Sitting back-to-back with Pulou in the gathering dusk, Tristan watched the brush for the slinking shapes of jous and
chewed on a strip of dried meat. Shifting enough to tip his
head back, he studied the stars already visible over the
ridge behind them.

"Little brother," Pulou said, "jous don't come from
sky."

"There's no jou sign or howls for two nights," Tristan
said. "Flat-teeth scare them away from here, like peimus."

"You do what?" Pulou asked.

"Look at stars."

Pulou moved behind him, depriving him of his backrest,
and peered over his shoulder. "Your father is where?" he
asked.

"I don't know," said Tristan.

"Your mother knows?"

"Maybe."

"You don't ask her?"

"No."

"Why? It's *jwa'lai* for her."

Tristan lowered his head. "I don't tell her that I go."

Pulou twisted around fully, staring at him, eyes wide. "She doesn't *ask* you to do it?"

"No."

"*That* isn't *jwa'lai*—"

"It *is* duty!" said Tristan. "But if I tell her that I go, she tells me not to, and—" He shrugged with finality.

Pulou would understand that: disobedience to one's mother was sacrilege.

There was silence for several heartbeats, and then Pulou asked, "Why does she tell you not to go?"

Tristan sighed. "Flat-teeth are like jous to my mother," he said. "When I'm small there are big fights between my mother's people and other flat-teeth, and many are killed."

"Fights between clans?" said Pulou, and cocked his head. "That's stupid! Why?"

"I don't know," Tristan said. "That's why we stay with ganan and don't go live with flat-teeth when we fall from sky. But they have things that fly to stars. No other way to find my father." Tristan's tone turned serious; his mouth was dry. He glanced over at his companion. "It's dangerous, Pulou. You don't have to go with me."

"Hunter who goes alone," said Pulou, "can't watch for jous all ways at once."

His face remained almost expressionless but his tone was that of a protective older brother. Tristan met his amber eyes. Studied them for a long moment almost questioningly.

But Pulou just glanced around and rose. "It's dark

enough," he said, and paused to stretch. "Come on, little brother."

Tristan scooped up their canteen and balanced its cool weight in his hand. Half-full. He offered it to his companion first, then took a long drink himself and slung its strap over his shoulder.

Pulou chose their path down the side of the canyon, moving with an ease that still challenged Tristan.

The canyon opened onto a bench that rolled down to the human camp in a series of gradual slopes. At the bench's foot the brush and prairie grass ended, separated by a line of upright poles from grass that had been planted in rows, so tall that its seed tassels reached Tristan's chest. The breeze chased waves over its expanse like ripples from a pebble dropped in water.

"You lead," Pulou said. "You can see over it better."

But as Tristan strode past the nearest pole, crackling light struck his shoulder, knifing through bone, tendon, nerve. He staggered back with a cry, gripping his arm.

"Tsaan Jwei!" said Pulou behind him. "You're hurt, little brother?"

"I . . . don't think so." The tingling was receding already, dissipating to his fingertips. Tristan flexed his hand. "It's all right."

"It comes from poles?" Pulou asked. "It looks like lightning." He reached past Tristan.

His hand seemed to jerk back from the flash by itself. He shook it, hissing quick breaths through his teeth. "Tsaan Jwei!" he said again, and jabbed at his forehead.

Keeping his distance, Tristan eyed the pole. Its surface was too smooth to be bark, the marks on it too much alike to be knotholes. It was taller than himself and probably four full arm-lengths from the next pole, which looked exactly the same. He paced back and forth a few times, studying them.

Perplexed, he scooped up a stone from beside his foot and hurled it between the poles. It spun an arc, untouched. Startled when it wasn't struck by lightning, he flung another after it.

"You don't hit anything," Pulou said.

"I know," said Tristan. "But there isn't lightning." He considered that, picked up another stone, hurled it *at* the pole.

It connected with a shatter of blue light and dropped.

"*Tsaun Jweil*" hissed Pulou, and touched his brow again.

Tristan barely heard him. The first two stones hadn't touched anything, even the ground; he could imitate that with a long jump. He backed up a few paces.

"You do what?" Pulou asked.

"Jump," said Tristan, "like stones."

He misjudged his leap, didn't quite clear the line of poles before he tucked his head to take the fall in a roll. A scintillating blow caught him across the chest, smashing the breath from his lungs, stiffening his spine. He collapsed into the long grass and lay there gasping.

He didn't see the lightning behind him, didn't hear its sizzling strike. He heard only an urgent voice calling his name, felt a quivery hand on his head and shoulder as the pain began to recede. He opened his eyes. Pulou was squatting beside him. He turned over and sat up slowly, still gulping for breath.

Pulou was panting, too. Sweat gleamed about his nose and mouth and matted his mane on his forehead. His eyes were vicious with the aftermath of *tsaa'chi*, the ganan's physiological threat response. "Be calm," Tristan said. "I'm all right, Pulou. Be calm. I'm not hurt."

He watched Pulou's breathing steady, watched the fury fade from his eyes. They rose together, and Tristan took the lead, wading into the field.

The second and third moons had risen by the time they

came out of the grass onto a trail wide enough for four or five people to walk shoulder-to-shoulder. It ran down between the square lodges like a stream bed at the bottom of a gully, and Tristan, chewing his lip, paused to look for white walls above the rooftops. "This way," he said at last, and slipped into an alley.

Behind him, Pulou said, "Too close, too hard; flat-tooth lodges," and ran his fingers in a soft, rapid thudding along the ribbed shell of one. Tristan signed at him to be quiet and ducked beneath a square hole that shot yellow light across their path.

Pulou didn't duck. "Look, little brother," he said.

When Tristan glanced back, Pulou had stretched up to look into the square hole. The light escaping from it made garish patterns across his striped face. Wary, Tristan slipped up beside him.

There was a hand of humans, four adults and a child, sitting in a circle to eat from something flat and stiff that seemed to rest on their knees. Tristan studied clothing not made of peimu hide, which covered all but their hands and heads, eyed skin as bare and stripeless as his own, recognized snatches of words in Standard that sounded monotonous compared to his mother's. They were his own kind, and yet everything about them seemed strange. More alien than the striped face at his shoulder. It sent a shiver up his spine.

"Look at their hair!" said Pulou. "It grows on their faces!"

On the three men it did, covering their chins as if to make up for its shortness around their ears and across the backs of their necks.

Tristan felt sudden disgust. "Mine doesn't!" he said.

Pulou scrutinized him, touching his chin with the back of a finger. He grinned. "It starts to."

"It does not!" Tristan raised a curled hand.

He started at a noise somewhere, a trilling like insects in the evening, but louder and harsher. One of the two young men stood and left the room and the trilling stopped. He came back in a few minutes, securing a belt about his waist. Tristan recognized the object in its pouch; his mother had called hers an E-gun.

The older man began to question him, and the woman and child stopped eating. Tristan could only pick out a few words of their conversation.

"Something came through . . ." he heard. "Have to find out what . . . where it went. . . . monitors went crazy."

". . . know what it was?" That was the woman.

". . . thinks it's a couple of wild boys," the young man with the pistol told her. "Animals would run off. . . ."

The woman again, sounding worried: "What would they want?"

". . . don't know. We'll find out."

Tristan looked at Pulou, furrowing his brow. "Wild boys?"

Pulou shrugged. "They don't look for us. Come on."

They crept to the lodge's end, squatted to peer around its corner—and saw the man with the pistol step through a square opening that slid shut behind him. He paused to pull on a hat, glanced up and down the row of lodges, and then strode off in the opposite direction, leaving a trail of crunching sounds under his boots. They watched until he disappeared around a corner.

The lane between the lodges was flooded with moonlight and a breeze that stirred up swirls of dust. Tristan and Pulou sprinted across it, into a narrower alley. They chose a zigzag route through the human camp, keeping close to the ground—once crouching in a corner at the noise of nearby boots and voices.

Waiting for them to pass, Tristan plucked nervously at bits of a brown skin that peeled from the wall he huddled against, like skin from fruit. Huddled there, he listened to the sounds that came from inside: a baby's cry, a woman's quiet song.

He jumped when Pulou nudged him and beckoned him to follow.

Occasional humans moved among the long buildings beyond the lodges, busy at a purpose only they knew. Watching them, Tristan and Pulou crept from shadow to shadow—like peimus being stalked by a pack of jous, Tristan thought.

Open areas stretched between the long buildings and the walls of the spacecraft nests. They were scattered with stacks of crates and barrels and the long-necked machines that lifted them. Plenty of cover. Pulou surveyed it, pointed; Tristan, teeth tight on his lip, slipped toward a pile of boxes.

Halfway across the loading yard, he signaled Pulou to stillness and froze on hands and knees, his heart hammering. A human paced among the pallets with a long weapon on his shoulder. He passed so close to their concealment that Tristan might have touched him if he had put out a hand. He pressed himself against the crate instead, and held his breath.

The human went by, oblivious.

"Stupid as lomos," Pulou said quietly. "But lomos know when there's danger. Flat-teeth don't."

Tristan glowered at him, and Pulou grinned. "Come on, little brother," he said.

A curved wall loomed like a cliff's face ahead of them. They slipped toward an opening at its base, pausing to listen before moving down into the darkness, into a cave that opened at the bottom of the bowl.

Two moons hung almost overhead by now, and their light silvered the skin of the waiting spacecraft. Tristan cocked his head, comparing it to the images in his memory. "Lifepod," he whispered in Standard.

Pulou was eyeing it, too. "We go where in this?" he asked.

"To my father's home," said Tristan. "Topawa. Maybe he's there."

"Maybe," said Pulou. "Maybe not."

Tristan ignored him; the spacecraft held his attention. He strode its circumference, raising a curious hand to run his fingertips along its hull, tracing lines meant to carve an atmosphere and slice through cold space, studying its symmetry—until he heard footfalls in the entry.

He twisted around.

A tall human emerged through the arch, taller still in armor borrowed from figures in Tristan's unforgotten nightmares, with his long weapon leveled in his hands.

Tristan froze, his blood suddenly cold in his veins. It was a Dominion legionnaire.

TWO

The soldier shifted his weapon to one arm, a posture that looked no less threatening, and his free hand moved to an object at his waist. Light shot across the bowl.

Tristan winced, expecting a shock, but there was none. The light ate concealing shadows, slid into corners like water—found him, and then Pulou, by the ship's ramp. He squinted at its brilliance, showing his teeth.

Without lowering his weapon, the man spoke rapidly into the palm of his hand. His light never wavered from Tristan's face.

In moments three more legionnaires, dark shapes on dark beyond the blinding light, entered the bowl running. They spread out, invisible but for the noise of their boots, to close from both sides.

Tristan had seen jous hunt: surrounding a lone peimu, worrying it, springing clear of striking forefeet and horned head while one attacked unguarded flanks and disemboweled it on its feet. The legionnaires seemed to be using the same tactic. Glancing from one side to the other to keep them in sight, he began edging clear of the ship, backing toward the wall; he saw Pulou at his periphery doing the same. He dropped his game bag, took his knife from his belt and gripped it in his teeth.

"Back to me, back to me!" said Pulou. He was hyperventilating in the onset of *tsaa'chi* and his mane stood on end. Tristan sidled closer, taking an attack stance, teeth clenched and hands flexed.

Lights closed on them from three directions, mesmerizing, blinding. Pulou grimaced at it, plainly in pain, and when one lamp was thrust too close to his face, he lashed out. The light went spinning in a spatter of red and its bearer sank back with a yell, clutching his torn hand with the other. The rest hesitated.

In that half moment, Tristan lunged. He seized the nearest soldier in a bear hug, throwing his whole weight forward. The man staggered, losing weapon and lamp. The beam cut a crazy arc across the blackness, struck and rolled between the combatants' feet. Pinning his opponent with one arm, Tristan reached for his knife with the other, twisting its point to the man's throatpiece.

The soldier got his left hand free. He caught Tristan's wrist and pushed it up and back, hard, behind his head. Pain lanced through his wrist and shoulder blade but he didn't lose his knife. He felt the man's heavy breath in his face, felt a twinge in his shoulder at an increase of pressure. "Drop it, wild boy!" he heard, close to his ear. He hissed through his teeth, tried to duck out of the hold. It only tightened, abruptly forcing his arm down, backward, behind his neck. He gasped, and the knife fell from his fingers.

The man wrenched him around, gripping both his arms, and someone shoved a light at his face. "This ain't no wild boy," he heard. "Look at his eyes and skin—his stripes are rubbin' off! What's going on here, kid?"

Heart racing, still panting, Tristan turned his face away from the heat of the light—and a gloved hand smacked his jaw. He snapped his head up, teeth locked.

"I said, what d'you think you're doing, kid?" the soldier with the lamp demanded.

Tristan only swallowed. He slid a glance sideways, looking for Pulou, and the hand struck his face again.

"Somebody get over here!"

The voice came from a few meters off to Tristan's right. His captor jerked him around, and the lampbearer turned his light on the spot.

The man who had been hit first, bloody hand pressed between his other arm and his side, stood over two shapes stretched motionless on the ground, one armored, one not. He held his weapon clumsily, like a club, in his uninjured hand and shouted, "Get some links on him before he comes around, will you? I had to hit him four times to drop him and he almost tore out Kreg's throat first!"

"Pulou!" Tristan's heart contracted. He lunged against the restraining hands as the legionnaires crouched over his companion, but his captor wrenched his arm up behind his back. He went to his knees, his breath catching with pain— and was shoved facedown onto launch-kilned tarmac.

"Hey, Scully, hurry it up! This one isn't unconscious!" his captor called.

The lampbearer came back to crouch at Tristan's shoulder. Metallic rings glinted in his hand. He seized Tristan's pinioned wrist and crossed it over the other, clamping cold bands around both. There was no opportunity to resist. One of them hauled Tristan to his feet. Steadying himself, he twisted to look around for Pulou.

The gan was coming to. Using only feet and legs, he shoved himself onto his side, and Tristan saw the heaving motion of his ribs. He didn't sit up, just lay in a tight huddle.

"How's Kreg?" asked Tristan's captor behind him.

"Dead." The other legionnaire turned to glance over his shoulder at the shape sprawled beyond Pulou. His breastplate was splashed with crimson that looked black in the moonlight.

Tristan had seen the result of *tsaa'chi* before. He turned his face away.

There were more legionnaires now, almost two hands of them: covering and carrying away the dead man, flashing their lights all around, picking up flint knives and game bag and human weapons lost in the fight, staring at Tristan. He glared back from beneath disheveled hair, baring his teeth at them, and most of them laughed.

He watched two of them drag Pulou up by his arms, saw how he swayed, still dizzy; but they pushed him with the ends of their long weapons to make him walk. He seemed lost until Tristan called his name, and then he raised his head and came toward Tristan unsteadily. His nose had been bloodied.

They were prodded from the spacecraft nest and across the loading yard to one of the long buildings. Tristan stopped at its threshold, staring into the square cavern beyond, and someone pushed him forward. He glared at the armored man—tried to steady Pulou when he stumbled.

Three soldiers marched them along the passage to a boxy space at its end, and one man touched a panel of small lights on its wall. Another wall slid across the way out, and the ground dropped beneath their feet. Tristan's stomach dropped, too. When he glanced around, startled, the soldiers were watching him and grinning.

The fall stopped abruptly, and Pulou almost buckled against him. The box opened. Tristan shrugged away from the legionnaire's prod—but the tunnel he found himself facing was darker and colder than the one the door had closed on. He felt a cave's dankness on his skin, smelled it on the air. Confused and a little frightened, he planted his feet.

Someone caught him by the shoulder and shoved him forward, out of the box and up to a wall, face first. He tried to twist away, hissing through his teeth, but the hand between his shoulder blades pressed hard enough to take his breath away, to make him gasp. Hands probed around his waist, ran down one leg and then the other. He shifted his feet, trying to escape them. They grabbed the canteen still dangling over his shoulder, cut its strap and took it away.

The pressure between his shoulder blades let up only so the soldier could shove him into another box, larger than the moving one and built of stones. They thrust Pulou in, too, hard enough that he fell into Tristan. Unable to catch himself, the gan sank to his knees, grimacing, and slumped forward on the floor.

Tristan dropped down beside him. "Pulou!" He struggled to loosen wrists locked at his back, but the rings bit into his skin.

He jumped, his head jerking up, when the legionnaires slammed a heavy door across the way out. He swallowed as its echoes rang between the stone walls.

Brigadier General Jules François scowled at the bundle on his desk and glanced at his console screen for an explanation. Its message was brief:

FROM DEPARTMENT OF SECURITY AND INVESTIGATION
2234L HOURS, 5/8/3307 SY
THE FOLLOWING REPORT WAS FORWARDED BY COL
LANSILL, OIC DS&I, RE: INTRUDERS APPREHENDED
IN LAUNCH BAY #2. POSSIBLE INTELLIGENCE
VALUE; SAFEGUARD PENDING CLASSIFICATION. SEE
CONFISCATED POSSESSIONS.

François secured the office door before he sank into the molded chair behind his desk. He entered his access code to call the report up on his screen and deliberately left the voice synthesizer turned off.

The military policeman's report contained only the circumstances of the apprehension, listed two casualties, and gave physical descriptions of the intruders. It was his commander, Colonel Lansill, who had safeguarded the report.

François caught the skin bag with a sweep of his hand and upended it over his desk. He had no idea what he was looking for—certainly not the handgun which clunked onto the desktop. Leaning forward in his chair, he poked among several strips of dried meat, a handful of nuts in wrinkled shells, a pair of ID tags on a chain. He took up the weapon and turned it in his hands, weighing and balancing it. It was a type of energy pistol, probably close to twenty-five standard years old. Not of Dominion make, and the Issel Sector hadn't produced its own arms then. He scratched at a raised place on the grip and crusted grime chipped away to reveal part of a crest: an oval enclosing an eagle's head with a planet held in its beak. "Unified Worlds," he said.

Setting down the sidearm, he took up the chain, activated the desk's illuminant with a motion, and held one tag up to its light.

His fingers tightened on it as his casual gaze turned to intense examination. He punched the intercom to his exec's office, and when the major replied, he said, "I want to see Colonel Lansill from the DS and I in here ASAP."

Turning back to his console, he called up the stills retrieved from the guardhouse vid monitor for inclusion with the report.

The first two were of the native, curled up on his side in the middle of the cell floor, grid-marked with his own stripes and the sunlight that breached the small window. His eyes were closed and his mouth open. The third showed the youth stretching up to the window bars, wrists still crossed in restraints at his back.

François flicked through the frames until he found one that focused on the boy's face.

His hair was sandy-blond and shaggy, brushing his shoulders, and his skin was tanned under the smudges of dust on his face and torso. François noted blue eyes and a cleft in the chin. He dredged his memory.

Boot heels clicked at the doorway; the colonel said, "Lansill reporting as ordered, sir."

"Come in. Have a seat." François motioned at a chair and leaned back in his own. "Your soldier's report neglected to state how the prisoners entered the base compound and what their intentions were. Weren't they interrogated?"

Lansill said, "No, sir. Neither speaks Standard. But I doubt that's your foremost concern."

"You're right; it isn't. Does your man know that you forwarded his report to me?"

"No, sir."

"Leave it that way." François's glance dropped briefly to the sidearm on his desk and he reached for his intercom again. "Major, contact the anthropology unit and get an expert on indigenous races over here. And while we wait, load the colonial history files and send me any references to contacts with the Unified Worlds over the last twenty-five standard years."

To the colonel he said, "If the kid doesn't speak our language, we'll find somebody who speaks his."

Tristan had spent the rest of the night crouched beside Pulou; the restraints didn't allow him to do much else. As darkness gave way to gray he'd tried to curl himself up for warmth, but the restraints made that awkward and uncomfortable.

Pulou slept now, uneasily, but Tristan couldn't. Anxious, he stretched up to the ground-level sill again to watch disciplined squads of boots tramp the gravel; he sneezed at the dust they raised, and squinted at the sunlight beyond them.

The grating shriek of metal tore his attention to the door. He jerked around, swallowed hard. On the floor, Pulou stirred and opened one eye.

The barrier scraped open. Legionnaires paced outside, shiny shapes in the dimness; but the man who entered wore no plating. He dropped to a squat, rested forearms on knees with his hands hanging down, and said, "Peace in you."

Tristan stared, embarrassed at being approached with a greeting given only to mothers, and startled at hearing a human speaking gan at all. He moved away from the window to place himself protectively between the human and Pulou. "You are who?" he demanded.

"I am Nuan to ganan," the man said, and paused. "I ask you questions."

Tristan said nothing, just studied him through narrowed eyes—a message in itself if this intruder knew ganan. A message of distrust, of warning.

"One man is dead," said the human. "Another is hurt."

"They attack us," Tristan said. "*Tsaa'chi* comes."

"Why do you come here?" the man asked. "Why are you in"—he resorted to Standard—"launch bay?"

"*Jwa'lai*," Tristan said, and turned his back.

He heard a long pause, and the man rising with a grunt and crossing to the barrier, and voices outside, and the noise of the barrier closing. He kept his back turned to it.

"It's what, little brother?" Pulou asked from near his knee.

"Flat-tooth. He asks questions." Tristan glanced down at him. "Your head is better?"

Pulou tried to lift it and winced. "Hurts to move."

"Sleep more." Tristan settled himself on the floor, awkward with his arms bound. "I sleep, too."

But he was too scared to sleep. He was still wide-awake, every muscle in his body taut, when the barrier scraped open once more. He twisted just enough to glance over his shoulder—and struggled to sit up, to free one hand to touch his brow. The best he could do was to duck his head.

The woman who had entered the stone room was about the age and build of his own mother, but with hair the color of fire. She didn't crouch down, but Tristan didn't expect her to. He whispered, "Peace in you, mother."

Her smile wasn't cruel, but it wasn't warm, either. She said, "I am Marna. You are who?"

He eyed her. "Tristan," he said, and ducked his head. "Why, mother?"

"Flat-tooth name," she said, "not gan. Why are you with him?" And she pointed at Pulou with her fingers straight, threatening.

Tristan tensed his bound hands at his back. "He's my brother. We hunt together."

"You come from where?"

"Out there." Tristan indicated the general direction with a motion of his head.

"Why?"

"*Jwa'lai*," Tristan said, watching her.

She nodded, and her smile warmed. "You live with ganan for long time?"

"When I am very little," Tristan said.

"Other flat-teeth are there?"

It seemed a harmless query but something about it made Tristan uneasy. He cocked his head. "Flat-teeth, mother?"

"Yes. Like me, like you. Humans. Think when you go to live with ganan. Other flat-teeth go with you?"

Tristan hesitated. "I'm little then," he said.

He hadn't answered her question and he saw her recognition of it. But she asked, "You come here for *jwa'lai*? Why?"

He hesitated again; his mouth had gone dry. "I hunt for . . . my father."

Her eyebrows lifted. He studied her, fidgeting with an increasing discomfort.

"He's in this—camp?" she asked.

"No, mother."

"He's where?"

"I don't know," Tristan said. He hunched lower, still watching her face. "Why do you ask me, mother?"

She paused this time, and then said, "We try to help you."

He cocked his head, questioning that.

"You're hungry?" she asked. "You and—your brother?" She pointed at Pulou again with her straight fingers.

"Yes," said Tristan.

She reached out then, slowly, and touched his forehead with her fingertips—not the backs of her fingers that kept her claws curled toward herself—and he braced himself and bore it. She might be the *jwa'nan* here; he wouldn't risk her *tsaa'chi*.

"I tell them to bring you food," she said, and the legionnaires opened the barrier and let her out.

"Well, Doctor." François indicated a chair facing his desk and waited until the woman was seated. Then he asked, "How do your interrogation methods differ from those of your colleague?"

"Ganan are matriarchal, sir," she said. "Your prisoners would have talked to any female older than themselves."

"Humph." The general shifted forward in his chair. "What were you able to learn?"

"It's rather difficult to take someone's history in a language that has no past or future tenses," the woman said, "but the boy claims to have come here out of *jwa'lai*—'duty to mother' in the gan language."

"What's that?" the general asked. "Some sort of native idolatry?"

She smiled. "You might call it that."

François raised an eyebrow.

"One's mother," said the anthropologist, "is his personal incarnation of *Yung Jwei*, the life-giving deity. Because of that, a request from, or promise made to her takes higher precedence than life itself. One even approaches his mother—all mature females, in fact—with a gesture"—she touched her brow—"symbolic of putting his head—his life—into her hands. That's *jwa'lai*."

"Interesting." François leaned back in his chair. "So what's the story on the native that came with him?"

"The boy referred to him as his brother and said that they hunt together," the doctor said.

"His *brother*?" said François.

She gave a single nod. "Male ganan practically live in pairs," she explained. "It takes two individuals to carry the large game they use for food and shelter, and it provides mutual protection against natural threats. After one's mother, a male gan's strongest allegiance is to his hunting partner, who usually is a brother." She hesitated. "It's not all that different from the cohesion you'd want your troops to have in battle, sir."

"Hmm." François stroked his chin, considering that, and nodded.

"But I've never heard of a human-gan bonding of this type before," the anthropologist continued. "It suggests that the boy is deeply assimilated into the gan culture. This is definitely worthy of further study."

"Perhaps," said François. He shifted in his chair. "So you think we have a couple of . . . kids down there who're trying to do their mother a favor?"

The doctor locked her hands in her lap and looked at François directly. "I don't think so, sir. The boy may use the language and mannerisms like a native, but he made a few crucial errors in our interview. First, ganan have no concept of deceit, and he was evasive about answering some of my questions. That shows a human influence.

"Second, he said he was looking for his father. Ganan don't mate for life, and few youngsters even know what male fathered them. None would ever consider it important to find him."

François nodded, and toyed with the ID tag on its chain. "You believe that his mother is out there, too, then?"

"Probably. Or at least, she was. I also suspect that he *can* speak a human language. Thought patterns and language are necessarily connected. And he said that his name is Tristan—certainly not a native name."

"Humph." The general studied her. "Did he say anything about why and how he got out there in the first place?"

"Just that he joined the ganan when he was very small." The doctor spread her hands. "One can only speculate from that."

"What about his father? Did he expect to find him here?"

"No, he didn't. He said that he didn't know where he is."

François glanced at the ID tag again—DARTMUTH, DARCIE—and furrowed his brow. "We appreciate your time, Doctor."

Lansill pushed a stylus and memory pad across at her. "Nondisclosure statement," he said. "Sign it. It verifies your understanding that what you've seen, heard, and said doesn't leave this office."

She signed it, suddenly solemn.

François nodded; the colonel opened the door for her, closed it, touched his superior's vision with his own. François dropped the chain on the desktop and said, "Let's look at that colonial history."

Lansill moved to the console and called up contacts with the Unified Worlds. Several entries on the monitor index highlighted themselves. "Document number one," he said. When its text appeared on the screen he said, "Here we go, sir," and offered the general his chair.

It was dated 12/6/3282 Standard Years, a month after

the battle at Enach, in which the Unified Worlds had dealt its final blow to the Dominion and ended the War of Resistance. A message originating from the government of Kaleo, one of the Unified Worlds, had been received by Comm Central, demanding the return of all passengers and crew from a captured personnel transport. When Comm Central denied having any knowledge of a lost ship, it had been included in the prisoners-of-war issue at the Enach Accords. The negotiations produced an agreement which allowed each side to search, for a period of one standard year, any enemy world believed to be holding personnel who had not been accounted for.

Six weeks after the Accords were ratified, a team from the Unified Worlds had arrived in the Korot system to begin an intensive search of Ganwold and its surrounding space. The team had employed every technology, every method allowed under the treaty, but no trace of the missing ship or its passengers was ever discovered. At the end of the year, the searchers had sealed the required documents confirming that no Unified Worlds personnel, military or civilian, were held on Ganwold.

That had been almost twenty-five standard years ago: François' estimated dating of the ruined energy pistol.

The next highlight was dated 23/7/3291 SY, the first entry detailing an incident serialized over several days' message traffic.

A lightdrive craft had entered the Korot system with no identification signals, and Colonial Defense had tried to raise communications. Receiving no response, Defense dispatched two skirmish craft to identify and investigate. The damaged transport, bearing Unified Worlds crest and registration numbers, had opened fire. The skirmishers took out its weapons and propulsion systems, boarded, and found it to be under the control of masuk slavers.

The legionnaires had secured the ship and made a thorough tour of it. The captain's log listed Aeire City spaceport on Adriat, on 4/6/3282 SY, as its place and date of departure. Two lightskip points had been charted but an officer of the bridge had dumped the rest of the nav program. He hadn't lived long enough to dump the crew and passenger rosters as well. Those had prompted a search.

The only survivors not taken earlier by the masuki were a young woman and a small male child. They were tentatively identified as mate and son of one of the Unified Worlds' most decorated Spherzah. They had escaped the legionnaires, leaving a pair of holodiscs in the soldiers' possession, and had evidently reached the lifepods. Five had been jettisoned into landing orbits around Ganwold.

The skirmishers had destroyed the transport before tracing the pods' locators. Colonial Defense had been instructed to take occupants of all lifepods into custody and inform the Sector General at once. Hours later, the first transponder signals were picked up. Over three days, surface troops recovered four pods, including one from a southern ocean. Each was empty. The fifth had been tracked briefly by radar but it lacked a functional transponder. It had taken more than two weeks to find it at the bottom of a canyon.

Unlike the others, it had been found with its hatch open; but all evidence to confirm human occupation had been obliterated by marauding animals. With the trail already cold, search efforts had been abandoned as futile after a few days.

But its occupants had surfaced at last. That was explanation enough for the Unified Worlds sidearm in the skin bag. And reason enough for its owner to evade questioning.

Pursing his mouth, François called up images of the holodiscs which had been confiscated years before.

One showed a laughing young man with a toddler riding on his shoulders, gripping his hair. The other was a joining portrait: the same young man in a ceremonial uniform with several medals, and a girl in pale blue standing in the circle of his arms, one hand resting on his chest.

François noted the young officer's sandy-blond hair, blue eyes, the cleft in his chin . . .

He had never seen any of the Spherzah in the flesh—and quite frankly, he hoped he never would. They were the Unified Worlds' special operations force. Having originated on Kaleo, they took their name from a Kalese bird of prey, a night hunter that swooped and struck without warning. The word's literal translation was "talons of the night," and by all the accounts he'd heard, it fit the crack force very well.

François also remembered how, like a phoenix from his father's ashes, Lujan Serege had flown in the attack on Dominion Station when he was only a few years older than the youth in the guardhouse.

"Well, sir?" Lansill said at his shoulder.

François glanced away from the screen. "No question in my mind of the kid's identity, Colonel. But we still have a few unanswered questions, like why he came *here* looking for his father, and where the woman is these days. If the anthropologists are correct, the kid's not ignorant of who he is or of the danger to himself in coming here."

He pushed himself back, rose to pace a few steps, paused to meet the colonel's look directly. "Sector General Renier must be notified at once, in any case."

THREE

"Captain, you're to report to the Department of Security and Investigation immediately."

"Security and Investigation?" Reed Weil's finger slipped off the comm button.

He punched it again, caught an electronic "—still there, sir?"

"Yes. Is it a medical situation?"

"No, it isn't."

He hesitated. "Can you tell me what it is, then?"

"Not over the comm, sir."

Weil rose, finger still on the button, and said, "I'm on my way. Out here."

His palms were damp. He wiped them on the front of his lab coat—then took that off, on a second thought, and removed his service jacket and cap from their hook.

In the base clinic's outer office, he fumbled the jacket's clasps as he asked the NCO receptionist to reschedule his next appointments.

He was surprised to find François in the Security office, too, but the brigadier general just returned a perfunctory salute and said, "At ease, Captain," when he reported in. Shoving a handful of papers aside, François added, "You're being sent on a new assignment. Your change-of-post orders are being cut as we speak."

"Sir?"

"I apologize for the short notice, Captain. This morning I received orders from Governor Renier for the immediate transfer of a prisoner to his headquarters on Issel. Colonel Lansill"—he indicated the security commander—"and I have discussed it and concluded that sedating him would be the most practical method, so I'm putting the case under your charge; you may use whatever method you prefer. You'll leave Ganwold aboard the merchant ship *Bonne Fortune* at twenty-two hundred this evening."

"Yes, sir." Weil glanced from one to the other. "Excuse me, gentlemen, but I wasn't even aware there had been a court-martial."

"There wasn't," said Lansill.

Weil didn't understand until he stood outside the cell with them later, wearing his lab coat once more. Peering through the grid in the door, he asked, "Who is he, sir? How long has he been in here, and how did he get the bruises on his face and chest?"

"He's been here five days." Lansill clipped his words. "The bruises are the result of his lack of cooperation under interrogation."

Weil winced. "May I ask what he's done to deserve Issel?"

The security officer's voice and features turned hard. "You have no need to know that, Captain. Your duty is to get him to Sector General Renier alive."

The security briefing he'd received burned in the back of Weil's mind. "Yes, sir," he said. And, after a moment, "I recommend medical stasis. It'll guarantee his controllability and prevent trauma due to lightskip travel."

The colonel only said, "Humph," and motioned at the guard. "Open it up."

The door grated back. Two armored soldiers pushed up

from behind Weil but he motioned them away. "No. Let me try it alone first." Ignoring the way one of the men shook his head, he stepped into the cell.

He didn't see the native, crouched on the bench beneath the window with his knees drawn up against his chest, until his eyes reflected dull light out of the shadows. Weil hesitated, then turned his attention to the youth who sat on his heels with his back to the wall, his face showing suspicion between the bruises. He took only a few steps, then dropped down in a squat—a less threatening posture—and said quietly, "I'm not going to hurt you, kid. Can you understand that?"

The youth glared at him and shifted like a predator gathering for a spring. His right eye was swollen half-shut.

"Those thugs!" Weil said under his breath. He put out a hand, empty palm up. "Look, kid, I want to help you, okay? Will you let me close enough to help you?" Still crouching, he advanced a few steps.

Like a cornered animal, the boy showed his teeth and hissed at him.

He paused. "It's all right, kid. If you don't take it easy they'll be in here beating you up again. Understand?"

When he moved, the boy raised his hands before his chest, palms forward, fingers curled like claws. Restraints had chafed his wrists raw and his left hand was swollen and discolored; the fingers didn't curl well.

"Watch it, Doc," someone behind him said. "That's a warning."

"I'm sorry, kid," Weil said, showing his empty hands in return and sidling nearer a centimeter at a time. "It's okay, it's okay. I can help you if you'll let me." He was close enough to detect fear behind the defiance in the blue eyes. His hand closed gently but firmly on the boy's right wrist.

A hissed threat distracted his attention to the native crouching in the shadows—

—directly into a blow across the face that bowled him

backward, cheekbone throbbing, skin burning with deep scratches. The boy was on his feet, hands still curled, eyes wild.

Weil hadn't even picked himself up before the legionnaires lunged in, closing on the prisoner from both sides. The youth launched himself at one soldier, a tackle at the waist that threw him to the floor. The native erupted at the second, staggering him under a rain of cuffs at his helmet. The man tore at the clinging fury until he freed one hand enough to grasp his nightstick, and then he lashed out.

It connected with a crack like a rifle-blast above the scuffling. The gan crumpled, mouth bleeding.

The youth saw it and stiffened. Horror etched his face, drained it of all color. He gasped out an alien word—screamed it over and over as he tore at his opponent with hands like claws.

Watching as the boy fought to free himself, teeth bared and limbs flailing, Weil couldn't help wondering if he was entirely human, or if there might be as much alien biology as upbringing behind his attack.

The legionnaire was larger of build, and heavier. He found leverage with a foot and wrenched himself over. Straddling the boy's chest, pinning his arms, he panted, "Here . . . you go . . . Doc. He's—all yours!"

Weil dropped down beside them—looked up at the sound of footfalls. Lansill and François stood over him, but the colonel motioned at the second soldier. "Put the wild boy outside the electrifield—if you haven't killed him already."

"Yes, sir." The man hauled the limp native up over his plated shoulders.

On the floor, the youth kicked and strained against his captor, screaming that alien word again.

"Get the drug into him," Lansill said.

Weil reached into his coat pocket for a plastic packet. He

pulled it open, revealing two pads like coins made of stiff gauze. Peeling the backing from one, he reached for the prisoner's face.

The youth twisted his head away. The soldier, knees planted on his upper arms, leaned forward to seize him by the hair. The boy stiffened, paled under the shift of weight, choked on a gasp.

"You'll break his arms!" said Weil.

"Yes, sir. You want him hitting you again?"

Weil glared at him. He pressed the pad to the boy's temple—couldn't meet his eyes, wide with fear, as he turned his head to apply the second patch.

In moments the youth's rigidity subsided, his clenched hands uncurled, his bent knees went slack. He lay turning his head from side to side, blinking, his panting reduced to sighs.

"That's good," the colonel said behind Weil, and unclipped an audicorder from his belt. "Sit him up against the wall, Gerik."

"What, sir?" Weil stared up at him.

The soldier caught the youth under the arms and propped him against the wall; his head lolled; he shook it, tried to lift it. He barely managed to hiss when the colonel squatted in front of him.

"Now then, *Tristan Serege*." Lansill drew two pendants on a thread from an inside pocket and dangled them before him. "You can stop playing ignorant; we know who you are. We've had these for several years. Do you know what they are?"

The youth's eyes widened, fixing on the slowly revolving holodiscs. He only swallowed.

The colonel's sudden hand snapped his head to the side. "Answer me, Tristan! Where is your mother? Why did she send you here?"

"Sir," Weil said, "the drug's disoriented him."

The colonel scowled at him. "It'll also break him, Captain. We need answers." He faced the youth again. "Where is she, Tristan?"

"Sick . . ." the boy said, "fr'm th' coughing sickness. . . ."

"Why did she send you here? Where is she?"

"Ou' there . . . man' nights away. . . ." Tristan shook his head, trying to hold it up.

Weil recognized the drug's effect in slurred words that spilled without reservation. He knotted up his hands.

The broad hand struck the other side of Tristan's face. Last daylight through the window grid showed a red print there. Lansill tapped the patch adhered to his temple. "You'll give us answers sooner or later," he said. "It'll be easier for you if you don't keep me waiting. . . . Now, why did you come here?"

The youth sagged, his eyes showing confusion. "T' find . . . m' father."

His interrogator grasped his chin, jerked up his head. "Your father. Where is *he*? Where are you going?"

"Don' know." Tristan tried to shake his head but the hand at his jaw prevented it. "I don' know. . . ."

"And *why* must you find your father, Tristan?"

"Gotta help 'er. She's sick," Tristan said. "Gotta . . . find 'im t' help 'er. . . . Don' know where 'e is."

Weil cringed when the colonel slapped the boy once more, but it roused him only enough to make him shudder this time. Lansill switched off the audicorder, rocked back on his heels, rose up. "Give the doctor a hand with him, Gerik."

"Yes sir." The soldier let the boy slump sideways to the floor and motioned at a cohort to bring in a med sled.

"With your permission, sir," Weil heard the colonel say, "I'll set up a low-level aerial search for the woman." He didn't glance up, just eased the youth onto the sled and drew its cocoon over him.

"Good," the general said behind him. "Governor Renier doesn't want her taken into custody yet, but she must be kept under surveillance in case that becomes necessary."

When Weil straightened, turning the sled over to the soldiers, the general was already gone. But Lansill stood in the doorway. "The shuttle lifts in two standard hours, Captain," he said.

Weil clenched his teeth, watching the soldiers place the comatose youth on the ER surgical table. Only when they withdrew to stand near the door did he move away to scrub.

He removed the boy's aboriginal clothing, washed him, and shrouded him in the metallic chill of a hypothermic sheet. Reaching over the table, he uncoiled wires from the monitor bank in the medical capsule which waited like a coffin on a wheeled cart. He switched on its computer, scanned the temperature control and life-support units, and put the thermostat on its lowest setting.

He applied cardiopulmonary sensors to the boy's chest, inserted an internal thermoprobe, catheterized him. Placing intravenous shunts in his external iliac artery and vein required minor laser surgery. Weil eyed the vital-signs monitor when he had finished, noting blood pressure and body temperature, pulse rate, respirations, and blood chemistry. The computerized infusion system purred on, managing oxygenation and dialysis and maintaining the boy's electrolyte balance.

The temperature reading already showed a marginal drop. Weil stepped back, peeling off bloodied gloves, and said quietly, "Good."

Waiting for temperature and pulse rate to drop further, he placed the youth's battered left hand under the holoscanner and examined it for fractures. There were none, but he applied medication and braced the hand, then spread salve over the contusions on the boy's face, arms, and chest.

"Maybe you should cut his nails so he don't claw you again, sir," said Gerik from near the door.

Weil touched the discoloration swelling on his own cheekbone. "Get out of here, Sergeant!"

The boy's pulse had dropped to fifty and his respirations were slow and shallow when Weil glanced at the monitors again. He reached for the electrocardio patches.

Peeling the backing from the metallic discs, he adhered one over his patient's heart, the second in the corresponding spot on his back. He checked wiring connections, then synchronized the computer's weak impulse to the rhythm already sketched on the monitor. Opening the current, he watched the pulsemaker's green line parallel the youth's heartbeat—his body didn't twitch at the mild shock.

Pressing his mouth tight, Weil keyed in the stasis program: twelve heartbeats and three respirations per minute with body temperature maintained at 22 degrees Celsius. Coordinating the data, the vital-signs monitor and computer would gradually reduce the boy's metabolism to the set level and support it there. Once established, stasis required only minimal IV nourishment and no anesthetic.

Weil watched the pulsemaker's oscillating pattern shift into the primary rate decrease, the critical point of initiation: there was always a small chance of fibrillation or total arrest.

The first hesitant heartbeat faltered—then was caught up, righted, on the second shock. Weil released a breath he didn't know he'd been holding.

Assured that the transition would progress smoothly, he called the guards back in to help move his patient from the table into the capsule. Untangling monitor wires and re-wrapping the hypothermic sheet, he avoided looking at the youth's face.

An hour later he switched on the capsule's repulsors. The military police maneuvered it through automated doors toward a freight hauler with terrain treads, and two more legionnaires eased it aboard.

Colonel Lansill glanced at the form beneath the transparent capsule cover as it slid past him, then thrust a strongbox at Weil. "Proof of the prisoner's identity," he said. "Give it *only* to Governor Renier." He inspected his timepiece. "The crew of the *Bonne Fortune* is waiting. You'll go with them as far as Adriat, where the Sector General's personal voyager will make rendezvous. Questions, Captain?"

Weil set his jaw. "No sir."

"Very good. You're dismissed."

Weil clipped off the expected salute and mounted the freight hauler; thought for a moment that he'd glimpsed amber eyes blinking up at him from between its treads. He shook his head. Still, huddled with the soldiers under the hauler's shell, he shuddered with the feeling that something in the shadows was watching him, questioning him, assessing him.

He couldn't shake it even in the shuttle, kept thinking he'd felt something brush his leg as he helped maneuver the capsule aboard.

In another four hours he was strapping the medical capsule into a berth in one of *Bonne Fortune*'s cabins. He tested the bands with a tug and looked around the cubicle before he snapped out the illuminant, half expecting to glimpse a ghost in a corner. Latching the door, he found that someone had attached a handmade placard that read AUTHORIZED PERSONNEL ONLY. He left it there when he retired to the crew lounge for departure.

Thrusters bore the merchant ship clear of the orbital station where the shuttle still hung in dock. Real-space engines cut in, and Ganwold gradually began to shrink on the lounge viewscreen.

Three days until lightskip to Adriat, Weil thought. *What am I doing here?* He glanced about the compartment at twenty-six merchant spacers and three legionnaires, and felt again that someone was watching him.

When a voice over the intercom gave clearance, he rose and went back to his own cabin, next to the one with the placard on the door.

He had just stretched out in his berth and pulled the microreader with the anthropologist's report out of his front pocket when he heard the wail. He tried to ignore it at first, but he found himself listening as it swelled to a mournful pitch and ebbed to a sigh at irregular intervals. It rose over the throb from the engine room belowdecks; it emanated from the bulkheads. Weil felt his scalp prickle.

After a few moments he rose and slid open the portal. Listening, he stepped into the passage.

The moan reached him clearly, coming from the compartment with the AUTHORIZED PERSONNEL ONLY sign. He'd known that had to be its source. He stood still, heart beating hard against his ribs—and in a distracted, clinical way, he briefly wondered at its rate. *Be sensible,* he chided himself. *There's a logical explanation for this.* He seized the lever, flung the door open.

Amber eyes glowed at him out of darkness. The keening turned to a hiss. Weil substituted several jabs at the light button for a gasp—and missed three times before he connected.

Crouched in the lower berth beside the capsule, with clawed hands spread on its cover, the alien drew back bloodied lips from his teeth. A bottom canine was broken. He raised one hand like a readied weapon.

Weil sank back from the door frame, his heart still racing. But when the alien began groping at the capsule's seals, he shook his head. "Don't! Don't! You'll hurt him, understand? He's not dead. He's—he's asleep. Don't hurt him!"

The frantic hands paused. The striped face tilted and the eyes narrowed, questioning.

"That's it," Weil said, nodding. "That's it." He felt his tension ebbing, felt his heart rate beginning to calm. He drew a long breath and said, "He's all right." He kept his tone calm, soothing. "I won't hurt him. . . . I won't hurt you. It's going to be all right, understand?"

Hunched by the capsule, the gan eyed him for a long time before he gave a single, acknowledging blink.

Sitting alone in the spacers' mess, Weil placed the meat portin of his meal in a paper towel, wrapped it carefully and slipped it into his jacket pocket. It was synthetic, a protein concoction of some type instead of real meat, but it would have to do. He rose, slid his utensils and tray into the collection bin, and made his way back to the prisoner's cabin.

The alien peered down at him from the upper berth when he stepped inside. Weil pulled the package from his pocket, unfolded the wrapping, spread it out in front of him. "This won't taste like what you're used to," he said, "but it's all there is."

The gan sniffed at his offering, wary. Wrinkled his nose at it. But he was plainly hungry: in another moment he picked it up, smelled it more carefully, then ventured a cautious bite. He cocked his head as if puzzled by its flavor, but he continued to eat.

Feeling oddly relieved, Weil returned to his own cabin.

The anthropology report still lay on the berth where he had left it. He scooped it up, sank into the cabin's single seat and flicked it on.

As he read, questions began to curl up in his mind like wisps of smoke. What would the authorities do with the alien if he were discovered? Dispose of him out of an airlock? What would they do with him if he made it all the way to Issel? Weil was certain they wouldn't trouble themselves to return him to Ganwold. And how would the boy react when he learned what had happened to his friend? Remembering the way he had fought in the guardhouse—so that he'd seemed more animal than human—Weil set his teeth.

The questions kept him awake through the ship's simulated night, kept him restless in his berth. They tangled themselves up with portions of the anthropology report and ran through his memory again and again as if caught in a loop.

The anthropology report! That was it! The scientists had emphasized the depth of the fraternal bond between gan males. Could he perhaps claim a psychological link as well? That the companionship was as necessary for psychological stability as it was for physical safety? What he had witnessed in the cell would certainly tend to support that!

Weil shoved himself out of the berth, his heart racing. He fumbled through the stowage compartment, among his clothes, for the microreader containing the report. All he had to do was create a medical record for the prisoner, documenting his instability and his tendency toward violence when separated from his alien companion. He could even claim, after watching the alien try to tear open the capsule, that the instability went both ways. He'd have to embellish it some—but then, that would be nothing new. Every officer evaluation he'd ever written or received had been more fiction than fact.

Halfway through tapping his conclusions and recommendations into his microwriter, another set of questions crossed his mind: *Why are you doing this? What does it even matter to you?*

He sat for several minutes trying to rationalize his actions, but there didn't seem to be any reasonable answers. The kid was supposed to be a criminal, after all. He could end up being court-martialed himself if his attempt to obstruct justice was discovered.

He didn't believe the "criminal" story. There was something else behind this, something about it that left him uncomfortable. He felt as if he'd been made an unwitting accessory to an abduction.

Waiting inside the hangar shell out of the early winter sleet, Dylan Dartmuth scanned the roiling darkness for flashes of a shuttle's approach lights.

Nothing yet. It left him with an odd sense of reprieve, a sense that there might still be a chance, if he could come up with a plan. . . .

Better forget it, he counseled himself. *He's a prisoner being transferred—probably a dangerous prisoner, to be transferred that way. . . . So there's an uncanny resemblance; that's all it is.*

He narrowed his gaze on the outline of *Bonne Fortune*'s landing boat. Its skin still seemed to shimmer with its receding heat. Around it, the private landing area was a topographical map of icy lakes.

Shivering, Dylan crossed his arms over the Academy flightline patches and tech sergeant insignia on his field jacket. There was no regular crew for the Sector General's private spaceport; Dylan had been conscripted for duty here today much as he had been conscripted into the Sector General's service in the first place.

He felt a lot older than thirty-five. The War had ended his childhood before he was ten, in a single night of torture which had left him maimed and his twin brother dead. There hadn't been access to medical care then, to repair the damage done by his mother's interrogators; he still limped. His gray eyes had hardened to steel, his mouth to a serious line beneath his dark mustache, and most of his hair had already gone gray.

Leaning against the pressmetal siding, he couldn't keep himself from glancing over his shoulder toward the center of the dome hangar. His cohorts ranged about in pairs and small knots, some leaning on the grain drums stamped

GANWOLD which they had unloaded and stacked. They all kept their distance from the soldiers, the alien, the med capsule whose cover was beaded with rainwater that hadn't rolled off.

Helping to unload that capsule, Dylan had glimpsed its occupant's face and found himself remembering a childhood hero: a combat pilot with a Topawan accent and a ready smile, who had flown in the battle that bought Adriat's short-lived liberation, and survived to join with Dylan's older sister.

It had been years since Dylan had seen the man that young pilot had become: hero of all the Unified Worlds now, but very much alone despite his place in the public eye.

Riveted by the youth's familiarity, Dylan had asked the medical officer, "Who is he, sir? What's the matter here?"

He'd read wariness in the captain's appraisal of him, had half expected the younger man to disdain replying to an enlisted man's curiosity. But the medic said, "He's a prisoner being transferred to Issel."

Dylan had recoiled. "To Issel? He's bloody young for a sentence like that! What's he done, sir?"

The doctor flicked a glance backward and, noting how the legionnaires stood off, cradling their rifles, he said, "I don't know; they wouldn't tell me that."

In another moment the soldiers turned and began to saunter toward them, and the captain had swallowed and said, "Dismissed, Sergeant."

Dylan had turned away, but not before he'd read the distress that creased the medical officer's face, and he knew the captain didn't believe the boy was a criminal any more than he did.

FOUR

Tristan was first aware of being cold, shivering, and then voices, and hands massaging feeling into his limbs, and moving him, and wrapping him in something warm. It was a long time before the shivering began to ease. He tried to open his eyes, tried to lift a hand to rub them, but the effort left him exhausted.

A hand slid under his head and neck, raising him slightly, and a voice above his head said, "Come on, kid, try to drink a little now." Another hand put a drinking tube to his mouth. Suddenly aware that he was thirsty, he took the water in gulps, so that he almost choked on it.

The tube drew away. "Easy there!" the voice said. "You'll upset your stomach. That's enough!" The hand eased him down.

Without any warning discomfort, he was retching. Hands supported his head until it ended, then wiped his mouth and nose and chin. The voice was apologetic: "I was afraid of that. Your stomach's been empty for too long. Go back to sleep now. We'll try some more later."

There were moments of rousing—vague memories of the drinking tube and vomiting, and hands, and a shadow leaning over him—between timeless stretches of sleep.

Tristan sensed that several more hours had passed by the time he woke enough to perceive his surroundings. Dim light from his left drew his attention; it filtered through a cover hung over a large opening. Turning over to face it, his hand slipped off the surface he was lying on. He jerked back with a gasp.

Through eyes that wouldn't focus he scanned ceiling and walls. The room was about four arm-lengths wide and maybe twice as long—half the size of the stone room he'd lost consciousness in. And he was alone.

"Pulou!" he whispered.

He struggled the covers off, puzzled at the effort it required, and pushed himself to a sitting position. His vision spun—momentarily tunneled. Waiting for the dizziness to pass, he tried to shed the loose garment that hung from his shoulders, but it was twisted around his thighs. He got it untangled enough to slide one leg over the edge and reach for the ground with his foot; the other leg followed. He stood up slowly—and staggered, strengthless as a newborn peimu. Gaining a little balance, he stumbled toward the opening, pushed its cover away with one hand—

—and crashed into something as solid as the walls.

He crumpled, robbed of wind, weak, his nose and forehead throbbing. It took all the strength he had left to drag himself to his knees, panting hard. He groped for a way out of the curtains, but they clung like a spider's web, and dizziness swallowed him. He reached out for something to steady himself. One hand found smooth solidity; he leaned against it.

As the giddiness ebbed, he opened his eyes—and his breath snagged in his throat. He shrank back as if the wall might give way into the thin air it appeared to be.

Beyond it, open space dropped away to a depth so vast he didn't want to glimpse the bottom of it, and stretched across smoky daylight to a skyline of cylindrical towers. The scent of the wind burned his nostrils, made him wrinkle his nose. He saw movement against the skyscape, vehicles that careened between the towers like insects through tall grass. His stomach turned under his ribs.

He was still staring, not daring to move for fear of losing his balance and falling out, when something clicked and rasped softly behind him. He turned slightly, in time to see part of the wall sliding closed behind a man in uniform.

The face was shadowed but Tristan recognized him at once. He swallowed, mouth suddenly dry. Tried once more to push himself back from the edge, to gain his feet, and raised one hand like bared claws in a desperate attempt to warn the man back.

But the man set down the box he was carrying, crossed to him in two strides, and dropped to his heels beside him. "Good grief, kid!" he said. "I leave the room for two minutes and you get out of bed!" He caught Tristan by the shoulders when he swayed. "Are you all right?"

Tristan managed to hiss at the grip on his shoulders—combat posture among the ganan—and tried to struggle.

The man didn't let go. "I'm not going to hurt you," he said. "Come on." He steered Tristan against his will back to the bed and settled him in. "You're still groggy," he said. "You shouldn't be getting up unassisted like that. The oxygen level here is lower than you're used to, and the grav is higher, and stasis always leaves a person weak and shaky for a few days anyway. . . . Now, how did you get that knot on your forehead?"

Tristan tried to touch the bruise but he could barely raise his hand to it. "That looks open," he said with a random wave toward the curtain, "but it's hard—like stone." His speech sounded garbled even to himself; his lips and tongue and mind all seemed thick, fuzzy, disconnected. And that increased his sense of urgency. "Have t' find Pulou," he said. "They hurt 'im." He tried to push himself up.

"Take it easy." The man pressed him back down with a

hand on his shoulder. "There's no need to get upset. Your friend is fine; he's asleep in my room. I'll bring him in later. Let's just take care of you right now, okay?"

He opened the thin cloth over Tristan's shoulder, uncovering a blue circle near his armpit.

"What's that?" Tristan asked. "Will it—make me sleep again?"

"No. It's a thermodot," the man said. "It would change color if you were feverish, but it looks normal right now." He reached out toward Tristan's throat.

Tristan twitched away from him, baring his teeth.

"Hey, relax!" the man said. "I just need to count your pulse!"

Tristan swallowed and watched his eyes, tense under his touch.

"How's your stomach?" the man asked. "Are you getting hungry yet?"

"N-no," Tristan said.

"Does it still feel upset?"

"Yes."

"We'll wait to give you anything else, then." The man closed the cloth back up over his shoulder and reached for his box. Tristan watched as he selected a small vial. "This is for that bruise on your forehead," he said, pressing something white onto his fingertip. "It should be pretty well healed by tomorrow."

Spreading the salve, he added, "I'm Reed Weil. I'm a captain in the Isselan Surface Forces Medical Corps. I'm really sorry about all of this."

Tristan said nothing, just watched him.

"Look," Weil said, "I don't blame you for not trusting me. You're thinking I'm just another of the thugs who beat up on you—"

"You didn't stop them!" Tristan said. "You put—those things—on my face!" The thick feeling was gradually leaving his mouth.

The medic winced at his accusation. "I didn't want to, kid, but it would've been a lot worse for you if I hadn't." He sighed. "I'm sorry. I'm just trying to help you."

Tristan didn't answer.

"I'm trying to help your friend, too," Weil said. He leaned closer and lowered his voice. "I told the—the people here—that you and he would both become violent and dangerous if you were separated."

Tristan straightened abruptly and stared at him. "Why did you say that?" he demanded. "That isn't right!"

The medic motioned him to be quiet. "I did it to protect you," he said. "I had reason to believe they'd take your friend away and harm him."

Tristan's puzzlement deepened. He furrowed his brow. "Why would they do that?"

The other hesitated. Shook his head. "Because they don't have any use for him," he said at last. "They . . . think he's not important because he's not human, and that he's just in the way. Do you understand that?"

Tristan understood the meaning of the words but not the thinking behind them. He nodded, but his forehead stayed wrinkled.

"Okay," the medic said. And then, "Even if the part about being dangerous isn't true, it's important that you and your friend act like it is if anyone tries to take him away. Got that?"

Tristan swallowed hard and nodded again.

"Good." The medic straightened and returned to his normal tone of voice. "How's your hand?" he asked. "The left one. Can you move it?"

Tristan lifted it—and stiffened. His fingernails had been cut off. He looked at his right hand, too, and felt shock. "You cut off my claws!" The words were an accusation. "Why did you do that to me?"

Weil appeared startled. He put out his own hand. "Look at mine."

"It's naked!" Tristan said. "Only babies don't have claws! I need them to hunt and to—"

"You won't have to hunt here," said the medic. "There's no need to have claws here."

Chagrined, Tristan knotted his hands together between his knees and turned onto his side, his back to the man. His throat suddenly seemed so tight he could scarcely breathe.

It was several seconds before Weil asked quietly from behind him, "Tristan, is there any pain or stiffness in your hand?"

"No," he said into the pillow.

"It was very badly bruised. What happened?"

"I—hit one of the humans wearing the—shiny shells."

"You mean armor?" the medic said. "You're lucky it wasn't broken!"

Tristan didn't reply, didn't stir. Just squeezed his hands more tightly together.

"Tris," Weil said after another pause, "I'm not done patching you up yet. I need you to turn onto your back again."

Tristan waited for several more seconds before he complied, and then he watched, wary, as the medic drew the covers away, applied more salve to his finger, and reached for the thin cloth covering his groin. He stiffened, suddenly suspicious, suddenly angry. "What are you doing?"

"I had to make a couple of cuts in your thigh to place some tubes," Weil said. "They need fresh salve, too." He paused. "Would you rather do it yourself?"

"Yes," Tristan said.

"Hold out your finger, then."

He did, and Weil wiped the salve from his own finger onto it.

The healing cuts in Tristan's upper thigh were still pink, still tender. "Why did you put tubes in my leg?" he demanded.

The medic drew a deep breath. "You've been in—hibernation—for over two weeks, except in medicine we call it stasis. The tubes were to feed you."

"*Weeks?*" Tristan furrowed his brow again at the unfamiliar word. "How many nights is that?"

"You were asleep for fifteen."

"Fifteen!" The shock came back. And the dry-mouthed fear. "Three hands of nights!" Tristan stared at the man. "Why?"

Weil studied him briefly, looking uncomfortable. At last he sighed. "They wanted to move you," he said. "I did it to make the trip easier for you. It took almost fifteen days to get here."

Tristan looked away from him, toward the gray skyscape. His throat felt tight again. "It's . . . too close in here," he said. "It's—ugly."

"Yes, it is," Weil said, very quietly. "I'm sorry." He pulled the bedcovers back up over Tristan's legs and sighed once more. "You're doing fine," he said, "but I think you should try to sleep some more. I'll be here if you need help."

Waking again later, Tristan thought maybe he had only dreamed it all—until the medic brought him more water and he drew one hand from beneath the bedcovers to take the cup and saw his naked fingers.

He turned back toward the wall and didn't sleep after that. When a dull ache began at the back of his skull, he curled deeper under the covers, wrapping his arms over his head. He heard the medic moving around the room and ignored him, until he heard the wall open and close. Then he shifted onto his back, grimacing with the headache.

Evening was coming. The walls were pink with light reflected from a red sun that slid down behind the faraway towers. He watched the smoky sky turn bloody, then black. There were no stars, no insect noises, no jous howling. Just lights that winked on in the silhouetted towers and sounds he didn't recognize.

He lay for a long time staring out on it all, lay with his

violated hands clenched together, wanting to keen out his loss, his fear and confusion; but the sound was caught like a bone in his throat, swelling the ache in his chest.

He didn't hear the wall open and close again, just glimpsed a shadow's motion from the corner of his eye. He thrust a hand from under the covers in an ineffective shove. "Leave me alone!"

Another, swifter hand caught his, and claws gripped it in brief reprimand. "Little brother."

"Pulou!" The tension left Tristan's hand. He freed it to nudge his companion's chest with his knuckles. "You're all right?"

Pulou grinned, a flash of teeth in the dimness. A bottom one was broken, but Pulou said, "I'm all right."

He crouched close, stroking Tristan's hair with the back of one hand while the medic read the thermodot and counted his pulse again.

"How are you feeling now?" Weil asked.

"Head aches," Tristan said.

"What about your stomach?"

He shrugged.

The medic opened his box, removed the seal from a tiny cup of dark liquid. "Drink this. It'll stop the headache and help you relax. Can you take some more water with it?"

He accepted the water as well, drank it with Pulou and the human watching him—and kept his hands curled so Pulou wouldn't see that they were naked.

He waited only until the medic had gone to get out of bed. He tried to tug its cover off but he was still shaky, still weak. "Help me," he asked of Pulou.

"You do what, little brother?"

"I sleep on ground," Tristan said. "I don't like this; I'm afraid I fall off."

When he sank into sleep again, rolled up in the bedcover, Pulou was sitting cross-legged beside him, gazing out on the skyscape with his head cocked in bewilderment.

There was light coming through the curtain, and Pulou was already curled up in sleep beside it, when Tristan woke to a clinical touch on his forehead. He shifted onto his back and blinked up at Captain Weil.

"Why are you on the floor?" the medic asked. "Are you all right?"

"Yes," Tristan said. And then, "I need the bushes."

Weil appeared puzzled for a moment. Then he said, "Oh," and offered a hand. "Let me help you up and I'll show you where the latrine is."

He took Tristan by the elbow and helped to steady him on his feet before maneuvering him around the bed toward a curtain over the wall at its foot. Tristan flinched, putting out a blocking hand when the medic pushed the curtain aside.

Behind it was a tiny room full of shiny things, oddly shaped. Weil explained their use, showed him how they worked, but Tristan hung back, wrinkling his nose with revulsion.

He felt the medic eyeing him. "What's wrong?"

"At home we go away from camp for that," Tristan said. "We never do it in the lodge! It's not clean."

He saw several expressions flicker across the other's face, but the eyes that met his held only sympathy. "Look, I know this is all really strange to you," Weil said, "but you can't 'go away' here. I'm trying to make it as easy for you as I can. You'll get used to it. Do you want me to wait outside?"

"Yes," Tristan said.

Even then he stood staring at the toilet until his bladder left him without a choice.

When Weil came back, he indicated a cylinder in the corner, like the trunk of a large tree. Its side slid open when he touched it, revealing a hollow big enough to stand in.

"It's a hygiene booth, for washing yourself," he said, and pointed to small holes in a ring around the top. "The water comes in through those. You push the buttons here"—he tapped a panel just inside the door—"to start it and make it cooler or warmer. It'll stop by itself when the ration's spent. I think you'll feel better after you've washed."

Tristan held on to its doorframe with both hands and let the medic assist him out of the loose garment. Wadding the cloth and tucking it under his arm, Weil helped him into the booth. "If you start getting shaky or faint," he said, "just call; I'll be right here."

Tristan watched him push the buttons; stiffened when Weil slid the door closed. Tristan glanced around the enclosure, tested the door panel's seam with his fingers until a soft hiss jerked his vision to the water ring over his head. Remembering the creeks he'd bathed in since childhood, he braced himself for a downpour of icy water. It was warm, but he gasped anyway.

And then he realized that he'd seen no way for the water to escape. Wet hands clawed at the door's seal, pulled at the grid in the ceiling. "Stop it!" he said. "I'll drown in here!"

The water turned into lather, white and slippery. It matted in his hair; he shook it out—and lost his balance. Staggering, he flung out an arm to catch himself and caught a swath of white spray across his face instead. He gagged on sudden bitterness in his mouth, swiped at burning eyes, began to choke and spit.

From outside, Weil's voice asked, ". . . all right, Tristan?"

"Let me—" Choking cut him off. He coughed, spit, managed to drag in a breath. "Let me out of this!"

One hand brushed the button panel. He slammed at it

blindly, and an icy deluge broke over his head. It took his breath, but it swept away the lather.

Shivering violently, he reached out to save himself when his legs gave way. His fingers slid down a seam in the cylinder's wall. He tore at it, scrabbling on wet metal. Yelled again: "Let me out of here!"

Pale light shot over his shoulder through the opened door; the waterfall ceased simultaneously. "Are you all right, Tristan?" asked Weil.

He was facing the wrong direction, his fingers tearing at the wrong seam. He wrenched around, glaring at the medic as he pulled himself to his feet. His hands shook, and his legs. "Am I—all right?" he said, teeth chattering. "Y-you—put me in this—this water thing . . . like a lomo in a burrow—with no way out . . . and th-that white slime—almost made me go blind, and—" He broke off, coughing again. "Why didn't you—just kill me—before?"

"Tristan, calm down," Weil said. "I'm sorry. That 'white slime' is just body cleanser; you're not going blind. I should've told you what to expect. I'm sorry." He reached out, but Tristan, still shaking, raised a curled hand and bared his teeth. The medic hesitated. "All right," he said after a moment. "Do you see the square black button? Push that one."

Tristan eyed him, suspicious. "What'll that do to me?"

"It'll send in warm air through the vents above your head and dry you off," Weil said. "If you stand there cold and wet much longer, I'll be treating you for pneumonia instead of just stasis shock."

Tristan fixed him with a warning look from beneath his dripping forelock as he reached for the square black button.

It took a few minutes for the shivering to subside, even in the rush of warm air. It took even longer for him to begin to relax.

The medic held out a fresh tunic when he stepped out of

the hygiene booth. Tristan took it, wrapped it snug around his waist, knotted it.

"That's not how—" Weil began.

"It's like a loincloth this way," Tristan said.

The other didn't argue, just helped him back to the bedroom and asked, "Are you hungry yet?"

"Yes," Tristan said. He sat down on the floor, deliberately avoiding both the bed and the medic's look.

Weil collected a container from beside his box and twisted off its lid. "This is a cracked-grain gruel," he said. "It's good nourishment but it'll have a laxative effect. Stasis tends to make your bowel sluggish."

Tristan eyed the thick liquid, smelled it, stuck a finger into it and licked it off to taste it. It was vaguely sweet on his tongue, chewy in his teeth. His stomach growled. He tipped up the container for another mouthful.

"You're making a very good recovery," the medic said, "but I suggest that you rest again today. I'll come in from time to time to see how you're doing."

Occupied with eating, Tristan didn't answer. In a few minutes he put his head back for the last bit of gruel, then swept a finger around the inside of the container to make sure. Licking his finger clean, he thrust the empty canister at the medic.

Weil accepted it with a dim smile. "Are you still hungry?"

"No."

"Fine. I'll wait awhile to bring you anything else, then. Just go ahead and rest for now," Weil said, and picked up his box and stood.

Tristan watched, eyes narrowed, as the wall simply parted when the man approached it and closed again after he stepped through. Glancing back once at his sleeping companion, he rose.

The wall didn't open when he drew up to it. He tried to

force his fingers into seams that his nails might have succeeded at, sat down to brace his feet against the wall, and strained to slide the panel back.

The effort left him weak, left his arms and back sore. He searched with eyes and fingers for latches or buttons, but there were none. Realizing at last that it must be secured from the outside, he gave up and sat down to stare out on the skyscape.

But in another moment he was back on his feet, pushing the curtain aside. He held to the wall, still not certain that the pane wouldn't give way when he pressed his face to it to look down. The view made his stomach roll as it had before. He squeezed his eyes shut, pushed himself back, and released his breath.

The pane had been set into a square hole in the wall that reached from the floor almost to the ceiling; it was sunk several finger-widths into the wall. He tried to get a purchase on it, around its edges, but he couldn't without fingernails. He hissed his annoyance through his teeth.

Behind him, Pulou stirred, opening one eye. "You do what, little brother?"

He curled his naked hands against his body. "I try to find way out."

"Not that," said Pulou, and motioned in the general direction of the opening wall. "That's only way out."

"I try that," said Tristan. "It doesn't open."

Pulou shrugged one shoulder; he was lying on the other. "It's daytime, little brother. Go to sleep."

Sighing, Tristan dropped down and stretched out on his belly beside the gan. He wasn't sleepy; he was too restless, too frustrated—and more than a little anxious. He began an agitated picking at the fleecy floor covering with the hand that wasn't supporting his chin.

"Pulou?" he said after a minute.

"What?"

"We are where?"

He heard a noisy yawn, and Pulou said, "Far away."

"We go out how?" he asked.

Pulou turned his head, blinked at him. "I don't know. It's like tsigis nest."

Tristan remembered a honey tree he'd seen once, pocked and tunneled through until it was nearly hollow, and crawling with the insects. He questioned Pulou with his look.

"Go to sleep," the gan said. "We talk at night."

Pulou was asleep again in a moment, but Tristan wasn't.

He had not slept before the medic brought them supper in the evening: bowls of food and a pair of tiny sealed cups.

"You'll need to take one of these before you eat for the next few days," Weil said, peeling the seal off the cups. He gave one to Tristan, the other to Pulou. "The food here is different than what you're used to and this'll help your bodies adjust without the typical upset. I'm sorry that I couldn't just immunize you for this along with everything else while you were still in stasis."

The liquid was white, but it caked Tristan's mouth like mud. He grimaced, fighting the desire to spit, and watched Pulou wrinkle his nose over his own.

Weil put a bowl into his hands: a red soup with meat in it. He smelled it, felt its scent bite his nostrils, and glanced up. Pulou was already fishing meat out of the broth with his fingers. Tristan did the same.

It tasted like— *Burning!* He managed three or four chunks before thirst drove him to tip up the bowl and drink. But that only worsened it. Choking, he pushed the bowl away. "I want water!"

Weil poured a cupful from a jug. "Never drink water from the faucets in the latrine," he said. "It's not safe."

"Why?" Tristan asked—and suddenly thought of a

whole string of questions: "What is this place? Why won't the wall open for me? Why can't we go outside?"

The medic made a calming gesture. "You'll only have to stay in here until you're well. Governor Renier wanted to let you recover without disturbance."

"Governor? What's that?"

Weil looked briefly bewildered. "He's the—the leader over this sector of space. Do you understand that?"

"Of *space*?" Tristan furrowed his brow, feeling more confused than before. "Why does he want us here?"

"I don't know."

Something about the medic's expression and tone paralyzed Tristan. He held the steady gaze and swallowed hard. Then, glancing at Pulou, he pushed himself back, started to rise. "But we can't stay here! My mother is—"

Weil caught him by the arm. "Tristan, listen to me!"

His reaction to the grip, just above his elbow, was sheer reflex: a sharp, warning hiss; a flexed hand.

The medic let go, almost recoiling. But he said, "Sit down, will you, kid? Listen to me for a minute."

Pulou had already set down his bowl, and Tristan saw the wariness in his eyes. He felt a tightness in his own stomach as he squatted again, facing the human but staying beyond his reach.

"You're not on Ganwold anymore," Weil said. He kept his voice quiet. "We've traveled to a different planet in a different star system. Do you understand that?"

Tristan felt disbelief. He glanced over at Pulou. When the gan confirmed it with a single nod, he said, "In a . . . spacecraft?"

"Yes," Weil said. "That's why I—made you sleep. Lightskips and gravity changes are sometimes hard even for experienced spacers. Your friend was sick most of the way."

Tristan looked back at Pulou, who nodded again.

"The Sector General," Weil said quietly, "is in exile in

this system—but I guess you wouldn't understand any of that, would you?" He glanced uneasily about the room and lowered his voice still more. "I think he wants revenge, mostly. He knows that your mother is sick and that you're trying to find your father. . . ."

"Revenge?" Tristan cocked his head at the unfamiliar word.

"That means to get even. Somebody hurts you, so you go and hurt them back." Weil hesitated. "Doesn't that happen where you came from?"

"No." Tristan exchanged looks with Pulou. "There's only *tsaa'chi*."

"What's that?"

"It comes into your blood when there's danger," Tristan said. "It makes your heart beat fast. It makes you so you don't feel pain and so you want to fight, and when the danger is over, it goes away. You can't go hurt someone back; it's already over."

"Always," Pulou said quietly in gan, "someone dies. It's better to turn your back to anger."

Weil looked at Tristan for a translation, and then nodded. "Too bad most humans don't have that kind of sense." He sighed. "Look, kid, just be careful, okay? Don't believe everything you may be told. . . . And if you ever need help, you can trust me."

Tristan met his eyes. Searched them with his own for a long while before he gave a slight nod.

The medic forced a smile. "You haven't eaten very much."

"I'm not hungry anymore," Tristan said.

"I'm sorry," said Weil. He gathered up the discarded bowls and left the room.

FIVE

Captain Weil didn't come back in the morning.

Tristan was already awake and watching daylight pale the smoky skyscape when the wall sighed open. He turned his head, then reached over to nudge Pulou and sat up.

The men who came in were strangers: one tall, with gray hair and features that made Tristan think of a hawk; the other a little older than himself, stolid of face and stocky in his uniform.

Tristan got carefully to his feet, eyeing them, and in his peripheral vision saw Pulou slipping up to stand at his shoulder. "Where's Captain Weil?" he asked.

"It's all right, Tristan." The old man smiled and came toward him stiffly, leaning on a walking stick. "The captain has been transferred to a more urgent position. You don't need his treatment anymore."

Something about that left Tristan uneasy—left him remembering what Weil had said the night before. He studied the old man's face, studied his eyes through his own narrowed ones—and read suffering in them, as plainly as if it were a scar upon his face. That startled him.

The other must have seen it. He smiled again, dimly, and said, "It's good to see you again."

The tone was warm, not threatening, and Tristan's wariness gave way to bewilderment. "Again? I've never seen you before," he said.

The man appeared amused by that. "You wouldn't remember, I think. You were only a baby the last time I saw you."

His puzzlement increasing, Tristan cocked his head. "Who are you?"

"Governor Mordan Renier," the man said. "I'm an old friend of your parents'. It's been a very long time."

He knew the name. Knew it from something his mother had once told him. A chill shot up his spine; he edged back a step, shaking his head. Let his hands curl at his sides. "You're not my father's friend!" he said.

The governor looked at him with hurt in his eyes, in his features. "Didn't your mother ever teach you to forgive and forget, Tristan? To let bygones be bygones?"

He shook his head, backed up again. A ball of ice seemed to have settled in his stomach. "Why do you want us here?"

The governor smiled once more, still with that suggestion of hurt. "To help you, of course. I was told that your mother is seriously ill and you believe that your father can help her. Isn't that right?"

Tristan remembered again what Weil had said. He hesitated, then said, "Yes."

"Do you know where your father is, or how to contact him?"

"No."

"Well then, you're going to need some assistance, aren't you?" And the governor reached out and placed a hand on his shoulder.

Tristan cringed under the long fingers; his stomach lurched, too. He locked his teeth to hiss a warning—but then he glimpsed the other's eyes. They were full of gentleness, completely devoid of the provocation implied by his grip. Thoroughly confused, Tristan braced against reflex, keeping his curled hands close to his sides.

The voice was gentle, too. "It may take some time to contact your father, you understand. I hope you'll find this room suitable until then."

"No!" Tristan said at once, and made an angry gesture toward the skyscape. "It's ugly! We don't like being kept in here!"

"I'm sorry, my boy," the governor said. The gentleness left his tone; it took on a hard edge. "I would like to return to my own motherworld, too. But neither of us has that option right now."

He motioned at a sensor near the window and a white panel slid out from its frame, covering it the same way the sliding wall covered the doorway. With another motion the panel seemed to vanish, giving way to a view from a grassy hilltop that sloped down to sand and water. Water that rolled out to the sky like prairie grass in a wind and curled to white crests that crashed on the sand. Sunlight painted rainbows in the spray and flashed on the wings of circling birds whose cries sounded over the water's thunder.

Then the roar was silenced. The water turned to desert sand as white and hot as the sky it reflected. Rock and dust stretched to the horizon, rippled by a wind that tossed the sand and rattled the brittle plants.

Then the desert was swallowed up by the growth of a forest floor, by trees whose trunks were wider than the room, and ferns which were drawn up from black loam by fingers of light reaching down between the shivering leaves. An unseen bird called.

Tristan reached for the window frame, tried to push the panel back, wondering what had happened beyond it. He cocked his head at the governor.

Renier smiled. "The city is still out there," he said. "This forest and the desert and seashore are just recordings made on my motherworld. They provide a little variety."

He left the forest on the screen and moved away from it. "I expect that you're hungry by now, Tristan. I would be pleased to have you join me for breakfast."

"Pulou's hungry, too," Tristan said. Remembering what Weil had said, he curled his hands and gave the words a threatening tone.

The governor flicked a glance at Pulou. "He can come, of course. But first"—he reached for a strand of Tristan's hair, lying loose on his shoulder—

Too close to his throat. Tristan evaded the touch, bared his teeth—

—and saw fury shadow the other's face, hardening his eyes and jaw.

It was just as swiftly controlled. The governor's voice was gentle again when he said, "You need proper clothes and grooming first, Tristan, beginning with your hair." He drew two crystal pendants from his breast pocket and displayed them for the young man in uniform. "Cut it like this, please, Rajak."

Tristan eyed the pendants in the governor's hand, recognized the woman in one. "That's my mother!" he said, and the thing she had told him flashed across his mind once more.

"Yes, it is." The governor nodded. "These belonged to her once. Please sit down on the bed."

He stood still for a moment, looking the other in the eye. Finally sat. And immediately wondered if he had made a mistake when Rajak advanced on him with a shiny tool that looked like a weapon. He shot a half-panicked look at Pulou.

The gan crawled up on the bed beside him, fangs bared and ears pinned back, and crouched close enough to strike should it be necessary.

Rajak didn't seem to notice. "Sit still," he said. "Don't move your head."

Tristan recoiled when the instrument came too near his ear, buzzing like a tsigi. He felt Pulou stiffen, heard his warning hiss.

Rajak barely paused. "Hold still," he said.

Tristan squeezed his eyes shut, clenched his hands and teeth hard—until he felt the instrument's vibration at the nape of his neck. Then he reached up to shove it away. "Don't—!"

"Move your hand or it'll get cut," said Rajak.

Tristan saw shock in Pulou's face; he bit his lip. Hands knotted hard on his thighs, he bore it until the buzzing stopped and Rajak withdrew and the governor moved closer. His face heated up under the old man's scrutiny; he kept his head lowered.

Renier said, "Well done, Rajak. The resemblance is truly remarkable." He returned the holodiscs to his pocket and continued. "I'll send in Avuse with clothing for him. In the meantime, you will show him how to use the hygiene booth and beard foam. Breakfast will be served in one hour."

"Yes, sir," said Rajak.

When he heard the wall rasp open and then closed behind him, Tristan lifted his head just enough to slide a glance across at Pulou. His voice was barely audible: "It shows?"

"Yes." Pulou looked away from him, too decent to stare.

He felt as if he'd been stripped and put on display before his whole clan, more violated than he'd felt when he found his fingernails cut off. Reaching to the nape of his neck, he pressed his hand over the tiny raised tattoo there, the clan mark meant only for the eyes and touches of mates. His face burned with his humiliation.

"Come on, Tristan," said Rajak.

Hand still covering his clan mark, he rose and strode past Rajak without looking at him.

Emerging from the hygiene booth several minutes later, he caught a glimpse of himself in the reflector on the wall. A fresh wave of humiliation made him twist his face away.

But something about that split-second image caught at his memory, drew his reluctant gaze back up.

The face was undistorted by ripple or shadow, like the reflections he'd always seen of himself in water. But that wasn't it. He found himself startled by a sense of familiarity, a realization that he'd seen the same features somewhere else, in a way detached from himself. He turned his head to study his face from different angles, to see if that would make the connection. Paused to smooth his shorn hair down over his ears and neck—

—and familiarity became recognition: he looked like the young man in the holodiscs.

The trousers pinched where he was used to having only his loincloth. Tristan shifted from foot to foot and tugged at a chafing inseam, trying to relieve it. "I don't like this," he said. "It's too tight!"

"Stand still," said Rajak. He adjusted the shirt across Tristan's shoulders, made tucks at his waist, fastened the collar.

"That's too tight!" Tristan said.

The other thrust a finger between fabric and flesh. "No it's not."

"Yes it is!" Tristan pulled at it, but the catch didn't give. He slid his hand around to the back of his neck . . . felt a measure of relief when he discovered that it concealed his clan mark.

"Put on the boots," Rajak said, pointing.

They were tall and black, and as stiff as peimu hide that hadn't been tanned properly. Tristan picked one up, studied it. "How?" he asked.

Rajak looked at him as if he were stupid. "Push your foot down into it. . . . The other foot," he added when Tristan tried. "It's easier if you sit down. And tuck your trousers into the top."

The tops rubbed at Tristan's shins; the foot part chafed his ankles and heels. Their stiffness from ankles to knees made it difficult to walk, made him stumble.

"Here's your jacket," said Rajak, holding it out.

"I don't need that," Tristan said. "I already have this one on." He indicated his shirt.

"This goes over that one," said Rajak.

"Why? It's too warm in here even for this one!"

"It's proper. Put your arms in."

Tristan glowered at him but obeyed; and then he braced himself while the other tugged at shoulders and sleeves and fastened the clasps.

The jacket was binding across his chest and upper arms, restricting his movement. It made his shoulder blades and ribs itch and then made scratching futile. Turning away from Rajak, he glimpsed Pulou out of the corner of his eye, studying him. He didn't dare meet the look, didn't want to see Pulou, with his mane and his claws, grinning at him. A fresh wave of heat swept over his face. "Stupid!" he said under his breath.

"Come on," said Rajak. "The governor is waiting." He held the wall open for Tristan.

Beyond lay a passage that went left and right, wide enough for three people to walk at once, and gradually curving away so that Tristan couldn't see either end. Its walls were smooth and white, its floor quiet under a covering that looked like short gray fleece.

Rajak went to the left. Following him, Tristan trailed a hand along the curving wall and tried to ignore the way he already sweated under his shirt and jacket.

They passed a smaller corridor on the right with a door at its end, and three or four doors on the left that were indistinguishable from his but for the numbers on them. He hadn't noticed what number was on his own.

"Here," said Rajak. He stopped at double doors on the right; they parted as he approached. He said, "Tristan, sir," and stepped aside, beckoning.

Tristan's room would have fit inside this one nine or ten times. He looked around it, barely noticing the chairs at one side for the fireplace they were gathered around, scarcely seeing the cabinets that lined the back wall for the way they drew his vision up to sunlight flooding through panels in the ceiling. It didn't even occur to him to wonder whether or not that sunlight was real; it was the first bright, cheering thing he had seen here.

"Come in, Tristan." The governor, standing beside a table in the center of the room, looked him over and smiled. "That's much better," he said. "Now you do look like the son of an admiral."

Tristan said nothing.

Behind him, the doors opened once more and someone said, "Lady Larielle, sir."

He turned—and his hand went immediately to his forehead.

She appeared to be only a few years older than himself, tall for a woman, and willowy-slender, with dark hair that framed her face in loose ringlets. She said, "Good morning, Papa," and placed her hands in the governor's and allowed him to kiss one side of her face and then the other.

Tristan watched her unabashed, until she seemed to sense it and turned toward him—and then he ducked his head and touched his brow again and murmured, "Peace in you, mother," in gan. It was the only proper way he knew of to address her.

"My daughter, Larielle," the governor said, and his features tightened with some deep but indiscernible emotion as he added, "The last blossom left to the House of Renier."

The young woman's expression turned solemn at that; she pursed her pink lips and lowered her eyes.

"Lari," the governor said, "this is Tristan Serege, son of Admiral Lujan Serege, the Commander in Chief of the Unified Worlds' Spherzah. He will be staying here with us for a time."

Larielle reached out and took both of his hands. "Hello, Tristan," she said. There was genuine warmth in her voice, in her gentle squeeze of his hands. But her eyes, searching his, showed fear. Fear for him. Tristan saw it and swallowed hard.

"Please be seated," the governor said, and Tristan glanced up as he motioned to chairs beside his own and Larielle's.

Tristan watched them draw their chairs back from the table and seat themselves. He imitated them, feeling awkward. Eyeing the space between the chair and the floor, he braced his feet and held on to the edge of the table.

Pulou refused a chair altogether. "Flat-tooth things," he said, and stood studying the trays of food on the table. But he didn't reach for any of it, and Tristan didn't, either. Mothers ate first.

A boxy machine entered the room on hidden rollers and produced hot dishes and mugs of bittersweet black liquid from racks inside of it. The dishes contained circles of meat, crumbly chunks of white bread under dark gravy, slices of green fruit with black seeds clustered in the center. The smell of the meat made Tristan's stomach growl. He pressed a quick hand there to still it and glanced up, embarrassed. The girl and the governor hadn't noticed; they were already eating.

He watched as Pulou gathered up his dish and knife and settled in a squat on the floor, placing his plate before his feet. Familiar and practical. Tristan took up his own knife, started to lift his own plate—but the governor looked up at him. "Aren't you hungry, Tristan?"

"Yes," he said.

The governor studied him for a long moment. He stayed in the chair.

. He could see no use for any of the utensils except the knife; he ate the chunky circles of meat from its point. Then he broke up the bread and mopped up the gravy with its pieces, salvaging the rest with his fingers and licking them clean. The gravy's saltiness left him thirsty but the aroma from the mug made him wrinkle his nose. He pushed it away.

"Here, little brother," said Pulou, reaching up to leave a handful of green fruit on the white tablecloth. "I don't like this."

Tristan picked up the slices one by one and sucked at their sweetness. They assuaged his thirst. He licked the green juice from between his fingers.

"Tristan!" the governor said.

He looked up.

"There are handcloths for that!" The governor pointed. When Tristan cocked his head, puzzled, the governor took up his own and demonstrated.

"But that would dirty it!" Tristan said. "You clean your hands first so you won't dirty things."

The governor looked annoyed at that; but Tristan noticed the girl hiding a smile behind her hand. A smile about *him.* He turned away from her and shoved himself back from the table. "We don't have things like this at home! This is a stupid way to eat!"

The governor pushed himself to his feet, his expression a forced calm, his words a controlled quiet. "Come here, my boy. I think it's time that we talked."

Already on his feet, Tristan watched him cross to the fireplace and lower himself stiffly into a chair, but he didn't follow. The governor turned, favored him with a stern look, and indicated the facing chair with his walking stick.

Tristan went past it to the hearth and put out his hand to the flames. There was no heat. "This isn't a real fire," he said, accusing.

The other chuckled. "No, Tristan. It's a holoprojection, like the scenery in your room. A real fire is unnecessary where technology provides more efficient means of heating. . . . Come sit down."

Tristan glanced from the governor to the chair and back, and leaned up to the mantelpiece instead. He watched the servos clear the table, let his gaze wander the room again. Larielle had already slipped away, he saw, but Pulou squatted in the shadow of the chairs, vigilant with half-closed eyes.

"I'm being patient with you," the governor said at the edge of his awareness, "because I know this is all new and different to you. But don't try me, young one; I'm not a good man to press too far." He pointed his walking stick again at the empty chair and his tone went taut, like his jaw: "Sit down."

Tristan held his place. Watched the governor turn the walking stick in his hands so that artificial firelight reflected, red as blood, up and down its metallic length. Watched him curl his hands about its handle as if it were a knife or a club. He touched the governor's vision once more with his own, saw the controlled fury there . . . and waited as long as he dared.

Then he deliberately settled into a squat in front of the indicated chair.

The trousers pinched. The boots made balancing on his heels almost impossible. He leaned back against the chair's leg and locked his teeth against his discomfort.

The governor fixed a narrowed gaze on him. "Tristan, you are a human among humans," he said. "It's time that you began to behave like a human instead of like an animal."

Tristan glared at him. "Ganan aren't animals! Pulou is my brother, and if—"

"Your mother was an officer." The governor cut him off. "She was a refined and accomplished woman in her own world. Your behavior would be an embarrassment to her."

"My mother taught me what was right in *my* world," Tristan said. "She had important things to do, like helping sick people."

The governor was silent for a moment at that; then his features softened. "I'm sorry," he said. "I can't begin to imagine what she's suffered all these years!"

"She's sick!" Tristan said.

"I know that. And I admire the way in which you are trying to help her. But you have no idea how vast the galaxy is, young one. No concept of what you've taken on. You can't possibly accomplish it without assistance."

"Then take me to my father!"

"I wish it were that simple." The old man grew momentarily distant. "But it isn't. Not now."

When his vision came up again, he locked it on Tristan's. "I don't doubt that your father will want to help you and your mother when he finds out," he said. "In all of the years since you and she were lost he's never joined with another woman, never sired other children." His tone and expression were enigmatic. "There is no question that he'll want you back."

Something about his tone, about his choice of words sent a chill up Tristan's spine. Sent his mind racing again through the story that his mother had once told him. He glowered. Curled his hands.

"Perhaps we should send him a message," the governor said. He beckoned to the uniformed man standing near the double doors. "Avuse, please bring us the strongbox that General François sent out from Ganwold."

Avuse nodded, wordless, and went out.

Tristan could no longer resist the urge to put space between himself and the governor. He shoved himself to his feet and went back to the mantel, his vision fixed on the old man. "My mother told me that you tried to kill my father once. Why did you tell me that you were his friend?"

The governor met his look, seeming only mildly surprised at his accusation. "We *were* friends once," he said. "Good friends—until he betrayed me. It almost cost me my life."

"Betrayed?" Tristan cocked his head. "What does that mean?"

"It means to deliver or reveal one's friend to his enemies."

"My father didn't do that!" Tristan said. "You—"

"He betrayed me out of fear, I think," the governor continued. "All men fear what they do not understand, and they all judge issues of which they have no knowledge."

Tristan said nothing, just let his eyes narrow.

"Perhaps I should tell you what happened," the governor said, "so that you'll understand."

"Yes." Tristan snapped the word.

The governor regarded him briefly. "We were stationed at an emergency outpost on Tohh during the War of Resistance, rebuilding the forces we'd lost trying to save Issel, when I received word that my brother Sauvere, World Governor of Sostis, had died. It was a terrible shock to me— more so because his death put me next in line for the governorship."

His brow creased and his gaze grew distant, remembering. "I returned home to Sostis at once, to my mates and my children. It was the first time I'd seen Larielle; she was five months old by then." His jaw tightened. "That was also when I learned that my brother had been murdered, by the man who had been the chief minister of his cabinet and would now be mine."

Tristan stared. "Why?"

"Some members of Sauvere's cabinet had learned that the Dominion intended to strike Sostis next, while our forces were too weak to defend it. They had no desire to see their world devastated as Issel had been, and so they conspired to surrender it peacefully. My brother had refused to seal the documents.

"The thought of it sickened me. But Minister Remarq informed me that the Dominion's agents had already sealed their part of the documents. I could comply, or I could share Sauvere's fate; the deed was already done."

The governor paused. Sighed. "I sealed the surrender. Only a few of my cabinet and the Dominion agents knew of it. It allowed me, at least, to hold the governorship under Dominion authority." He looked up. "I did it out of love for my children, Tristan—and for my people. I did it to save them from the horrors I'd seen here on Issel . . . but I couldn't even tell them what it was I had done. They wouldn't have understood.

"When Sauvere's memorials and my own installation as World Governor were completed, I was informed by Remarq that I had to return to Tohh to finalize my separation from military service. I was still en route there when the Dominion seized power. Word of it reached Tohh even before I did, and I learned of it immediately upon my arrival. There had been a coup, I was told, and I couldn't return to Sostis. My former commanders had no idea what part I'd played in it, but it made no difference: the Dominion had my homeworld.

"They removed me from flying status at once, claiming that as the new World Governor I was far too valuable to be risked in combat—and that my distress at the situation might make me a danger to my comrades in battle." The governor's voice and his eyes, fixed on the artificial flames, revealed his disgust at the last.

"The humiliation might have been worse," he said. "I was appointed executive officer to the Wing Commander instead of being sent to the orderly room as a clerk. Still, it wasn't as demanding a job as I'd hoped it would be. In my spare time I discovered how to access the interstellar comm nets, and when I was alone in the office I used them to conduct my governmental correspondence with the cabinet on Sostis.

"Then one day your father came in to see the Wing Commander, just as I was preparing to release a message to Minister Remarq." The governor looked briefly at Tristan, then turned away again. "I told him that the Commander was out, but he didn't leave right away; he stood there and talked with me for several minutes.

"Unfortunately, there was no way for me to conceal what I was working on. I didn't know how much of it your father might have seen, but I couldn't take a chance of him telling anyone about it. So, knowing that he would be flying a training mission a little later that evening, I went out to the flightline and made some minor adjustments to his fighter—things that wouldn't be noticed in the preflight check but which would be attributed to ground crew carelessness afterward."

Tristan stared at him, feeling weak with shock—as much from the governor's emotionless retelling of it as by the actual deed. His palms were clammy, his mouth dry.

"I deeply regretted having to do it," the governor said. He shook his head. "Lujan had always been a good friend, and a good man to have at my wingtip in battle. But no one would have understood, had word of what he'd seen gotten out. They didn't know the situation. . . . Not even *he* would have understood."

"You almost killed him!" Tristan said. Every muscle in his body had gone taut.

The governor shook his head again; raised a hand in a

calming gesture. "No, Tristan," he said. "He received only minor injuries when he bailed out.

"But the crash investigators discovered what I'd done when they examined the fighter's wreckage. The ground crew was blamed at first, but then someone said that they'd seen me on the flightline. They questioned your father in the hospital, and he told them all about our conversation in the commander's office."

The governor's vision turned back to the flames; his features appeared hard as flint. "What he said resulted in a court-martial, Tristan. I was charged with attempted murder and high treason, and your father was the chief witness against me. Conviction would have meant the death sentence, and your father would have been the one most responsible.

"The only thing that saved me was the Dominion's attack on Tohh." The governor's voice had quieted, but it was still laced with bitterness. "I was liberated by Dominion troops and returned to Sostis.

"The next time I saw your father was across the treaty table at the Enach Accords. By that time he was wearing the uniform of a Spherzah assassin."

"Assassin?" said Tristan. "What's that?"

"A person who is paid to kill others," said the governor. "It's one of the dirty jobs that the Spherzah are best at."

"That's not right!" The shock that had enveloped Tristan gave way to a sudden fury. "That's not what my mother said! She told me the Spherzah—"

"Your mother"—Renier cut him off—"couldn't very well tell you about things she wouldn't know herself, Tristan. It isn't one of the things the Spherzah openly admit to. Assassination is frowned upon in most sectors of the galaxy."

Tristan searched the governor's face for several seconds at that. He swallowed hard. Shook his head against churning confusion, against an edge of doubt. "That's not right!" he said. Repeated it then to convince himself: "It's not right!"

The governor was watching him, his eyes still smoldering, but his features were relaxed now. "Your father is not really so different from me, young one," he said. "Every man has something in his life for which he will sell himself. I had mine; your father has his; you have your own. Remember that."

He turned then to motion at the servant who had resumed his place near the doors, and said, "Thank you, Avuse," when the man brought him the box. He opened it on his lap, withdrew a pair of ID tags on a chain and a gray object that fit in his palm. "Your mother's identification," he said, "and a recording of your voice. Shall we include the holodiscs as well?"

Tristan, eyes narrowed, said nothing.

But he watched as the governor drew the pendants from his pocket. Caught a glimpse of their images—the young man with the baby, the joining portrait—before he put them into the box, latched it and returned it to the servant, and asked, "When does the *Nebula Wind* leave Delta Station?"

"In two days, sir," the servant said.

Renier nodded. "Convenient. Mark this 'Personal for Admiral Lujan Serege' and entrust it to the *Wind*'s captain. It's to be delivered to our embassy on Sostis and couriered to Spherzah headquarters."

Tristan stripped to his shorts when he got back to his room, hurled boots and trousers and jacket into a corner on top of each other, and squatted before the holograph screen. He fingered its edge—pulled once, experimentally—but it didn't budge.

Moonlight had turned the ferns and grasses silver and made silhouettes of the foliage above. He wanted to run his hand up and down the roughness of a tree trunk, to take up a handful of soil and crumble it, moist and spicy, between his fingers. Maybe that would help him to relax.

His stomach was in knots. He hadn't eaten much at dinner; thought now that he shouldn't have eaten at all, though he knew it wasn't the food that had caused it.

He started when Pulou squatted beside him, nudging his shoulder. "Something's wrong, little brother."

He nodded but didn't look up. Pulou's mane and claws reminded him of his own nakedness. Shamed him.

"It's what?" said Pulou.

He shrugged. Tried once more to sort out the turmoil in his head before he sighed and said, "He tells me things about my father."

Pulou questioned him with a blink; Tristan caught the flash of amber from the corner of his eye.

"He tells me different things from what my mother tells me," he said. "He tells me bad things she doesn't know about."

Pulou cocked his head. "Why?"

"I don't know." Tristan stared at the carpet between his feet and shook his head. "He says they're right. I don't think they are. I . . . don't want them to be right!"

The knot in his stomach tightened—a knot of fear, he realized. Fear that perhaps the things the governor had told him were true.

SIX

The hallway was a circle. Four short corridors crossed it in the center, intersecting at a row of doors. Tristan watched the man called Avuse approach one, touch a square of metal on the wall beside it, and step into a tiny box of a room when the door opened.

It was one of those rooms that moved, he knew, the room they called a "lift," which carried people up and down to different places in the building. He touched Pulou's vision with his own. "Maybe one of those goes to the way out."

Pulou looked doubtful. "Maybe," he said.

Tristan waited until the door closed behind Avuse to touch the metal square on the wall as the servant had done.

The door didn't open.

He tried each lift in turn, but none of them opened. Punched each panel harder, two or three times. There was no response.

Glowering his frustration, he strode all the way around the circular hall with Pulou at his shoulder, trying one door after another. None yielded to his efforts.

At one place the corridor widened into an observation lounge with chairs and small tables. Only tinted panes separated him from the skyline. He stayed well back from the panes, gripping the back of a chair when the view made his senses reel.

There were mountains beyond the city of towers, faintly visible as hazy silhouettes through the thick air. Catching Pulou's attention with a glance, he pointed, wordless, with a motion of his head.

He stood there gazing out at them for some time, his chest aching with homesickness the way it had when he'd first looked out on the darkening city three nights before. Throat tight, teeth tight on his lip, he glanced at Pulou again and then turned away and went back to his room.

He came to dinner sullen that evening. Kept his attention fixed on his plate until he felt the governor watching him. Then he looked up, glowering.

Renier said, "You've been very quiet this evening, Tristan. Is something wrong?"

"The doors won't open for me," he said. It was an accusation.

"This one and your bedroom door open, don't they?"

"Yes."

"Well then, there's no need for concern," Renier said. "The rest haven't been programmed to accept your hand scan."

"Why?" Tristan demanded.

"Because you have no business in those rooms." The governor gave him a stern look. "This world and its people and their customs are completely unfamiliar to you. You must realize that this confinement is for your own safety."

Tristan questioned that with a wordless scowl. When he looked over at Larielle for her confirmation, she wouldn't meet his gaze.

He suddenly had no more appetite.

* * *

The governor wasn't there when Rajak led him and Pulou to the dining room the next morning; only Larielle, who was already seated at the table. Tristan hesitated in the doorway—touched his forehead when she turned toward him.

"Come in, Tristan," she said, and beckoned him to his place. "My father will be late. He had a message this morning."

Tristan sat down. Watched without speaking as the servos distributed the plates. When Pulou retreated under the table with his food, Tristan picked up the knife from the collection of utensils spread before him.

He looked up when Larielle said, "It's really easier to eat this way. Try these two." She showed him her own utensils. "Watch how I do it."

He watched her, his utensils motionless, feeling awkward in his hands. His mind wasn't on the lesson. "Who is the message from?" he asked.

His question startled her; she stopped what she was doing. "I don't know," she said. "Why, Tristan?"

"He sent a box of"—he shrugged—"*things* to my father the other day."

Larielle shook her head. "The box wouldn't even have gotten to your father yet," she said. "I'm sorry."

They both jumped when the double doors abruptly opened. ". . . make the arrangements right away," the governor was saying to someone outside. "We'll leave directly after breakfast tomorrow."

Striding into the room, he came briskly around the table to Larielle without the aid of his walking stick. "Good morning, precious," he said, running a hand down the mahogany tumble of her hair, and bent to kiss her forehead before he seated himself.

Tristan watched him unfold a linen napkin over his lap. "Was the message from my father?" he asked.

The governor glanced up, frowning. "No, it wasn't." For a moment he seemed about to add something else, but then he changed his mind. He turned to his daughter instead. "Lari, it's become necessary to make an unscheduled inspection tour of the mines on Issel II. It'll take about a week at the moon residence. I'd like you to go with me."

Tristan saw how she froze. Then she met the governor's gaze. "I really don't want to go, Papa," she said. "Besides, examinations will be starting soon at the university and I still have a lot of work to do on my presentation for Intersystem Issues."

"You can work on your studies at the moon residence." The governor's tone was firm. "You don't have to accompany me on the actual inspections."

Larielle hesitated. Lowered her gaze. "Yes, Papa," she said, very quietly.

In the brief silence that followed, Renier looked over at Tristan. "You and your little friend will go with us, too, of course," he said.

"Level, please?" said a female voice as the lift's door slid closed on the governor's party.

Tristan turned to see if Larielle had said it, but her attention was fixed on some troubled distance.

"Shuttle bay," said Renier, and the floor rose up under their feet.

Tristan steadied himself, glanced around again. "Where's that girl?" he asked.

The governor smiled. "There isn't really a girl," he said. "The voice is synthesized by a computer, which is programmed to recognize certain words and take the lift to that level."

Tristan furrowed his brow, even more confused by the explanation. But before he could ask what *synthesized* and *computer* and *programmed* meant, the lift's ceiling spiraled open, revealing sky, and its floor rose until it became part of a larger floor. They stood on the round tower's roof, a platform that was hollowed like a dish and blackened by the fire of launch. It had no walls like the shuttle bay on Ganwold—not even a rail! Just the city and the distant mountains rising on all sides and a warm fitful wind, laden with the bitter smell of burning, which tugged at their clothes. Tristan stood paralyzed, surveying the view. It was like standing near the edge of a cliff on Ganwold.

A shuttlecraft waited at the center of the platform. The governor paused at the foot of its boarding ramp to shift his walking stick to his other hand and offer Larielle his arm. "Come, Tristan," he said. "We're on a schedule."

The ramp led into a passenger lounge furnished with reclining acceleration seats, and viewpanes that arched high enough for Tristan to see the sky beyond. He cocked his head at a series of handles running the length of the overhead. "What are those for?" he asked.

"They're for moving around the cabin after we reach zero gravity," said Renier. "Take that seat over there." He motioned to a chair close to the viewpanes.

Tristan settled into it and beckoned Pulou to the one beside his own.

Movement outside caught Tristan's eye; the curved viewpanes reflected it upside down. He looked up from the buckles of his safety harness, reached over and nudged Pulou. "Look!"

Steam erupted from beneath the shuttle, lit pink and gold by the fire from the thrusters. Sudden pressure crushed Tristan into his seat. He gasped, wind-robbed, and blinked at the blur of the horizon falling away. It tilted precariously, sweeping past far below in a replay of a nightmare he had never forgotten:

A lifepod. An acceleration seat big enough to swallow a child not quite two. He wanted to cry, to reach out for his mother, but it was pushing too hard, and the rushing starfield made him dizzy.

He locked his teeth, closed his eyes against the memory,

clenched his hands on the upholstery. Beside him, he heard Pulou's breath coming in hisses through his teeth.

The pressure eased gradually until there was none at all. By the time he opened his eyes, the craft had fled the atmosphere, but the planet, a turquoise globe veiled in white, still filled the viewpane. He watched it recede, almost imperceptibly at first. Wondered if Ganwold had looked the same way.

The thought of that sent a pang of homesickness through him. Swallowing against a sudden constriction in his throat, he tore his vision away from the viewpane.

"We are now on course for the Issel II Command Complex," said a voice from the overhead—a voice like the one in the lift, except that this one was a man's. "Flight time will be approximately nine and one-quarter standard hours."

Across the aisle from him, the governor asked, "Haven't you ever flown before, Tristan?"

Suddenly self-conscious, he made himself let go of the chair's arms. "When I was small," he said. His mouth was dry.

"A pity," the governor said. "Your father was already an accomplished pilot at your age."

Tristan eyed him. Renier's features were neutral but his voice held the barest suggestion of mockery. Tristan didn't answer.

The governor shrugged. Releasing his straps, he pushed against his seat—and shot toward the overhead, leaving the deck completely! Tristan stared.

The governor caught a handhold and pulled himself up. "Feel free to move around the cabin," he said, ignoring Tristan's surprise. "Just do so with care until you're comfortable with zero gravity." Using the handholds, his body drifting parallel to the overhead, he made his way forward with less effort than if he had been swimming, and disappeared through the forward hatchway.

Tristan didn't move; his stomach felt as if there were a

large stone slowly turning inside it. He closed his eyes and breathed through his mouth to ease the discomfort, keeping his face turned away from Larielle and the servants.

Some time later, looking out on unfamiliar constellations, a glitter against the starfield caught his eye. He unfastened his straps and tried to stand—and found himself falling toward the overhead! His hands shot out to catch himself, grasped for anything to save himself; the handholds were too far away.

One foot struck the back of his chair, sending him into a somersault. He flailed, expecting to strike the deck with his shoulder. Seizing the chair back as his roll brought it within reach, he pulled himself down, struggling to bring his feet back to the deck.

More upright than not, he held on to the chair, gulping for breath; glimpsed Pulou staring at him with eyes wider than lomo's eggs.

"Are you all right, Tristan?" Larielle asked. Her features showed genuine concern, but behind her Rajak and Avuse were laughing.

Tristan tightened his jaw. "Yes," he said. But his face burned with humiliation.

He didn't move for several minutes, until he found that he could reach the rail that ran along in front of the viewpanes. He let go of the chair with one hand, stretched, locked it hard around the rail. Holding his breath, he tried to step up to the pane. His feet left the deck again. His other hand clamped on to the rail, too. Reorienting himself, he spotted what looked like more handholds on the deck below the rail, and he shoved the toes of his boots under two of them to keep his feet planted.

The cluster of lights had brightened by now, taking on shape and dimension: a structure adrift in space. Tristan studied it, brows knitted, and when the governor joined him, he asked, "What's that?"

"It's our main orbital station," Renier said. He floated

between overhead and deck, anchored with a single hand-hold. "It's the port of entry to the Issel system. We'll pass close by it on our way to the moon."

A few more minutes cast the station into silhouette against Issel's bright globe. It appeared as fragile as spider's webbing, a scaffolding of girders and gantries around a rotating cylinder, festive with red warning lights and green guidance beacons. Tramcars glided between the cylinder and vessels as massive as mountains, caught like flies by docking umbilicals.

"What are those?" Tristan asked, daring to let go with one hand long enough to point.

"Freighters," Renier said. "They're part of our trade fleet."

The shuttle slid over a long line of berths, and Tristan pointed at three ships docked in a row, bristled as hedge-hogs. "Are those freighters, too?"

"No, they're destroyers. They're being refitted for return to service."

"Destroyers?" Tristan cocked his head.

"Warships," the governor said. Clipped it.

Tristan studied his eyes for a moment, and didn't ask anything else.

In another half hour the orbital station had slipped from view in the shuttle's wake, and Tristan pulled himself back to his seat.

He was actually dozing when the voice came from the overhead speaker again: "We are now on approach for landing. Please secure your harnesses and remain in your seats until landing and pressurization are completed." Blinking awake, he pushed himself up in his seat and looked out through the viewpane.

The shuttle seemed to be gliding over a black desert, craggy and cratered and lifeless, its features finally fading into a bowed horizon. Only red pulses of light from occasional man-made towers and the reflected flash from scattered metallic domes—like shelled water creatures half-submerged in silt, he thought—proved that the moon was inhabited at all.

Tristan watched the descent, felt the trembling roar of the retro rockets that illuminated the terrain below and turned it ruddy, until it was obscured by billows of dust and vapor. He glimpsed only a moment's flash of lights encircling the dome they hovered over, then saw the dome spiraling open like an alien mouth to swallow them. He curled his hands hard around the chair arms as the craft sank into the opening.

As they settled, the roar subsided and the billows of fire-lit steam dissolved. Tristan looked out on launch-bay walls like the ones on Ganwold—had that been only three weeks ago?—and watched the dome, above them now, spiral closed. The noise of wind surrounded the shuttle. It was several minutes before lights came on in the bay and several doors in its walls opened, admitting a number of men, some in uniforms and others in coveralls.

The weight of his own body, like carrying a peimu across his shoulders, pushed Tristan down the ramp after the governor and Larielle. At the bottom, Renier conversed briefly with the men in uniform. They eyed Tristan with masked expressions. He met their looks, held them, said nothing.

They left the launch bay through an airlock with shield doors as thick as his body, and strode down a passage bored from dark stone. Tristan saw how Pulou wrinkled his nose, sniffing. How his eyes widened, catlike, in the dimness. Following, he trailed his hand along the wall, feeling its cragginess, brushing off loose bits with his fingers; the ceiling was low enough that he could have trailed his hand along it, too. Underfoot, a grating made of hard plastic muffled the noise of their footfalls.

They passed through another air lock into a lift the size

of a small room, and when a masculine voice said, "Level, please," the governor answered, "Command Section."

The lift dropped swiftly. Tristan watched a light blink its way down a graph on the wall, passing levels identified as Flightline, Shuttle Maintenance, Supply and Storage, Personnel Maintenance and Quarters, Mine and Life Support Offices.

Shield doors opened, two levels from the bottom of the shaft, into a corridor with a carpeted floor. Its walls were hewn smooth, a neutral tan color, and lit with hidden illuminants.

"The residence area here is two kilometers below the surface," the governor said.

Tristan stared up at him. "Two *kilometers*?" He remembered how his mother had measured gan migrations, tried to imagine those distances turned on end underground, and couldn't. He shook his head. "That can't be right! It can't be that far!"

Renier smiled. "There's a stairwell at the far end of this hallway, for emergencies. If you doubt me, you have my permission to climb it."

Tristan scanned the corridor and its low ceiling seem to settle on him. "Why?" he asked. "Why do you live under the ground?"

"You saw the surface," the governor said. "It can't support life. There's no atmosphere or light, and no protection from radiation and meteors. Our survival depends on putting solid rock and shield doors between ourselves and the outside."

He turned to the servants. "Show Larielle and Tristan to their rooms, please—and Avuse, we'll dine in my suite for the duration of our stay."

Avuse, carrying the travel bags, acknowledged with a stiff nod; Rajak said, "This way, Tristan."

The room was smaller than the one he'd had on the

planet, and its latrine connected with another room: Rajak's. Tristan wrinkled his nose at its musty smell, almost willing to believe it was a cave, except that the walls were dry and the floor was even.

There was a white screen on the wall. A holoscreen. He found the sensor that activated it and flicked through the choices of scenery twice. There wasn't a forest; he settled for a fishing stream tumbling through a meadow, then sat down on the floor to pull off his boots and shirt.

That was when he spotted three small openings in the floor, spaced along the base of the wall. Each was about as long as the width of his hand and about two fingers wide. Cautious, he slipped his hand into the nearest one and felt warm air blowing up around his fingers. He reached as far as he could and felt moisture on the sides of the duct, but he couldn't find its bottom. Withdrawing his hand, he peered into the duct. It was dark—he couldn't see anything—but the air that brushed his face bore the moist odor of a cave. He sat back, grimacing.

Pulou was watching him, head cocked. "You find what, little brother?"

"Where air comes in," Tristan said. "It smells like cave."

Pulou only blinked, as puzzled as he was.

He hadn't even taken his seat at the dinner table that evening before he asked, "Why did people come here if it isn't safe to live on the outside?"

"Because this moon is one of the richest sources of carmite ore in the known galaxy," the governor said. "It's a mining colony."

"Ore?" Tristan cocked his head. "Mining? What are those?"

"Mining is the method of collecting the ore," Renier said. "The ore looks like red rock when it's first brought from the ground. But when it's refined it produces a red metal which is heat-resistant, a nonconductor—valuable for the construction of starcraft and high-powered weapons. It was a great asset during the War of Resistance. . . . It still is."

"Who brings it from the ground?" Tristan asked.

"We have workers for that."

"Where are they?"

"At the various mine complexes." The governor studied him briefly. "Perhaps you would like to go with me when I begin the inspections tomorrow. It's often easier to understand a thing if you can actually see it."

Larielle looked up, shaking her head. "No, Papa. Tris, you don't—"

"I want to go," said Tristan.

They rode the lift up only to the level marked Mine and Life Support Offices and emerged, Tristan and Pulou and the governor, into another carpeted corridor with doors on either side. Lettering identified them: Oxygen and Water Development, Laborer Control and Maintenance, Power Production, Ore Assessment, Mine Production Records. Tristan looked around, self-conscious, from trying to sound out the words when he sensed the governor watching him.

"I didn't know that you could read," Renier said.

"A little." Tristan ducked his head. "My mother taught me when I was small."

"Remarkable woman," the governor said. "I hope that you appreciate her."

Tristan's vision locked on those dark hawk's eyes. "You won't let me help her!"

"I told you at the first that it would take time." The governor leaned on his walking stick, turning back up the corridor. "At the moment I have more pressing concerns. Come now."

Tristan glanced at Pulou and followed, glaring at the governor's back.

The door at the end of the hall said Control Center.

Beyond it was blackness broken only by the minimal glow of monitors, and the heat and scents of people and machines working together in close quarters.

"Sir!" said someone at Tristan's right. He jumped, and as his eyes adjusted he made out the form of a man with a paunch standing before the governor. "We weren't expecting you so early in the day."

"Will that disadvantage your presentation?" the governor asked.

"No, sir," the other said hastily. "Not at all. Follow me, please."

The man guided them through the monitor room, talking too rapidly of things Tristan didn't understand—*tonnage* and *labor lines*—and pointing at screens with red lights scattered at random among green lines that twisted like a river seen from the rim of a canyon.

Tristan followed them down a close aisle between terminals and illuminated maps, past people who seemed to be only shadows seated at the keyboards, except for their faces, tinted garish colors by the displays on their screens.

"I received a message from Production Records," the governor said, "stating that for the past two periods the Malin Point mine's production has dropped to less than fifty percent of its quota. What do you know about this?"

Tristan saw the man's face contort as if he'd been struck. "Only the most sketchy facts, sir. Come over here." He led them to a terminal across the room and said, "Put the Malin Point map on-screen."

The young man seated there bent over his keyboard.

A shape that resembled a spread hand appeared on the monitor, with one of its fingers colored red.

The man began rubbing nervous hands together. "There was no explanation given for closing the shaft, sir. The officer in charge said only that it was an emergency."

"I want an explanation." The governor looked hard at

the other. "Contact the OIC. He will report to my office at thirteen hundred tomorrow."

"Yes, sir."

The governor paused, then asked, "What about terrarium development in the Beta segment?"

The man visibly relaxed. "Ahead of schedule, sir."

"Good." Renier turned away, seeming to remember only then that he wasn't alone. "What do you think, Tristan?" he asked.

Tristan pointed at a screen full of illuminated dots and lines. "What are these for?"

"They're maps. Each red light marks a mine complex." The governor tapped one. "This is Malin Point."

"Where are we?"

"Here." Renier indicated an amber light near the map's center.

Tristan traced a green line with his finger. "What's that?"

"One of the terrarium caverns, the moon's life-support system," said the governor. "They run for kilometers among the mine complexes. We'll see one in a little while."

Tristan leaned closer to study markings, names, notations, and the way the red lights seemed to be linked by the twisting green lines. He didn't touch the screen, just glanced over at Pulou.

After a moment he asked the governor, "Will we see a mine, too?"

"Not today. Each complex can be reached only by flight to its own shuttle bays."

"But you said those green lines—"

"No, Tristan," the governor said. "Those are connected to the mines only by shielded ventilation shafts and water lines, to ensure against depressurization accidents. If you want to see a mine, look at the patrol monitors." He gestured at a bank of screens tucked up next to the ceiling.

Tristan studied rows of narrow wire cages enclosing huddled dusky figures on one screen; figures in coveralls and oxygen masks wielding laser boring tools; figures loading reddish rock and soil into pneumatic transport tubes on another; shadows shuffling single file through a ragged tunnel on a third. Their expressionless eyes stared out of faces thin as death and caked with grime. Their bodies moved stiffly, slowly, as Tristan had seen only the very old and feeble move.

He recoiled. "What's wrong with them? Why are they in those—cages?"

He could actually feel the silence, the shock in the stares of the people around him, before the governor said, "Because they're criminals, Tristan. They're dangerous, both to other people and to the security of their motherworld."

Tristan shuddered. He didn't want to look any longer, but he couldn't tear his vision away.

"Come now," the governor said behind him, and his tone was taut.

The lift took them down past the Command Section to a level that said Life Support Facilities, and opened onto a passage as bleak as the one from the shuttle bays. It had little lighting. Glowpainted arrows on the wall pointed toward Utility Plants 1–5 on the left, Utility Plant 6 and Terrarium Main Access on the right. Tristan mouthed the words to remember them.

A worker in coveralls emerged from the dim office of Plant 6 to lead them down a clanging metal stairwell guarded by shield doors, through the hot near dark to another door with a cipher code box. The man punched in the sequence. Electronic locks clicked, an unseen bolt grated back; the door swung inward at his push.

They stepped from black into teal green.

It looked like a canyon without a sky above its walls, Tristan thought. Walls and ceiling glowed turquoise under ultraviolet globes floating like small suns at regular intervals. The air was warm and heavy with the scent of mildew, and moisture lay in clouds along the floor.

"Our life-support system," said Renier. He moved out onto a walkway of plastic grating, planting his walking stick with care. "We've cultivated the indigenous lichens with imported light and water until they can provide enough oxygen to support the entire population. We're even experimenting with growing edible plants in some of the caverns."

Tristan wrinkled his nose at the odor—the same musty scent that came up through the ducts in his room—and scrutinized boulders and walls layered with blue fuzz and sparkling with crystal humidity. Behind his back he signaled "*Go*" to Pulou and asked the governor, "How does the air get up to my room from down here?"

Renier described the collector vents that drew oxygen into personnel areas or into condensation systems where hydrogen was infused to create water. He explained power plants supported by their own production, elaborated on recycling systems and rationing. "It's a most delicate balance," he said. "We could have water brought from the primary in an emergency, but not sufficient oxygen to sustain life here."

Tristan understood almost none of it, but it didn't matter. He felt knuckles nudge his shoulder and he glanced around.

Pulou's expression was smug. "We talk at night," he said.

When the lift stopped at the Command Section, the governor said, "There's one more visit to make, the Command Post." The lift's back wall retracted; they stepped through another shield door into an office area where a man in uniform rose from his desk. "The troops are waiting for your inspection, sir."

"And the areas have been properly sanitized?"

"To unclassified, sir."

"Thank you, Major." The governor gestured. "You may come, Tristan."

The major escorted them down a corridor with tiled floors that echoed underfoot, past doors with markers that said Operations Planning, Advanced Warning, Communications, Command Post. He stopped at the door to Operations Planning and fingered a rapid code. As the door clicked open he called, "Room, atten-*tion!*"

Tristan heard movement—abrupt, stilled as suddenly as it started—and then silence weighty with expectation. He followed the governor into a room full of empty tables, blank wall screens, and a crystal pillar in the center so large it would take four people with outstretched arms to encircle it. But his vision came back to the soldiers.

They stood motionless, stiff. Expressionless. Unblinking.

"They look dead," Pulou said at his shoulder.

The governor surveyed them and smiled. He strode about the room among them, glancing at ribbons and gleaming boots and faces with shorn hair. Following him, Tristan studied eyes that wouldn't meet his own, saw tension in hands curled at trouser seams.

Renier said, "Carry on." The soldiers relaxed, almost as one, and the governor nodded to their officer in charge. "Commendable, Colonel." To Tristan he said, "In wartime, this room is used to develop battle plans and campaign strategies."

He moved to the pillar in the center of the room and touched a switch at its base. Images appeared inside: a globe that Tristan recognized as Issel, orbited by two moons and—

"What are those?" he asked, pointing at smaller objects drifting around it.

"Orbital stations," said the governor. "Most of those near this moon are smelting plants where the ore is purified and tempered and loaded aboard freight ships as carmite for trade with other worlds. The rest are defense posts. Some are bases for fighter squadrons, others are maintenance depots. They are all directed in wartime from the command post at the end of this hall."

Renier touched the buttons. The planet was replaced by a three-dimensional astral map.

Tristan leaned up to the column, searching. "What are these worlds?" he asked. "Is my father at one of them?"

More buttons clicked; the rest of the starfield vanished as one system was magnified, focusing on the planets circling one yellow star. "He's on the one in the center," said Renier. "Sostis. My motherworld."

"Sostis." Tristan stared into the holotank, fixing its position in the astral map in his mind.

"This way," the governor said behind him.

They went from Ops to Communications, a cooled room equipped with vidphones of different colors, a row of comm terminals and printers—all idle or covered at the moment—and receiver banks with headsets hung on their hooks. They were guarded by more soldiers standing at stiff attention.

". . . all information that enters or leaves this system passes through this center," the governor was saying; but Tristan felt someone watching him. He glanced around, over his shoulder—

—into the face of a man with skin as black as a midnight sky and NIEDDU on the patch over his uniform pocket. He couldn't have been any older than Captain Weil, but his eyes were ancient, dangerous. Tristan drew back, curling one hand in warning.

*   *   *

When the governor's party was gone and all the equipment was put back on line, Tech Sergeant Nieddu turned back to his terminal keyboard.

His name wasn't really Nieddu—it was Ajimir Nemec—and he wasn't really a tech sergeant in the Isselan Space Forces. In fact, as a lieutenant commander in the Unified Worlds' Spherzah, he outranked the OIC of the Comms Center.

Meticulous effort had gone into developing his alias and getting him an assignment to the command post on Issel II. Providing him with an Isselan military ID—even creating a complete military record for him and slipping it into Issel's central military database—had been relatively easy. But Spherzah Research provided far more than that for its deep-cover operators. Nemec had spent months learning the dialect and culture of his "native" region on Issel; learning the customs and courtesies of the Isselan military forces; and memorizing the details of all his "previous assignments"—from descriptions of the bases as they had been at the time, to the personnel he had "worked with" and the places they had frequented off-duty. Anyone who had served tours at any of the locations would be able to corroborate the details. His cover—his life—depended on it.

Memorizing secure frequencies and call signs had been easy by comparison.

Keeping one eye on the OIC as he moved about the room, Nemec set up a directional transmission which would evade the Command Post's myriad receivers and typed out a cryptic message:

URGENT
021247L 9 3307SY
TO RELAY RACER
FM CHAMELEON II
TOP SECRET

GOVERNOR RENIER COMPLETED AN UNSCHEDULED IN-
SPECTION TOUR OF THE ISSEL II COMMAND COMPLEX
APPROXIMATELY ONE STANDARD HOUR AGO. DURING
THE INSPECTION, THE GOVERNOR WAS ACCOMPANIED
BY A MAMMALIAN HUMANOID ALIEN AND A YOUNG
MAN, APPARENTLY IN HIS LATE TEENS, WHOM THE
GOVERNOR ADDRESSED AS TRISTAN. NO FURTHER IN-
FORMATION IS AVAILABLE ON THE IDENTITIES OF THE
VISITORS OR THE REASON FOR THEIR PRESENCE. CON-
SIDER THIS HIGHLY UNUSUAL. WILL CONT TO REPORT.
DNT ACK.
END OF MESSAGE

Nemec glanced once over his shoulder when the MES-
SAGE RELEASED line blinked on his monitor. Let out his
breath. A few more keystrokes deleted the record of his
message from the terminal's log.

SEVEN

"Here, Tris." Larielle placed a flat box on the table, barely longer than Tristan's hand, and opened its lid to reveal a monitor and a compact keyboard inside. "This is my Pocket Tutor," she said. "Let me program it to respond to your voice and then I'll show you how to use it."

The dishes of their midday meal had been cleared from the table in the governor's sitting room and Tristan leaned on it with both arms, watching without speaking as Larielle touched the Tutor's ON button and waited for the monitor to light up. As it did, a distinctly masculine voice said, "Identify user for access."

"Larielle Renier," said Larielle.

"Voice pattern of Larielle Renier recognized," said the Tutor. "You may continue." A menu appeared on the monitor.

Glancing at Tristan, Larielle indicated the first item and said, "Expand work parameters." When a new menu replaced the first, she pointed at the fourth item. "Identify additional user for access."

"Please enter voice pattern for additional user."

Larielle turned to Tristan. "Say something now, Tris."

He stared at the monitor for several moments, his mind

suddenly gone empty. "What should I say to it?" he asked at last.

"Start with your full name," Larielle said, "and then tell it something else about yourself—just enough for it to establish a voice pattern."

Tristan nodded and returned his attention to the monitor, half wondering if the owner of the masculine voice were staring back at him from behind it. "Tristan Lujanic Serege," he said, and stopped. He caught sight of Pulou, napping under the table. "Pulou is my brother, and . . ." After a long pause, he shot a desperate look over at Larielle. "I can't think of anything else to say."

"That's probably enough," she said, and then: "Please confirm identity of additional user."

"Additional user is identified as Tristan Lujanic Serege," said the Tutor.

"Good. Now then, Tris," Larielle said, "let's see what we can find for you to read. . . . Open library, please. Show titles available."

Three columns of titles filled the monitor, from right to left, and a line at the bottom read SCROLL DOWN FOR ADDITIONAL TITLES.

"These are my university texts," Larielle said. "I bought the memory-chip versions for this"—she tapped the unit—"but you can get them by on-line subscription as well."

She must have realized when she glanced up that that didn't mean a thing to him. "I'm sorry," she said. "Would you like to try some history?"

"Okay," Tristan said.

"Open 'A Concise Account of the Resistance,'" said Larielle. "Begin at chapter eighteen, with dictionary and discussion options on and read-aloud option off." As the titles list disappeared and the requested text came up in its place, she pushed the box over in front of Tristan. "Start from the top," she said.

Eyeing the screenful of characters, Tristan shook his head. "I don't know those words!"

"Sound them out, one word at a time," Larielle said. "After you read a little, we'll put on the voice option and you can listen as you follow along. . . . Now then, what's that?" She pointed at the first word.

Tristan furrowed his brow, cocking his head at the characters glowing on the display. "El-e-men-ta-ry."

"That's right," said Larielle. "Every character makes a whole sound, or syllable. Just put the sounds together, one after the other."

Tristan nodded, but his hands, gripping the sides of the Tutor, were tense. Even some of the characters were new. There were over seven thousand in the Standard language, various arrangements of basic marks and shapes. The words they formed were longer than those his mother had taught him to read. Some of them had five or six characters instead of two or three—and almost none of them meant anything to him. He drew a breath like a sigh and started again: "Ele-men-tary log-ic suj-ges-ted—"

"No, no!" Larielle stopped him. "That's *sug*-gested. That's a different character."

"It is?" said Tristan. "How is it different?"

"The tail here is slanted. See?" She pointed out the difference on the display.

"Oh." Tristan eyed it. Sighed his frustration. "My mother didn't have things like this," he said, waving at the Tutor. "All she had was sand and a stick to write in it with, and the characters didn't all look square like this."

He glimpsed sympathy in her eyes. "You'll get used to it," she said. "It just takes practice. You're doing fine. Go on now."

He shifted forward, planted his elbows on the table, put his chin in his hands. "Elemen-tary logic *sug*-gested that it was—what's *that*?"

"Sound it out one character at a time," she said.

He furrowed his brow. "Es-sen-tial?" He glanced sideways at her, cocking his head.

"That's right!" She smiled. "Essential."

"Essential," Tristan repeated. "But what does it mean? I don't know what *any* of this means!"

"Ask the Tutor," said Larielle. "The dictionary option is on, you know."

"Dictionary?" said Tristan. He wrinkled his nose.

"That gives you the defi . . . the meaning—of the words," she explained. "Like this: Please define 'essential.' "

"Essential," said the Tutor. "Of great importance. Necessary; requisite."

In the outer office beyond the living area, the servant Avuse said, "Sir, Captain Krotkin, officer in charge of the Malin Point mine, is here."

Tristan looked up in time to see the governor nod acknowledgment from his seat at his desk. "Admit him, please, Avuse."

Tristan watched Krotkin come in. Studied him briefly as he stood inside the office door, with jowls taut and hands clenched white on his cap, before returning his attention to the Tutor.

"Captain," he heard the governor say, his tone cool but cordial as he rose from his desk. "Come in and be seated."

"Go on, Tristan." Larielle touched his arm.

"Ele-mentary logic sug-gested that it was es-sential to the . . ."

Krotkin approached the chair facing the governor's desk, sidling as if to keep his back to a wall. "Thank you, sir. Thank you." He stayed at attention even seated, his spine rigid, and kept wringing his cap. "There's a good explanation, sir, actually."

The governor moved behind his desk, out of Tristan's

line of sight through the doorway, but not beyond his hearing. "Would you please make it, then, Captain?"

"Yes, sir. Yes." Krotkin swallowed visibly, kneaded his hat. "It's the new line of workers, sir. When they proved to be unmanageable as a unit, we divided them among the other lines—"

"And now they've stirred up the others, too," the governor said.

"Yes, sir," Krotkin nodded. "Exactly, sir. In fact, last week the guards over the oh-eight-hundred Chi line moved in to discipline a couple of them—some big men from Thrax Port, sir—and they'd sabotaged the supports to make them collapse. It knocked one guard senseless and practically buried the rest of the line before reinforcements got there."

"How many casualties?" The question fell without emotion.

"Seven wounded, sir. Four seriously, including the guard. There were no fatalities."

A moment's silence. "There should have been several," the governor said. "The ones who were caught under the cave-in."

Tristan stopped reading. Looked up. Swallowed.

"But sir, they weren't the ones who caused it," said Krotkin.

"It doesn't matter. It would've caused second thoughts for anyone else considering such a tactic." The governor paused, then said, "Put the men from Thrax Port, and any other troublemakers, through a disciplinary session. They don't have to survive it. And cut rations for the rest of the Chi shaft lines—or double their shifts—until they've got it cleared and workable again."

"Keep going, Tristan," Larielle said beside him. "That was very good."

He glanced at her, actually startled.

Her eyes bore a confusion of emotions, dominated by fear and shame. "Please," she said, "just keep reading."

"But, sir," the captain was saying, "the production level will drop even—"

"Krotkin, Malin Point's attrition rate is even lower than its production rate. Fear of being culled promotes diligence and prevents collusions. If you doubt me, talk to Captain Sylte at the Firnis mine. He turns over the equivalent of two lines per month but his tonnage is increasing."

The governor had risen; he paced, crossing past the doorway, oblivious of the two young people beyond it. "You won't lack for replacements," he said. "I recently had to stiffen the sentence for rioting in three regions on the primary." He shook his head, hands interlaced at his back. "Ungrateful young people! They'll learn what it means to work for the good of their motherworld if they don't put an end to their troublemaking!"

"Yes, sir," said Krotkin.

The governor paused in his pacing, turned to face the officer. "Malin Point will see an improvement of twenty-five percent or better in a month's time. There are smelting quotas to be met."

"Yes, of course, sir."

"You're dismissed, Captain."

"Yes, sir. Thank you, sir." Krotkin snapped to his feet, saluted, and withdrew in haste.

When Larielle touched his hand, Tristan jumped. He shifted the Tutor between his hands, thumbed its scrolling button over and over—but his concentration was shattered. He could hear the silence, the deliberate footsteps coming across it, and his pulse pounding in his ears. He looked up.

The governor stood in front of the table. "Please forgive the interruption," he said, drawing out a chair. "How is your reading coming, Tristan?"

From the corner of his eye, Tristan saw Larielle's hands

clench in her lap, her lips press into a firm line. He traced the characters embossed on the Tutor's cover with a tremulous finger and said, "I wasn't . . . reading. I was listening."

The governor shot a swift look at his daughter—she met it, her face unreadable—and he said, "Well, I suppose that listening can also be instructive." He interlaced his hands on the table. "What did you learn from listening, Tristan?"

He hesitated, looking at the governor's eyes. "Do— frightened people—really work harder?" he asked at last. His mouth had gone dry.

He saw how Renier's mouth pursed. "In a labor camp, yes," the governor said. "They can always see the consequences of disobedience."

"Why are the young people . . . ungrateful?"

"They're unhappy at the measures we've had to take recently," Renier said. "I can't blame them entirely, but their strikes and marches won't resolve anything." He sighed. "They don't remember the War. They don't remember when Sanabria was a city of charred shells, or what my generation sacrificed to rebuild it and our other cities." He shook his head. "I'm sorry that so many have had their educations interrupted to fill the shock forces in the factories, but it can't be helped just now. Other goals must be reached first. It's very hard, Tristan."

He cocked his head. "Why?"

Renier sighed again. "I was installed as Sector General during the War of Resistance," he said. "Issel had already been devastated. While the young men of Sostis were conscripted and its industries utilized to support the Dominion war effort, I revitalized Issel's mining guilds. Under my governorship, the carmite in this system was used to finance Issel's reconstruction and rebuild both worlds' economies.

"Then the Dominion's back was broken at Enach with the attack on its orbital command station and the assassination of its leadership by the Spherzah. All Dominion-sponsored trade ended. We were pariah to the Unified Worlds for the role I had played, and—" He cut himself off, his jaw tightening, and stared for a long while into some bitter distance of time before he shook his head again.

"Issel finished reconstructing alone," he said at last to the tabletop. "It's been difficult. We've struggled. We've known starvation—deprivation of all kinds." He made a loose gesture with both hands. "I understand the young people's unhappiness, but unlike most of them, I know their real enemy." He lifted his gaze and looked directly at Tristan. "We're in a position to stand up to that enemy now. The mines are paying off again. We've signed new trade contracts sufficient to raise the standard of living and our levels of defense, and we've made new alliances."

He paused. Eyed Tristan again. "Aren't you a little curious, Tristan, as to how you fit into all of this?"

"How *I* fit into it?" Tristan stopped tracing the Tutor's embossing and stared at him, shocked. "I don't want to fit into it! My mother is sick!"

"I know that." The governor sat back, looking thoughtful. "It will be most interesting to see how your father responds to our message."

Tristan paused before the holoscreen when he came into his room, gazing out on its meadow as he peeled off his jacket and shirt and dropped them on the bed. He settled to the floor to tug off the boots, and flung them after the jacket.

Sitting cross-legged, he smoothed a patch of carpet with his hand and closed his eyes. The map of lines and lights from the monitor room glowed in his remembered vision; he traced it in the carpet's nap with his finger. He studied it for a few moments—then shook his head abruptly in frustration and erased the sketch with a sweep of his hand.

Watching, Pulou asked, "You do what, little brother?"

"I think how we go away from here." Tristan leaned forward, elbows on knees. "There are stairs and lift. We make lift go down so they chase it, and we go up stairs to shuttles."

"Too easy to hunt us," said Pulou.

Tristan cocked his head, questioning him.

"Think of lomos in burrows."

"Lomos?" Tristan wrinkled his nose. "But they're stupid!"

"Maybe," said Pulou. "Maybe not. Lomos do what when children pour water into burrows?"

"Go out other burrow."

Pulou nodded, watching him.

And Tristan grinned. He began tracing the map in the carpet again. But then he stopped and looked at Pulou. "But governor says you *can't* go out of caves another way."

"Not right," the gan said. "You can."

"You find what?"

"Green cave goes on and on for long way," Pulou said. "It has places to hide and water to drink and burrows that go up to gray cave we walk in. Small caves go out like tree branches from big cave, and I find flat-tooth footprints that come out of one but none that go in."

"That come *out*?" Tristan held Pulou's amber gaze for a long moment, considering that before he returned to the map etched in the carpet. He finished the drawing. "We go down stairs here," he said, pointing, "and hide in caves if they hunt us, and"—drawing a finger along one mark—"come out over here, or here, or here." He looked at Pulou. "Like lomos from burrows."

"Good." The gan gave him a fanged smile. "You learn to think like hunter, not like flat-tooth." He evaded Tristan's playful cuff and said, "At night, little brother?"

"Yes," said Tristan.

* * *

Sleepless night paled too slowly to angry dawn.

When the stars over the screen's projected meadow began to fade, Tristan reached up to turn it off, letting the blanket slide from his shoulders. He stood slowly; his thighs ached from hours of sitting cross-legged. He limped into the latrine.

The face that stared back at him from the reflector as he washed looked older than it had the day before, he thought. He pushed dripping hair away from his eyes, unsure of what caused the illusion. Except that he couldn't meet his own gaze.

When he'd come into his room after dinner the previous evening, he'd dismissed Rajak and held the door for Pulou—held it until he heard the valet's door close down the corridor. Then he'd fished in his jacket pocket for the clasp he'd pulled from it, placed it in the door's track, switched off the automation—and held his breath as the door slid to the blockage and stopped. It had cost him an afternoon of studying the electronic latches, and pinched fingers from testing the door's recoil mechanism, to figure it out.

He'd smiled as he tossed his jacket onto the bed—taking a moment to lock the door between Rajak's room and the connecting latrine before he crouched to sketch the tunnel map in the carpet again. Pulou squatted beside him, watching as he traced one of the longer lines. He tapped the spot at its end and nodded.

"He says cargo shuttles are there," Tristan said. "We hide in one and ride away in it."

"To where?" asked Pulou.

"To—orbital station." Tristan found himself having to intersperse his gan with Standard words for which there were no equivalents. "Think about round picture of stars in white room." He pantomimed the shape of the holotank in Operations Planning. "He says big ships are at stations. Maybe one goes to my father's world."

"Maybe not," said Pulou.

Tristan had ignored that, smoothing away the map with his hand. They'd settled on the floor to rest while they waited for the living level to grow quiet.

Tristan hadn't slept. He'd just lain there with his eyes closed, seeing the glow of the monitor room's map in his mind.

When they'd risen, what seemed half the night later, the door had responded easily to his push. He signed at Pulou to wait while he knelt at the doorjamb to ease the door into its lock—and felt someone watching from behind even before Pulou nudged him. He turned slowly, swallowing, and looked up.

Rajak leered down at him. "It isn't very smart to go for a walk by yourself at night, Tristan."

He came to his feet in one motion. "What are you doing here? We don't want your help!"

"You may need it, though. The doors to the lifts and the emergency stairs aren't as easy to sabotage as your bedroom's."

Tristan glowered and said nothing.

"Aw, come on, that's what you had in mind, wasn't it?" Rajak reached past him to punch the door's OPEN button. "Take out your doorstop."

Tristan studied him: about twice his own weight, a couple finger-widths taller, but with sluggish reflexes. . . .

"Hurry up," said Rajak. "Take it out."

Without shifting his vision from the servant's face, Tristan knelt, picked up the broken piece of clasp and curled his fist around it. He locked his teeth.

"Give it to me," said Rajak, holding out his hand and waggling his fingers. "Would you rather tell Governor Renier about this yourself, or should I do it for you?"

"If you say anything to anyone, Rajak, I'll see that you won't need first pick of the women prisoners anymore."

The voice was quiet, menacing, and female.

Rajak wrenched around. Tristan and Pulou hunched lower still, hands going to their foreheads.

Larielle had come down the corridor, silent on bare feet and draped only in a dressing gown and her loosed hair.

Rajak made a snorting sound. "You little vixen! You wouldn't dare—"

"Yes I would." The smile that flickered at her lips was almost evil. "I'd only have to tell my father that you behaved improperly toward me and you'd be lucky to keep even your life!" She interposed herself between Tristan and the servant. "Get out of here, Rajak."

He hesitated.

"Get out!" She swung at him, something needlelike flashing in her hand. He staggered back, flinging up an arm to shield his face, and retreated.

She had waited until Rajak entered his room, waited until they heard its door click shut before she turned back to Tristan. "Don't do this," she had said, her voice quiet but urgent. "Be patient, Tristan. If you're caught trying to run away again, your mother will suffer for it as much as you will."

EIGHT

A light on the keyboard blinked red; a persistent beep announced a priority message coming in on an out-system frequency. It would be encrypted, Nemec knew. He punched the ACCEPT key, overriding the material already on his monitor, and entered his release code to unscramble the text.

It was dated 3/9/3307 SY—two days earlier—and classified Confidential. Nemec's vision narrowed on green lines spilling onto the screen from an electronic ether, noted the imprecise translation from a language not human. He kept his face impassive, concealing both interest and surprise as he read it.

He touched the HARDCOPY key and glanced up. The officer in charge was across the room. Quick fingers set a directional transmission and hit DISSEMINATE.

Relay's communications receivers would have the message in its entirety before the printout was completed in the Issel II Comm Center.

Nemec hit DELETE as he rose, tore off the printer paper, and handed the message to the officer in charge. "This just came in, sir."

The other read it through quickly. "The governor will want to see this right away."

"Yes, sir." Nemec enclosed it in a folder before crossing through the lift to the residence area, where a large man wearing the insignia of the governor's personal security force met him and motioned for him to wait in the office.

Beyond was a dining room; the governor and his household were at dinner.

The security man said, "Messenger from the Comms Center, sir."

"Thank you, Avuse. Show him in." Renier rose from the dining table and came into the office. "Sergeant?"

At the table behind him, the youth named Tristan looked up—and froze. Nemec could almost sense how his hand tightened on his knife. He felt the boy watching him as he opened the folder on the governor's desk and handed over the sheaf of papers. "This just came through, sir."

Renier scanned the top sheet. "Mi'ika. From the Bacal Belt," he said half-aloud. "This is much sooner than I had expected." He read through the remaining pages, concentration deepening the lines around his eyes and pursed mouth. After long moments he said, "Return word to the Pasha of Mi'ika that I look forward to accepting his son and the other candidates from his world into the military colleges of Adriat, and that I'll arrange my schedule to be in Aeire City when they arrive, in order to receive them personally."

"Yes, sir," Nemec said, and saw from the corner of his eye how the youth's attention jerked up at that; saw how he glanced under the table at the alien squatting near his feet.

"Please send notification to the ministers of Internal Security and Alien Relations on Adriat," the governor was saying, "regarding the date of our allies' arrival there. Arrangements for their accommodation and entrance into the academies should begin at once." He paused to study the message again. "Please inform my staff at Aeire City of this change of plans, also. Order tripled security, and assure them that I'll arrive far enough in advance to oversee most of the preparations myself."

"Yes, sir," Nemec said again. "Will that be all?" Relay's analysts, he knew, would be working double shifts over this!

"Destroy these." Renier returned the handful of papers. "Thank you, Sergeant."

Returning the message to the folder, Nemec gave a curt bow from the neck—and managed to meet the boy's eyes before he about-faced on his heel.

Tristan watched him leave the room. Watched the governor return to the table and resume his seat.

"I'll be concluding the mine inspections this afternoon," Renier said, taking up his napkin, "so that we can return tomorrow. We have another journey to make next week which we must begin to prepare for at once."

"Papa?" Larielle said.

"We'll be taking our holiday on Adriat early this year," the governor told her, and smiled. "I trust that won't disappoint you, Lari."

She smiled. "No, Papa."

"And what of you, Tristan? What do you know about your mother's homeworld?"

Tristan studied him, trying to read his shadowed eyes. "I know the name of where she lived," he said. His knuckles had grown white gripping his utensil.

The governor smiled again. "I believe you'll find it an interesting diversion from the histories you've been reading these last few days. You'll have the opportunity to see history in its making."

The shuttle seemed almost familiar this time. Still, Tristan gripped the arms of the acceleration seat through the crushing thrust of launch and closed his eyes against the sight of a spiraling horizon as the craft banked over the towered city of Sanabria.

Hours later, with Issel a sunlit globe filling the shuttle's rear view, Tristan spotted the glitter of the orbital station drifting ahead. He released his straps, pushed himself toward the pane. Catching the rail, he pulled himself into an upright position and anchored his feet. Against the perpetual night, the spiderweb structure gradually became visible in the midst of its artificial constellation.

As the shuttle circled around the station, Tristan observed the freight vessels at their loading docks and wondered at their destinations. He found his attention drawn to the bristled destroyers in the maintenance docks. One was missing, he noticed. It had been replaced by two smaller but equally-bristled ships.

"We are now making final approach," said the voice from the overhead. "Please take your seats and secure your harnesses until docking is complete."

Lying in his couch, Tristan sensed the shuttle's change of direction mostly by the way the starfield swung around past the viewpanes. The docking berth slid up around the shuttle, an enclosure of girders and guide beacons like the reed spokes of a gan fishtrap, which the craft seemed to be swimming into. Tristan pushed himself back in his chair, willing the shuttle not to pass through the opening, which allowed no escape. He felt a mild bump, and the structure outside stopped moving.

He glanced over at Pulou. Finding him curled asleep in the seat, Tristan nudged him awake.

They exited through a tunnel sealed over the hatch, corrugated so that Tristan thought of a caterpillar turned inside out. The tunnel bent around and downward and emptied into a transparent corridor. Tristan held on to a rail on the bulkhead, steadying himself in the buoyancy of low gravity after the shuttle's complete lack of it, and looked back to see the craft floating at its moorings in a cage of girders.

The corridor joined a concourse where a dozen men waited, some in the uniform of the Isselan Space Forces, others wearing the bandoliers of ambassadors and various ministries of Isselan government. The officers drew themselves up as the governor strode into the passage, and their commander stepped forward and saluted. "This way, sir," he said. "Your voyager is standing by for departure."

Another caterpillar tunnel led into a passenger lounge similar to the shuttle's, but larger. The voyager was designed to have artificial gravity, but there were handholds along the narrow passage between the cabins, and when Rajak pushed open a door and said, "This one's ours," Tristan saw that its furnishings were anchored to the deck and bulkheads.

"You're in the top berth," Rajak said, dumping duffle bags in a corner.

There were only two berths, stacked one above the other. Tristan said, "What about Pulou?"

"You'll both fit up there," Rajak said. "Or you can take turns, I don't care. Right now you need to go back to the passenger lounge so we can launch."

They were three days out of the Issel system, in the middle of the ship's simulated night, when they made their first lightskip. A sudden siren echoed from the bulkheads and went on and on like a trapped banshee, snatching Tristan from sleep. He stiffened, lying back-to-back with Pulou, and strained to see across the black of the cabin.

Nothing. It only helped to conjure undimmed images in his mind:

A locker intended only for a pressure suit. Hot darkness. The fear in his mother's whispers and touch as she tried to calm his own confusion.   ❋

Beside him, Pulou shifted, tried to sit up despite the low overhead. "It's what, little brother?"

Rajak turned over below them, making his berth creak. "We're gonna make lightskip," he said, sounding half-asleep. "Strap yourselves in and lie still up there!"

Tristan reached for the safety netting rolled up on Pulou's side of the berth, turned onto his back and pulled it over them both. His mouth was too dry to even whisper. The sound of his heartbeat hammered in his ears. It took several tries before he could control his hands' shaking enough to secure the net into its latches.

The warning horn changed pitch, became a shriek. Nearly choking on fear, Tristan closed his eyes, clenched his teeth—

—and felt like he was melting. Evaporating. Being pushed through solid stone one molecule at a time. He wanted to scream, but there was no sound—no breath for sound.

Then he was lying on his back in the berth again, sweat-soaked and shaking.

He tried to move. There was no strength, and only enough reflex left to retch. He heaved until he couldn't anymore.

Below him, Rajak swore, his voice sounding dim and distorted. Tristan heard his foot hit the deck as he tumbled from the lower bunk, and his unsteady movements before lights came on in the cabin. The heaving had ended by then; Tristan shifted a little and put his left hand in slippery vomit. Its smell made him gag again.

Still muttering, Rajak staggered against the hatch and fumbled to open it. "I'll get you stuff to clean it up with, but you're doing it yourself," he said, and disappeared into the dark of the passage.

Raising himself on his elbows, Tristan glanced at Pulou. The gan lay still, eyes closed, breath raking over bared fangs, sweat gleaming around his muzzle. Tristan nudged his shoulder with a curled hand. "You're all right?"

Pulou opened his eyes to slits, showing a veil of nictitating membrane. "Maybe," he panted. "Maybe."

"Get down here," said Rajak, coming back into the cabin.

Tristan turned over and released the safety net and reached for the deck with one foot. He lost his grip on the berth. His legs wouldn't support him, gave way. He caught himself on hands and knees on the deck, and Rajak shoved a self-contained cleaning unit at him. "If you're smart, you'll take a patch before the next 'skip," he said.

"A patch?" Tristan asked, and grimaced. His mouth was still sour and gritty.

"You stick it on your forehead and it knocks you out for a couple of hours."

Tristan remembered a legionnaire kneeling on his arms on the floor of a stone cell and a man with a pair of metallic discs in his hand leaning over him. All of that seemed surreal now, like part of a nightmare.

There weren't any legionnaires this time, or even any patches—yet—but the queasiness in Tristan's stomach seemed to be a warning that the nightmare was going to get worse.

NINE

Lujan Serege shrugged off the wet weight of his coat, handed it to the servo that whirred up to him, and ran his free hand through hair grown gray but not thinner.

"Good morning, sir." His executive officer offered a mug of hot shuk. "Still sleeting?"

"Just raining now.... Thanks." Lujan accepted the mug, took a sip as he turned toward his office. "Anything new, Jiron?"

"Just the usual message traffic, sir," the captain said, "and this." He picked up a metal box from his desktop. "A courier from the Isselan Embassy delivered it after you left last night."

"Isselan?" Lujan raised an eyebrow and smiled beneath his mustache as he took the case. "What is it, explosives?"

"No, sir." Jiron was serious. "Hobarth ran it through scan. Nonlethal contents."

Lujan chuckled. "Thanks." Entering his office, he activated lighting with a motion at the sensor and set down the mug to turn the strongbox in his hands. It was marked PERSONAL FOR ADMIRAL LUJAN SEREGE, CHIEF COMMANDER, SPHERZAH, but it was the place of origin that held his attention.

He tried the latches. They gave at his touch; the cover

fell open. He tipped the contents into his hand. . . . Two crystal pendants, an audicorder, a pair of ID tags dangling on their chain. The tags bore a flight surgeon's symbol.

Her tags.

Light caught the image suspended in one pendant. He took it up to look more closely.

It was a joining portrait: a young pilot in ceremonial grays holding a girl in pale blue in the circle of his arms.

"Darcie," he whispered. His throat was suddenly too tight for sound. He swallowed against the constriction and stood paralyzed, remembering.

Adriat, her homeworld, had been liberated for less than a month when they were joined there. He still remembered the solemnity of her face when they kissed over the altar at the rite's conclusion, how tightly she had held him on the dance floor later, and how quiet she had become when they were finally alone.

"Is it Berg?" he'd asked gently.

"No," she said first. And then, "Yes—sort of." She'd been widowed once already, and she said, "I'm so afraid that I'll lose you, too!"

He remembered how she had gripped his hands through her labor with Tristan, closing her eyes to concentrate on her breathing as he coached her, and how he'd stroked the sweat from her face with a cloth as each spasm passed. He remembered how once, in a lull between contractions, she'd taken the cloth from his hand and reached up to mop sweat from his forehead, asking with a weak but mischievous smile, "How are *you* holding up, Luj?"

Issel had fallen a few weeks later. All of the noncombatants, including Darcie, had been withdrawn to Topawa while the fighter squadrons were stationed forward on Tohh. Lujan remembered the cartons of rich Anchenken nutloaf called *urdisch* and the audicorded letters with Tristan's first babblings that she had sent out from Topawa.

He remembered how she had come on emergency leave

to Tohh when he was injured in a flying mishap. By the time she arrived he was back on his feet, though still limping, and he'd needed her moral support more than her medical skill. A fellow pilot and good friend was on trial for attempted murder and treason, and he was the prosecution's key witness. She hadn't understood why he'd found it so hard to testify, but she had accompanied him to the proceedings. And when the guilty verdict was announced, she had mourned along with him.

He'd only seen her once more after that. They'd had a few days together on Topawa before he began six months of Spherzah basic training on Kaleo and she accepted an assignment to a medical unit on Adriat. He remembered walking up the flightline with Tristan riding on his shoulders, and kissing her good-bye in the golden light of dawn before he boarded the transport.

There had been no audicorded letters or cartons of *urdisch* on Kaleo; Spherzah training demanded celibacy of the mind as well as of the body.

His first mission had taken his Spherzah team to Enach. They had penetrated the Dominion's command station a few hours before the Unified Worlds launched its attack, and accomplished their mission as they had been trained to do. The battle that followed had been the final blow to the Dominion.

He had sent a message to Darcie four days later. He wanted to return to her on Adriat, but the Unified Worlds' Command had required the Spherzah to be mediators and witnesses at the Accords. So she had taken leave and booked passage for herself and Tristan on the next transport out of Aeire City.

He would never forget how he'd learned that she was lost. The messenger might as well have been his older brother. Also a pilot, he wore the patches of Lujan's old interceptor squadron—and an atypically grim expression.

"Sean!" he said. "You look like you just flew into a field of space mines. What's wrong?"

The taller man had taken him by the shoulders and pressed him backward to a bench. "Sit down, buddy," he said, and his tone was oddly quiet. "I have to talk to you."

Puzzled, Lujan yielded to the physical insistence to sit. "Look," he said, "if this has anything to do with the negotiations, you know I can't talk—"

"Blast it, just listen to me, will you?" Sean's face showed strain. His hands tightened like twin vises on Lujan's shoulders, and he muttered, "I don't even know how to tell you this."

Studying his eyes, Lujan felt bewilderment give way to premonition. He swallowed, but his voice stayed steady. "Just tell me, Sean," he said.

The older pilot turned his face away, and his grip produced pain. "Darcie and Tristan are . . . dead, Jink—or worse."

"What?" He stiffened, staring at Sean. "That's impossible! They're supposed to dock . . ." His voice trailed off when Sean shook his head. The hands on his shoulders loosened only enough to start a nervous kneading; he saw pain shared in his friend's eyes.

"Dead?" He could manage only a strangled whisper. "Are you sure? How?"

Sean straightened, began to pace. "All I know is that a message came in through the Comms Center. It was a transmission from the Korot system—part of one, anyway; it was cut off. Something about masuk slavers and the transport being boarded." He shrugged. "And then nothing. It just—broke off."

"Slavers?" Lujan said. "In the Korot system?" His blood turned to ice water. "Have its planetary governments been contacted?"

"Yeah. There's only one, on Ganwold, and they claim

they don't know anything about it." Sean lowered his head. "I'm really sorry, buddy."

Lujan couldn't even nod—just sat staring at nothing until the full weight of it washed over him. Then he slumped forward, elbows on his knees, and buried his face in his hands. "Slavers!" he whispered. "No!"

He had joined the team that searched the Korot system for missing personnel, after the Accords were sealed, but the year's efforts had yielded nothing. At its end he'd put his seal to the required documents and had tried to accept his loss. But night after night he had dreamed of Darcie running through a ship's passage, panting and pale and clutching his son to her breast.

That had been twenty-five years ago.

He had never stopped missing her.

He shifted the objects in his hands and raised the second holodisc to the light.

Tristan. About a year and a half old, perched up on Lujan's shoulders and gripping his hair. The image still made him smile.

Tristan would have been a man by now.

He set the holos and ID tags on his desk and examined the audicorder. His thumb found its PLAY button.

"—stop playing ignorant," said a male voice. The tone belonged to a practiced interrogator. "We know who you are. We've had these for several years. Do you know what they are?"

Short silence. A slap.

Lujan recoiled as if he'd taken the blow himself.

The interrogator's voice suggested threat: "Answer me, Tristan! Where is your mother? Why did she send you here?"

"Sir—" A younger voice, anxious. "—the drug's disoriented him."

"It'll also break him, Captain. We need answers. Where is she, Tristan?"

"Sick . . . fr'm th' coughing sickness. . . ."

Lujan knew the boy's voice, despite the drug's slur, despite the lost years. "Tristan!" he said.

"Why did she send you here?" he heard. "Where is she?"

"Ou' there . . . man' nights away. . . ."

Another slap, an audible catching of breath.

Lujan punched the OFF button, locking his teeth.

It was several moments before he could steel himself to reactivate the audicorder, to hear the rest.

Comments originally meant for the Sector General followed the interrogation. Lujan played through them twice:

"Sir, I have included several articles for your examination which should be sufficient to prove the boy's identity. At the time he was apprehended he had in his possession the enclosed ID tags and a Unified-issue energy pistol dated circa 3280 Standard Years.

"The holodiscs have been in the possession of the Department of Security and Investigation since 3291, when Lieutenant Dartmuth escaped our legionnaires after the transport on which she was a passenger entered the Korot system in the control of masuk slavers."

Lujan couldn't prevent a slight smile. "Escaped. That's Darcie."

"According to your orders, sir, we have pinpointed the woman's location via reconnaissance flights and will continue surveillance. We are standing by for further orders.

"This is Brigadier General Jules François, Commander, Ganwold Forty-second Defense Squadron, concluding this report on the tenth day of the eighth month, 3307 Standard Years."

Barely a standard month ago! Lujan realized. He checked the dispatch date on the metal box: 27/8/3307. Two weeks ago.

More recent than that—only one week ago, in fact—there had been that unusual message from Nemec about the boy called Tristan accompanying the Sector General on his inspection tour. It had to be *his* Tristan! A standard month was more than enough time to transport him from Ganwold to Issel II. . . .

When the audicorder shut itself off, Lujan set it down and moved to the diaphametal wall behind his desk. Leaning against it, he looked out over the lights of Ramiscal City toward the glacier-jagged mountains rising beyond, pink in the predawn light. His mind kept shifting back to Darcie. "She's on Ganwold," he whispered. "Sick. . . . But—*thirty-two ninety-one*?"

The puzzle provided its own solution: "Timewarp!" he said. "It must have been. No wonder we could never find them!"

He glanced back at the articles on the desktop and his hand tightened into a fist. "No demands. Blast it, Mordan, what do you want?"

He already suspected the answer.

"There's a greater threat in this than to my family alone," Lujan said.

He sat in conference with the World Governor of Sostis and with the Triune, the three executives of the Unified Worlds Assembly. As civilians with ambassador rank, the four hundred sixty Assembly members under the Triune represented the major cultures of the nine Unified Worlds at the highest level of interplanetary administration.

Though Lujan was on the Defense Directorate, which came under the Assembly's jurisdiction and included the top military commanders from each member world, the nature of the Spherzah kept his forces separate from that chain of command; he answered only to the Triune.

Pite Hanesson of Mythos glanced across at his counterparts and kept his arms folded over his chest. "In what way, Admiral?"

"It may have been intended as a provocation."

Hanesson raised an eyebrow. "To what? Surely not to war!"

"Perhaps not directly," Lujan said, "but it can't be ruled out. Hostages have been at the origin of many conflicts."

Hanesson looked skeptical. "I don't understand why—"

The other members of the Triune moved uneasily in their chairs, and Kedar Gisha, Governor of Sostis, put out her hand to touch his arm. "Pite, you're too young to remember the Enach Accords, or how Sostis and Tohh were lost during the War of Resistance. Mordan Renier was commander of a Unified fighter squadron when he sold them out to the Dominion."

"I've studied history," said Hanesson. Of Lujan he asked, "What evidence is there to suggest that Issel may be preparing for war?"

"We've seen several significant indications in the past few months," Lujan said, "including changes in the Isselan space fleet's order of battle." He opened his folder and removed several plasticine image sheets, which he passed around to his counterparts. "At the Secret level, Kaleo Sector sources have in the last two weeks observed eleven war ships—two spacecraft carriers, three frigates, and six destroyers—in space docks at Issel and Adriat for apparent refitting. And message traffic from Yan has reported the delivery of fourteen training craft to the piloting academy at Aeire City. A major expansion was completed there last month, which will allow classes to be increased by fifty percent.

"Last week, Sostish sources also noted shifts from Issel's machine and light industries to support increases in the military area—the second time this has occurred within the last eight months," Lujan emphasized. "The spacecraft plant at Sanabria is capable of rolling out a fighter every three days or commissioning a battleship through space dock in less than six months." He glanced around the table. "Issel has five of these plants and Adriat has two. Lately they've been operating around the clock.

"They're producing newly-developed munitions as well as spacecraft. We haven't been able to determine yet what they are but I consider it a matter of importance.

"Most recently, we've received notification from the planetary governor of Adriat that they're going to conduct military exercises in that system next month. They're supposed to run for about three weeks. That's the normal time frame for Adriat's training, but the expected number of participants is unusually large: they're including divisions from Issel, Saede, Na Shiv, and three Bacalli worlds."

"Bacalli?" Kun Reng-Tan of Kaleo straightened in his chair. "Then those reports of talks between Issel and the Bacal Belt were true?"

"Yes." Lujan placed a sealed pouch on the table. "Spherzah Intelligence has acquired a copy of their Cooperation Pact. Among other things, it provides for the sale of Isselan weapon systems to three worlds in the Bacal Belt, and for admittance of Bacalli candidates into Issel Sector military colleges."

"But what's the payoff?" asked Alois Ashforth of Jonica. "The Bacalli worlds can barely even feed their own populations!"

"That's what we need to find out." Lujan paused. Then he said, "I know Sector General Renier. When he and the Na Shivish holdouts were finally forced to the Enach Accords, he vowed that he'd someday regain what he'd lost. He knows he can't gain that objective with anything less than force of arms. Even five years ago that would have been impossible, but today the Issel Sector's military capability rivals our own."

Hanesson still looked doubtful, but a glance at the expressions of Gisha, Kun, and Ashforth apparently made him think better of what he'd seemed about to say. Instead he asked, "What are you going to do, Admiral?"

"With your approval"—Lujan addressed them all—"I'm sending a Spherzah surveillance ship into the Issel system. There's too much we don't know."

"No rescue operations?" asked Hanesson.

Lujan fixed a look on him like blue fire. "No," he said. "That's exactly what Mordan would like us to try. It would be all the excuse he'd need to initiate hostilities."

The depiction on the screen was true enough to make Lujan feel that he stood on the bridge of a ship, observing the orbits of Issel and her two moons in real-time from within the system.

Cerise Chesney, Commodore of the Spherzah, traced the ingress route through narrowed eyes and slapped the folder of MISSION PLAN 891 against her leg. "Well, Jink, it looks like we'll get to see how good *Sentinel*'s new cloaking system really is."

"More chance for that than you may want," Lujan said with a grim smile. "Even orbiting in the moon's radar shadow, you're going to be avoiding three watchdog satellites. Their ephemerides are given in the mission folder."

"Nice." Chesney tossed back her shoulder-length honey-blond hair. Then she furrowed her brow. "Why does the command post on Issel II bounce all of its comms off the other moon, anyway? That just seems to be asking for interception."

Lujan said, "It's only used as a relay for intersystem transmissions to avoid interference from surface mining and shipping comms. The facilities on Issel I will be your major source, but you'll also be receiving messages from our people on the primary and on Issel II itself."

Chesney favored him with an inquiring look.

"Most of them are already in place; we've had deep-cover agents in the Issel system for some time," Lujan said. "Your call sign will be Echo; you'll receive the code specs and secured frequencies at your pre-mission brief. Any questions?"

She hesitated, studying him for a moment before she said, "One thing, Jink. What about Tristan?"

The Chief Commander of the Spherzah lowered his gaze, even though he knew he couldn't conceal the raw emotion in it. Not from Chesney. He drew a deep breath before he said, "Tristan's not in danger—yet. Any attempt to recover him at this point would only jeopardize both him and Darcie, and probably trigger the conflict we're trying to prevent."

"But if the situation should change?"

Lujan looked at her directly. "The mission plan assigns a Spherzah combat company to your ship. We'll also have our own people on the inside. If it should become necessary, Ches, you know that I trust both your judgment and your capability."

TEN

Retro rockets vaporized the ice that layered the landing pad as the ship-to-surface shuttle touched down. Encircling lights shot luminous pillars through eruptions of steam, obliterating visibility from the passenger hold.

As the clouds of vapor dispersed, an enclosed passenger carrier grumbled up to the craft backward, and crewmen wearing insulated coveralls and gloves connected a boarding tube between shuttle and vehicle. Still shaky from the descent, Tristan shoved himself out of his acceleration seat and followed Larielle and the governor.

The sight beyond the carrier's windows as he came aboard made him stop in midstride and stare: the whole world, as much of it as he could see, was *white*.

He had sometimes seen patches of Ganwold's prairie that looked white—or yellow or blue or red—when the wildflowers bloomed in the spring; but this whiteness lay over everything as thick and heavy as a peimu robe. Amazed, he dropped into the carrier's nearest seat and rubbed frosty condensation from the window with his sleeve so he could see out. He barely glanced up when Pulou settled beside him, huddling deeper into the blanket he'd wrapped around himself. He couldn't tear his vision away from the whiteness.

It was night, and shuttleport lighting illuminated white particles as large as lomo feathers drifting down from the sky. Tristan watched the crewmen shuffle around in it on the ground. When a piece of it struck the window in front of him, he studied its six-pointed structure, intricate as the lace on one of Larielle's dresses, until it slid down the pane and disappeared.

"It's what, little brother?" asked Pulou, peering over his shoulder.

"Snow, I think," Tristan said. "My mother tells me about it. She says we live too far south on Ganwold to have it."

Pulou blinked, cocked his head at that, and said nothing more.

The crewmen disconnected the passenger carrier from the shuttle and folded its ramp closed, and it drew away from the landing pad and lights and burrowed into the early-winter storm with a growl of engines.

Several minutes later it began to crawl up a hillside, under trees that rose like skeletal black hands clawing at the gray veil of snowfall. The Governor's Mansion stood at the crest, a tower of cantilevered blocks extending to the eight points of the compass. White under floodlighting, it appeared to have been constructed out of ice. Tristan shivered, studying it.

At the mansion's entry, they stepped out of the carrier's steamy shell into a wind laden with snow. The layer on the ground made a brittle crunch under their boots. Tristan paused to trail his hand through a drift, felt its crystalline cold bite his fingertips, and jerked them away. Behind him, Pulou urged, "Go, little brother," and placed his feet gingerly in Tristan's bootprints.

At the threshold, Pulou stopped to shake snow from his mane—and froze, nostrils working. His eyes widened, his nose wrinkled; he drew his lips back.

Tristan, shrugging off his coat, saw him and stiffened. "What's wrong?"

Before Pulou could answer, he started at a whine, a whimper, and the noise of claws clattering on the stone floor. When three furred beasts bounded into the vestibule, he bared his own teeth, his hands curling hard, and Pulou pressed up behind him, hissing and hyperventilating.

The beasts' broad heads reached to Tristan's midsection. He stared at slavering jowls, at small eyes rimmed with red, at ears almost lost in mottled haircoat as long as Pulou's mane. He backed up a step.

"Jous!" Pulou hissed over his shoulder. "Jous!"

They shoved around him, their tails beating his legs, to thrust their muzzles into the governor's hands. Renier smiled, stooping to fondle their heads and speak to them with words Tristan didn't understand.

"My pets," Renier said. "Their breed, Sybrin bearhound, is almost extinct now. I don't like leaving them here but they're not suited for our residence on Issel." He snapped his fingers and pointed, and the largest dog shifted its head toward Tristan.

Tristan swallowed, started to draw back, but Renier said, "Reach out to him slowly. Bearhounds don't readily accept strangers; they were bred as much to be bodyguards as to be bear hunters."

Tristan felt Pulou's claws dig into his shoulders, heard his hissing heighten near his ear, and wondered if Pulou was going to climb his back. But he gritted his teeth and put out a hand to the beast.

Its black nose touched his palm, cold as a fish. He flinched away.

"Hold!" said the governor. "Bearhounds can smell fear. They know threat and flight, and either one may provoke attack. If you pull your hand back too suddenly, Tristan, it might be torn from your arm."

Mouth pressed closed to keep from hissing, he stood rigid and let the dog snuffle at his hand. Let it butt and sniff at him from belly to boots until the governor called it back.

"He's identified you now," Renier said, smiling. "Abattoir never forgets a scent."

Tristan followed Rajak to a suite at the outermost end of one upper wing, relieved to leave the dogs behind.

He didn't wait until the valet had gone to push aside the drapery covering the far wall. The pane behind it was tinted gray, dimming the floodlights and snow below. It was cold when he leaned on it, and it clouded with his breath: this was no holograph screen.

Beyond the hill and the park, clouds above and snow below held the glow of nighttime city lights.

Aeire City.

His mother's home city.

Tristan stood looking out into the dark for a long while.

The shuttle sent thunder across the low sky, appearing first as a flash, then as a streak like a meteor. It hovered, firing landing rockets, and descended gradually over the VTOL dish until it touched on pillars of fire that shook the ground and boiled the ice around it. Steam rolled as it settled, making its skin seem to shimmer, and even the members of the honor guard turned their faces away.

Tristan braced himself against a wall of wind, still heavy with moisture, although last week's snowstorm had passed. He felt the cold as an ache in his legs and his chest; he fisted his bare, stiffened hands and tried to resist shivering.

He heard a clipped order, saw the honor guard snap to attention and bring weapons to present arms, forming a double file that faced the shuttle. The order and the stamp of boots rippled through four companies of soldiers assembled on the tarmac behind the receiving party. Tristan slid a glance sideways, at the governor in military cloak and medals, and Larielle in furs.

A hatchway slid open on the craft's underside and a ramp lowered. Tristan saw shadowed movement within as the first figure emerged onto the ramp, and then the others followed.

They were taller even than Renier, wearing tunics and cloaks of various colors that brushed their knees with golden fringe. The darkness of their exposed arms and lower legs was hair, thick on ruddy skin; their faces were more bearded than not, and their hair tumbled longer and wilder about their shoulders than a gan's mane. Heavy brows could not conceal ursine eyes, nor did mustaches hide fanged smiles more menacing than a jou's.

Tristan recoiled, remembering the hirsute shape that had seized his mother in the dark of a damaged transport's hold.

They wore leather boots, strapped tight around ankles and muscled calves. Scuffing footfalls up a ship's corridor echoed in the pulse pounding hard in Tristan's ears.

He glimpsed knife hilts stuck into belts among the rich fringe—saw again the flash of a blade at his mother's throat, close to his own face.

There were ten of them, representing Mi'ika, the chief world in the Bacal Belt, and they approached the governor's party as if they owned Adriat. They paused barely two meters in front of Renier, and the one foremost raised a hand before his chest in greeting, his palm forward, his fingers tensed.

The wind rolled itself into a cold ball in Tristan's gut. His hands curled involuntarily, hard as claws. He bared his teeth. "Masuki!" He hissed it. "They're masuki!"

ELEVEN

The Commander of the College of Surface Warfare clasped wrists with b'Anar Id Pa'an, son of the Pasha of Mi'ika; they embraced briefly and smiled for the bank of holocorders at the rear of the viditorium. All around the half-circle stage, humans and nonhumans rose cheering and applauding from tiered seats.

The cheers echoed in the amphitheater, continuing as each of Pa'an's fellows came forward to salute the Commander in similar fashion, and be presented to the college's assembled officials.

Two junior officers in the center of an upper tier exchanged looks as everyone resumed their seats and the Sector General took the podium. Neither was Isselan; one was nonhuman. Both wore instructor's badges.

"Here comes another load of 'Progress Through Cooperation' rubbish," said the human under his breath. A native Adriat, he leaned back in his seat and folded his arms over his chest.

His counterpart, an umedo from Saede, agreed with a brief darkening of its ashen skin, and swept a damp pad over features that resembled thumbprints in firm clay. Its whisper was a rasp through the translator worn at its throat. "I am not concerned for advantages to growing the industry and the economy. We do not need a conflict against the Unified Worlds."

"Especially not in an alliance with the Bacal Belt," said the Adriat. "Establishing even trade relations with a species that deals in slave markets would make me uncomfortable. But this—" He twisted his features in distaste.

"Trading of slaves has been a crime in the galaxy since the Stedjaard Convention," the amphibian said. "Did the masuki not seal it?"

The human shook his head. "*Some* of the masuk worlds are party, for what that may be worth. We're dealing with nonhu . . . uh, I mean uncivilized—mindsets and amorality here, for whom compliance with laws is determined mostly by convenience.

"Masuki," he said, "value life only by what it'll bring on the market. Our new allies have nothing to lose and quite a bit to gain by selling off their undesirables as mercenaries."

"What is this, Ian?" said the umedo.

"Didn't you know? That's how the Bacal Belt is paying for all the weapon systems we've given them—with mercenaries. Proxy soldiers to carry out the Sector General's 'progress.' "

He would have continued, but an officer seated in front of them shot a look over his shoulder. Ian sat through the rest of the speech with his jaw set, stood mechanically when the Sector General and his entourage departed for a tour of the college, and sat again to watch the viditorium empty around him, the assemblage moving down the sloped aisles like water rolling to the bottom of a basin.

Beside him the umedo said, "I am not understanding how the Sector General will prove the need for a war against the Unified Worlds."

"It's revenge, Katja, pure and simple," said Ian.

The other stared at him. "That is *niijik*—insane! Does it desire a Tarssyginian Peace?"

"No. The governor's public motives are to free his

homeworld from its subjugation to the Unified Worlds." Ian looked sideways at his counterpart. "You heard what he said about liberation."

Katja's skin seemed to undulate with wave after wave of dark coloring. "It is *niijik*! It is not worth the elements of cost and risk, the expenses for the procurement, or the distances of transport. And it is estimating too low the Unified Worlds."

"And overestimating the complicity of the *masuki*," said Ian.

The umedo's shade stayed dark. It appeared pensive, thoughtful.

Ian sighed resignedly and rose. They were alone in the amphitheater now. When his companion stood, too, he began moving toward the aisle. They strode down it together, Katja mopping at its face again.

Stepping outside, Ian glanced around the portico as he put on his service cap and fastened his coat collar against the wind. "Did you notice the boy sitting near the governor in there?"

"Yes," said the amphibian. It drew up the hood of its coverall uniform and touched a patch on the chest that activated heating filaments in the fabric. "Was it not an aide or a page?"

"He's the son of Admiral Serege, the Chief Commander of the Spherzah—the boy that's been missing for twenty-five standard years."

Katja darkened under its hood. "How does it have to do with this?"

"He's the catalyst," said Ian. "A hostage. He's the insurance for Serege's cooperation."

Boarding the carrier in front of the college administration building, Tristan deliberately trod on a foot thrust into the aisle to trip him, and shoved his way between shoulders broader than a bull peimu's. With Pulou close behind him, he glared back at ursine leers, wrinkling his nose at rankness that rose from masuk bodies like steam in the cold. Dropping into an empty seat at the back of the carrier, he pressed his forehead to the one-way windowpane in feigned boredom.

As the carrier began to move, he peered out between bands of violet bunting meant to disguise the vehicle's armor, and focused on landmarks: the hillside that rolled down from the campus to the city beyond, the distinct shapes of buildings against the winter sky. A couple of times he nudged Pulou and pointed, wordless.

At the back of his mind he envisioned the city map he'd studied, an historical work painted like a mural in one of the administration building's vaulted concourses. Comparing map symbols and landmarks, he began to estimate distances and directions.

The vehicle entered the grounds of the Governor's Mansion, and Tristan squinted through the dusk at something he hadn't noticed before. The forest was hemmed by a line of slender poles. He noted their height and the intervals at which they were set: a lightning wall, like the one he and Pulou had gone through on Ganwold.

He kept his gaze on the forest for the rest of the ride, thinking. Planning. The trees were a tangle of black on white, fading into shades of blue in the approaching dark. He scarcely noticed.

He and Pulou hung back when the carrier drew up before the mansion, letting the masuki disembark ahead of them so that they and the governor would intercept the bearhounds' greetings. He let his hands curl, watching them lumber from the entry.

"Whelps!" The word was a snarl. b'Anar Id Pa'an flattened his ears, bent to show his fangs, and the dogs cringed, hackles raised but tails between their legs. Pa'an straightened, grinning at his companions. "Whelps!" he said again.

Behind them, Tristan flexed his hands and locked his teeth in a hiss.

He turned on lighting when he came into his room, and Pulou slipped past to settle himself on a rug in the corner and remove his wet leg-wrappings. Tugging off his own boots, Tristan squatted down, too.

"In big . . . picture of this camp"—Tristan described the map in gan—"on wall of big lodge where we go, I find Elincourt, where my mother lives when she is small. It takes maybe part of one night to walk there."

Pulou cocked his head. "Her family is there?"

"Yes."

"You know that, little brother?"

He didn't. Not now, not for sure. He lowered his eyes. "They are when I'm small," he said.

In another moment he'd risen, crossed to the drapery, and pulled it aside to look down through dark diaphametal on darker woods. "She's sick, Pulou!" he said. "Where else can I go to help her?"

There was a moment's quiet, and Pulou said, "You think of what?"

"They take jous out to run at night," Tristan said. "When they do that, we dress in warm clothes and wait. Keep your knife at dinner."

"We go out how?" Pulou asked. "Lodge only has one door, at bottom."

"In latrine," said Tristan, "there's hole in roof."

Pulou blinked at him and grinned. "Like lomos from burrow."

Tristan found his vision fixing on Larielle at dinner and kept remembering what she had whispered to him in the corridor the last time he'd tried to escape.

She looked up at last. "Is something wrong, Tristan?"

"No," he said, too quickly, and fingered the handle of the steak knife he'd stuck into the waistband of his trousers. "I'm just tired."

He switched off the door's automation when he and Pulou came back to their suite, locking it to the outside. He gathered up his warmest clothing and divided it into two piles.

Struggling to put on human garments, Pulou said, "Skin that," and gestured at the bed.

"Clothes are warmer," said Tristan.

"No, not for warmth. Why do I teach you to make stripes on your body?"

Tristan looked out on a forest wrapped in white, and grinned. "To hide!"

Shrouded in a sheet, he paced before the partially-opened drapes, watching the floodlit grounds. He saw handlers leaning against leashes as the hounds came into the open. The diaphametal shut out the noise of their baying but his hand still tensed on the pane.

They were more than an hour coming back. Tristan watched until they disappeared toward the entry, though it wasn't visible from his window. He waited until he heard commanding voices and barks and claws rattling on the floors below. Then he motioned to Pulou.

There was a ventilation duct in the ceiling of the hygiene booth. Tristan yanked out its fan, revealing a shaft less than a meter long, with wind whistling through the vented cover at its top. Standing on a chair he dragged into the booth, he squeezed into a space almost too narrow for his shoulders and reached for what appeared to be latches holding the cover on.

He tugged at one; it didn't budge. He reached for the second; it moved sideways. He twisted it experimentally and it loosened—came off in his hand. A wingnut. He dropped it, reached for the first again.

It still wouldn't turn. Glancing down at Pulou, he saw the fan lying on the floor and said, "Give me that."

Two fan blades bent together served as pliers to grip the wingnut. With a few quick twists, it bounced down on his head and shoulders. He used the fan blades on the third and fourth wingnuts, too. The vent cover shook in the wind and a sharp gust ripped it away. Tristan dropped the fan and pulled on his gloves and reached up for the rim.

Pulling, straining, he thrust arms, then head, out into a blizzard. Sleet in his face took his breath. He ducked his head away from the wind, gasping, and pushed himself up on his arms until first his hips were clear, then his legs. Lying flat in the snow on the roof, he reached back into the shaft for Pulou's hand. In another minute the gan emerged onto the roof beside him.

They hugged the core of the spiraling structure, shaped like a cantilevered staircase of three-meter steps. Helping each other slide from one level to the next, landing lightly on the balls of their feet with knees bent to take the shock, they stayed as wordless as if they were stalking a peimu. Once on the ground, they crouched in a shadow to catch their breaths and listen. Pulou sniffed the wind, grimaced at its iciness; but he motioned "Go."

The snow was nearly knee-deep, wet and heavy. Too heavy to just plow through and too deep to continuously step over. Almost like walking upstream in knee-deep water, Tristan thought. Maybe harder, because the snow concealed everything underfoot.

"Stupid things, flat-tooth boots!" Pulou said once, and flung out his arms to keep his balance. "I can't feel ground where I walk!"

Tristan could only nod agreement; he was panting with his own efforts, actually sweating under his coat.

They were a kilometer into the forest when the wind brought distant baying like a warning. Pulou heard it first and stiffened at Tristan's shoulder, baring his teeth. "Jous!" he said.

Abattoir never forgets a scent, the governor had said. Tristan stared about him—saw a broken branch protruding from a drift. "Go on," he said, nudging Pulou, and tugged the limb free.

Baying swelled on a gust of wind, closing on them. The wind was at their backs but it wouldn't cover their trail. Not in time. "Hurry!" Tristan said. He was panting. "Lightning wall is close. They won't follow through that! Run, Pulou!"

Something slammed into his shins; the snow came up to catch him in its cold. Tristan shoved himself up on shaky arms, gritting his teeth at the pain in his legs, and saw Pulou in the snow beside him, trying to gain his feet, trying to shake the whiteness from his coat. He glanced back as he struggled up.

Drifted snow had concealed the trunk of a fallen tree.

The bearhounds' cries carried to him. He saw Pulou stiffen, and retrieved his branch. "Hurry! They're closer!"

In the splintered lantern light swinging after them, three shapes became visible, lumbering easily through snow that lay as deep as their bellies. Their baying echoed from trees stripped by the elements.

"Too close!" Pulou's voice was a hiss. His claws closed hard on Tristan's shoulder and his eyes were vicious on the verge of *tsaa'chi*. "Too close to run from!"

On impulse, Tristan pushed him toward the nearest tree. "Get up there! Hurry! I come behind you."

There wasn't time. Pulou was barely out of reach when the lead bearhound crashed through brittle brush and launched himself over the fallen log. Pursuer's bay died to a killer's snarl. Tristan seized his branch like a quarterstaff and put his back to the trunk of Pulou's tree.

The dog leaped for his throat—

—he intercepted with the limb.

Fangs grazed his glove. One broke on the frozen wood, but the bearhound held on.

The dog shook his head, snarling, tugging as if to wrest the limb from Tristan's hands. A dark splash stained the back of his glove; he gasped, surprised that he felt no pain.

Paws broader than his hand raked his shoulders, shredding the sheet. Teeth flashed around the gag of the branch, straining to reach him. Tristan smelled steamy breath in his face.

He shifted his grip on the limb, abruptly twisting it up to the right. It threw the dog off his feet, rolling it over in the snow.

But the other two lunged in, growling, before the first had regained its feet. One took the thick end of the limb in the chest and reeled back, yelping; the other caught a swipe across the face with the branching end.

And the first dog sprang again, slavering blood.

Lights flared over the area and a voice, sharp on the wind, brought the dogs to a quivering stance. The leader licked its abused mouth, questioning its master with its eyes as its mates drew up at its flanks.

Tristan didn't lower his weapon.

Renier strode across the clearing, the lanterns at his back casting him into stark silhouette. His face remained in shadow, indiscernible, and Tristan shifted his hands, tightening his grip on the branch. He was shaking.

"What is this, Tristan?" The governor's tone was taut, but whether with anger or exertion Tristan couldn't tell. "What's going on here?"

"My mother's sick!" Tristan said. He couldn't keep the anger from his voice. "Her family is here and you know it! All I want is to help her!"

Renier gestured. Two shapes carrying lamps detached themselves from the darkness to leash the hounds. Masuk shapes. Tristan ignored them, waiting, aware that they had withdrawn only by the snow's crunch under their boots and the dogs' diminished whuffing. He kept his vision locked on the governor.

When they stood alone in the icy dark, Renier said, "If your mother's life is so important to you, Tristan, this will not happen again."

TWELVE

Tristan turned his head, squinting against gusts that slashed his face with liquid ice. He raised one hand to shield himself, and stumbled. Staggering to stay on his feet, he paused, panting.

Whuffing came hard behind him, eager, encouraged by a handler loosening the leashes. Tristan glowered over his shoulder. b'Anar Id Pa'an leered back through a mustache matted with snow, showing his teeth, and shook the leashes again. "Move, pup." It sounded like a snarl.

Moments later, Pulou's boot caught in underbrush. He tugged at it twice to free it and lost his balance. Both hands flailed out to catch himself. He got to his knees, snow-covered—and flung up an arm when the bearhounds lunged, teeth bared.

They were jerked up centimeters from closing on him, and Pa'an's laughter rose over the wind as he twisted the leashes about his wrists.

"Jou's whelp!" Tristan interposed himself between gan and dogs, his hand hovering near the knife in his belt. "Don't do that again!"

Pa'an raised bushy eyebrows. "Look what's whining whelp!" He loosed the leashes—

—and the knife flashed free in Tristan's hand.

Something slapped it away, caught at his wrist; the knife sliced into a drift at the foot of a tree and vanished. He wrenched around—and recoiled from the fury in Pulou's eyes.

"Don't," the gan said, still gripping his wrist.

Pa'an showed his canine teeth in a leer and played with the bearhounds' leashes.

Tristan shot a glance at the spot where his knife had disappeared, and felt Pulou's hand tighten.

"Turn your back, little brother."

He hesitated. Glowered at the masuk.

And turned his back to him.

An hour later he sank to his heels in the mansion's lift, away from Pulou, and leaned his head against the wall, his eyes closed against the others' gazes. He gulped in the warm air, coughing at the cold that ached in his lungs, shivering in his sodden clothing.

The lift didn't stop on the level where his rooms were. He looked up, questioning the governor with his eyes.

Renier said, "Your room is too badly damaged to go back to, Tristan. Avuse is moving to let you have the servants' quarters outside my rooms."

The lift door sighed open. Tristan didn't move, just sat until Rajak poked at him with the toe of his boot. Then he shot to his feet, twisting about with his teeth bared and his hand raised, curled like a claw—

Pulou caught his arm, gripped it hard enough that he could feel the claws through his sleeve; but it was the expression in his eyes that made Tristan wince.

Rajak only grunted and gave him a shove toward the door, and the others followed him into the foyer.

"This way, Tristan," said Renier.

The servant's room was smaller than his quarters on

Issel's moon had been, no more than a curtained antechamber outside the governor's sleeping room, as chilly as his suite downstairs had been. It had no window, no lavatory of its own. Only a bed, and a storage compartment in the facing wall.

He didn't go in until Pulou nudged his shoulder, and then he kept his back to the governor as he tore off what remained of his camouflage sheet, wadded it, and hurled it onto the bed. When he glanced up again, Renier and the others were gone.

His right glove was bloodstained. He examined it, found no tear in it, no mark on his hand when he pulled it off. He remembered teeth closing on frozen wood, hot breath in his face, the bearhound slavering blood as it held him at bay. He shuddered and flung the glove into a corner.

Wet parka and boots and trousers came off with difficulty. He tugged at them with stiff hands, shivering, his teeth still chattering. The bruises on his shins were already swollen and discolored.

Pulou offered him a blanket from the bed and said, "Sit down" as he wrapped himself in it.

He sat, sullen, with his back to the gan.

"I'm sorry," said Pulou, "that I take your knife when masuk watches."

Tristan glared at the wall. "Then why do you do it?"

"*Tsaa'chi* is serious thing, little brother. Always, someone dies."

Tristan snapped around to face him. "You let *tsaa'chi* come when we fall!"

"Yes." Pulou nodded once, slightly. "Because I can see no way out. You show me, in tree. If jous are too strong for you, I let it come again; but they're not."

"But masuk turns jous on you when we come back!"

"Not real danger," said Pulou. "He teases, like jous at home when they're not hungry. To turn your back is best."

"He makes me angry."

Pulou looked at him, eyes narrowed to amber slivers. "Yes. But *tsaa'chi* brings death. Is anger important enough to die about?"

Tristan lowered his head, turning his face away. "No," he said after a moment, and sighed. "I'm sorry, Pulou." He felt suddenly exhausted.

But, curled close beside Pulou for mutual warmth, he stared at the wall. Half-sleep brought nightmares of the woods and the governor standing like a threat between himself and the lights of Aeire City, a threat that left him with no way out.

The overcast had blown away by the next morning, uncovering a sky bright enough to make Tristan squint at its reflection on the snow. The wind hadn't died though; it drove snow before it like sand, shaping ripples and dunes that glittered in the sunlight. It reddened faces and stiffened hands in mere minutes, and watching it even from the enclosed gallery made him shiver.

. . . Until he looked down on the landing strip, on four starcraft waiting in a row like so many needles. He raised a pair of televiewers to his eyes.

For a moment he thought he'd been transported to the side of one craft; he was surprised that he couldn't hear the voices of the crewmen moving over and around it. He began to put out a hand to touch its skin—and then drew back, feeling foolish at being caught in the illusion. He glanced at Larielle and Pulou to see if they had noticed. They hadn't.

Its wings were short and swept close to its fuselage, its canopy rode like a streamlined bubble where a fish's dorsal fin would be, and it had twin vertical stabilizers. Scrutinizing it, Tristan felt his breath catch in his throat. He nudged Pulou. "My father flies in things like that," he said.

"These IS-30 Javelin fighters are the most recent addition to our arsenal," he heard the governor telling his guests. "They are transatmospheric craft capable of deploying either from surface bases or spacecraft carriers. Although they are not lightskip-capable, they can reach hypersonic speeds within the atmosphere to achieve escape velocity, and they are exceptionally maneuverable in both atmospheric and space flight, as you'll see. They're armed with two internal plasma cannon and have six internal wing rails for launching a variety of ordnance."

Tristan shut out the monologue and watched as the groundcrew scrambled clear of the craft and stood rigid in a file behind the mounting ladder. Movement at his right caught his attention; he focused on four men in silver flight suits, egress packs on their shoulders, helmets in the crook of their arms. They strode across the landing field in step, heedless of the snow-laden wind, and each pivoted sharply to his own ship. Tristan watched one man hand his helmet to his crew chief, romp up the mounting ladder, settle into the cockpit; he watched the groundcrew secure his harness and help him with helmet and oxygen mask.

"Our pilots," the governor said behind him, "are trained here at the Aeire City Academy. We'll take a tour of the facilities after the aerial demonstration. These particular pilots are instructors with at least three thousand hours' flight time each, mostly in interceptor-type craft."

His masuk guests grunted acknowledgment.

In a moment the crewmen withdrew. Crew chiefs and pilots exchanged hand signals; engines fired up one by one. Walking backward before the lead Javelin's starboard wing, its crew chief beckoned. The needle rolled forward, pivoted to starboard; the others fell in line. Tristan saw the leader's afterburners flare orange, baring black tarmac behind it as it began to move. He felt its thunder as it accelerated; his heart rate accelerated with it. It shot down the strip, forward landing gear thrusting its nosecone to the sky, and rotated.

It rocketed vertically from the surface, and the others followed in a wedge.

Thrusters' echoes shook the gallery. Tristan felt breathless; his hands tightened on the televiewers. There was only him and the starcraft, one in flight.

Flashing splinters left vapor trails across the frozen sky, twisted them into a helix, braided the wind. Wingmen rolled out in opposite directions, turning on ailerons into level attitude, and banked around to cut a crossover with their leaders before rejoining the formation like fish swimming close in a school.

An hour later they screamed into final approach as one. Landing gear reached for the surface; they taxied to a halt before the gallery. Canopies popped, oxygen masks fell away, gauntlets touched helmets in salute.

Tristan studied the pilots' faces.

He and Pulou lagged behind the others when they walked through the academy's hangars. He paused to run a hand along a trainer ship's short wing, to fix its stiletto shape in his mind for a dream he wouldn't have to wake from.

And that night, lying on his belly in a shroud of blanket, he traced the Javelins' aerobatics in the carpet with his finger.

Tristan glanced up from the Pocket Tutor when Renier entered the sitting room flanked by Avuse and two masuki, but Larielle patted his arm and said, "Go on, Tris. You're doing very well."

Conscious of the governor pausing across the table from him, he returned his attention to the display, and his reading: "De-spite their limi-ted role in de-ter-min-ing the final . . . out-come?" He glanced at Larielle for confirmation.

She nodded. "That's right. It means how something turns out in the end."

"Oh." Tristan shifted in his chair and went on. "—the

final outcome of the con-flick . . . What's *that*?" He pointed at the miniature monitor.

"Just a minute; one at a time," Larielle said, and tapped the monitor. "What's that again?"

"Conflick," said Tristan.

"Close, but not quite. What does that little mark on the second character do to it?"

"Oh. Con-*flict*." Tristan planted an elbow on the table to support his head in his hand. "What does it mean?"

"Ask the Tutor," said Larielle.

Tristan sighed. "Define 'conflict,' " he said.

"Conflict," the Tutor responded. "War; struggle; disagreement between opposing ideas or forces."

"Do you understand that?" Larielle asked.

"Yeah."

"Good. Now," she said, "look at the other word, one character at a time."

Tristan said, "Na Shiv-ish?" and questioned her with his look.

"Yes," she said. "That means people from Na Shiv. It's another world in the Issel Sector."

"Na Shiv-ish," Tristan repeated to himself, and continued. "—troops formed the ma-jor-ity of the sur-face forces."

Larielle nodded. "Good. Why don't you ask the Tutor to read that passage back to you now?"

Tristan shrugged and opened his mouth to make the request, but the governor chuckled. "I think that's enough reading for this evening, my dear. Come now." He turned away. "We'll have chelle tonight, Avuse."

Reaching for the Tutor's OFF button, Tristan nudged Pulou with his foot and rose, and the gan emerged from under the table. They joined the others before another fireplace with artificial flames, and Tristan took the chair farthest from the masuki.

In a moment, Avuse brought a tray of goblets and a crystal carafe from the vacuwaiter. Tristan watched him place the tray on the table at the governor's elbow and pour a crimson liquid from the carafe.

He accepted the glass he was offered. The red liquid smelled spoiled to him, but the others either didn't notice or didn't mind. He took a sip; it tingled on his tongue. He grimaced and set the glass down.

Across from him, the governor said, "I'm pleased with your progress over this past month, Tristan."

He glanced up but said nothing.

"Your reading skills and confidence with the Tutor are improving," Renier pointed out. "I sense your hunger for the education that you've never had." He ran a finger around the rim of his own goblet and looked at Tristan directly. "I think it's time you were granted that opportunity."

The words were generous but there was something about his tone that Tristan didn't trust. "Why?" he asked.

The governor appeared mildly surprised. "Your father would have wanted the best for you, my boy. Since he has not been able to provide it, I feel that I should."

In his periphery Tristan could see the masuki grinning at him with their bared teeth and tongues. Something about all of it put him on edge, made him increasingly uneasy. "Why?" he said again. "You don't even like my father!"

The governor's expression turned suddenly cold. " 'Why' is of no concern to you, Tristan. I expect only your compliance in this matter. The arrangements for you to enter the Aeire City Academy next month have already been completed."

"Next month!" Tristan stared at him, stiffening in his chair. "I can't do that—!"

"You can and you will," the governor said. His voice was quiet, his jaw taut, but it was his eyes, locked on Tristan's, that bore a warning. "It is very important to me, my young Spherzah," he said.

Tristan studied him. Swallowed. But then Weil's advice slipped across the back of his mind. "What about Pulou?" he demanded abruptly. "If I have to go, then Pulou does, too!"

The governor looked annoyed. "Don't be ridiculous, Tristan!" he said. "Your friend can't read! . . . He doesn't even speak a human language! I doubt that—"

"That doesn't matter!" Tristan curled his hands tight about the arms of his chair, digging his fingernails hard into its upholstery, and gathering himself as if for a spring. Near his feet, Pulou had let his mane bristle, had bared his teeth, and Tristan said, "You won't take us away from each other!"

The governor's jaw worked; his dark eyes fixed on Tristan's—and Tristan met that gaze and held it, letting feigned fury mask his mounting fear. Several silent seconds passed before the governor said, "Very well, I'll allow him to go with you. But you *will* attend the Academy, young one."

Tristan said nothing else after that. He let his vision drop to the drink in his hand, red as blood in the goblet, and slid his thumb and first finger up and down its stem several times.

He could feel the other's vision still fixed on him; sensed suppressed threat when the governor said, after a long minute, "Tristan."

He looked up, glaring.

"Most young people in the Issel Sector can only dream of attending the Aeire City Academy," Renier said. "It would be very poor manners not to thank someone who gives you such a gift."

Tristan met his narrowed gaze. Held it once more—and let the silence stretch for as long as he dared before he said sullenly, "Thank you."

* * *

He lifted his attention from the Pocket Tutor only enough to glower when Larielle entered the sitting room the next afternoon and sat down before the desk terminal. She actually winced when she met his eyes, and her dim smile melted into a sigh. "You're still upset about going to the academy, aren't you, Tris?" she said.

"Yes." He clipped the word.

"But you *want* to learn piloting, don't you?" she asked. "I saw how that demo flight affected you, and the way you admired that starcraft in the hangar."

He ducked his head. "Yes. . . . But I can't do it right now."

"You're worried about your mother."

He nodded without looking up.

She sighed again. Sat silent for several moments before she said, "Remember how, the first time you tried to run away, I told you to be patient?"

He studied her, wondering at her. Said warily, "Yes."

"It's even more important that you be patient now," she said.

"But there isn't time!" He made a desperate gesture with both hands. "I have to find my father!"

"Tristan." Larielle placed a firm hand on his arm—cast a furtive glance back at the doorway and then leaned nearer him. "Listen to me for a minute: your father knows where you are, and where your mother is."

"How do you know that?" he demanded.

"Because my father made sure that he knows," she said. "He—"

"Your father doesn't like my father," Tristan told her. "Why would he tell him that?"

"Because he wants to use you and your mother to force your father into . . . a very dangerous situation," Larielle said. "You're the bargaining pieces in a complex political game—the bait in a massive trap."

Tristan stared at her, shocked. Shook his head. Started to

shove his chair back from the table, to rise. "I have to get away from here."

Her hand tightened on his arm. "No!" she said.

The urgency in her voice—the suggestion of fear—caught him up short. She pulled him back down, kept her hold on his arm. "That's the worst thing you could possibly do right now, Tris!" she said. "This is a very precarious situation, for a lot more people than just you and your mother. It could cost the lives of thousands—maybe millions—of people, on Sostis and Issel and who knows how many other worlds if . . . something goes wrong.

"Your father knows that, too, and he doesn't want it to happen. He's going to have to be very careful to get you and your mother out, and that's going to take time. You've just got to trust him. Do you understand?"

He didn't know if he did or not; the whole thing seemed impossible. Whole worlds at risk—over him and his mother? He sat stiff in his chair, every muscle so tight that he shook; and his mouth was so dry he could barely ask, "How do you know all of that?" The words came in a rasp.

Larielle looked down. Let go of his arm. Rubbed it a little with her fingers. "My father told me," she said quietly. And sighed. And didn't look up. "He feels it's important for me to know about these things, since he's named me to be the next Governor of Issel. He's—trying to prepare me, he says." She shook her head, spilling her hair about her shoulders. "I know this is wrong but I haven't been able to change his mind about it."

She looked up at last, into Tristan's face, and he saw in her eyes the same fear he'd seen there on the morning he first met her. "I'm so sorry about all of this," she said, and lay her hand over his. "Right now, Tris, the best way you can help your mother is to cooperate with my father. Don't complicate things. Just go to the academy, and be patient."

Tristan only nodded. He felt too shaken, too drained to do anything else.

THIRTEEN

The lecture hall was already darkened, the instructor pointing out the components of an altimeter as a diagram of one rotated in the holotank behind his podium, when Tristan slipped into the viditorium. Motioning Pulou to stay back with Rajak, who positioned himself at the door with his arms folded over his chest, Tristan made his way to an empty seat in the middle of a row near the back.

The cadet to his left, a narrow-faced young man named Siggar, glanced up as he dropped into his seat. "Five more demerits for coming late to formation, Serege," he said, holding up his hand with fingers spread as if to let Tristan count them.

Tristan, taking off his coat and flinging it over the back of his chair, shot him a glare but didn't say anything.

"That's about six tardies now, isn't it?" the other persisted. "Man, you're gonna spend your whole off-day on the drill field!"

"Shut up, Siggar," said the cadet on his other side. "I can't hear what McAdam's saying."

With Siggar momentarily distracted, Tristan switched on the desk attached to his chair. The altimeter diagram in the holotank appeared in its display. He studied the labeled parts.

"... The only time your altimeter will show the true altitude," the instructor was saying, "is when the actual air temperature and pressure match those of the 'standard atmosphere.' Since that seldom happens, your altimeter reading will usually be off, and how much it's off depends on how much the in-flight temperature and pressure differ from the standard. Anybody who *doesn't* understand that?"

Tristan furrowed his brow, trying to make sense of it, but with Siggar watching his every move he didn't dare tap the button on his desk to request a repeat or a more basic explanation. The instructor looked across his audience and continued. "All right, then, even though you have the right altimeter setting, changes in in-flight temperatures are going to cause differences in your indicated altitude. For example, colder temperatures are going to put your 'craft at a lower altitude than what your altimeter shows, and warmer temps will put it higher. Any questions?"

None must have appeared on his podium monitor because he said, "Good. Do the problems on your desks."

The diagram on Tristan's desk display was replaced by fifteen questions. He began to read through them, slowly, to be sure that he understood what they meant:

4.1   The altimeter is essential only to the pilot of an atmosphere-bound craft flying in IFR conditions. (True/False)

4.2   Identify the components of the altimeter diagrammed below and explain its operation.

Tristan keyed in FALSE for the first question. He labeled the altimeter components and then paused. "I didn't hear him explain how it works," he said.

"Maybe you would've if you'd been here on time," Siggar said without looking up from his own desk.

Tristan ignored him. "Sajatte?" he asked of the cadet at his right.

"Nothing to it," said Sajatte. "When your 'craft climbs, the air leaves this outer case"—he tapped the diagram on his display—"and these discs spread apart. That makes your readout change. It works the opposite way when you descend."

"What?" Tristan wrinkled his brow.

Sajatte's expression showed mild exasperation, but he explained again anyway. "Get it now?"

"Yes," Tristan said. Hesitantly. "Thank you." He looked over the next few questions:

4.3   According to Ministry of Aerospace Activity regulations, an atmospheric craft flying at or over 5486.4 meters above planetary sea level (PSL) will have its altimeter set to _____.

4.4   Determine density altitude when launching from a spaceport at 1609 meters PSL. Reported temperature is 30°C, altimeter setting is 75.69 cm, and pressure altitude is 1646 meters. Note: Set your altimeter to 76.00 cm.

Tristan keyed in 1646 and P/ALT, entered 30, then wavered between Indicated°C and True°C before he chose Indicated°C and hit COMP.

A cue line appeared at the bottom of the display:

ERROR. WORK PROBLEM AGAIN.

He sagged back in his chair and scowled at the screen for a moment before he reached out to jab the CLEAR key. The cue line vanished.

From his left came a muttered curse and the thump of a fist on the computer desk, followed by the rapid tapping of fingers on keypads.

Tristan didn't glance up. Brow furrowed, he entered the

givens again and closed his eyes to sort out the formulas i his mind. He deliberately touched the COMP key.

The cue line reappeared:

ERROR. WORK PROBLEM AGAIN.

Frustrated, he locked his teeth in a hiss and punched the CLEAR key again.

The instructor's voice interrupted his third effort. "Al right, if you're not done with all the questions yet, do them during study period. We've got more material to cover on altimeters before we move on to vertical speed indicators. . . ."

Tristan lingered over the problem for some moments before he hit SAVE, watched his display go blank, and hit WRITE.

His monitor was still empty when the instructor cleared the holotank behind his podium and said, "We'll wrap up Instruments tomorrow. Your test will be the day after that, and then we'll start on Propulsion Systems. Those of you who are having trouble with this stuff, I want to see you in the multimedia booths during study period. You know who you are."

Siggar looked at Tristan, flicked a glance at his empty desk, and smiled. "So do we."

Glaring, Tristan turned off his desk and shoved it away. "You didn't do very well on the last test yourself!"

"At least I passed it the first time."

"By one point!" said Tristan.

Sajatte was collecting his coat and cap. "Get moving, Siggar, you slime-sucking swamp worm," he said. "You're holding up the rest of the row."

Siggar only grinned and started toward the aisle, and Tristan and Sajatte and the others followed.

Tristan didn't so much as glance in Rajak's direction, but

he felt the servant's presence like an unwanted shadow as he filed into the corridor. Glimpsing Pulou, however, watching everything through half-closed eyes, he let out a sigh of relief.

Stay in line, stay in step, no talking while in formation. Only the rhythm of boots rang in the hallway. *Square your corners, keep your vision caged—show some discipline!*

Tristan could almost hear the drill master's voice in his mind. "This is stupid!" he said under his breath.

After a month and a half it seemed even more stupid than it had at the outset. It heightened his impatience, increased his frustration. He knotted his hands into fists at his trouser seams, hard enough that his fingernails bit into the heels of his hands.

The line turned a corner where the corridors intersected, and entered another viditorium's double doors. The cadets marched down its steep aisle and filled its encircling rows of seats, as in a small stadium, one after another.

"There's one good thing about Isselan history," Siggar said as he slouched way down in his chair. "It's a chance to catch up on your sleep."

"This is better than having to read it," said Tristan.

"Aw, this War of Resistance stuff isn't so bad," said Sajatte. "My old man's war stories are finally starting to make sense." He watched Siggar settle his head back against the seat and looked over at Tristan. "Did your old man fight in the Resistance?"

Tristan hesitated. "Yes."

"Does he talk about it all the time, too?"

"No," Tristan said. "My mother told me."

In the darkness, the other's face was only an oval with shadows for eyes, but Tristan could see the question in them. "I was about a year and a half old the last time we saw him," he said.

"Oh," Sajatte said. "Sorry."

Tristan only shrugged.

This viditorium's "stage" was a globe-shaped holotank whose life-size projections gave the impression of being on location in history, instead of viewing it as a series of holo-cordings compiled from decades of newsnet transmissions. Blocky words appeared in the tank, three-dimensional, white against a starfield:

A UNIFIED BLOW: DOMINION STATION

The words faded; the projection took the cadets aboard a shuttle making final approach to a battle station orbiting a green world called Yan. As if through tinted viewpanes they surveyed communications towers, antispacecraft emplacements, docking arms for resupply and warships. Monotone narration cited statistics on manning, on firepower, on basing for strategic operations.

Holography provided passes into briefing rooms and command councils conducted by participants who were long since dead or deposed, and documented dramas of decision as the Dominion's leadership sought to bring a collection of balking worlds under its galactic government. When those worlds had joined as allies, Dominion war efforts had begun to meet coordinated resistance. The Unified Worlds forces used unconventional tactics and struck from unpredictable quarters, but their direction came from the ruling house of Sostis. The resistance had to be killed in its cradle.

Yan's station was the staging area and command post. Dominion destroyers and troop ships arrived in the system one after another and prepared to move against Sostis.

But on the eve of their departure, the Unified Worlds had attacked. A spacecraft carrier group had erupted from lightskip into Yan's space, and squadrons of one-man attack craft penetrated the station's defenses. Despite heavy losses from low-altitude surface guns, the Unified forces decimated the Dominion fleet in its berths with men and munitions aboard. The station itself was left dead in space, eighty percent of its solar-power production and all of its communications down, and a third of its area lost to depressurization.

Three-dimensional graphics diagrammed inadequacies in the defenses and demonstrated how the enemy ships had reached their targets, undetected until it was almost too late.

As the Resistance gained momentum, the Dominion had gathered dossiers on its most important enemies: warriors, political figures, spies. Pilfered portraits appeared in the holotank, accompanying biographies pieced together by war correspondents and historians.

Tristan gave it little attention until the narrator said, "Lujan Serege, fighter pilot from Topawa. Credited with twenty-six kills in space combat throughout the war, his career is believed to have begun with the attack on Dominion Station. He was instated as Chief Commander of the Unified Worlds' Spherzah in 3304 and still holds that position. . . ."

Tristan sat forward in his seat, studying the image of a young man in a flight suit, his eyes narrowed and hair disheveled in the wind: a young man whose image he'd seen before only in a holodisc.

Siggar leaned over and poked him with an elbow. "You any relation to that Topowak, Serege? He looks enough like you to be your father!"

Tristan met his look. Held it for a long moment. "What if he is?"

"They're all religious fanatics," said Siggar. "The only good Monotheist is a dead one!"

"Monotheist?" The word was a new one to Tristan, different from those his mother had used as she taught him of her beliefs. He gave Siggar a quizzical look. "What does that mean?"

"It means they believe that a supernatural man created

the universe." Siggar's tone was derisive. "All their men become priests, and they spend the rest of their lives fasting and praying. No drinking, no women—no fun at all."

Tristan eyed him for several moments, taken aback by the mockery. "What's wrong with that?" he demanded at last. "They're the best pilots in the galaxy!"

"Yeah?" said Siggar. "Then what happened to you? You're probably the only one in the whole tribe who can't tell an altimeter from an attitude indicator! That's probably why they sent you here instead of to the Sostis Aerospace Institute, isn't it?"

Tristan let his hand curl, clawlike. "I'll beat you out for Alpha Flight, Siggar!"

"Aw, you couldn't beat me out for anything but the commandant's cut list!"

"Cadets Siggar and Serege!"

They both turned around.

An instructor stood at the end of the row, barely discernible in the amphitheater's darkness. He said, "Write up three, both of you, for talking in formation."

Siggar waited until the officer had moved out of earshot to mutter, "Thanks a lot, Serege! That's eighteen demerits this week!"

When his eyes would no longer focus on the display's configurations and the ERROR line appeared for the fifth time on problem 6.3, Tristan touched CLOSE to disconnect from his on-line text subscription, and fumbled for the OFF switch. Without the monitor's glow, the only light in the sitting room came from the projection of the fire on the grate. Waiting for his eyes to adjust, Tristan rubbed at his temples, trying to ease their throbbing.

The governor and b'Anar Id Pa'an had come in earlier, after dinner, with the bearhounds wagging thick tails against their legs and whuffing at them for tidbits. When one of the dogs followed the governor over to the table where Tristan was working, Pulou retreated into a chair, pulling his legs up away from the dog's nosiness and baring his teeth at it.

"Well now, Tristan," the governor said, "what's so important that you'll miss dinner for it?"

Tristan said, "Aerospace Dynamics, sir. Exams are next week and if I fail, I'll be cut from the program."

The governor smiled. "There's no need to be so concerned. I rather doubt that you'll fail."

His expression was enigmatic, and Tristan questioned it with his look until Renier turned away.

He'd paid no attention to them after that, giving his full attention to his studies until the ERROR line appeared three times in a row on one problem. Then, teeth locked, he brought his fist down hard on the tabletop.

Sudden silence replaced the conversation going on in the circle before the fireplace, and b'Anar Id Pa'an said, "The pup is learning new tricks at the academy. What other new tricks have they taught you, pup?"

He met the masuk's leer. "I'm not a pup, you slime-sucking swamp worm!"

"Tristan!" Renier had said, and his hand tightened on his walking stick as if it were a weapon.

Tristan had met his gaze, still glowering, and felt Pulou's claws close on his forearm in wordless correction.

Pulou had slipped out of the chair to sit near the fireplace when the others left, taking the bearhounds with them. He was still squatting there on the hearthstones, facing the artificial coals. The light showed serenity in his silhouetted posture.

Tristan pushed himself from his chair and crossed to the fireplace and dropped to his heels beside Pulou, and the gan turned his head ever so slightly, slitted eyes widening just enough to reflect the light, like golden embers themselves. He said, "You're finished, little brother?"

"No," Tristan said.

"But you stop."

"I'm tired. Can't think."

Pulou studied him, unblinking. "You're always tired, little brother. You don't eat enough; you don't sleep enough. You do *that*—rub your head like it hurts."

"It does," Tristan said.

"You're sick?"

"No."

He felt Pulou still watching him doubtfully, and took his hands away from his head to fold his arms over his knees. "I don't like academy," he said. "It's stupid." He stared numbly at the projection. "Stupid to walk everywhere in straight lines and call all the teachers 'sir,' and if we do it wrong they shout at us. I never even see any starships!" He made a loose gesture with both hands. "How does that help my mother?"

"Who tells you it does?" Pulou asked.

Tristan hesitated. "Larielle."

"Why?"

He wondered how he could explain it to Pulou—realized that he still didn't understand it himself. "I don't know," he said. He couldn't look at Pulou; it sounded foolish even to himself. He said, "She says it's important."

There was a long silence.

"You think she's right?" asked Pulou.

"I don't know." Tristan shook his head. "We're here long time; I don't like it."

On an impulse, he paused to count on his fingers. Fifteen nights from the gan camp to the flat-tooth camp, five nights in the stone room, fifteen more on the ship from Ganwold to Issel—more than one month right there! Almost another month traveling to Issel's moon and back, and then to Adriat. And they'd been on Adriat for . . . about three months now!

The tally left him stiff, made him swallow. "It's five flat-tooth months when we go away from camp," he said. "*Five*, Pulou!"

He felt suddenly sick. Too shaken to sit still, he shot to his feet and strode about the room, back and forth, aimless. "We're here too long!" he said. "If we stay here, she dies!"

A shadow slipped up at his periphery as he paced; a familiar hand caught his wrist and held it fast, gently, without claws. "Stop, little brother," Pulou said. "You're tired. No good to think and to work when you're tired. Time to sleep."

Wrapped in a couple of blankets, Tristan curled up on his side on the floor and closed his eyes, but he couldn't relax. Memories of his mother, pale in the light of the cooking fire, filled his mind. Memories of his mother, and visions of the funerary pyre at the top of the hill. Tension tightened his huddled limbs and his chest until they ached; fear made his breath come too fast, made his heart race.

He turned onto his back, his eyes still closed. His stomach was in knots, like a hard fist in his middle.

When he dozed, he found himself crouching in the center of the lodge on Ganwold. His mother's things were there—her tools, her storage pouches, her sleeping robe—but she was gone. And instead of peimu blood on his hands, as there was after a hunt, there was black, powdered ash.

He woke abruptly in the dark, breathless. His heart was pounding again, as if he'd been running.

The little anteroom was chilly. He drew the blankets up closer around his shoulders, turned onto his belly, concentrated on drawing slow, deep breaths to calm his pulse—

—started from another doze at a creak somewhere in the mansion. He turned onto his side again, drawing up his knees and wrapping his arms over his head.

He shouldn't have left her, he thought. It would have

been better to be there with her when she died than to get back to Ganwold and find her already gone.

He hadn't fallen sleep again before there was a step near his head, and Rajak's boot toe nudged his arm. "Get up, Tristan."

He stayed silent, pulling on his uniform physical-training shirt and shorts. The motions were mechanical, accomplished only out of routine; his hands seemed detached from himself, his body numb—except for the heavy pain in his heart. He stayed silent in the skimmer on the way to the academy, too.

Mist lay over the parade ground, pale in the dark, idle in the wake of an early spring rain. Tristan's gaze settled on it without seeing it as he waited in the skimcraft; he barely heard Rajak yawn beside him.

Reveille startled him from his numbness; he actually jumped, his head jerking up. He groped for the skimmer's hatch handle and popped it and forced himself to climb out.

The mist was cold, clammy in his light clothing, on his face and hair. It made him shiver but he didn't care. Not waiting for Rajak and Pulou, he picked up his gym bag and moved across the puddled tarmac to fall in with the dim shapes spilling out of the barracks.

"How're your bodyguard and your pet whatever-it-is, Serege?" someone asked, jerking a thumb at Rajak and Pulou on the sidelines.

"If you were smart," put in somebody else, "you'd make your bodyguard do your calisthenics for you!"

Tristan didn't answer—didn't even look at them.

The cadet class leader, hair tucked into her cap and damp shirt clinging across her breasts, called them to attention and marched them double-time to the drill ground.

Sore muscles were long past but calisthenics still produced sweat, despite the morning's chill. Tristan scarcely felt the tiny bits of gravel that pierced the heels of his hands with each push-up, scarcely felt the cold when his shirt back and shorts got soaked doing sit-ups, checked his stride to the others' to run five kilometers in formation. His lungs ached from the cold by the time it was over—but the ache in his soul was far worse.

The sky had turned predawn pink while they worked out. The cadets fell out in front of the barracks and raced for the hygiene booths. Tristan deliberately hung back to avoid all the jostling.

He was still waiting in line when someone shoved at his shoulder. "Hey, Serege, have you seen your last test score yet?"

It was Siggar, looking smug.

Tristan favored him with a glower. "No."

"If I were you," said Siggar, "I'd start reaching for the yellow handles." He twisted one hand in an arcing nose-dive toward the floor and said, "Bail out! Bail out! Bail out!"

It rained again the night after final exams, a downpour which held on into the morning as a cold drizzle: weather like the winters Tristan had known on Ganwold—

—where he wished he was right now.

He scowled at the overcast. "Stay here," he told Pulou, and slammed the skimmer's hatch closed without a glance at Rajak. Hunching his shoulders under his jacket, he strode toward the cadet squadron offices.

A couple of noncoms in the coveralls of flightline mechanics stood in the entry, peering out at the grayness and grumbling to each other. They shifted away from the doors just enough to let Tristan come in, and he brushed past them, half expecting one or the other to put a foot into his path as b'Anar Id Pa'an would have done.

The hallway was full of cadets, most gathered around the monitors outside the orderly room. Gray light etched distress on some faces, relief and even excitement on others. Tristan saw Siggar in the crowd at the same moment the other spotted him—saw his expression turn colder than the drizzle outside as he pushed clear of the group and approached.

"So, how much did your old man pay for your slot in Alpha Flight?" Siggar asked.

"Alpha Flight?" Tristan tore his attention from Siggar to scan the nearest screen—and found his name fourth on the roster traditionally filled only by the top cadets in the class. He shook his head. "That's wrong! I didn't earn that!"

"Maybe you should remind your old man of that," Siggar said. "Not all of us have fathers with reputations big enough to ride through on. It's not very fair to the rest of us who have to work for our grades."

The implication in the statement went over Tristan's head, but Siggar's tone of voice didn't. "What do you mean by that?" he demanded.

"Aw, c'mon, Serege," said Siggar. "Everybody knows you're the Spherzah Commander's brat. That's the only reason you haven't been washed out of here yet!"

Two days of numbness abruptly shattered; Tristan let his hands curl. "My father didn't have anything to do with this!"

"Oh yeah?" Siggar looked him hard in the face. "Why don't you live in the barracks, then? Why don't you have to march off demerits like the rest of us? How'd he even get you into an Issel Sector academy, anyway?"

Tristan felt the sudden silence in the corridor, felt the crossfire of the others watching. "My father didn't send me to this lomo's-hole academy—"

"Sure, Serege! Who else'd buy a slot in Alpha Flight for you? Or did he use political pressure?"

"*Buy* it?" The thought of that pulled Tristan up short, wrinkling his brow. He glimpsed mockery in the encircling faces and shook his head. "He didn't do it!" he said.

"You know he had to!" said Siggar. "He couldn't let you make a laughingstock of him at SAI."

"You tell him, Siggar!" said someone from the sidelines, and others took it up, jeering.

Tristan ignored the others. "Take it back, Siggar!" he said, and brought his hands up before his chest, hard as claws.

He saw how Siggar darted a glance around the circle of cadets and sneered, hunching himself in a parody of Tristan's stance. "Am I supposed to be scared?"

"Don't push me," Tristan said through his teeth. "I've killed bigger animals than you!"

Siggar laughed at that. Sidled a few steps back and forth. Made a swipe at him.

Tristan's right hand caught the left side of his opponent's face, snapping his head to the side and leaving four livid gashes across his face from his ear to the corner of his mouth. Siggar swayed but recovered, eyes blazing and jaw tightening. "Snotty Spherzah brat!" he said, and shot out a fist.

It met Tristan's cheekbone just under his left eye, made him stagger. He ducked the punch from the right and retreated a step.

The jeers were shouts now: "Get him, Siggar! Get him, Siggar!" Someone behind Tristan shoved at his shoulder, pushing him toward his adversary.

Siggar advanced on him, grinning. "What'll your old man do to me if I bloody your nose, brat?"

Tristan went under the next swing. Siggar's blow missed, overextending him, and Tristan caught him like a charging peimu, by the head and shoulder, and wrenched.

Siggar's feet went over his head; his free arm flailed. Tristan saw it crumple under him at an impossible angle when he hit the floor, saw his face go white. There wasn't enough breath left for him to scream.

Straddling his antagonist, Tristan held him with one knee, seized a handful of hair, jerked his head back—

There was a sudden stir among the cadets; they sank back, opening up the circle. Suddenly wary, Tristan stood, letting Siggar sit up. The other grimaced and clutched his arm to his body.

Tristan held his ground when the first noncom came up to them. Met the man's steely gaze—and saw a split second's shock there, like abrupt recognition, before he demanded, "What's going on here?"

Tristan kept his head down, his face turned away. "I warn him," he said. "He hits first."

Pulou didn't say anything, just cocked his head and looked at the bruise on his face through half-closed eyes.

"He says things that aren't right."

"So you hurt him." Pulou narrowed his eyes still more. "You're with flat-teeth too long."

Tristan said nothing.

"Is it important enough to die about, little brother?" asked Pulou.

Tristan hung his head. "No," he said. And after a little silence, "Pulou, I'm afraid—"

"Tristan," said Rajak from outside the anteroom's curtain, "the governor wants to talk to you."

Tristan looked at Pulou.

And Pulou said, "Turn your back to it."

Tristan got stiffly to his feet.

The governor rose from behind his desk when Tristan and Rajak drew up, wordless, in front of him. He came forward, strode a slow circle around Tristan, touched the discoloration beneath his left eye. "I was informed that you got into a fight, young one."

"Yes, sir." As if on the parade ground, Tristan kept his eyes caged.

"Why, may I ask?"

Tristan addressed the wall: "One of the cadets said that—my father—bought me the slot in Alpha Flight, and he called me a Spherzah's brat."

The governor chuckled. "I told you that you wouldn't fail, Tristan. But I think you should be thanking *me* for buying your slot."

Tristan jerked his head up to stare at him, and his hands clenched into fists at his sides. The fury which had seized him outside the orderly room welled up again, uncontrolled. "Why should I thank you?" he demanded. "My mother's dying and you're keeping me here! I don't want that slot! I don't want your help! . . . I don't even want to be here—"

The governor's walking stick struck like a viper, knocking Tristan to the floor. It left a welt from his cheekbone to his chin. Scrambling back to his feet, he let his hands curl— but Pulou's words still echoed in his ears. He drew himself up, clenching and loosening his hands, and looked the governor in the face instead.

"I would appreciate it if you showed a little more gratitude for my efforts in your behalf from now on," Renier said very quietly.

The stripe throbbed, hot as a burning brand across Tristan's face. He didn't answer.

And the governor turned the walking stick in his hands. "You would also be wise to remember that I have my own reasons for your attendance at the academy. I won't take your noncooperation lightly, Tristan."

The people from the newsnets stood in the walkway between the Physiological Training and Simulator class buildings like a pack of jous waiting to ambush their quarry. Seeing the holocorders on their shoulders, Tristan pulled the bill of his cap further down on his brow and hunched deeper into his jacket. But he couldn't lose himself in a knot of cadets with Rajak at his elbow.

One of the media people detached himself from the covey, a voice pickup in his hand. "Tristan Serege! May we talk with you for a moment?"

"No," Tristan said, and tried to brush past him. "Leave me alone."

Rajak's hand on his shoulder jerked him up short. "Answer their questions."

He eyed them all, suspicious. "What do you want?"

"Mostly, to congratulate you on your position in the academy's top flight of first-year cadets. Your father would be proud of you, if he knew."

Tristan tightened his jaw—but then he lowered his head, turned it away. "No, he wouldn't," he said. "I didn't earn it."

The man didn't seem to have heard him. He said, "We understand that you and your mother have spent the past several years living among the natives on Ganwold. Was she rescued at the same time you were?"

Sudden fury jerked Tristan's head back up. "I wasn't rescued!"

The newsman paused for half a heartbeat, but he didn't change his line of questioning. "Is your mother still on Ganwold?" he asked. "The common belief is that she's ill and you're trying to find your father. Is that true?"

"What if it is?" Tristan didn't try to mask his anger. "What does it matter to you?"

The newsman actually blinked at that, but he kept his tone neutral. "It might matter a great deal to your father," he said.

Tristan could only stare at him, his hands flexing and unflexing at his sides.

"Then again, it might not," said the media man, watching him. "We understand that he's never responded to the message Governor Renier sent at the time of your rescue from Ganwold. Do you really believe that a man you haven't seen since you were a baby would still care enough to help you?"

The question struck Tristan like a blow to the face, a blow which cut far deeper than the governor's walking stick had. He actually recoiled. Stared at the man. Swallowed convulsively.

That possibility had never even crossed his mind before now. What if it were true? What if his father *didn't* care? His throat and heart and lungs suddenly seemed to constrict, so much that they hurt. He shook his head, let it droop. "I don't know," he managed to whisper. "I don't know."

FOURTEEN

Lujan stepped out of the bathroom with his hair still damp and accepted his shirt from the waiting servo. Shrugging it on, he gave a short whistle, and the dog, lying near the foot of the bed and watching him, rose up on legs like stilts, stretched and yawned, and came up to him, wagging its tail. It lay its head in his hands, and Lujan rubbed its ears and said, "Ready for breakfast, boy?"

He turned when the visiphone on the night table buzzed. The red button blinking at its base indicated the exec office downstairs, on the main floor of the flag officers' residence. That meant a call from Headquarters. Fastening his shirt with one hand, Lujan punched the button with the other, securing the line, and said, "What is it, Kierem?"

"There's a call from the Watch, sir. Stand by."

Kierem disappeared from the monitor in a moment of static and was replaced by the watch officer, a young man who said, "Sir, we've got a new development in the hostage situation. The newsnets are running an interview with your son."

Lujan hit the remote button beside the visiphone. The holovid in the far wall came on with a ripple of iridescent color and focused on a sullen youth who said, "What do you want?"

Tristan!

Lujan's jaw tightened. "Call the imagery section and get someone on this," he said with a glance back at the watch officer.

"We have, sir. They've got a team on the way."

"Thank you."

In the holovid, a newsman was saying, ". . . to congratulate you on your position in the Academy's top flight of first-year cadets. Your father would be proud of you, if he knew."

Lujan saw a moment's fury in the youth's eyes and taut jaw before he turned his face away. "No, he wouldn't," he said. "I didn't earn it."

"Son," Lujan said. Whispered it.

He watched silently for a few seconds, then turned back to the lieutenant on the visiphone. "I'll be in by oh-seven-hundred," he said, checking his timepiece. "Can you have a preliminary report ready by then?"

"Yes, sir," the lieutenant said.

"Thanks," said Lujan. "Out here." He touched the disconnect, then buzzed the exec office. When Kierem's face reappeared in the monitor, Lujan said, "Please call my office and warn Captain Jiron that the local newsnets will probably jump on this. We don't need their people underfoot while we're working on it."

"Right, sir."

Lujan's attention returned to the holovid.

". . . he's never responded to the message Governor Renier sent at the time of your rescue from Ganwold," the interviewer was saying. "Do you really believe that a man you haven't seen since you were a baby would still care enough to help you?"

Lujan saw how the youth stiffened at the question, then let his head droop. "I don't know," the boy whispered, and the words went through Lujan's soul like a knife. "I don't know."

It was several moments before he realized that he was still holding down the visiphone's disconnect button, so hard that his finger hurt.

His staff must have already put them out of the Command Section, Lujan thought when he spotted the people with the holocorders. They were standing just off the VIP skimmer pad atop the Unified Worlds Tower, huddled together near the doors.

His driver saw them, too. "Would you prefer one of the mid-level platforms, sir?" he asked.

"No, this is all right." The skimmer set down and Lujan released its hatch. He smiled as he stepped out. "There're only three of them."

They stood between himself and the entrance, coats wrapped tight and breath clouding on the morning's crisp air. Waiting for him.

He strode directly toward them.

"Admiral Serege," said one, thrusting a voice pickup at him. "You're no doubt aware of this morning's news interview with a young man purported to be your missing son. Is there any—"

Lujan looked the reporter in the eye and said only, "Excuse me, please."

The man stepped back from him, and Lujan strode past the others toward the entrance.

"Sir?" the man said from behind him.

He didn't look back.

They didn't follow.

Tinted panels parted at his approach, letting him into an oval lobby made of marble. He surveyed it with a glance, spotted two more media personnel over by the controller's desk, and turned toward the nearest bank of lifts. Stepping into one, he said, "Spherzah Intelligence Section."

He emerged in an entry control booth and paused before

the visual monitor to place his hand on the square plate below it, where an infrared scanner read the pattern of the capillaries in his hand. The monitor's synthesized voice said, "Serege, Lujan, Admiral: identification confirmed," and the security door swung open.

He turned right, strode down a tiled corridor to a door marked Imagery Interpretation, and punched in its entry code.

Half a dozen junior officers and NCOs started up from their work stations as he stepped inside, but he made a small gesture and said, "Carry on," before anyone could call the room to attention.

"This way, sir." The officer in charge came around a desk, offering a cup of shuk. "Lieutenant Brookes is set up in the conference room."

Like Chesney and Ashforth, Brookes was Jonican: blond, and taller than himself. She slipped an image chip into the laser scanner beneath the holotank on the wall and, when Lujan was seated at the table, touched the ON switch. "Sir, this briefing is classified Secret, releasable to the Unified Worlds," she said.

The holotank lit up and she took a pointer from her pocket. "We have determined that the interview was conducted at the Aeire City piloting academy; this building in the background has been confirmed to be the Physiological Training facility. Analysis of the conversation suggests that the interview took place no more than three days ago. The Academy's winter term concluded on the twenty-eighth day of the twelfth standard month, and student appointments for the next term would have been posted a day or two later."

"No, he wouldn't," said the youth in the recording. As he turned his face away, Brookes pressed a couple of buttons on her remote, and the image froze and magnified. With her pointer's beam, she traced a shadow below the boy's left eye and another mark that angled across his left cheek. "Sir, these marks are bruises," she said. "Depending on the treatment given, they could be as recent as two days or as old as two weeks."

Lujan felt something twist in his gut. His jaw tightened. He gave a curt nod and motioned for her to continue.

"He's also under guard, sir. The uniform and insignia worn by the man standing here behind your son are those of the Sector General's personal security force."

"Which would indicate that he's in Renier's direct custody," said Lujan.

"Yes, sir."

Lujan nodded again. "Go on."

"Was she rescued at the same time you were?" asked the Adriat newsman in the holovid.

The youth's head snapped up, his features hard with fury. "I wasn't rescued!"

"Where did this come from?" Lujan asked.

"The Adriat Ministry of Public Media, sir," said Brookes, "via Intersystem Broadcast transmission."

"Normal news channels. . . . Have our psychological warfare analysts seen it yet?"

"Yes, sir; we prepared this briefing together," said Brookes. "They believe it's an attempt by the Issel Sector to apply pressure through public outrage."

"Apply pressure." Lujan raised an eyebrow. "To whom? Me?"

Brookes glanced at her superior, who stood at Lujan's shoulder, and said, "Yes, sir."

"That fits Renier's methodology." The recording ended, and Lujan said, "Thank you, Lieutenant." He turned to the division chief as he rose. "Tell your people that I appreciate their extra efforts."

The lieutenant commander nodded. "We'll have a more complete evaluation ready in time for the staff briefing at oh-nine-hundred, sir."

* * *

The cockpit rocked again, throwing Tristan against his acceleration harness, and all of the lights went red. His fingers worked the thruster switches, fighting to maintain control. He punched DAMAGE CONTROL, and the flight computer's screen filled itself with hopeless data. He braced himself against another rolling lurch. The red lights were hot; his hair clung to his forehead in sweaty strands under his helmet.

Another light began to flash; the screen blanked, and a new message glowed out of it:

> LIFE SUPPORT HAS FAILED
> ESTIMATED RESERVE: 3 MINUTES
> PREPARE FOR EGRESS

He heard his breath catch in his earphones before he realized he'd done it—felt the instructor pilot watching him through narrowed eyes. The airflow through his oxygen mask already seemed to be diminishing. He fought the urge to gulp at it but his heart slammed into full throttle and his hand shook as he thumbed the comms button. "Base, this is Hammer Four-three requesting clearance to punch out! I say again—"

"You don't have time to ask for clearance, 'specially when your radio's already gone," the other said without emotion. "Just do it."

The screen flashed:

> EGRESS! EGRESS! EGRESS!

Tristan braced himself: heels planted hard at the seat's base, spine straight, shoulders and head pressed into the chair back. He reached for the yellow handles on either side of the seat and closed his eyes as he jerked the handles up.

He heard the explosion of ejection, felt the egress capsule blast clear of the cockpit under a pressure that made his consciousness reel and threatened to snap his collarbones and neck. He clenched his teeth to prevent an outcry.

The pressure lifted almost immediately; the seat bumped and stopped. Through his headset, the IP said, "Debriefing's in ten minutes, Serege."

"Yes, sir," Tristan said without looking at him.

Riding the simulator's seat back down its rail, he pulled off his gloves and fumbled with hands that still quivered to unfasten one side of his oxygen mask. Then he sat back, breathing through his mouth and waiting for his pulse to steady.

The cockpit's lighting had returned to normal; the sensors and readouts were functioning again. Tristan disconnected his helmet's intercom and oxygen lines, released the flight harness, pushed himself to his feet. His knees were weak.

Captain Coborn was already at their table in the classroom when Tristan came in from the support room. He gestured at one of the two students' chairs opposite his own and said, "You got an unsatisfactory on that ride, Serege. If that'd been the real thing, we'd be conducting this debriefing in the morgue."

"What, sir?"

"Watch the recording," Coborn said, "and tell me what you did wrong." He turned on the desktop holovid.

Tristan watched himself at the simulated controls, listened to the radio dialogue. He cocked his head at the instructor when it was finished.

"Off the top," the captain said. "What's the first thing you do when a malfunction light comes on?"

Tristan recited the Emergency Procedures text:

"Maintain control of the 'craft."

"You did that right. Then what?"

"Check Damage Control to determine the nature and

extent of the damage and take necessary action to correct it."

"All right, you did that. You had a mechanical failure. Now what?"

"Declare a distress condition and request assistance immediately," Tristan said. "Squawk mode three-alpha, seven-oh-seven Emergency Code, and establish communications with the ASTC facility."

"Good enough. You're still alive to that point. But look at the egress sequence again." Coborn hit FAST-FORWARD on the holovid.

Tristan said, "I was in the proper position, sir!"

"That's not going to do you a whole lot of good if you haven't switched over to your capsule's emergency life support," said Coborn. "You're just committing slow suicide by suffocation."

"Yes, sir," Tristan said quietly.

The IP studied him. "I don't get it, Serege. You've never blown a written Emergency Procedures quiz. Never blown a stand-up EP—you rattle those things off like an audicorder!" He rose, shaking his head. "You've got one more shot at this. Nobody goes to the flightline until they've passed the EP simulator ride."

"We missed you at dinner again this evening," Larielle said from the antechamber's curtained doorway.

Tristan, sitting cross-legged on the bed with his back to the wall, didn't look up. "I'm not hungry."

Through his peripheral vision he watched her cross the little room toward him, felt her sit down on the edge of the bed near him; but when she reached out to lay a hand on his shoulder, he jumped and stared up at her, almost raising a hand to touch his forehead.

"Tristan," she said, "are you ill?"

"No," he said. He looked down at hands knotted white

in his lap and drew a long breath. His stomach felt like a stone in the middle of his body.

"Something's wrong," she said gently, and moved closer to him. "You've missed dinner more often than you've come lately, and even when you do come you hardly eat anything. You're tense and jumpy all the time—"

"How long do I have to keep doing this?" he asked abruptly. "Going to the academy, I mean. It's been almost six months since I left my mother! She could be dying by now!"   •

"Shhh!" Larielle twisted around, and he followed her look toward the doorway. She didn't relax. "I don't know, Tris," she said. "I'm sorry." Before he could say anything else, she asked, "Did something happen today? Is it something I can help you with?"

He shrugged and ducked his head. "I failed the simulator test. I forgot a couple of things, and if it'd been real, I would've been dead."

She said, "You'll remember the next time."

"I don't know if I will or not—and I don't even care anymore. How can I think about piloting things when my mother is dying?" He made a desperate gesture with both hands.

"Tris," she said, trying to comfort him.

He shook his head and didn't glance up. "I can't stay here!" he said. He shoved himself off the bed to his feet, and began to pace the cubicle. "I need to be with my mother! I shouldn't ever have left her. I . . . didn't even tell her good-bye!"

"Tris," Larielle said again, and rose and crossed to him. Standing in front of him, she studied his face for a moment before she raised both hands and began to gently knead his neck.

Her touch, where his clan mark was, sent a shiver down his spine. Sent heat up over his face. He felt his heart speed up; he couldn't take his vision from her face.

"Tristan," she said suddenly, "you're blushing." She sounded surprised.

His mouth was dry—hanging open. "Why are you doing that?" he asked. His voice rasped.

"You're so tense." He heard her as if from kilometers away. "Your muscles are in knots."

Her fingers sent sensations through him that he'd only known in dreams from which he awoke embarrassed. He stood paralyzed, watching her, waiting for the caress to turn to claws at the clasps of his jacket.

"Peace in you, mother!" he said in gan. He used the word for one's mate. He gasped it: "Peace in you!"

Larielle drew back her hands. Her eyes showed perplexity. "Tristan, what's wrong? Did I hurt you?"

"No." He shook his head and drew a wary breath, still watching her. "No."

"Then, what—?"

"Gan females do that," he said, "when they choose their mates." His face throbbed. He lowered his eyes. "It's part of mating."

"Oh." Larielle's face grew pink. After a pause she said, "I'm sorry. I didn't know."

"No," he said, and dared to look at her. "Don't be sorry."

And then he recoiled, shocked at himself for saying it.

She studied him for several moments, her expression gentle, almost a smile. Then she raised one hand cautiously, as if he were a wild creature that might bolt, and touched his temple. She slipped her fingers through his hair, running them lightly above his ear. "Humans have a different way to show their affection," she said, and her voice was very quiet. "Would you like me to show you?"

He was breathless again. He swallowed hard and said, "Yes."

She leaned up to him, closing her eyes. Her hand slipped to his neck again, drew his head down; her mouth met his, warm and firm, and made it tingle. He started to lift one hand, to reach for her, and froze.

Her hand slid from his neck, from his shoulder. She stepped back, and her gaze touched his, her smile suddenly shy. "You'll do fine on the sim ride," she said, still quietly, and turned and left the room.

He watched, wordless, as she went. And he thought about her for a long while after he curled up in the warmth of the blankets.

But he dreamed he was back on Ganwold, standing alone beside a smoldering funeral pyre. He woke up cold, his body rigid and his hands and teeth and stomach clenched up.

When the nightmare didn't fade with waking and the tension didn't ease, he sat up in the dark, drew the blankets about his shoulders against the chilliness, and released a despairing sigh.

I shouldn't have left, he thought. *None of this would have happened if I had never left. She would've died but I would've been with her. Now, because of me, she's dying anyway—alone.*

His heart and mind felt weighted, burdened with guilt. He shook his head; he couldn't lift it up.

He felt someone watching him. He glanced over his shoulder without turning around.

Pulou sat cross-legged on the cot behind him, grooming his mane. He cocked his head. "You do what, little brother?"

"I think," Tristan said, and sighed again. "It's my fault that she dies like this."

Pulou blinked at him, puzzled. "Why?"

Tristan shook his head once more—couldn't answer for a moment. When he did, he said, "If I stay there, she isn't alone when she dies. If I stay there, there isn't all this—" He gestured all-inclusively. "—this trouble with the governor and my father and—" He let his hands drop.

Pulou studied him for some moments. "You try to help, little brother," he said at last. "You do what you think is right. Maybe it helps, maybe it doesn't. There's no fault in that."

He thought about Pulou's words for a long while afterward. Wished he could believe them, but the ache inside, the deep fear, wouldn't let him.

He was still sitting there, wrapped in the blankets, when Rajak came in to wake him up.

"Deflectors full front, nose down thirty degrees, thrusters at one and two to make one-three-five, roger." Tristan's fingers moved over the thruster switches. His gloves' linings were damp with sweat.

The cockpit rocked again, throwing him against his harness. The impact was from port this time. More red lights came on. He hit DAMAGE CONTROL; the screen lit up. "Base," he said, "I've lost my forward port thrusters, too."

"Acknowledged, Hammer—"

The comms went dead with an electronic shatter in his earphones, and the impact it seemed to anticipate threw him back in his seat. The instruments went blank, except for the computer screen:

LIFE SUPPORT HAS FAILED
ESTIMATED RESERVE: 3 MINUTES
PREPARE FOR EGRESS

Tristan took a deep breath. "Emergency life support," he whispered, and heard it in his headset. He felt Coborn watching from beside him. The ring lay over his left shoulder where the oxygen hose was attached. He fumbled for it with gloved fingers and tugged. Cool air rushed into his oxygen mask.

The screen flashed:

EGRESS! EGRESS! EGRESS!

He stiffened into egress position, reached for the yellow handles, locked his teeth against the launch.

When the simulator seat bumped to a stop, he heard the IP release his breath. "See you in the classroom, Serege."

Tristan stood at attention before the table, his vision fixed on the back wall, his face expressionless.

"You passed," the captain said, "but I hesitate to recommend you into the flight program. You're already exhibiting MOA; you'll never make it through elementary flight training if you don't get over it."

"MOA, sir?"

"Manifestation of apprehension," said Coborn. "I'm passing you, Serege, but only on conditional status. I need your sponsor's name so I can submit the report."

"Governor Renier," Tristan said. His throat was tight.

The IP looked up at him, hard, for a full minute. "Oh," he said at last. "Then I guess you'll be flying whether you should be or not."

Whether I want to or not, Tristan thought.

FIFTEEN

Dylan Dartmuth pulled two food trays from the warmer and placed one in front of the old man before he took his own seat. He dropped into the chair stiffly, grimacing.

"Dampness bothering you again?" Beaumont asked.

Dylan glanced up. "Yes, Uncle. The damp and the overtime." He picked up his utensils and bent over his meal.

He felt the old man observing him but he didn't raise his vision; he concentrated on his food. He had nearly emptied his tray before Beaumont said, "The bum leg isn't the only thing, eh, lad? You've not been this grim since the lieutenant refused to submit that request for spare parts. What's it this time?"

"Masuki," said Dylan. His gaze locked on the old man's, smoldering. "The colonel told us today at commander's call that the academy's to admit the first masuki into pilot training within six months."

Beaumont raised sparse eyebrows. "A provision of the Cooperation Pact?"

"The same." Dylan's hand fisted around his utensil. "It was masuk scum that took my sister and her baby."

"I remember," said Beaumont.

The old man rose from the table then, as if suddenly recalling something, and made his slow way across the room to pull a packet from a cabinet near the door. "A courier brought this for you today."

Dylan accepted it, flipped it over. It bore the seal of the Topawan Embassy. "What in great space—?" he said, and slid a finger under the packet's flap to tear it open. He withdrew a single sheet of paper, folded in half.

It was the hardcopy of a message transmitted from Ramiscal City, nation of East Odymis on Sostis. "What the—?" he said again, and pushed his tray aside to spread the sheet out on the table.

He read it twice, and then sat staring at the tabletop.

"What's the matter, lad?" asked Beaumont.

The old man's voice cut across a distance like a dream. Dylan started, looked up. "It's from Admiral Serege," he said. "He's putting me on assignment."

"On assignment?" Beaumont lowered himself back into his chair and folded knobby hands on the table.

"Yes. Remember how, early in the winter, I told you about the boy in the med capsule? The prisoner transfer from Ganwold? And the cadet who got into the fight over a slot in Alpha Flight a couple of weeks ago? He *is* my sister's son. And he's at the academy on the governor's sponsorship!"

"The governor's?" Beaumont arched his brows. "That's an interesting twist."

"Right. And it all smells very bad."

Beaumont said, "What's Lujan asking of you?"

"He wants me to look out for Tristan," Dylan said. "Make sure he's all right—that sort of thing." He pushed himself to his feet and collected the empty trays. "For now."

"What does that mean?"

Dylan paused at the disposer in the kitchen. "It means

that if there's a change in defense status," he said, "I'm to take Tristan to safe haven at the Topawan Embassy."

Governor Renier crossed to his chair at the head of the conference table and the two masuki followed, flanking him, to their places on either side of him. He paused at his chair to look around the table, to study the faces, human and non-human, of the members of his war council. He saw the veiled shock, the questions forming in narrowed eyes and creased brows, and he smiled. He motioned the council to be seated, but he remained standing.

"Gentlemen," he said, "I present to you b'Anar Id Pa'an, son of the Pasha of Mi'ika and emissary of our allies in the Bacal Belt." He scanned the circle again. Smiled again at its grimness. "We have much to offer one another," he said. "All of our peoples—human, umedo, and masuki—have much to gain by this alliance." He turned to face b'Anar Id Pa'an.

"My sire thanks you, Sector General." Pa'an inclined his head slightly. Narrowed eyes and the curl of his lip lent irony to his smile. "Your enemies will become the wealth of the Bacal Belt."

Human and umedo advisors and generals moved in their chairs, uneasy and repulsed. Renier saw how many couldn't prevent it from showing in their faces.

Pa'an saw it, too. He smiled on them all, baring canine teeth thick as tusks. "Be pleased," he said, "that we are your allies. Be careful that you remain that way. One human slave is worth to us three slaves of our own kind."

The booth was just large enough to stand in, a closet for a medical monitor with two screens: one at waist level, angled like the keyboard beside it and marked with the outline of a hand, the other at face level, like a reflector. The upper screen displayed instructions:

1. ENTER NAME AND STUDENT ID NUMBER.
2. PLACE RIGHT HAND ON SENSOR PANEL AS SHOWN WITH
   FIRST FINGER THROUGH SPHYGMOMANOMETER SENSOR
   BAND.
3. MAINTAIN HAND PLACEMENT UNTIL READOUTS APPEAR.

Tristan followed the instructions without reading them; it had become part of his daily routine by now.

The upper screen cleared itself. After several seconds its cursor began to shoot back and forth, unrolling a block of information:

SEREGE, TRISTAN, ID#TS9392, CLEARED.
BLOOD GASES: NEGATIVE FOR INTOXICANTS CONSUMED
WITHIN PREVIOUS EIGHT HOURS.
BLOOD PRESSURE: 142/83*
PULSE: 86/MIN*
TEMPERATURE: 37°C
*PASSING BUT IN CAUTION RANGE. IF CONDITION
PERSISTS, PLEASE CONSULT FLIGHT SURGEON.

He didn't have to read that bottom line, either; it had appeared six days in a row now. He withdrew his hand, wiped it down the leg of his flight suit, and flexed it.

He felt the med tech watching from his own console as he stepped out of the booth. Tristan avoided his look but the man asked, "What's wrong, cadet?"

Tristan hesitated. *My mother is dying on Ganwold!* he wanted to shout, *and I'm being held prisoner here as bait for my father, and no one will let me help her!*

But he was too afraid; the governor's threats echoed in his mind: *If your mother's life is so important to you, Tristan, this will not happen again. . . . I have my own reasons for your attendance at the academy. I won't take your noncooperation lightly.* In his memory, the stroke from the governor's walking stick still burned across his face.

"Nothing," he said instead, dry-mouthed.

"It doesn't look like nothing to me," the medic said. "You're hypertensive. You're too young for that sort of thing. You should see the flight surgeon."

"I'm all right," Tristan said.

The medic shrugged. "All right. But I'm keeping an eye on you."

Tristan felt him still watching as he walked away.

In the support room he collected his helmet and egress pack. He tested the oxygen and radio lines mechanically. The door sighed open at his approach, letting him out to the slideway where Coborn and Pulou waited.

The slideway sloped down into a subterranean corridor that ran as far as Tristan could see. They stepped onto the outbound conveyor. It carried them in silence, but for the *shush-shush* of its track, past one arched portal after another. With a glance at Pulou, Tristan placed his egress pack between his feet and mentally reviewed the lesson plan, his call sign, his ship's number.

They stepped off the conveyor at the sixteenth arch and rode its lift up, emerging in a launch bay domed only with sky, crisp with predawn chill. Floodlighting lit the bay like daylight, glanced from the skin of the trainer ship, etched into sharp detail the men and machinery moving around it.

Tristan shifted his helmet in his hands and paused beneath an abbreviated delta wing. He reached up with his free hand to touch it, releasing a shaky breath.

—And felt someone watching him.

He froze. Turned his head slowly, just enough to look over his shoulder.

His crew chief stood there, a man with gray hair and mustache and eyes like steel. The man who had broken up his fight with Siggar. Tristan nudged Pulou and pointed with his chin before he turned his back to make his walk-around check of thruster nozzles and landing gear.

In the pilot's seat, he lost his harness clasps twice before he got them secured, and then they seemed to constrict his heart; he could feel it pounding against the webbing. His breath raked through his earphones. He curled his hands into fists on his thighs.

". . . checklist," Coborn's voice said in his helmet. Tristan jumped, looked at him.

"Start your checklist," Coborn said again, with a note of impatience.

"Yes, sir." He whispered it. Swallowed. Reached for switches and buttons, exchanged hand signals with the crew chief as he tested each system—glimpsed Pulou watching from the doorway of the maintenance room beyond him. When he finished the checkout, the man gave him a thumbs-up and limped clear.

"All systems green, sir," Tristan said.

"Then start your engines."

A gloved finger flicked the switches, one at a time, and the roar mounted around the ship as each engine came to life. The craft trembled with contained power.

"What're you waiting for?" asked Coborn.

Tristan started again. "Huh?"

"Call for clearance."

"Yes, sir. . . ." Tristan drew a long breath, carefully, so it wouldn't be audible to the IP. His voice was steady when he said, "Clearance Control, this is Hammer four-three— Disregard, disregard! Hammer three-two requesting clearance for launch."

"Hammer three-two, you're cleared to space station papa tango via SID foxtrot tango two-two-niner. Do you copy?"

"Roger that," said Tristan.

"Now what?" Coborn prompted.

"Ground," said Tristan, and thumbed the comms button. "This is Hammer three-two—"

He heard chuckling through his headset. "Hammer three-two, where are you calling from?"

He swallowed again at being caught in such a state of distraction. "Launch bay zero-one-six, sir."

Beside him, Coborn folded his arms over his chest and stared straight ahead through the canopy.

"Hammer three-two," said Ground, "there are ten ships ahead of you; bays on both sides of you are filled. Wind is from zero-three-zero at twelve knots, and . . ."

Tristan listened to the final weather report, adjusted his altimeter for atmospheric flight, and when Ground instructed him to switch to tower frequency, he said, "Roger."

The tower frequency was filled with chatter. He called, "Tower, this is Hammer three-two—"

"Hammer three-two," a sharp voice came back, "you are eleventh in launch sequence. Please do not acknowledge until we give you clearance. . . ."

He nodded. Shot a sideways look at Coborn. Waited. His mind was on Ganwold.

The insides of his gloves were already damp.

He heard, "Hammer three-two, please hold. . . . Hammer three-two, you now have three launches ahead of you, please hold for launch time. . . . Hammer three-two, you have clearance to launch. You have traffic ahead and will have traffic behind. . . ."

"Roger, Tower," he said, and glanced at Coborn again.

"So take us out, Serege," the captain said.

Locking his teeth, he spread his hand over the thruster switches.

"All at once," said the IP. "If you don't, you'll lift at an angle and hit the bay dome. Cadets who do that don't get their crests even if they live to tell about it."

"Yes, sir." Sweat plastered Tristan's hair to his forehead. "This is Hammer three-two lifting," he said into his pickup.

"I've got four green, no red or amber, line on line, point on point, eight good engines, and squawking normal." He toggled all eight switches together.

He felt the tremor increase, the roar swell to a scream. It flattened him into his seat, pushed his stomach down like a stone dropped into a pool. His teeth closed on his lip.

They were out of the bay. He heard Coborn release his breath.

He brought up the landing gear and leaned back in his seat.

"You forgot something," said Coborn.

Tristan jumped. Stared at him. "What?"

"Make contact with Departure."

"Yes, sir." He licked dry lips before thumbing the mike. "Departure, this is Hammer three-two requesting vectors to space station papa tango."

"Roger, Hammer three-two." The voice rattled through his earphones; he winced. "Have you on radar, passing point one-niner-two. Proceed on your present course. . . ."

Predawn pink riddled a northeastern horizon filled with clouds. Tristan glanced at the vertical speed and attitude indicators; his right hand rode the thrust switches, holding his course until the controller gave him a heading.

"When we break atmosphere," the captain said, "switch over to the space station's frequency and start trying to establish communications. It won't take long to come into range."

Surface detail diminished, disappeared beneath cloud, and then the craft broke clear of white billows into a sky so bright that Tristan squinted despite the dark visor of his helmet. But the blue deepened and darkened, and the pressure eased, and constellations appeared beyond.

For one mad moment, Tristan thought of wrenching the craft out of its flight profile and aiming it at one of those constellations and running—

—but only for a moment. He wouldn't leave Pulou. Besides, even if Coborn didn't seize control of it, he knew the craft would never make it to the outskirts of Issel's solar system.

Teeth locked, he reset his radio to the space station's frequency and listened for its VOR signal. "Station papa tango," he said, "this is Hammer three-two requesting vectors to bay one-four-echo."

"Station to Hammer three-two," he heard. "Continue on present course and stand by for heading."

The lesson plan included landing in and launching from three horizontal-plane bays in the academy's training station. "Approach angle and speed are critical," said Coborn. "Cut your engines and drift; you've got enough momentum to carry us in. Watch your approach guidance lights. If you come in at an angle, you'll crash into the bulkhead."

The bay loomed up like a square mouth lighted from within, and the AG lights above and below showed amber.

"You're too high," said Coborn. "Pull up and around and make another approach."

"Roger," said Tristan. "Station, this is Hammer three-two on the go."

The AG lights showed green on the second approach. Tristan cut the engines again and kept his hand tense on the switches.

"Watch your speed," said the IP. "Fire retros one second on, one off."

Tristan's lower lip was numb, clenched between his teeth, by the time the ship slid into the bay.

"Request clearance for departure," said Coborn. "We're not going to stay long enough to go through the pressurization cycle."

Launch was easy by comparison: fire thrusters at two and one to clear the bay, ignite the engines, roll out. As he cleared the space station after the final docking, Coborn said, "All right, get us home now."

He hit turbulence six thousand meters from the surface.

Descent built a painful pressure in his ears and made his stomach rise into his throat. The craft bucked like a peimu caught by the horns. He fingered the switches, fighting to maintain control.

"Give it here," said Coborn.

He relinquished the controls without a word and put his head back, eyes closed.

"Feeling green, Serege?" he heard in his headset.

"Yes, sir. . . ."

"Switch your oxygen to a hundred percent."

He opened his eyes only long enough to find the switch; he concentrated on breathing. Sweat broke cold around his nose and mouth. His stomach turned under his ribs.

The ship lurched up again; his stomach went with it. He gagged on his gorge and sat rigid, swallowing over and over to keep it down.

"Get the blasted oxygen mask off!" Coborn said in his earphones. "You want to drown yourself in it?"

He had to pull off his glove, and his hand was white and wet and shook so that he could barely release the mask. He pressed his fist to his mouth and kept his eyes closed, felt the craft rock in the crosswind and heard Coborn's breath sucking through his mask as he fought it. He swallowed down the retch reflex. The ship dropped, dropped, and then settled in a tremor and a roar—

"We're down!" Coborn was shouting into his pickup. "We're down! Get your tail out of here! If you puke in this cockpit, you're cleaning it up!"

Tristan groped for his hatch handle and popped it. Wet wind struck him cold in the face; he gasped. He tore his straps loose and his helmet off. Stumbled on the mounting ladder. His legs gave out; he caught himself on his hands on hot tarmac and gave in to the heaving.

From the corner of his eye, he saw the IP standing over him, watching him spit and wipe at his mouth. He didn't look up.

"And you're Lujan Serege's brat." Coborn slapped his gloves against his leg, and the wind laid bare his disgust like a knife cutting to the bone. "He'd probably disown you if he saw you puking all over the bay like that!"

Tristan's head jerked up; his throat went tight.

"Don't keep me waiting for debrief," Coborn said.

Tristan spat again and didn't answer. He watched Coborn walk away.

Pulou slipped up, crouched beside him, stroked his pressure-suited arm with curled fingers. And then abruptly those fingers closed about his arm. Tristan looked up, wrenched around . . .

He found himself face-to-face with his crew chief. Humiliation burned his cheeks, ached in his chest. "Leave me alone," he said.

"It happens to more of 'em than it doesn't," said the sergeant, and he held out a drinking bottle. "Here now, wash out your mouth and don't take it so hard."

Tristan eyed him briefly before he accepted the bottle and took a mouthful.

"How'd the bird go?" the crew chief asked, still crouched beside him. "Any problems?"

Tristan swished the water around in his mouth and spat it out on the tarmac. "No."

"We'll give her a look. You hit a nasty bit of weather."

Tristan raised the bottle again and felt the sergeant studying him. "What's wrong?" he asked.

"Your mother, Tristan," said the crew chief. "Where is she?"

Tristan slammed the water bottle down and shot to his feet, abruptly angry. "On Ganwold!" he said. "Dying—if she's not dead already! What does it matter to you?"

"She's my sister," the sergeant said.

Tristan stared at him. Then drew back. "How do I know you're not just telling me that?"

The crew chief made a helpless gesture with both hands

and rose, too. "I can't prove anything to you," he said. "You probably don't remember living in Elincourt before you were lost on Ganwold."

Suddenly subdued, Tristan said, "I remember some things."

"Do you remember the boy named Dylan who used to pack you about piggyback?"

Tristan studied him, cocking his head, recalling distant images of a solemn boy with a crooked leg, dark hair, gray eyes . . . "You're—Dylan?" he asked.

"Yes."

"Help her!" Tristan said. "Tell my father! The governor won't let me—"

"Your father knows," Dylan said. "But he's concerned about you, too."

Tristan's vision dropped to the vomit on the tarmac at his feet, and Captain Coborn's parting words burned through his mind again. He said nothing.

"It may get worse before it gets better," Dylan said. "Will you be able to trust me if it comes to that?"

Tristan looked up. The steely eyes held him, as dangerous as the eyes of the black man in Issel's Communications Center. He swallowed. "Yes," he said at last.

"Right, then," said Dylan, and forced a smile. "You two"—he glanced at Pulou—"better get going now before Coborn's back out here looking for you."

Tristan dropped to his heels before the artificial fireplace in the sitting room and chewed at his lower lip. His mind kept skipping back to that morning, to the conversation with his crew chief in the landing bay. Frustrated, he sighed and shoved himself to his feet again and paced back toward the table where Larielle sat.

They were alone in the sitting room. He glanced around to be certain of that before he leaned on the table with both hands and said, "I talked to Dylan this morning."

"Dylan?" Larielle looked up from her studies. "Who's that?"

"My mother's brother. He's my crew chief. I . . . think he's talked to my father."

"What?" Larielle straightened, looked him hard in the face.

"I knew my mother's family was here somewhere," he said. "We lived here—for a while—when I was little. I remember Dylan."

"You're very sure this is the same person?" Larielle asked. "Not just someone telling you this?"

"Yes." Tristan said. And after a hesitation: "He asked me if I could trust him if it came to that."

"Can you?" she asked.

"Yes," he said again. Firmly.

Larielle reached out and lay her hand over his, but her eyes were serious and her voice was only a whisper. "Then, Tris, if he suddenly tells you to go with him, do it. This is probably what I've been telling you to be patient for."

Her gaze softened. She let go his hand to stroke his hair back from his ear. "I'm so relieved—but I'll miss you, Tristan."

He didn't know what to say to that, but she didn't give him a chance to think of something before she pressed her mouth to his.

In his dream, their mouths melded again and again, and her hand roamed down across his chest and belly, heightening his breath to hyperventilation. He reached out for her—

"Get up, Tristan," said Rajak from somewhere over his head. A boot toe nudged his shoulder. He rolled over in a tangle of blanket, sweating, and flung up an arm against the sudden glare of lights.

He pushed himself up, blinking, and squinted at the timepanel on the wall: 0214. "What are you doing, Rajak?" he demanded. "It's still two hours before I have to get up!"

"Get dressed," said the servant. "The shuttle is waiting. There's trouble on Issel and we have to go back right now."

Lying propped against a rolled peimu robe, Darcie watched listlessly as Shiga stirred the cooking pot. She couldn't smell whatever was in the pot, but it didn't really matter; she had little appetite anymore.

She had forced herself to eat at first, to try to keep her strength up, but the illness was too advanced for that to make any difference now. She could no longer get to her feet without assistance. Couldn't walk more than three or four meters without tiring.

There was pain now, too, in her spine and her shoulders and legs, an aching that seemed to throb from the very marrow of her bones. And there was nothing to deaden it with but herbal remedies that only made her dizzy and light-headed. She would welcome death when it came, would open up her arms to it as it embraced her.

Perhaps it would be Tristan who would come from the other side to take her. Perhaps it would be Lujan.

A change in Shiga's posture, the way she suddenly stiffened, brought Darcie out of her reverie. She had stopped moving the ladle in the cooking pot and sat staring past the doorflap, head cocked. She stayed motionless for several seconds, nose wrinkled with her sniffing.

"It's what?" Darcie asked, watching her. The question was a bare whisper; she could manage no more.

"Something comes, mother," said Shiga.

Darcie turned her head slightly and listened.

There were only twilight sounds at first: crickets trilling in the grass, a baby wailing somewhere, the first stirrings of activity among the lodges. And then she heard a throbbing sound, a long way off but coming gradually closer. Engines? She couldn't be sure; it had been almost seventeen years since she last heard engines.

Within minutes it was unmistakable. The thrumming stilled the crickets, overpowered the music of the creek, made the ground tremble. Shiga moved to the doorflap in a silken motion, pushed it aside—and recoiled as brilliance flashed across her face. Darcie saw how her eyes narrowed to slits, her lips drawing back in a silent snarl.

Outside, the engines cut to an idle; there were bootfalls and shouts. *Human* shouts.

"Shell people!" said Shiga. Mounting *tsaa'chi* turned her voice to a hiss, made her mane stand on end.

Shell people? Darcie thought. *Humans in armor. Legionnaires!* Her heart contracted. "No!" she whispered, and struggled to sit up.

The effort shot pain through her body, took her breath and made her cough. Eyes closed against a wave of dizziness, she gulped for air like a swimmer too long submerged. "They . . . do what?" she asked Shiga.

"They hunt," said Shiga. "They go into lodges." Still crouching, she reached for the work basket beside the door. Her clawed fingers found the hide-fleshing knife and curled around it.

"They hunt—for what?" Darcie asked.

"I don't know," Shiga said.

Sudden screams mingled with shouts over the roar of a lodge on fire. The evening wind turned heavy with ash and heat.

"No!" Darcie gasped. She choked on smoke; its bitterness brought up involuntary tears. She squeezed them back, blinked away the burning.

She knew what they were hunting for. Knew there was only one way to keep them from burning the entire camp. She reached out for the lodge's nearest support pole. Her hand—her whole arm—shook; there was no strength left to pull herself to her feet. "Shiga, help me!" she cried.

Shiga only hunkered down, gathering herself for a

spring. Firelight emphasized her taut muscles, flashed off the fleshing knife in her hand.

A rifle's muzzle tore back the doorflap. Darcie saw the glint of a sooted shoulderplate, a helmet—and the swift shadow of Shiga's attack.

Fleshing knife drove at throatpiece. The soldier staggered back, swinging his weapon up like a club. Its stock struck Shiga's face with a noise like a nut cracking and she crumpled, overturning the cooking pot, scattering coals across the floor. Emberlight briefly showed a long gash in her forehead before it was obliterated with blood.

Gasping, Darcie crawled from the sleeping hide on hands and knees that barely supported her, reached out for Shiga—but a human wall moved between them. Reflex stopped her breath in her throat, brought up her hand against the hot armor of his chest to hold him off.

His gauntlet closed around her wrist, dragged her to her feet. She sagged, bracing herself to avoid contact with him, as over her head he shouted into his helmet's pickup, "Captain, I have her!"

SIXTEEN

"**According to a message received at oh-eight-hun-**dred local," said the briefer from the Spherzah Intelligence Section, "Governor Renier's personal voyager left Adriat a few standard hours ago. Though the stated reason was to settle the factory strikes on Issel, the actual destination is believed to be the command post on Issel's second moon. The passenger list included the governor's highest-level military advisors from Adriat, Issel, Na Shiv, and the Bacal Belt, as well as his immediate household. The ship is expected to arrive in the Issel system in seven standard days."

Around the table in the command conference room of the Unified Worlds Tower, the members of the Defense Directorate exchanged glances. Lujan tapped a note into the microwriter under his hand: NOTIFY CHES.

"In possibly related activity," the lieutenant continued, "a transport left Adriat for Saede a few hours before Renier's departure. A military exercise is slated to begin in Saede's western hemisphere this week. Indications suggest it will be small, but this is outside the normal Saedese training schedule and the participants will consist mostly of Bacalli surface forces. Imagery received at oh-four-hundred this morning revealed two Bacalli troop ships in synchronous orbit over the Unkai Peninsula."

The holo changed from a map of Saede to a view of the vessels, and the lieutenant said, "On the ship in the foreground you can see that all eight launch bays are empty of their landing craft." He drew his finger across the video repeater on his podium and an arrow moved through the holotank behind him. "The absence of the shuttles suggests that a full complement has been transported to the surface. Each of these ships is capable of carrying two thousand heavily armed troops, plus surface assault vehicles and weapons."

The lieutenant scanned his audience. "Coinciding as it does with other indications briefed in the last two weeks, we believe that this exercise could possibly be cover for a forward deployment. Our patrol craft are closely monitoring all activity in the Saede system." He paused. "This concludes my briefing. Are there any questions?"

"Yes." The Commander-in-Chief of Jonica's space fleets raised her hand. "What led to the factory strikes on Issel, and how are they affecting its military production?"

"Production in heavy industry has fallen twenty percent short of quotas in the past week, ma'am," the lieutenant said. "The strikes began with the diversion of transports from public commuter systems. One report states that some workers have been unable to leave the industrial centers for several days because there aren't enough seats available on the limited number of transports still operating."

"Where have the transports been diverted to?" CINC JONSPAFLT asked next. "Are you seeing any deployment support activity?"

The briefer said, "Not yet, ma'am, but we suspect that's what the transports were pulled for. With minor work they're capable of transporting armed troops, heavy equipment, or a combination of both."

Silence settled over the head table, emphasizing narrowed eyes, taut jaws, concentrated features.

The commander of Sostis Surface Forces leaned forward. "When the exercise begins on Saede," he said, "I want to know what kind of training the Bacalli are conducting, what weapon systems they're using, and how well they're accomplishing their objectives."

"Yes, sir." The lieutenant keyed some notes into his microwriter. "Are there any more questions?"

"Yes." An admiral from Mythos gestured. "In the event of an Isselan offensive, what do you see as the probable course of action?"

"Sir, we expect an attack on the Sostish Protectorate of Yan first," the lieutenant said. He touched a button; a constellation like a kite with a tail appeared in the holotank. "Sostis would be the real objective, but Yan is nearer the Issel and Saede systems." He moved the arrow over the map. "Control of Unified early-warning and communications complexes on Yan would be vital in a campaign against Sostis. It would give Issel a forward staging area and reduce our opportunities for isolation of enemy forces or interdiction of their supply routes.

"With Yan secured, Renier would probably move against Sostis in a two-pronged attack." The arrow traced flight paths from Yan and Saede.

Lujan straightened in his chair, eyes narrowed, to study the diagram.

After several silent moments, Sostis's Chief of Planetary Defense said, "How soon could the Issel Sector be prepared to launch such an attack?"

"At their present level of readiness," the lieutenant answered, "we believe they could possibly do so within a month."

There were no more questions after that. The briefer left his podium and the audience dispersed in a murmur of subdued discussion. The Sostish Defense Committee withdrew to a smaller conference room and turned to the representative of the Triune at the head of the table.

Pite Hanesson, arms folded over his chest, said, "You may proceed, Governor."

Kedar Gisha made a slight bow in his direction and addressed her Chief of Planetary Defense. "General Choe, I need a list of requirements for putting Sostis and Yan into wartime postures and an estimate of how long that will take."

"There are sufficient ground troops and equipment already on Yan," the defense chief said, and the Commander-in-Chief of Surface Forces confirmed it with a nod. "But," he went on, "there's only one space fleet based there."

"What will we need?" Gisha asked.

"At least two numbered fleets, Your Honor."

Gisha looked at CINC SPAFLT. "What have we got?"

"Ch'on-dok's eighth fleet is at dock at the Shinchang, Ro, and Qarat orbital stations," the space-fleet commander said, "and several carrier groups of the East Odymis sixth have just returned from nine months of out-system patrol."

Gisha said, "How quickly could they be prepared to launch again?"

"Not in less than a week, Your Honor."

Gisha considered that. "Start making the preparations," she said. And then, "What of Sostis?"

Defense Chief and planetary commanders made their statements, laying out numbers and proposing strategies, and Hanesson moved impatiently in his chair. "This is beginning to suggest a pre-emptive strike."

"No," said Gisha. "It's a demonstration of commitment. By the time our defenses are mobilized, I will have prepared a statement advising Sector General Renier that we're watching Issel's activities closely, that I am concerned about it, and that actions perceived as threatening will not be tolerated."

Hanesson pursed his mouth. "And if Issel fails to be impressed by your commitment, Kedar?"

"Then we'll be prepared to fight." Gisha paused. "Should it come to that, we'll need the support of the Unified Worlds."

"That must come through the Assembly," said Hanesson. "The Triune cannot commit the forces of the other worlds without the consent of their governments. We can only call up the Spherzah."

Gisha met Lujan's look across the table. "That will be enough," she said.

"Sir," said Jiron as Lujan crossed the outer office, "the Isselan ambassador requested a meeting with you today."

Lujan checked his stride. "Isselan. Did he say what for?"

"No sir, except that it's extremely important."

Lujan let his eyes narrow. "Schedule him in—and inform Governor Gisha and the Triune's offices of it. I'll meet with them at their earliest convenience afterward."

Jiron said, "Yes, sir," and handed over a chip containing messages from Yan.

He looked up when Lujan emerged from his office shortly before oh-nine-hundred. "Fourteen-thirty for the ambassador, sir."

"Thanks," Lujan said. "I'll be off the pager until the briefing's over."

The command conference room had grown crowded with more of the Unified Defense Directorate in attendance lately. Aides and junior officers from the various worlds stood against the angled walls behind their respective senior officers, displaced from even the last rows of seats. Lujan took his place near the head of the table and returned the others' nodded greetings.

The lieutenant at the podium appeared grim. "Ladies

and gentlemen, this briefing is classified Unified Worlds Secret. The information is current as of oh-seven-fifty local."

He touched a button, lighting the holotank with an image of Saede. Standard symbols and dotted lines arcing out like planetary rings depicted the world's territorial space and the operation areas of Unified and Isselan spacecraft. "At approximately oh-two-twenty local," he said, "the Sostish patrol craft *Prevoyance* was fired on by an Isselan-flagged ship, probably an observer of the Saedese exercises which began four days ago.

"*Prevoyance* was patrolling parallel to but outside the boundary of the planetary defense zone at the time." The officer slid an arrow along the reported heading, pointing out the locations of the vessels involved. "According to the captain's report, the Isselan ship was following a parallel course along the edge of the planetary zone, apparently shadowing *Prevoyance*. Its captain claims that *Prevoyance* violated the planetary zone and that he attempted twice to establish communications to warn the Sostish craft away before opening fire.

"Another Sostish vessel and a Topawan patrol craft operating within tracking range of *Prevoyance* confirmed that the stricken ship was well outside the planetary defense zone and moving farther from the area when the Isselan craft closed on it from behind and began shooting. Captain Claydor of the Topawan vessel *Chermenke* reported that she had been monitoring the Isselan ship for some time because it had already crossed into interplanetary space twice in the course of its patrol."

The holotank blinked to display a broadside view of a Sostish patrol craft with a gouge across its stern. The briefer said, "This hologram, made by personnel aboard *Chermenke* as she approached to assist, shows that the bursts were probably fired from a position one hundred seventy degrees relative to *Prevoyance*'s heading. *Prevoyance* sustained damage to her external hull, but she was reported capable of powered movement as of oh-three-forty. Five crewmembers injured in the attack are in satisfactory condition. The incident is under investigation by both Unified and Isselan authorities."

That was probably the reason for the ambassador's visit, Lujan knew. But why did the man want to see *him*? And why was Issel so nervous about the Unified Worlds observing an exercise on Saede?

When Jiron came to his office door at fourteen-thirty and said, "Sir, the ambassador's here," Lujan switched off the message traffic on his terminal, closed it down into the desktop, and nodded to his executive officer.

He appraised the man who entered with only a look. "Ambassador Kapolas," he said, and gestured. "Please be seated."

Kapolas lowered his bulky frame into the indicated chair and pressed his fingertips together in a steeple. "Admiral Serege," he said, "my government appeals to the Unified Worlds to cease its threatening postures toward Saede. The Saedese want only peace and security; they have no aggressive intentions against Sostis or the Unified Worlds."

Lujan concealed surprise. "What particular activity does your government perceive as threatening, Mr. Ambassador?"

"Don't toy with me, Admiral," the ambassador said. "Several of the Unified Worlds' patrol craft are operating along Saede's planetary defense zone at this moment. Surely you are aware of this morning's incident?"

Lujan gave a slight nod.

"We regret that our captain found it necessary to fire on the vessel," said Kapolas. "We sincerely hope that it won't become necessary again."

"I'll relay your regrets to Governor Gisha," Lujan said

with the barest suggestion of sarcasm. His eyes narrowed on Kapolas and his tone turned serious. "The patrols will continue, however, until your government ends its military exercise on Saede. The unusual activity of the troops and combat vessels involved are a matter of great concern to the Sostish government. They see it as a threat to their own security."

He noted how Kapolas moved in his chair, shrugged. "We have provided the Saedese with some defensive systems, of course, along with the technicians and training necessary for their implementation. But I assure you, Admiral, that they are strictly defensive weapons."

The Saedese, Lujan thought. *No mention of the Bacalli.* He let his vision burn into the other man's soul. "In order that there be no mistake about the Sostish position on this," he said, "World Governor Gisha has prepared a declaration warning Issel to expect the most serious consequences if there is any escalation of activity in the Saede system. You will make certain that this message is unequivocally clear to your government, Ambassador."

"Of primary interest, ladies and gentlemen, is the increase in deployment activity in the Issel system since Renier's return five days ago." The ensign from Sostish Space Fleet Intelligence switched on the holotank. "According to sources on Issel, transports of the type diverted from the public commuter system have been observed in flight between several major transshipment points, including the spaceports at Sanabria, Rempel, and Gualata." She guided the arrow on her video repeater to each red dot on the projected map. "Shuttling to the orbital docks appears to have begun.

"In related activity, two probable Vuki-class destroyers and a starcraft carrier have been sighted at an Isselan orbital station that has served only freighters in the past. The number of vessels at the military space docks has continued to increase as well.

"Logistics activity has also begun on Saede." An image of that world appeared in the holotank, and the briefer continued, "Surface freight counts at the main transshipment areas on the Unkai Peninsula have tripled, and up to six transports have transitted from the continent in the last twenty-four standard hours.

"During that same reporting period, two more Bacalli troop ships have arrived in the vicinity of the peninsula. The additional troops are believed to be masuk transfers from Adriat military colleges.

"There have been dramatic changes in Issel Sector space-fleet orders of battle during the past week as well." The ensign pressed a button and a chart full of numbers came up in the holotank. "The first column gives the normal number of ships, by class, in Isselan, Adriat, and Saedese inventories," she said. "The second column gives the current counts by location."

She allowed her audience a few moments to study the chart.

On an impulse, Lujan began punching numbers into his microwriter and comparing the totals. His mouth tightened at the results.

At the podium, the ensign was saying, "There was another violation yesterday of Yan's planetary space by an Isselan reconnaissance drone—the second occurrence in four days." The holotank blinked, showing a map of Yan's eastern hemisphere with a flight profile marked over it. "The drone was visually identified by a Cathana-based pilot who intercepted and destroyed it.

"In both cases, the intruders were short-range platforms, probably launched by one of the Isselan vessels patrolling the Yan Sector. All are capable of carrying drones." A three-dimensional model of the intruder rotated in the holotank, and the briefer said, "We expect this collection activity to continue."

She paused, looking over the conference room. "Last

week our combined analysis team projected that Issel
would need a month to launch an offensive. If preparations
continue at their current pace, however, it's possible we
could see it launched in as little as ten days. This concludes
the briefing, ladies and gentlemen. May I answer any questions?"

"What tactics or techniques are being utilized in the Saedese exercises?" asked the Commander-in-Chief of Sostis
Surface Forces.

"Mostly airmobile assault and ground warfare in a rain
forest environment, sir," the ensign said. "The entire Unkai
Peninsula is heavily wooded. This type of activity would
suggest training for an attack on Yan's Cathana Range complex; the terrain is very similar."

"And their weapon systems?" CINC SURFOR persisted.

"Soldier-portable projectile launchers and energy weapons, sir," the briefer said. "The region isn't conducive to the
use of mechanized systems or troop vehicles. Much of the
activity has been carried out in a simulated chemical environment."

There was silence for several moments at that.

Then a general from Topawa said, "I understand, Ensign, that masuki are not subordinate as a species, particularly in dealing with races they consider to be inferior, such
as humans. What have these exercises shown about that?"

The briefer said, "There have been some problems
noted, sir. At least one human officer has reportedly been
killed by masuk soldiers for disciplining other masuki. In
their slave-keeping culture, which prefers taking prisoners
over killing the enemy, such a murder is the deepest kind of
insult, as it implies that the victim is without value. No action has been taken against the killers, probably out of fear
of further retaliation."

Whispered comments rippled through the hall.

"Are there any other questions?" the ensign asked.

"Yes," said Lujan. "I'd like to see the orders of battle again."

The chart materialized in the holotank.

He studied it for a long minute. "There's a discrepancy between the former and current totals," he said. "The equivalent of three carrier groups isn't accounted for here. Do you have locations for them?"

The ensign said, "We expect they're still in transit, sir."

"Confirm it," Lujan said, "or find them. I want to know where they are."

In the Strategy Center, Governor Gisha studied the images in the map table. "What's the status of our space forces?" she asked without looking up.

"The sixth and eighth fleets are assembled and on-loading," said CINC SOSSPAFLT, "and the planetary reserves are being mobilized. Our first and fifth fleets are continuing normal planetary defense ops."

"How long before the sixth and eighth will be ready to launch?"

CINC SOSSPAFLT said, "By tomorrow, Your Honor."

"Good. And the reserves?"

"They're mostly merchant ships for resupply. That may take up to ten days."

"We may not have ten days." Gisha pushed away from the table and began to pace. "How does our capability compare to Issel's?"

"The sixth fleet task force consists of seven spacecraft carrier groups, and the eighth has six. The first and fifth fleets each have six, and there are nearly five hundred reserve boats," CINC SPAFLT said. "You saw the Isselan orders of battle in the briefing, ma'am. Renier will probably reinforce his fleets with Adriat as well as Bacalli ships, since most masuk vessels are little more than troop carriers.

Adriat still has a large, viable space force, although most of its ships are Resistance-vintage."

Gisha nodded. "You expect a massive attack against Yan, then?"

"I doubt that Renier has a choice, Your Honor," said the Chief of Defense. "If he loses his bid for Yan, he'll have lost his campaign for Sostis, too."

Gisha came back to the table to study it again. "What's the EFT from here to Yan?"

"Seven standard days," said CINC SPAFLT.

"Seven days...." Gisha repeated, and glanced up. "And from Issel?"

"Five days. Four from Saede."

Gisha looked across at CINC SPAFLT. "By tomorrow I want the sixth and eighth fleets on standby to move out for Yan, along with every resupply ship we have ready."

SEVENTEEN

Avuse paused at the threshold of the dining room. "Messenger for you, sir."

Tristan glanced around as Renier rose from the table.

Behind Avuse stood the black man from the Communications Center.

Tristan put down his utensil. He couldn't hear the conversation but he saw how the sergeant looked at him around the governor's shoulder. Hard, like a blow to the face.

Like a warning.

He couldn't eat anymore. "I want to be excused," he said to Larielle, his mouth suddenly so dry he could scarcely get the words out.

She didn't ask why, just said, "All right," but he felt her watching as he pushed himself back and beckoned to Pulou.

Turning away from the table, he tripped. He barely caught himself, by the back of his own chair and b'Anar Id Pa'an's. The masuk withdrew his foot and leered at him. "Clumsy pup!" He reached over with his knife to spear the meat left on Tristan's plate. He tore half of it from the point and chewed so that it showed between his teeth and tongue.

Tristan glowered at him for a moment, hands knotted. Then he turned his back.

He could almost hear Pulou release his breath.

In his room, he stripped off boots and jacket and shirt and squatted down to trace a pattern in the carpet.

Pulou perched on the bed behind him. "Something's wrong, little brother. It's what?"

"I don't know," Tristan said.

"You know how?"

"Dark man in there." He nodded in the direction of the dining room. "He looks at me and his eyes say 'danger.'"

Pulou blinked, cocking his head. "You do what?"

"Think of ways out."

"At night?"

"Yes," said Tristan.

He was growing drowsy with waiting when he heard voices in the corridor outside his room. Fully awake at once, he sat still and listened: the governor's voice. And Pa'an's. But he couldn't make out all the words. On hands and knees he slipped up to the door, crouched, pressed his ear to it.

". . . transport from Ganwold docked at Delta Station earlier this evening," said the governor.

"At last," said Pa'an. His tone seemed a snarl. He asked, "What of its passenger? The woman?"

"The message which the captain relayed to me," said the governor, "stated that she was taken directly to the colonial medical facility after she was brought in from among the natives. The personnel there were able to stabilize her before she was taken aboard the ship, but they consider her condition incurable. They were unable to determine what it is." The governor paused. "Perhaps including that information with my next message will encourage my old friend Lujan Serege to take some action at last. . . ."

Tristan stiffened, listening. "My mother!" He pushed

away from the door, twisting around to stare at Pulou. "They bring my mother here, to Delta Station—and they tell my father!"

Striding on down the corridor, Pa'an shrugged. "Perhaps it would be more effective to let her die."

"No!" Renier's hand tightened on the grip of his walking stick. "That hasn't become necessary yet."

"I think that it has." The masuk stopped walking and turned, blocking the governor's way. "The Unified Worlds have not reacted to your provocations, Sector General, except to prepare their defenses."

"I'm aware of that," Renier said. "But it's of no concern to us."

"Your window for success is growing smaller."

"Not necessarily. Our real strike force will soon be fully assembled."

"My forces are already sufficient," said Pa'an, "to accomplish the Pasha's purposes."

"What do you mean by that?" The words were clipped; Renier's features turned hard.

Pa'an showed his canines. "My sire's world needs human slaves, Sector General, and it does not matter to my sire what world they are brought from. If the supply from Sostis is denied us, then slaves from Issel will suffice."

"You jackal!" Renier spat it.

"It is a necessity," said Pa'an. "Please remember, Governor, that I have command of the Pasha's soldiers and they are already within your system."

Renier stared at him. "You will not—"

Pa'an cut him off with a motion of his hand. "The hostages," he said. He smiled again, slightly. "It is ironic about hostages. Some must be killed to give the others value with which to barter." He eyed Renier. "Make a choice, Sector General. Which one of them is worth more to you?"

The governor hesitated. "Kill the boy," he said.

Pa'an reached for the knife in his belt and started to turn.

But Renier caught his arm. "No, that's too easy. I've waited a long time for the opportunity to teach Lujan Serege what it means to ache for the loss of what he loves. I'll take care of the boy myself."

Tristan fingered the lock panel. "Door's closed on outside!" He tapped the switch impatiently and glanced around the room. "This way, Pulou," he said suddenly. "We go through latrine and out through Rajak's room; it's not locked." Scooping up his boots with one hand, he said, "Be quiet," and reached for the latrine door—

—as Rajak, only a shape in the dark, stepped through it. "Not very smart, Tristan," he said.

The boots swung up, more out of reflex than by design, catching Rajak in the jaw and snapping his head back so that he staggered.

"Pulou, *go!*" Tristan said. "Go! I come behind you!"

He swung the boots at Rajak's head again and tried to duck past him. But the other countered the blow this time, struck the boots from his grip. He caught Tristan's arm and twisted it up behind his back. Pain lanced through his shoulder, forced him to his knees.

"That's enough, Rajak."

Tristan jerked his head up, startled, as the room's lighting came on.

The governor had come in through the hallway door behind Tristan with his walking stick in his hands. b'Anar Id Pa'an was with him. But Pulou had escaped.

Renier crossed the room to press the latrine door's switch, locking it. "Put him over the end of the bed and tie him," he said.

The hold on Tristan's arms eased just enough for Rajak to shove him forward, still on his knees, and push him face-down onto the foot of the bed.

"I'm sorry, my boy," Renier said from behind him, "but the situation has become such that I can't afford to keep you alive any longer."

While Rajak pinned him, Pa'an knotted cords around his wrists, stretched his arms over the bed, tied the cords to its legs. It made every breath an effort.

He heard a footstep behind him and started at the sensation of something blunt and cold gliding down his bare spine. "I wish I could assure you that your death will be quick and painless," the governor said, "but that wouldn't begin to repay what I owe your father."

The cold tip slid to the right, tracing his lowest rib. "His betrayal of me, Tristan, eventually cost the lives of my mates and my children and the loss of my motherworld."

The tip withdrew—then slammed into the same spot with a force that seemed to pierce Tristan's back. The floating rib snapped; he felt its stab when his body recoiled. His vision momentarily tunneled.

"I've borne all that ache for a long time, young one," the governor said somewhere above him. "It's time that he learned what I've suffered."

The end of the walking stick moved up Tristan's spine again; he shuddered.

"And he *will* suffer, Tristan. He'll ache as I have when he sees the holograms and realizes how long it took for you to die."

The tip paused at the nape of his neck—withdrew once more.

Tristan closed his eyes, clenched his teeth.

The walking stick whistled out of nowhere, settling red-hot across the top of his shoulders. He buried his face in the bedcover to stifle an outcry and felt sweat well up all over his body.

Pulou crouched outside the latrine door. The scent of human blood made him grimace, stirred his pulse, made him hyperventilate. The whistling whacks of metal on flesh made him pin his ears back; the muffled screams raised his hackles, drew his lips back from his fangs. The snarl that started low in his throat swelled into a banshee's shriek as he tore at the door.

One claw caught in the doorframe's seam and snapped off at the quick. He sprang back, hissing with pain, shaking his hand.

It would take another human to open the door and let him in, he realized. There was one who might.

He clawed at Larielle's door, mindless of the broken nail—

—and cringed when it opened. He touched his forehead over and over. "Peace, mother!" He panted it, beckoned. "Come! Come! Tristan is hurt!" He kept beckoning, "Come, come!" and backing away, and she followed, her expression puzzled and worried.

She was the *jwa'nan*, he knew. She could make them stop.

Tristan's hands closed around the cords, tried to pull up on them to relieve the pressure in his chest. He couldn't scream anymore—could barely breathe. His palms were slick with sweat and his fingers were stiff. He dragged in one breath before his hands went slack.

He didn't hear the door sigh open, heard only a cry that wasn't his own: "Papa, no! Papa, what in the worlds are you doing? Stop—!"

He heard the sound, too, like a nut being crushed with a stone. And the choke. And then the metal walking stick striking the wall and the governor's voice, sounding panicked: "Lari! My soul, I hit her! I didn't even see her! My soul, her throat! Oh, Lari, my dear one! Rajak, get the medics!"

"No . . ." Tristan's mouth was dry, the word only a

breath. He tried to raise his head, to turn it, but lightning shot through his ribs and spine.

He couldn't see anything but the masuk staring at something on the floor, couldn't hear anything but the rattling gasps of someone strangling and the governor sobbing, "My soul, my soul, she's all I have left! She's all I have!"

"Larielle . . ." Tristan moaned. He gulped and shuddered, and everything faded.

Something touched his jaw, his neck, and hesitated. A hand. He let his eyes flicker open.

"Lie still," a distant voice urged in a whisper.

He did.

The hands moved to one wrist, picked at the knotted cord until it loosened, then untied the other.

"Go limp; don't make a sound," the whisper said.

Hands lifted him from his knees and onto the bed. Something warm ran down his sides and the middle of his back and into the top of his trousers. His arms were useless, without feeling; his chest felt crushed; his back and shoulders were on fire. He locked his teeth on a groan and sweat broke over him again.

The hands eased him onto something that seemed to float—it rocked, gave as his weight settled on it—and then they pulled a sheet over his head.

Emerging from the lift into the dispensary, Captain Weil felt something brush his leg. He glanced down. Amber eyes blinked up at him, questioning. He nodded, motioned Pulou to stay back, and let his two corpsmen go ahead of him. "Take her down to the morgue," he said. "I can take care of this one in the trauma unit."

He didn't wait for the others to maneuver the second repulsion sled on down the corridor. When the doors of the trauma room slid closed behind him, he pulled the sheet away from Tristan's head and said, "It's going to be okay, kid. You're going to be all right."

The boy groaned when Weil moved him onto the surgical table. "I'm sorry, kid," he said.

The gan moved around the table, began to stroke the youth's hair with the back of his hand, began to keen; and Tristan, with an effort, turned his head. "Pulou . . ."

Weil switched on the hemomanagement system at the head of the table to prime its pump, and selected bloodsub over Parenteral-5. Reaching for packaged IV lines, he paused, reconsidered, then took a field pack from the storage cabinet instead. He tore it open on the counter and assessed its contents: medications for shock, for pain, for poisons, all in dermal infusers; aerosol cauterizer and suturing strips; two units of universal bloodsub in gravity canisters—primitive but mobile.

He hung one canister over the table, swabbed the youth's forearm and set the intracatheter.

Dulled eyes followed his motions but scarcely blinked at the momentary sting. *Shock.* Weil selected a dermal infuser, yanked off its cap with his teeth and pressed it to Tristan's shoulder. He turned on oxygen and slipped a mask over the youth's nose and mouth. Checked his pulse again, and blood pressure.

It was several moments before he relaxed.

Using buttons like a computer's cursor pad, he shifted scanner antennae above and below the table and adjusted the holographic display to eye level. Radio waves emitted and received between the antennae and translated into digital computer code produced a three-dimensional image in the display. Weil touched fine-tuning dials, deleting muscle and skin to focus on bone, and enlarged the cervical vertebrae.

"I'm going to put an electronic neural clip in the back of your neck, kid," Weil said as he turned away to scrub. "You won't be able to move as long as it's in place but it'll block the pain. Understand?"

No response; he wasn't sure whether the boy had even heard him or not.

It took only a moment and a small pair of forceps, using the scanner display for magnification. When the tautness left the youth's body, he sighed his relief behind his surgical hood.

The scanner revealed everything: five ribs cracked and one broken, all on the right side; seven cracked vertebral processes in the thoracic curvature; contusions and hemorrhage of both kidneys, particularly severe in the right; lacerations and contusions to a computer-estimated thirty-one percent of the dermal surface and underlying tissues.

Weil clenched his teeth.

Under Pulou's scrutiny, he stripped off Tristan's bloodied trousers and repositioned him on the table. "I've got to catheterize you, kid," he said. "He managed to bruise your kidneys."

". . . killed Lari . . . ?" Tristan moaned.

Weil paused, recalling what they'd found in the small room. The girl's larynx had been fractured when the backlash of her father's stroke caught her in the throat. By the time he and the corpsmen arrived, she was gone, suffocated by the larynx's swelling. Weil's stomach turned again at the thought of it. "She died quickly, Tris," he said, even though he knew that was a lie. He added, "I'm sorry."

Unfocused vision touched his for a moment. Then the boy turned his face away, teeth clamped tight on his lower lip, and Weil heard his breath catch.

Guided by the holographic display, he used a laser scalpel to cauterize and close the deepest lacerations, to fuse cracked ribs and vertebral processes.

Maneuvering the laser apparatus away on its robotic arm, he felt the youth watching him again dazedly. "We're almost done," he said, reaching for an aerosol container. He sprayed its contents over the boy's back with several sweeps. Mist settled into a transparent layer like a gel. "When that dries," Weil said, "it'll form an artificial skin that'll peel off as yours heals. It has a topical antibiotic as well as medication to reduce the swelling."

He set down the container, peeled off his surgical gloves, turned toward the medications locker. "I'm going to start you on a regen to help you heal more quickly and a sedative so you'll sleep, and I'll keep an eye on your vital signs for the first few hours. We should pretty well have you back on your feet in five or six days."

Tristan didn't answer.

But he jumped at a voice from outside the doors: "Need some help in there, sir?"

Staff Sergeant Ricker, one of the corpsmen.

Weil stiffened, too. "No," he said quickly. He forced himself to take a breath. "No, I'm just about finished." The timepanel on the far wall caught his attention. "You two might as well take off. The day shift will be in in a little while."

"What about the pictures?"

"I'll process them while I'm waiting for the day staff." He kept his voice under control.

A pause, and then Ricker said, "All right, sir. See you tonight."

Weil listened to two sets of footfalls retreat up the corridor. He met Pulou's inquisitive look and let out his breath.

Easing Tristan back onto the med sled, he collected the catheter and IV canister, a monitor kit, blankets and sterile towels, and concealed them under the sheet with his patient before leaving the room.

The morgue was chilly and it smelled of embalming fluids. Pulou wrinkled his nose and grimaced. Weil tried to ignore the cabinet with the new tag on it, but he felt the skin prickle at the nape of his neck.

The slab was at the back of the room, where light from the doorway didn't fall. The blankets would have to suffice for padding. Weil folded each in thirds and laid them out on the table. Then he shifted Tristan over from the sled, positioned limbs rendered limp by the neural clip, and placed folded towels to ease his pressure points.

Pulou slipped up on the counter and watched with his head cocked as Weil hung up the IV and infused it with the sedative and regen. Watched him attach the patches and probes of the vital signs monitor and make a final check of pulse and blood pressure, temperature and respirations.

"You're doing okay, kid," Weil said, "and Pulou will be here with you, but there's one more precaution I think we'd better take." He forced himself to meet the boy's eyes as he placed dressings and suturing tape on the slab near his head. "I'm going to bandage your mouth closed. We can't risk you moaning or something and being heard. Right now your survival depends on making people believe that you're dead."

. . . *And making sure the boy's father knows that he's still alive,* Weil thought a little later. He studied the death certificate format on the terminal's screen and wrinkled his brow.

The situation struck him with a sudden sense of déjà vu. Had it been only six months ago that he'd concocted that report about the psychological bond between gan hunting partners? *Here we go again,* he thought, and turned back to the task at hand.

Leaving the death date and time blank would be too obvious; so would be filling in "Unknown." He gave the correct date and approximate time of the beating.

MEDICAL EXAMINER.

On an impulse, he deleted the title and replaced it with ATTENDING PHYSICIAN before he entered his name.

CAUSE OF DEATH.

That was it. He chose the words carefully: medical terms

that cataloged his patient's injuries and stated their extent.
Precisely. They would mean nothing under scrutiny by
the governor or the Comms Center, but any physician in
known space would understand.

EIGHTEEN

The intercom on the desktop buzzed. Lujan reached for it without turning his vision from the document on his desk terminal, and hit its button. "What is it?"

Jiron's voice answered. "Intelligence has brought up the report you requested, sir."

"Tell them to come in."

It was the ensign who had briefed them the previous day. She removed a folder from her case, extended it to him over the desk, stepped back and stayed at attention.

"Thank you," Lujan said. And detected—awe?—in her face, in her rigid posture. That never failed to surprise him. He smiled to put her at ease, and gestured. "Have a seat while I look at this, Ensign Dicharia."

There was imagery, an astral map, a one-page summary. He read it completely and nodded. "That's what I suspected." He looked up. "How many combatants are out there now?"

"Thirty-nine, sir—almost four carrier battle groups—plus some resupply boats."

"And more are expected?"

"Probably, sir."

Lujan leaned back in his chair. "He's done this before,

once at Enach with the fleet he hid near Kvist, and again
when he took Adriat, five years after the Resistance ended.
There's always a concealed weapon." He straightened, re
placing the folder on the desktop. "Good work, Ensign.
There's one more thing: we'll need everything you can give
us about air and space defenses in the Saede system."

In the Triune's private conference room, Lujan said, "Issel is
assembling a fleet beyond Ogata, the sixth planet in the
Saede system. According to this imagery, it consisted of
thirty-nine ships at oh-one-hundred this morning, and
more will probably join them." He lay the pictures on the
table before the Triune and Governor Gisha. "In another
five days, Ogata's orbit will place it in an optimum position
for that fleet to launch against Sostis—"

"Sostis?" Pite Hanesson straightened in his chair. "Why
do you think it's not another force targeting Yan?"

"Because Renier has always worked this way," Lujan
said, "using multiple fronts to distract and divide his enemies. And because, although he wants Yan as well, his real
objective has always been Sostis."

Hanesson sat back, eyeing the astral map and stroking
his chin.

"Wouldn't that involve a considerable risk?" asked
Ashforth.

"Not if enough of Sostis's defenses were diverted to
Yan, which is what he seems to be counting on," said Lujan.

Silence: a weighted space that grew more so, until
Hanesson said, "What do you propose, Admiral?"

"The Spherzah fleet that entered your spaceports two
weeks ago is ready to launch again. You have the authority
to order it; I suggest that you do so. It should be in position
here at Buhlig—" Lujan pointed to a minor star system on
the astral map, "—when the Isselan strike force returns to
real space from its first lightskip. When that's contained,
we'll move on to Saede—"

"No!" Hanesson was on his feet. "That world—"

"—houses a main forward operating base," Lujan said evenly, "and ports which are vital links in Renier's chain of logistics support. If we don't eliminate those facilities now, they'll be used against us again."

"But our enemy is *Issel*," Hanesson protested, "not Saede!"

Kun Reng-Tan raised one hand in a conciliatory motion. "A world which aides your enemy is not your ally," he said.

Hanesson surveyed the circle of his peers and read a grimness in their eyes born of events and places they had survived and he had never seen. He let his hands drop to the tabletop, let his shoulders go slack. "Then you approve of the admiral's attack on Saede?" he said to Kun at last.

"Counterattack," said Kun. "Yes, I do. If that fleet launches, if it comes through the Buhlig 'skip point, then it has committed itself to attack. It has struck the first blow."

"And you, Alois?"

She gave a single nod. "I approve."

Hanesson turned to Lujan. "I can't in good conscience give you my own approval, Admiral Serege, but I am over-ruled. Therefore, do what you must to defend Sostis."

Lujan acknowledged him with a nod.

And Hanesson turned to the Sostis World Governor. "What of you, Kedar?"

She glanced across at CINC SPAFLT. "Are the fleets ready?"

"Yes, Your Honor."

"What of the resupply ships?"

"Only twenty-five have finished on-loading."

Gisha looked at Lujan. "The sixth and eighth fleets are standing by to launch for Yan today," she said. "According to the information you've presented, Admiral, we're at D-minus-nine right now. The flight to Yan will take most of that time, and the commanders will need the rest of it to establish their defense positions."

"The eighth fleet and the twenty-five resupply ships will be sufficient to defend Yan," he said, "at least initially."

"You're certain of that, Lujan?"

He said, "Nothing is certain in war, Your Honor."

She considered for several moments. "And the other fleets?" she asked.

"I suggest you keep the sixth ready to launch," Lujan said, "to reinforce Yan, should that become necessary. Keep your first and fifth fleets in a defense perimeter around Sostis. If the Spherzah fleet can't achieve its objective, you'll need those fleets here."

It was late afternoon before he returned to the Command Section. Jiron and most of the office staff were already gone, making final preparations for the departure. But the outer office wasn't empty.

Ambassador Kapolas stood in the center of the reception area, tapping the corners of two envelopes into his palm. He said, "I've been waiting for some time to see you, Admiral."

Lujan motioned the man into his office and said, "What is it, Ambassador?"

Kapolas ignored his gestured invitation to be seated. Said only, "I regret that I must be the bearer of bad news," and extended one of the envelopes.

Lujan accepted it. Examined it briefly before he slipped its catch.

"It's not an explosive," Kapolas said. "Not in the physical sense, at least. However, you would be wise to sit down before you look at the contents."

Lujan looked across at him, hard; but the other's expression was almost benign. Taking his place at the desk, he opened the envelope and reached into it.

Holography film. Two or three sheets of it. With another glance at Kapolas, he slid them out onto the desktop.

He felt the ambassador watching him with eyes like lasers, and masked his horror. All but a tiny twitch at one corner of his mouth.

He forced himself to look at all three holograms. Kept his face impassive. He noted the transmission codes along the top and bottom of each.

He studied the death certificate for several moments. The standard date and time caught his attention: 0423 on 7/2/3308. Only yesterday.

But there was something irregular about it. . . .

He looked directly at Kapolas. "Why?" he said.

"A number of reasons," said the ambassador, "some of which are known only to you and the Sector General. But mostly because of your failure to cooperate at earlier opportunities."

"To be coerced, you mean."

Kapolas shrugged. "Semantics are meaningless at this point, Admiral. But Governor Renier *is* offering you a final chance to cooperate." He handed over the second envelope.

Lujan pulled it open, withdrew another sheet of holography film.

Darcie.

She was very thin, very pale, and only the masuki on either side appeared to be keeping her on her feet.

"The picture was made yesterday as she was taken aboard the Bacalli vessel *s'Adou The'n*," said Kapolas. "Obviously, Admiral, she's in very frail health; she wouldn't last as long under torture as your son did."

Lujan crushed the envelope in his hand.

He regained control in the next instant and locked on to the ambassador's gaze with his own. "What are you leading up to?"

"The fact that it isn't too late to save her—yet. Nor is it too late to recall the warships which departed Issel a few standard hours ago. But that is up to you."

Warships have departed Issel—

Lujan masked that shock, too. "What does the Sector General expect me to do?" he said. "Sell out Sostis the way he did twenty-seven years ago?"

The ambassador betrayed a split second's surprise, and Lujan rose to his feet. "Treason is not an alternative, even at the cost of my family." He indicated the door. "Good day, Ambassador."

Kapolas paused at the threshold. "There are still forty-eight hours before the fleet reaches its first 'skip point, Admiral."

"Good day, Ambassador." Lujan let his eyes and voice turn hard.

Alone, he sank back into his chair, suddenly strengthless.

Warships have departed Issel.

He punched the secure phone and passed the message to the offices of the Triune and the World Governor.

His vision kept touching the holograms lying on the desk, finally fixing on them for several minutes until, nauseous, he turned his face away. . . .

But something about the death certificate drew his attention back.

ATTENDING PHYSICIAN.

"I've never seen that before." It was a murmur. He reached for the intercom button—remembered before he pressed it that Jiron wasn't there. He called the Command Surgeon's office instead, wondering if anyone would still be there.

Beyond the diaphametal wall, Ramiscal City appeared miragelike under the thin fog of early spring, but Lujan, leaning against the pane, scarcely noticed. He glanced over his shoulder when he sensed a presence at the doorway behind him, and turned away from the view.

"Surgeon's office, sir," said the woman who stood there.

She wore commander's rank. "You requested that someone come up?"

"Yes." He moved to his desk, reached for the death certificate lying there, passed it across to her. "There's something unusual about this," he said.

He saw how she glanced up once, swiftly, when she read the name of the deceased, but he said nothing. He only watched her and waited.

She read it through. Read it twice, in fact, and appeared to consider it for a long while.

Then she said carefully, "Sir, the way this is worded suggests to me that your son wasn't dead when this certificate was submitted. It gives a detailed description of his injuries but it makes no actual statement of death." She hesitated. "I suspect it was done that way intentionally. I'd guess that someone wanted to be sure that you'd know he was still alive."

Lujan only nodded; his throat was suddenly too tight to speak. He turned his vision abruptly back to the city outside, clenching his hands and his jaw.

The commander turned her eyes from him in apparent deference to his emotion. But she didn't withdraw. She waited until he'd regained control and then she asked, "Are you all right, sir?"

"I will be," he said, and managed to keep his voice steady.

"If there's anything we can do to assist you—" she offered.

He shook his head. "I don't think so, not right now, but thank you."

Lujan opened up his desktop terminal after the surgeon left. It took only a few minutes to draft a set of new orders: a few sentences, brief but explicit. He read them over, then added a directive: "Dispatch at highest precedent to Commodore of the Spherzah Cerise Chesney."

Two keystrokes released it into communications channels.

He glanced up at the timepanel on the wall: two hours until launch.

"Message just in for you, ma'am," said the ensign from Comms.

Chesney turned away from the personnel seated at the receiver banks. "Is it urgent?"

"Yes, ma'am. It's from Admiral Serege."

"I'll take it in my quarters."

Striding through the ship's passages, she said under her breath, "It's about time!"

In her cabin, Chesney secured the door before punching an access code and MSG REL into her desk terminal.

The text came up in green characters, barely filling a quarter of the screen. She scanned it rapidly first, narrowing her eyes. "Tristan!" she said. "I knew it!"

But the rest made her straighten in her chair. She read it again, slowly this time, her brow creasing with concentration. "Ogata? Holy Dzhou!" It was a whistle. "Brilliant as usual, Jink!"

Weil glanced over his shoulder as he touched the door switch. No one in the corridor. Stepping into the morgue, he said quietly, "It's just me, kids," and gestured at the light sensor.

Pulou, huddled at the base of the slab, blinked in the abrupt illumination, squinted, and came to his feet in a serpentine motion.

Tristan started when Weil pulled the sheet away from his face. His hair was a damp fringe stuck across his forehead, and his eyes showed fear and a pain which wasn't entirely physical. "What is it, Tris?" Weil asked, easing the gag off. "Nightmares again?"

"Yes." The boy gulped a breath. "I keep hearing Larielle scream . . . an' hearing 'em talk about my mother."

"I'm sorry," said Weil. "I'll give you a stronger sedative; that should help you sleep better." He checked the readouts on the vital-signs monitor.

"They've got my mother!" the youth said again.

"Take it easy, kid." Weil lay a hand on his head, looked into his face. "I know," he said. "I know, but we've got to worry about you first. Take it easy."

He waited a little, until Tristan seemed calmer. Then he said, "Let me look at your back now," and he drew the sheet down.

Under the dermal seal, red lacerations were just beginning to heal. Much of the swelling had receded. "In a couple more days," Weil said, "you'll be able to move around without risk of the skin injuries pulling open again."

"How long've I been here?" Tristan asked.

"Two days."

"Feels longer." It was a sigh.

"I know," said Weil. "I'm sorry. That's one of the reasons I've kept you asleep so much. . . . Are you starting to feel hungry yet?"

"A little."

"Good." He picked up the boy's arm. "I'm taking you off the IV and starting you on a soft diet with a high protein content—a step up from the ice chips and clear liquids you've been getting. It'll help you start to regain your strength."

Tristan said nothing.

"Your temperature's almost down to normal and your blood pressure's good," Weil said, "but we'll keep you catheterized a little longer to be sure you've stopped passing blood." He turned the youth onto his side and bolstered his head with rolled towels. "I'm going to put you through the range of motion exercises again, and then I'll feed you."

"I hate this, being fed and tended like a baby!" Tristan said.

Weil saw humiliation in his face. "I'm sorry, kid," he said again. "It was the best way to relieve your pain under the circumstances." He began the exercising with Tristan's right arm, manipulating each finger in turn, and his wrist, and then his elbow. "I'll pull the clip in a couple more days."

No answer, but the youth's listless gaze followed his actions.

"Sir?" It was Ricker's voice, in the corridor. "Are you down here? There's someone at the front desk to see you."

"Oh no," Weil said under his breath. He touched Tristan's gaze with his own and reached to draw up the sheet. "I'll be back in a few minutes. Stay with him, Pulou."

Sergeant Ricker, still standing in the hallway, eyed him when he came out of the morgue. "I misplaced something the other night," Weil said. "I think I must've lost it while I was moving the boy's body."

"It must be pretty important, sir," Ricker said, a suggestion of skepticism in his tone. "You've sure been spending a lot of time in there looking for it."

"Yes, it is important." Weil's mouth was dry. "It's—my grandfather's service ring." He forced his vision to meet the other's. "So who's at the front desk at this hour of the night?"

"Somebody from Communications," said Ricker, still studying him. "Says he's got stomach pains, but he wouldn't let me look at him. He said he knows you."

"From Communications?" Weil furrowed his brow.

He didn't recognize the man who stood beyond the counter, one hand pressed to his abdomen. "What's wrong, Sergeant?" he asked.

"It started aching right after mess," the sergeant said, "and it's been getting worse ever since. Now it feels like somebody hit me." He stood slightly hunched, as if doubling over would have been more comfortable.

"Food poisoning, maybe," said Weil. "Look, I'll give you some—"

"No, sir, I don't think so. This has been going on for some time."

"Why didn't you come in before, then?" Weil could hear impatience mounting in his voice and he didn't try to disguise it.

"Because it wasn't serious then," the NCO said, and there was suddenly something dangerous about his eyes, his tone of voice. "Now it is."

"What's wrong?" Weil asked, suspicious.

"Maybe you'd better find out, sir."

Weil eyed him for a long moment, feeling increasingly uneasy, before he said, "Come back here."

In the examining room, he touched the door switch and turned to see that his patient was no longer hunched. He swallowed, his heart suddenly hammering. "What's wrong?" he said again.

"You're not going to be able to hide Tristan much longer," the man said. "It's too dangerous. It's time to get him out."

Weil stiffened. "Who are you?"

"Lieutenant Commander Ajimir Nemec, Unified Worlds Spherzah."

"I don't have any reason to believe that!" Weil said.

"Except that right now you don't have a choice," said Nemec. "Your life is in danger, too, and I'm under orders from Admiral Lujan Serege to get both of you out of here."

Weil stared at him, still wary. "How?"

"There's a ship waiting. What condition is the boy in?"

"He's got cracked ribs and vertebrae."

"Can he walk?"

"He's been immobilized for two days," Weil said, "and I just took him off the IV. With one more day—"

"I doubt we have one more hour." Nemec punched the door switch—

—And Ricker almost toppled into the room when the door slid open.

Nemec felled him with the motion of one hand, like an ax at the base of a sapling, and bundled him onto the examination table. "Leave the light on and the door closed and go," he said. "It's a safe bet that he's already called Security."

NINETEEN

"I'm back, Tris." There was urgency in the medic's voice as he pulled the sheet away. Urgency in his face. He placed a backpack and a towel bundle on the counter and said, "Listen, we're getting you out of here. We'll do everything we can to make it easier for you. This is sooner than I'd planned but we don't have a choice."

"What?" Tristan watched as the medic peeled the monitor patches off his chest. He couldn't feel it. Still, when Weil reached for the catheter, he locked his teeth and squeezed his eyes closed.

"Your father sent one of his men in to get you," the surgeon said as he cut the tubes and withdrew them, "and one of my corpsmen overheard us talking. He'd probably called Security before we caught him."

Weil shifted him again and met his look. "I'm going to pull the neural clip, kid; it's going to hurt. I'm sorry we don't have time to place some specific clips for your ribs."

Tristan felt a twinge at the nape of his neck, and then—*pain!* Fire through his upper arms and chest and shoulders, a dull ache down his back. He closed one hand hard on the edge of the slab before he was fully aware that he could even do so.

"You'll have to sit up now," Weil said, and slipped a hand under his left side, up under his arm. "Here, let me help you."

The movement sent lightning through his spine and right side, took his breath, produced involuntary tears. He tried to swallow a groan, tried not to look over at Pulou.

"Just sit still for a minute," the medic said, and opened the towel bundle. "I'm going to put another layer of dermal seal on your back and give you another dose of antibiotic and something for pain, and then we'll put you in a brace to support your ribs."

Weil first applied a thermodot to Tristan's forehead, then took an aerosol container from the bundle, shook it, moved around behind him. The spray was cool up and down his back.

Weil traded the container for a dermal infuser. It made a small ache when he pressed it to Tristan's shoulder. Dropping it into a trash receptacle, he reached for an object that resembled a microreader: about eight centimeters long, five wide, and half a centimeter thick. It had a display and several buttons on one side and a backing on the other that the surgeon peeled away, revealing a duct in the center of an adhesive surface.

"This is a multiple infuser; it holds sixty grains of morphesyne," Weil said. "There's a miniature syringe here in the back." He indicated the duct. "When you push the pad on the front, it'll give you a small preprogrammed dosage and will record the time and amount in the memory. You can use it up to six times each hour if you need to. Frequent small doses control pain better than large doses at long intervals do." He checked the infuser's readout against the timepanel on the wall and pressed it to the center of Tristan's chest.

The brace was made of plastics and had a lining like fleece. "Sit up as straight as you can," Weil said, "and hold your arms away from your body."

Tristan sat motionless with his eyes squeezed shut and his breath hissing through his teeth. He didn't even have to watch the medic apply it; he could feel how each strap pulled through its eye, how each was fastened.

"Now the clothes," said Weil. "The best I could get you was a surgical suit."

Tristan opened his eyes as the surgeon pulled wadded blue cloth over his head, shook it out into a tunic, and said, "Put your arm through here. That's it; now the other one."

And then, "There's trousers, too. You'll have to get off the table."

Tristan looked down. There was half a meter of space between his feet and the floor. He swallowed and looked at Weil.

"Just slide off," the medic said. "Reach for the floor with one foot first. Yes, it'll hurt, but I've got your arm; I won't let you fall."

He took hold of Weil's shoulder with one hand, placed the other on Pulou's shoulder.

The jolt of his feet meeting the floor sent a shock through his ribs; his knees buckled. But Weil and Pulou held him by both arms, keeping him on his feet. He sagged until the swoon passed, until he could draw a cautious breath, and then he heard Pulou keening close to his ear.

"Easy," Weil said. "Easy. That's the worst part." And in a moment, "Can you stand now?"

Tristan only nodded. The thought of so much as saying yes was painful.

"Good. Hold on to Pulou," Weil said. "Right foot first."

The surgeon crouched at his feet, gathering up the trouser leg to make it easier. He stepped into the right leg, then the left, and let Weil pull the trousers up and draw the waistcord snug. "Not too tight!" he pled.

Behind him, the door clicked, and Weil jumped. Tristan turned his head.

It was the sergeant from Communications, the dark man with the dangerous eyes.

Tristan stiffened. He felt Pulou tense, too.

"They're coming in!" the man said. "Get him out of here!"

Tristan swallowed. "Who's coming?"

"Security." Weil flung his backpack over one shoulder and asked, "How?"

"There's an access to the emergency stairs from the ward," said the black man. "It'll have a pressure shield door. Go; I'll cover you."

Tristan hesitated, looked at Weil.

"It's all right," the surgeon said. "He's one of the Spherzah."

The corridor was a blur of bright light and pale walls and smooth floor. Lower lip caught between his teeth, Tristan pressed his right arm to his side and let Pulou and Weil support him up the passage, across a long room with several beds, to the door at its opposite end.

Somewhere behind them there were shouts and running bootfalls.

The Spherzah lunged at the door's security bolt, shoved it free. The door swung away, admitting enough light to reveal a stair landing. "Go!" the man said.

Tristan stumbled over a doortrack wider than his body; Pulou caught him, practically pulled him through, and Weil and the Spherzah came after.

"The stairs!" someone shouted from the room behind them.

The Spherzah punched the pressure door's manual trigger. With a small explosion, the shield slammed down over the doorway.

The sound of it rang on forever, above and below, in the sudden blackness; the platform they stood on shook with it.

The stairwell was hot, the air motionless and musty. The

Spherzah switched on a palm light and played it around the walls, over a sign with arrows marking an evacuation route.

"We're directly under the passenger shuttles," he said. "Start working your way down while I go up and seal off the access from the top." He slipped the light from his hand and gave it to Weil.

"What?" the surgeon said. "Why?"

"Because Security will expect us to try for the shuttles, and they may send someone down to meet us."

"But—what's down there?" Weil turned the lamp and peered through the grating under their feet, down a well webbed with steel stairs. It sank to a depth the beam couldn't find the bottom of.

"There're caves," Tristan said. He turned his vision away from the view and swallowed hard. "They go everywhere."

The black man nodded. "But they're almost two kilometers below us," he said. "Don't force your pace; there's enough time." He hesitated on the steps. "There will be an explosion, maybe two. Don't stop; I'll catch up to you."

Then he was gone, one with the dark and the quiet.

"Who is he?" Tristan asked of the medic.

"Lieutenant Commander Ajimir Nemec," said Weil. "He said he's one of your father's people."

Tristan saw, by the palm light, the lingering uncertainty in Weil's eyes. "Do you believe him?"

"Right now," the surgeon said, "we don't have a choice, Tris." He hesitated, then asked, "Are you doing all right?"

Tristan's mouth was dry, his limbs weak, and his whole body seemed to throb to the racing beat of his heart. He couldn't remember ever feeling worse in his life, but he nodded.

"Then let's go," said Weil.

The steps had narrow treads and steep risers and there were fifteen between each landing. Teeth locked, Tristan leaned on the handrail and reached down with one foot. Held his breath as that foot took his weight so the other could follow. The stretching, the shifting of weight made his ribs seem to jar and scrape against each other.

On the nineteenth landing he eased himself to his hands and knees. The movement produced new pain through his chest and back. He sank over and sat down.

"Little brother?" Pulou squatted close. "It's what?"

"It hurts," Tristan said. He hissed it, teeth clenched, and held the brace tightly to his side with one hand.

Weil, kneeling in front of him, checked the dot on his forehead and then his throat pulse. "Is it mostly your ribs?"

"Yeah . . ."

"Have you used the morphesyne infuser?"

"No . . ."

"Here." Weil reached under the brace and pressed the pad.

There was a tiny sting, like the prick of a thorn, in the center of Tristan's chest.

"Just try to relax and let it take effect," Weil said. He fumbled something from his backpack. "Here, try to drink some of this. You should have all the fluids you can take."

Tristan found a drinking bottle in his hands. He sipped at it, found it cool and vaguely fruit-flavored, but his stomach felt queasy. He handed it back.

The pain was already dulling, making it easier to breathe. Weil asked, "Feeling better now, kid?"

"A little," Tristan sighed.

"Let's go, then."

He crawled back to his feet, teeth gritted, and reached for the handrail.

In the haze of the morphesyne, the stairwell took on a nightmare quality: an endless repetition of effort that caused pain, that cost strength, and seemed to bring him no nearer the bottom. He lost count of the landings, lost count of the times he had to stop, and the times he had to press the infuser pad.

Once his legs gave way altogether, five steps from the next landing. Pulou caught him as he buckled, helped him sit down on the step. He rubbed the infuser on his chest once, then again, and felt nothing. "It's not working," he told Weil. "Hasn't it been ten minutes yet?"

Weil checked his timepiece. "I guess not. Is it getting worse?"

"Yeah . . ."

The surgeon felt his pulse and offered him the drinking bottle. "Try to take some more," he said.

Tristan managed two swallows and passed it back, his hand unsteady. "That's enough."

A distant concussion, a tremor through the landing startled him; made Pulou's eyes widen. He looked at Weil.

"That's Nemec sealing the shaft," the medic said. "—I hope." The palm light showed the tightness of his jaw as he looked up and then back at Tristan. "Ready to go on again?"

Tristan hesitated. "How much farther is it?"

Weil turned the palm light downward. "I think I can see the bottom."

Nemec caught up to them before they reached it: a voice first, and then a shadow materializing out of the dark above. His breath came hard, like a runner's at the end of a long race.

"What's going on?" Weil asked.

Nemec tapped his ear, and Tristan saw that he wore a receiver plug like those used by the air traffic controllers at the academy. "Right now they're staking out the stairway entrance to the shuttle bays," Nemec said when he could. "I triggered the shield doors into other levels as I went up to encourage that. But they won't hold those positions forever.

We'd better be gone by the time they start looking down here."

He unclipped a sensor from his gunbelt when they reached the bottom. Sinking down to lean against the wall, Tristan watched him run it over the doorframe. Its hum didn't fluctuate. "No electronic devices," Nemec said. He tested the door's security bolt, then threw it—and winced at its thunk.

They waited.

The echo exhausted itself up the stairwell behind them but there were no bootfalls, no alarms.

Nemec slipped through the door first, sidearm in one hand, sensor in the other. Then he was back, beckoning. "Still clear," he said in a whisper. "Hurry!"

Holding on to Pulou, Tristan regained his feet. He swayed, closed his eyes against a wave of dizziness.

They stepped into a maintenance tunnel, gray with a low ceiling. Weil's palm light illuminated glowpainted words on the wall: TERRARIUM MAIN ACCESS, with an arrow pointing the direction.

"I know where this goes," Tristan said.

But Nemec was kneeling, pulling up a circular cover from the floor. It scraped, shifted; he wrested it aside, and Weil flashed the palm light around a shaft with rungs down one side. Tristan remembered Pulou's description of burrows like a lomo's; it seemed ages ago.

"You first, Doc," Nemec said, "and then you." He pointed at Pulou. "It's about five meters down. Be careful; it's damp and the rungs will be slippery."

Weil disappeared into the hole first. Pulou hesitated, until Tristan said, "Go; I come behind you," and looked at Nemec.

The man nodded. "Sit down on the edge with your feet in the hole," he said. "It'll be easier to get onto the rungs that way." He took Tristan by the tunic, a handful of cloth at the nape of his neck. "I've got you," he said. "One at a time now. Take it slowly."

Bearing part of his weight on his arms was like having his rib cage pulled apart, Tristan thought. It strained the lacerations over his shoulder blades. He felt one pull open, felt warm fluid ooze down his back. It itched. Eyes closed, breath raking through his teeth, he hung motionless for long moments, hugging the ladder. Then he reached down with one bare foot . . .

He felt the grip on his tunic release only when Nemec could lean no further into the shaft to hold on to him.

Stretching for the next rung, he felt something give in his lower back. Its twinge made him gasp, stiffen. His foot missed its hold—

—his arms couldn't take the sudden weight. The tug as he dropped was like an explosion in his chest. He didn't feel the rung pull out of his grip as his consciousness collapsed on itself, or the arms that caught him when he fell.

He came to lying facedown on damp ground, roused by Pulou keening and stroking his hair. He moved one hand enough to nudge the gan and sighed, "I'm a' right, Pulou." But he didn't want to move anything else. A knot throbbed in the small of his back and the reopened wounds burned across his shoulders.

The others had seen him stir. "As soon as he can move . . ." Nemec said out of the dimness.

"He needs to rest!" That was Weil.

"Not here. We're sitting at Security's back door right here."

There was a little pause, and then Weil said, "Come on, Tris. You've got to sit up now." He offered a hand to assist. "Easy. That's it; just sit still for a minute."

Tristan closed his teeth on a groan. Dragged a hand over his face when his vision spun.

"What happened that made you fall?" Weil asked.

"Don't know." He rubbed at his back. "Felt like—something inside moved."

"In your back?"

"Yeah . . ."

He saw how Weil's features tensed. "Let's get you out of here," he said, and held out the brace.

Tristan realized only then that he was shirtless. He looked at the medic and cocked his head.

"A couple of the lacerations were bleeding," Weil said. "I had to take this off to apply the suture strips. Can you raise your arms a little?"

The thought of it made Tristan grimace. "No," he said. "I don't want that."

"You may need it later."

"Do it later, then."

He let Weil put the tunic over his head and guide his aching arms into the sleeves, though drawing it down to cover his back made his breath catch. He let Weil and Pulou help him to his feet. Dizziness swept over him again. He reached for the infuser's pad. This time there was a sting, a spread of sudden warmth under his skin.

He blinked at the cavern's floating lights, its turquoise walls. "Where're we going?" he asked.

"To Malin Point," said Nemec.

He saw the map of green lines and red lights in his mind. "That's almost thirty-four kilometers!"

Nemec said, "We have two days to get there. You'll be able to rest when you need to."

Tristan studied his dark face, his fierce eyes. He nodded acquiescence.

The knot in his back seemed to settle in his right side, hunching him that way as he walked, almost making him limp. He pressed his arm to his side and locked his teeth at the smart of sweat in his opened lacerations. Sweat soaked his tunic until it clung to his body.

He had to rest often. He stumbled frequently—went to his knees once. Pulou saved him, eased him down; and Weil, crouching beside him, said, "You're in shock, kid. I think we'd better stop for a while."

Nemec said, "There's a side tunnel up ahead. It'll be easier to defend, if necessary, than a spot here in the main cavern."

It was also dark, and its floor was rough and uneven.

"Put this under your head," Weil said, offering his pack.

Tristan did. But when the medic peeled backing from a silver patch and reached out, he turned his face away. "I don't want that!"

Weil said, "You've got to sleep, Tris, and I don't think you will without help."

He kept his eyes closed, unwilling to watch Weil press the patch to his temple.

It took effect almost immediately.

He woke what seemed hours later because he was too warm, and sweating again, and thirsty. It was dark and quiet. He turned his head—winced—and whispered, "Pulou?"

He felt Pulou's hand on his head. "Little brother?"

"I'm thirsty," he said.

Pulou was reaching for the drinking bottle when there was a stir nearby and a shadow leaned over him. "How do you feel, kid?" asked Weil.

"Ache all over." Tristan shifted onto his side—and decided against trying to sit up.

The surgeon pushed away his hair, damp with sweat, to read the thermodot, then felt his carotid pulse. "You're feverish," he said. Tristan couldn't see his face but there was concern in his voice. "I'd think it was an infection except that I've been giving you enough antibiotics to prevent that." He paused. "I think I should examine that sore spot in your back."

Tristan bore the careful prodding with his eyes closed and his teeth locked.

When he finished, Weil said, "By the localized tenderness I'd say that your kidney is out of position. Its connective tissues must have been injured, too."

Tristan swallowed. "Is that serious?"

"It can be," Weil said, "but we should have you under proper medical care before it gets that way." He drew a handful of dermal infusers from his pack and shuffled through them until he found the one he wanted. Snapping off its cap, he pressed it to Tristan's shoulder.

He glanced up when Nemec, standing at the tunnel's mouth with his sidearm prominent on his hip, left his post and came over to them. Dropping to his heels, he studied Tristan for a moment before asking, "Do you feel ready to go on again?"

"What is it?" Weil said. "Security?"

"Yes." Nemec indicated his earpiece. "I'm picking up radio chatter from several areas. A couple of patrols have entered the terrarium now, and they can move more quickly than we can."

"How much further to Malin Point?"

"About nineteen kilometers." Nemec looked back at Tristan. "Can you make it that far?"

He glanced at Weil. "I have to," he said.

He rubbed at the infuser pad on his chest as he crawled to his feet and was grateful for its pinprick. He wanted to rub at the knot in his back, too, but Weil said, "Don't do that. You'll only aggravate it."

He couldn't walk without limping now. He leaned on Pulou, holding his side. He had to rest more often but he couldn't sleep. He swallowed obediently, one or two sips, when the gan offered him the drinking bottle, although it made his stomach roll.

Hunched over, he focused his vision on his feet, on placing one in front of the other, until their motion mesmerized him. Until it seemed like only a dream of walking, for days, through a cave that never changed, never ended. And everything, including his feet, was the color of the lichens. . . .

He woke on the ground several times, woke to the chill of wet cloths being placed over his forehead and the back of his neck, and he couldn't remember that he'd even stopped walking. His mouth was so dry it felt fuzzy. He tried to catch the trickles that ran along his jaw from the cloths, but they only dripped from his chin. He tried once or twice to raise up, but it hurt; and a hand on his shoulder would push him back down and a voice would tell him to take it easy. The voice always sounded too far away to go with the hand but he knew they were both Weil's.

He heard voices each time he began to come around:

"I need water for cold compresses." Weil.

And Nemec: "I can get it from the misting system but it'll take a little while."

Once he heard Nemec ask, from somewhere above him, "How is he?"

"The fever's getting worse," Weil answered, "and he's stopped sweating. That concerns me." There was a brief silence, and then, "How much farther is it?"

"Just over six kilometers."

He drifted back out of awareness then, into a nightmare of a walking stick flashing across his back, laying open his flesh like a knife. He dreamed of being lost in a blue cave that never ended, and of falling down a stairwell that had no bottom.

His own scream and a hand clamping over his mouth shocked him awake. He gasped and tried to twist his face away from the hand. His eyes were open but they wouldn't focus.

Quivery hands stroked his hair. "Be calm, little brother, be calm."

Pulou.

And Weil, saying, "Relax, kid. Easy now," as he took his hand from Tristan's mouth.

And then Nemec, his voice grim: "They heard him. They're heading this way. We've got to get him out of here!"

He felt hands sitting him up again, hurting him, and snatches of talk half-lost in a swoon:

". . . don't want him walking . . ."

". . . carry him, then. Tie his hands."

He groaned, "No! I'm a' right!" But he heard cloth ripping—could almost feel it!—and bands being wrapped around his wrists. He tried to pull away. "Don't—!"

"Easy, easy!" said Weil. "It's going to be okay."

His arms were pulled over Nemec's head, around his neck. His body lay on Nemec's back, and Nemec wrapped arms around his legs so that he rode piggyback.

He blacked out at the jarring of Nemec's pace. Knew nothing else until hands lowering him to the ground roused him. Someone put the drinking bottle to his mouth. He pushed it away with both tied hands. "I can't. I'll throw up."

"You've got to," Weil said. "You'll dehydrate if you don't."

This time he was stretched on the floor of a dark tunnel and Weil was crouched beside him, applying wet cloths again. He sipped cautiously at the drinking bottle; there wasn't much left in it.

As his senses cleared he became aware of machinery sounds in the distance, and the dirty smell of burning. He said, "We're where?"

"At Malin Point," said Weil.

Nemec joined them. "This is where it's going to get tough," he said. "I'm going in to check out the complex and cause a distraction. Wait for me here. And if there's anything you can do to help Tristan travel more easily, do it. When I come back we'll have to move fast."

"What about Security?" asked Weil.

"That patrol is going on up the main cavern; it's about a kilometer ahead of us now."

The surgeon's sigh of relief was audible.

When Nemec had gone, Weil cut the strips binding Tristan's wrists and reached for the brace.

"No," Tristan said.

"You're going to need it, kid."

He grimaced as the surgeon helped him sit up, wrapped the brace around him, secured its straps. "It hurts!" he said.

"I'm sorry. It'd hurt worse without it."

Weil pulled the dermal infusers out on the flap of his backpack. Most had been used by now. He selected two, pulled the cap from one. "This is more antibiotic."

Tristan's shoulders were beginning to feel bruised. He twisted his face away as Weil reached for his arm.

"I'm going to give you a stimulant, too," the surgeon said, uncapping the second cylinder. "Let's see the other arm now." Pressing it to Tristan's shoulder, he said, "This'll trigger your adrenaline and help you keep going."

"Why didn't you give me that when we first started?" Tristan asked.

"Because it has a drawback," Weil said. "It'll increase the pain."

It made him restless, too. He couldn't lie still, couldn't sit. He tried to gain his feet, holding on to the wall, and staggered. When Weil caught him by the arm to steady him, he jerked away. "Leave me alone!"

He started at a noise up the tunnel and stiffened. It was Nemec, brandishing his sidearm and panting. "Come on! I shut down the containment field in the cellblock. The prisoners are trying to take the control room. That should keep Security busy long enough for us to reach the loading bays."

* * *

The shouting and thumping outside the control room were increasing. Captain Krotkin pressed the commceiver harder to one ear and covered the other with his hand. "We've had a power loss!" he shouted into the pickup. "The whole cell-block is down and we've got a mass breakout! Get some reinforcements out here!"

He paused, straining to hear over a steady banging at the door. "Say again, Command Post? . . . No, we don't know what caused it! There aren't any failure lights. They're storming the control room! We need reinforcements!"

Someone in the command post must have turned up the volume; the voice that came through the commceiver was loud and clear. "Negative on the reinforcements, Malin Point. We have reason to believe that your unexplained power loss may have been caused by the fugitives from the Headquarters dispensary. They were last noted heading your direction."

A veil of static dropped over Krotkin's channel and another voice cut in: "All patrols to quadrant delta-five! I say again, all patrols to delta-five!"

TWENTY

The tunnel made a corner and then became two, one going up, the other down. Nemec took the one that went up.

Its floor was a ramp. Tristan clenched his teeth, leaning into the climb. The knot in his back had become a fireball and his heart was beating too hard and too fast. He could feel it against his ribs and it made him breathe too quickly.

The machinery noise grew louder, the thrum of compressors and scream of valves, until Tristan's head throbbed. The smells of heat and lubricants turned the air bitter—turned his stomach.

He made it to the top of the ramp only because Weil and Pulou half carried him. He stood panting between them while Nemec ran his sensor around a door marked D-5 UTILITY PLANT—and saw him abruptly freeze. Touching his receiver plug, Nemec listened for a moment and let his jaw tighten.

"What is it?" Weil asked.

"They're diverting Security from the cellblock to the loading bays." Nemec waved at the door's trigger. The door scraped open; he urged Weil and Tristan and Pulou through and switched off its automation. "Keep going," he said, "straight up the passage. This door won't hold indefinitely as a pressure shield would, but it'll buy us some time."

The passage was narrow and dim. It echoed with the shriek and thump of machinery, and Pulou grimaced and pinned his ears back.

It was hot. Very hot. Tristan's mouth burned, but the drinking bottle was empty.

"This passage opens into the loading area," Nemec said. "It's a ring of five launch bays. The one they use for passengers has a lift from the mine complex below, and they're sending Security troops up in it. We could step out of here into a firefight."

He moved swiftly forward with his pistol in his hand. "If we do, I'll draw their fire while you get to the nearest cargo boat. We'll be setting a course for the other moon." He looked at each of them. "Got that?"

Tristan felt winded; he could only swallow hard and nod.

The passage ended at another automatic door with a pressure shield for backup, a necessity this near the moon's surface. Nemec eyed it, scowling, before he said, "Get behind me!" and waved the automatic door open.

Ribbons of energy sizzled across the loading area from several nooks and corners, searing holes into the walls and floor of the passage before the door slid closed again.

"Security's in position out there," Nemec said.

A series of muffled explosions began at the far end of the passage behind them: energy weapons blasting at its automatic door.

"They're closing from the rear, too," he said. "Let's go! The nearest bay is to your left as you go through this door." He pulled the receiver plug from his ear and adjusted a dial until it buzzed like a tsigi. "Simulated bomb," he said with a tight smile. "When I throw this out, run! There's plenty of cover. Stay low, keep moving, and don't clump together."

Up the passage behind them, the blasting had stopped. There were bootfalls instead, coming closer.

Nemec waved at the door trigger and rose up just enough to lob the receiver into a maze of starter carts and ore chutes. Its buzz filled the concourse.

A dozen Security troops dove for cover.

"Go!" Nemec said through his teeth. He twisted around, pistol leveled, to guard their backs.

Pulou, teeth bared and eyes wide with *tsaa'chi*, pulled Tristan's arm over his shoulder. "Run!" he hissed. "Run!" He ducked behind an ore chute, dragging Tristan with him. Meters away, the chute disappeared through a dark arch into a launch bay.

"Hey!" A shout rang across the concourse. "Hey, there they go!"

A bolt of energy seared across the top of the chute and smashed into the wall behind them. Its burst sent fragments of concrete flying.

Still at the mouth of the passage, Nemec squeezed off a shot at the sniper and gave Weil a shove as he spun to take aim at their pursuers in the passage.

The whole concourse flashed with flying energy, concentrated on the passage entrance. Bursts gone wild shattered off the pressure door's frame. One exploded on its trigger—

—and the shield slammed closed, sealing Nemec inside the passage.

Weil leaped for the cover of the ore chute. A burst caught him in midair, in the shoulder. Its impact smashed him to the wall, marking it with blood as he crumpled. He didn't move.

"Weil! No!"

The scream startled Tristan; it was a moment before he realized it was his own. But Pulou was pushing at him and panting. "Go! Run!"

Bolts followed them under the arch, glanced from the

ore chute, shattered upon the walls. Pulou fell headlong, taking Tristan down with him. It slammed the breath from his body, made his consciousness reel.

White heat screamed over their heads. It lit the launch bay beyond with a shower of sparks as it struck the deck; it showered the shuttle that waited with three of its cargo holds closed, the fourth still open.

Pulou grimaced, gaining his feet. His mane was on end, his eyes half-crazed. He staggered, pulling Tristan up. He was hyperventilating, and his breath seemed to rattle in his chest. "Run!" he said. "Run!"

They tumbled up the ramp to the shuttle's cockpit in a hail of fire. Panting, Tristan swiped twice at the hatch closure before he managed to punch it. The ramp bumped as it folded itself, clunked and hissed as its pressure seals locked.

A volley of energy ricocheted off the shuttle's hull and crisscrossed the launch bay like trapped lightning.

Tristan dragged himself up from his knees and pushed Pulou toward the copilot's seat. "Strap in!" he panted. "Gotta—get us—out of here!"

He winced, gasped, as he dropped into the pilot's seat. Fumbling for the harness, he saw Pulou doing the same, awkwardly, confused. "This way," Tristan said, reaching for the clasps.

The gan only nodded, watching him. The wildness had left his eyes—the nictitating membrane showed in their corners instead—but he was still breathing through his mouth, too quickly and with his tongue showing.

Sporadic bursts of energy showered the craft, each sounding like a small explosion.

Teeth locked, Tristan snatched up the headset from its hook and put it on, swept the instrumentation with a glance and released a full breath; it was standard configuration, like the academy's training shuttles.

One hand ran over the console, found the systems-check

switch and flipped it on. Blue readouts filled a tiny screen. All systems were green except a light that showed one cargo hatch still open. Two coolant reservoirs read low but all engines had maximum fuel levels. Tristan pulled the manual lever to close the cargo hatch.

"Start engines," he said under his breath, and toggled the switches.

In the dark of the launch bay, pink clouds erupted from beneath the craft as the engines screamed to life. The barrage of fire broke off and several dark shapes leaped clear.

Locking his teeth, Tristan hit the bay dome's remote control button.

Warning horns blared through the launch bay; lights flashed over its entry. The gunmen, shadows in motion, dashed for the arch before its pressure door slammed down.

Above him, the dome's fins spiraled slowly open, showing space beyond: stars and the mottled light of the other moon.

Tristan spread his hand over the row of thruster switches, eased them up one fraction, then another, and felt a tremor as their roar crescendoed and the hole full of sky expanded.

Blue letters began flashing on his screen:

DOME OVERRIDE ACTIVATED.

He glanced up. The fins, like petals of a flower, stood half-open. In his earphones, Control said, "Malin zero-five, abort launch sequence! You are not cleared for launch! I say again, you are not cleared for launch!"

The eye of space began to contract.

"No!" Tristan shouted it. "No!" He shoved at the thruster switches with a shaking hand, missed the three on the end—

—the craft lifted sideways; the attitude indicator

showed an angle of 54 degrees. The bay wall loomed up, tilted, before his canopy.

Cadets who do that don't get their crests, Coborn had told him once, *even if they live to tell about it.*

The impact threw him against his harness. He heard the crash and shriek of metal on metal, and the shuttle rolled. He caught a glimpse of twisted fins on opposite sides of the dome's eye as the shuttle hung momentarily over it, and he realized that he wouldn't have cleared it at all if he had lifted correctly.

He took the row of switches with both hands. As the craft came over in its roll, so that its thrusters were pointed toward the surface, he fired them all.

Its leap flattened him back in the seat, left him breathless. His vision tunneled.

A trilling, a red light on the console snapped him back to awareness. His gaze shot to the traffic scope, then out of the canopy.

Another shuttle, its red-and-white anticollision lights flashing against the starfield, banked hard to avoid him, mere meters away. Through his headset he heard, "Control, this is Malin zero-three. Where're your heads? You had us on a collision course with another craft!"

Suddenly weak, Tristan let his hands slide from the console. He couldn't control their shaking. They were hot and dry. But he must have been sweating: his tunic was wet and clinging to his back again, burning, itching. He shut out the voice rattling through the headset, ordering him to return, and closed his eyes for a moment.

A new voice in the earphones made him jump. "Malin zero-five, this is System Defense, Bravo Station. You are in violation of regulations nine-one-point-nine, nine-one-point-seven-three-delta, and—"

Tristan stared, then keyed his comms. "Shove off, Defense! I'm operating under regulation nine-one-point-three-bravo: a pilot in command may deviate from any rule to the extent required to meet the emergency!"

"Malin zero-five," said System Defense, "you are ordered to return to your point of departure and surrender to the authorities. Failure to comply will warrant destruction of your ship."

"Destruction?" Tristan stiffened in his seat.

"Malin zero-five." The voice remained impassive. "We are launching fighters with orders to engage and destroy. I say again, we are launching fighters with orders to engage and destroy. Acknowledge, over."

Tristan checked his traffic scope: empty, for the moment. With a hand that shook, he switched off the radio, tore off the headset, and reached again for the thrusters. "Hold on, Pulou," he said. "They're coming after us!"

He couldn't outrun them; he knew that. But he rolled the shuttle out like an attack ship over its target and aimed it at the other moon.

In a few minutes a beep from the traffic scope begged his attention. A point of light blinked at its edge, 195 degrees relative to his heading. *The fighters!* Clenching his teeth, he gave the shuttle full throttle.

The beep grew louder, faster. Tristan glanced down. The single blip of light had become two, close together and crossing the scope's outer ring toward the middle one. Closing the distance.

When the pair of blips split into four and penetrated the scope's inner ring, Tristan wrenched around in his seat, trying for a visual fix. Position lights blinked against the starfield. The fighters had come in high, ranging from 170 to 190 degrees relative to his heading and flying in fluid four formation. The leaders were close enough to turn the warning beep into a trill.

Tristan caught a flash at his periphery: he was being fired on! He reached out to activate deflector shields—

The shuttle didn't have any. His hand froze over the emergency release for the cargo holds.

The craft rocked at the hit. Hands hard on the thruster switches, Tristan brought it out of its tumble—and stared at a pair of damage lights blinking on the console. Starboard aft thrusters were gone.

Manipulating the switches, he put the shuttle into a series of banks and rolls, altering attitude and heading at random, trying to shake his pursuers.

The lead and one wingman stuck with him; their blips hovered near the center of the traffic scope, practically at point-blank range.

Tristan reached for the deflector shields again. His hand closed on the cargo release lever.

Three of the cargo holds were full. . . .

Yanking the lever back, he shoved the shuttle into a spinning dive.

There were thunks somewhere aft of the cockpit, scraping and sucking sounds, and jettison lights flashed on the console.

A silent explosion blossomed at the shuttle's 180—then another, nearly close enough to be a secondary of the first. Their light reflected red against the cockpit canopy.

Pulling the shuttle up, Tristan looked over his shoulder and saw two fireballs dissipating in a cloud of chunk ore that tumbled and spread like an asteroid field. He saw the remaining wingmen bank clear of it, one rocking as if he was hit.

Tristan let out his breath in a rush. His heartbeat shook his whole body.

He didn't relax. The traffic scope showed the two fighters regrouping.

They flanked the shuttle this time, keeping their distance but staying within firing range. Tristan fingered the thruster switches, jerking his craft about as if in a storm, rocking it on its longitudinal axis.

The blast that connected was sheer chance. It sent the ship into a flat spin that threw Tristan into the console and pinned him there. The starfield whirled in Doppler circles beyond the canopy.

Pressed to the instruments, stomach in his throat, Tristan dragged one hand to the thrust switches. Malfunction lights blinked over most of them. He toggled the ones that remained, to counter the spin, and kept swallowing down the gorge that burned in his throat.

As thrusters slowed the craft and the pressure began to ease, Tristan pushed himself back, panting, and scanned his console. Half the cockpit flashed red. A diagram on the screen showed depressurization lights in all but three compartments—the cockpit was sealed off. Structural stress lights blinked at six points. Five of eight engines were gone.

The traffic monitor still worked; its beep matched the throb of the damage lights. Tristan glanced at the scope.

There was a third blip in it now, bearing 75 degrees on his relative vertical and closing fast on a collision course. Its position put his shuttle at the center of a diminishing triangle, between it and the fighters.

He tore his vision from the scope to scan space.

The swollen glow of Issel I filled half of the canopy, almost over his head. As he stared, the ether between moon and shuttle seemed to ripple. He blinked, straining to make his eyes focus.

And a ship materialized out of nowhere, massive and black and bristled with weapons.

TWENTY-ONE

Tristan sat paralyzed for a moment, staring at it, watching its bulk gradually block out Issel's moon. His hand moved on the thruster switches, willing them to respond, to push the shuttle out of its way.

A pair of guns at the ship's bow swung around like fingers pointing at its next victim.

Tristan swallowed dryness. "So finish me off!" he whispered.

Red energy belched from the muzzles.

He locked his teeth, braced himself . . .

A blossom of light at the edge of his vision made him twist in his seat. The fireball was already dissipating, leaving behind a shower of debris which had been a fighter a moment before.

The ship held its collision course.

Tristan leaned on the switches. "Go!" he urged his craft. "Go!"

One thruster fired. Then another, feebly. The cargo shuttle began to slide backward, away from the ship; there wasn't even enough power to change course.

Tristan watched the guns swing around again.

"Jou!" he tried to shout at the ship, but it came out sounding like a croak.

Energy arced over his shuttle, sweeping the dark with tracers until it touched its quarry. On Tristan's traffic scope, the blip that was the last fleeing fighter flared and vanished.

The comm set buzzed for his attention—had been doing so for some time, he realized. Scanning the damage lights, he wondered what had shorted out to make it do that.

The traffic scope's warning beep rose to a trill; the ship was almost on top of him.

He reached across the console, shutting down everything he could, routing all the power he had left to life support and thrusters.

It wasn't enough. The ship slid over his shuttle like a hawk seeking its prey, blocking out the moonlight. Its hull panels parted like jaws and a bank of searchlights washed over his craft. Tristan grimaced, half-blinded even through the tinted canopy—and blinked at a flash like rockets being launched.

There was a thunk against the overhead. And then another. The craft lurched as if it had been brought up short at the end of a line, and something began to whine.

On his console, the comm set continued to buzz.

The shuttle began to haul toward the larger ship.

"No!" Tristan threw the thrust switches against its pull. "No!"

Thrusters flared; the canopy reflected their fire. Something metallic moaned and shrieked at the strain. Lights from the ship's hold cast shadows of quivering hawsers across the cockpit.

Tristan held the switches down until their ZERO FUEL and OVERHEAT lights began to flash, until the red lights in the cockpit dimmed and he had no more strength. Then he lapsed back in his seat, panting, shaking. "They've got us, Pulou," he whispered, and watched as the ship's hull enveloped them.

There was no answer. He turned his head.

The gan sagged in his straps.

"Pulou?" he said.

He struggled free of his harness, tried to rise from his seat—

His legs gave way. He hit the deck on his knees, and the shock blacked him out.

He came to with his head lying against Pulou's leg. He pushed himself back, slowly.

Pulou's eyes were open, unblinking, unseeing. There was blood on his fangs, on his tongue, on the hand that had been pressed to his body.

"No!" Tristan gulped it, shook his head. "No, Pulou!"

He fumbled with the buckles. When they gave, the gan crumpled forward on top of him.

Tristan caught him, pulled him from the seat, lowered him to the deck.

From outside the shuttle came a clatter, the squeal and bang of heavy equipment, the ring of bootfalls and voices. They echoed in the hollow of the ship's hold.

Catching his lower lip in his teeth, Tristan began to stroke the gan's mane.

He had been here before, waiting in the close dark, years ago. . . .

An outer hatch slammed open. Voices reached him— two or three of them, only meters away—but their words weren't understandable.

Boots rang in the outer compartment. Over the pulse in his ears, he heard an oscillating hum.

The hum shot to a sharp whine; the boots stopped outside the cockpit. Tristan heard an order—

—and then banging. Metal clashing on metal until he thought his head would split. He clenched his teeth to keep from crying out.

When the shield door tore away, Tristan stared up at three fire-suited shapes silhouetted against the dull light.

* * *

Motioning the others to wait, Chesney stepped over the wreckage of the shield door into the cockpit. Her palm light swept its interior, picking out the boy who huddled beside one acceleration seat, cradling another figure across his lap.

He recoiled from the light in his face, bared his teeth and lifted a hand curled like claws. "Leave us alone!" he cried.

"Oh, boy," she breathed into her pickup. "Brandt, I think we're gonna need some assistance in here."

The ship's surgeon shouldered past her.

"Get back!" the boy said. "Stay away from my brother!"

"Calm down, son." The surgeon edged nearer him. "It's okay now."

The boy shoved himself to his feet.

And buckled.

Brandt caught him under the arms, kept him from falling. "Get a sled in here!" he shouted into his pickup.

There was a moment's scramble, and Chesney moved back to let the medics through, guiding their repulsion sled.

Brandt eased the boy onto it and paused to pull off his smoke mask and heavy gloves. "Kid feels like a reactor gone critical!" he said with a quick glance up at Chesney as he accepted a medkit from a subordinate. She watched as he knelt by the sled and motioned at one of his techs. "Get his vital signs, Kerin."

When his patient stirred, gasped, attempted to sit up, Brandt pushed him back down and dodged a swipe at his face. He caught the boy's hand, and Chesney saw how he had to struggle to keep his grip. "Schey," he called, "we're going to need restraints here!"

"No!" Tristan screamed it. "Let me go! Leave me alone!"

"Calm down, calm down," Brandt said, and held on to his wrist while Schey slipped a padded cuff around it and clamped the cuff to the edge of the sled. He repeated the procedure with the other wrist and both ankles as well.

"Let me go!" the boy gasped. His eyes were wild with delirium and fear.

Brandt placed a hand on his shoulder. "Relax, son. It's all right now. Relax and let us help you."

He took an intravenous pump-pack, designed for use in zero-g environments, from the medkit. Normal saline, Chesney noticed. Brandt clipped it to his patient's tunic and reached for his arm.

Crouched across the sled from him, Kerin pressed the boy's other hand to a sensor screen. She looked up from its readouts. "Sir, temperature is forty-point-five degrees Celsius, pulse is one-twelve, and blood pressure is ninety over fifty-six. Respirations are shallow."

"Give supplemental oxygen and apply cold packs and a hypothermic wrap," Brandt snapped. He let go of the youth's arm. "Won't do. Schey, I need a cut-down kit and an extra hand here. We'll have to put the intracath in the subclavian." He seized the tunic near Tristan's neck and ripped it away from his shoulder.

It tore down the shoulder and side seam, revealing the brace and the morphesyne infuser.

Brandt raised an eyebrow, glanced up at Chesney. "Someone's been taking good care of him," he said. He touched the memory button; the last infusion had been almost three hours before. He pressed the pad. "This should help, son."

Schey unrolled the cut-down kit on Tristan's chest, smeared his collarbone with antiseptic and local anesthetic, sprayed liquid gloves over Brandt's hands.

At the hum of the laser scalpel, Tristan jerked at the restraints, trying to wrench away. "No!" The oxygen mask didn't muffle his voice much. "Leave me alone!"

"Hold him still!" said Brandt.

"I'll do it." Chesney pulled off her smoke mask and gloves and crouched down near the head of the sled. Taking the boy's head, cold packs and all, between her hands, she turned his face away from the scalpel and began to smooth back his hair with her fingers. "Settle down, Tris," she said quietly. "Settle down. You're going to be all right; Brandt's the best."

She felt him stiffen at the incision, saw the fear in his face, and kept smoothing his hair. "You'll be all right," she said again.

A few moments later, Brandt said, "Good," and sat back on his heels, studying the pump-pack as he peeled off the spray-on gloves. "Okay, move him," he said. "Get him nerve-clipped, catheterized, and onto the hemo system. He'll need only minimal sedation. I'll be in to run a scan as soon as I've seen to this other one." He jerked a thumb toward the slumped figure Tristan had been supporting.

Schey and Kerin maneuvered the med sled out of the shuttle, and Chesney followed.

They left her outside the trauma unit. She stood in its doorway and watched, hands knotted hard at her sides, as they moved the youth onto the table and attached its tubes and wires. He seemed to have given up struggling; he groaned only once at the handling.

Brandt followed minutes later, looking grim; he didn't appear to notice Chesney standing there. "How are his vital signs now?" he asked.

Kerin read them off, and he nodded and checked the tubes that ran from the hemomanagement system to the intracath near his patient's collarbone. "What about blood gases?"

"Stabilizing, sir, and the sedative has taken effect."

"Good." Brandt flicked on the holoscanner and studied its display from beneath lowered brows. "Necrosis has set in," he said as if to himself, and looked at the med techs. "Get him prepped for surgery."

Turning away from the table, he finally spotted Chesney, still standing at the doorway. As if reading the questions in her face, he crossed to her. "We'll have to destroy the right kidney," he told her. "It dropped when the connective tissue tore. That put a kink in the ureter and the kidney's been backing up; it's swollen to half again its normal size." He glanced over his shoulder and shook his head. "It would've poisoned him before long—if the fever hadn't killed him first."

Chesney swallowed. "What are his chances?"

"He should pull through," Brandt said, "but it's going to be touchy for a while."

She allowed herself a sigh. Then, recalling the battle she'd watched from the bridge, she asked, "What in great space kept him going?"

"Adrenaline, probably," said Brandt. "The blood work shows high levels of it. You can't predict how that will affect people."

She considered that for a moment, then looked at the surgeon directly. "Has the rescue team found any sign of Nemec or the doctor yet? There were supposed to be four aboard that shuttle."

"Not a trace," said Brandt.

She shook her head and let her vision settle to the deck for a while, pensive, before returning it to the youth on the surgical table. "Maybe he knows what happened."

"Well, if he does," Brandt said, "he won't be up to being debriefed until at least tomorrow. Excuse me, ma'am; I have to go scrub."

Through a window, Chesney watched him manipulate the surgical robot, using keys like a computer's cursor and the holoscanner's display to guide its skipping laser over Tristan's right side. Watched via the display as the laser gradually vaporized the damaged kidney and ureter and repaired the torn tissues. Watched as Brandt cleaned up and closed the opened lacerations across the boy's back.

"He'll make a complete recovery," Brandt said afterward. "I'm putting him on antibiotics and a regen, and we'll keep a close eye on him for the next few days, but what he needs most now is rest."

Chesney released a breath in a rush. "Let me know when he wakes up," she said.

He was in the blue cavern again, running, and soldiers that he couldn't see were shooting at him and Nemec and Weil. He was telling them to hurry when a shield door closed across the tunnel behind him. He tried to reach the door, to stop it, but Nemec disappeared behind it, a startled expression on his face.

He turned around in time to see a bolt of energy catch Weil in the shoulder and throw him into the wall. "Weil!" he shouted, and tried to go to him, but he couldn't move. And then Weil disappeared, too. "Weil, no!" he said. He stood alone, paralyzed, in crossfire that screamed around him. . . .

"Tristan." A hand closed on his shoulder. "Tristan, wake up."

The hand, the voice, seemed familiar. "Weil?" he gasped, and turned his head with an effort.

He didn't know the man who stood beside him. He swallowed. "You're not Weil," he said.

"No; I'm Commander Brandt, ship's surgeon," the man said. "You're aboard the Spherzah ship *Sentinel*."

"Spherzah?" Tristan hesitated. "Is—my father here?"

"No," said Brandt, "but he sent us. Just relax now. You were dreaming."

He lay a small screen with the outline of a hand on it on the bed and pressed Tristan's hand to it, like the computer in the academy's med booth. He scanned the readouts when they appeared and, seeming satisfied, put the screen away. "You're doing pretty well," he said. "How do you feel?"

"Sore," Tristan said. "All over."

"That's understandable. Can you sit up?"

He turned onto his side, wincing, and let Brandt help him sit up. He sipped at the cup of water Brandt brought him.

"Tristan," the surgeon said, watching him, "can you tell me who this Weil is that you were dreaming about?"

"He's the doctor who—" The dream flashed across his memory again, and he stopped, looking away from Brandt. "I think he's dead," he said, his voice a bare whisper. "Both of them are. The shield door closed Nemec into the passage." He shuddered, almost spilling the water.

Brandt took back the cup and studied him briefly, then said, "We need to get you up and walking a little. I think you'll feel better. Put your feet over the side first; that's it. Now hold on to my arm."

Pushing himself to his feet, Tristan locked his teeth at the rending ache in his muscles. He was surprised that there wasn't more pain in his ribs, or in his right side. He looked at Brandt.

"We applied some neural clips to specific nerves," the surgeon said, "so they'll block localized pain without immobilizing you. They can come out in three or four days."

He still limped a little, walking. Had to lean on the surgeon. But the effort cleared the grogginess and the clinging dream from his mind.

Coming back to his cubicle, he stopped at the door to scan each corner and then the shadowed space under the bed. He felt his chest tighten. "Where's Pulou?" he asked.

Brandt supported him to the bed before he said anything, and then he looked Tristan in the face. "He didn't make it," he said gently. "It was already too late when we found you. I'm sorry."

Tristan's head drooped. His throat constricted so tight that it hurt; he couldn't even whisper.

"I don't think he suffered much," Brandt said. "He

hardly knew he'd been hit; there was very little external bleeding."

Tristan shook his head, unable to speak. It made his whole chest ache inside, made it hard to breathe. Suddenly weary, unable to sit any longer, he turned away from the surgeon and lay down on his side with his face to the bulkhead. He waited for the sobs to come, but they didn't; the ache just swelled like a stream behind a logjam until he thought it would stop his heart.

TWENTY-TWO

There were no orbital stations in the Saede system. The Bacalli carrier *s'Adou The'n* and its convoy assumed standard orbit around the planet while the landing parties boarded their shuttles.

When his aide brought word to the bridge that they were ready, b'Anar Id Pa'an gestured to its captain, the human named Mebius. "You will leave this system when I order it," he said.

His boots rang in the corridor; his battle gear rattled as he walked. The sound of it heightened his pulse, heated his blood. Seeing his glower, others in the corridor pressed themselves to the bulkheads until he passed.

In the lift to the launch bays, he asked his aide, "Where is the human woman?"

"She is aboard the shuttle as you asked, sire."

She was seated by herself in a corner at the back of the craft, under guard. She looked weary but not frightened. Even when Pa'an pushed the guard aside and stood staring down at her, she returned his gaze.

He grunted and turned away. "She will stay with me at the command post," he told the guard.

They touched down on one of the shuttle pads serving

the Unkai Peninsula's main supply and transshipment depot, in a narrow valley ringed with mountains like a carnivore's teeth, except that they were green with jungle foliage. The air, when the shuttle hatch opened and it burst inside, was hot and wet and smelled of vegetation. Pa'an wrinkled his nose at it as he came down the ramp.

Masuk troops stood in loose formation among the trees that hemmed and half-concealed the landing pad, waiting to board the shuttle for the flight to their troop ship. As Pa'an and his party touched soil, umedo captains called their troops to attention, their translators carrying electronic words over the rasp of their natural voices. Pa'an disregarded their salutes, strode past with his canines bared at them, and boarded the waiting troop carrier.

It lurched forward, its tracks clawing into the loam. Pa'an saw how it almost threw the woman from her bench. She braced herself, ignoring his leer, as the vehicle left the clearing and rumbled along its track under a canopy of living green.

A few kilometers later, it came into a clearing before a tunnel entrance.

Command post and control facilities, vehicle shelters and storage vaults, had been bored into the mountains. At the entry control point, where umedo guards held the gates, Pa'an left his party with the carrier, left the heat and misty sunlight for the cool of underground.

With a umedo escort he crossed the hollow of the main loading area and the intersection of corridors beyond, took a lift down into the mountain's bowels, and emerged in another corridor. The amphibian led him straight on, to double doors that parted as they approached.

The command post was an amphitheater: four tiers of seats, all equipped with secure visiphones, facing a holotank that filled the opposite wall. At the moment, the holotank displayed an astral map of Saede and Ogata, Sostis and

Yan, and showed the positions of the Isselan and Bacalli fleets.

Pa'an surveyed it before he acknowledged the presence of the others: mostly human flag officers from Issel and Adriat, a few umedos, the masuk field commanders who had come for the exercise. He put out his hand to the masuki, palm forward in greeting, and each clasped it in turn, baring tusks in a grin.

He didn't approach the humans or the umedos. He held his place until they approached him, as befit a son of the Pasha of Mi'ika.

One of the humans addressed him, a man with many medals and thinning hair. "You've arrived earlier than expected, Pa'an. We've had no orders from the Sector General—"

"That is because I carry them." Pa'an reached into his tunic and produced a sheaf of folded pages. "They will be executed at my command."

"At *your* command?" Pa'an read the human's indignation in his face, saw distaste in his look and the sudden set of his jaw; but another, his features no less grim, put a hand on his arm.

Pa'an unfolded the sheaf with care, smoothed the creases, passed it over to the human who wore the greatest rank, and waited while he and his deputies examined the way the Sector General's seal was laser-burned through each page, making the document official—as if they disdained to believe him.

"The orders are plain," he said. "The Isselan first fleet and the Saedese fourth are to launch at once. The fourth will move against Yan; and the first, when it is joined by the ships I have brought from Issel, will depart Ogata for its strike against Sostis."

Captain Benjamin Horsch glanced at the timepanel over the navigator's station, then turned to Lujan. "Think I'll try to get some shut-eye while I've got the chance, sir. Who knows what we'll be in the middle of in another few hours."

"Good idea," Lujan said. "I'll probably turn in soon myself."

Horsch nodded and addressed the officer of the deck. "Mr. Dowlen, I'll be in my quarters if anything comes up before zero-six-hundred."

"Aye, aye, sir," said the OOD, and then, as Horsch stepped into the lift, "Captain off the bridge!"

Lujan returned his attention to the forward screen.

According to the message traffic, Issel's hidden task force had broken orbit from Ogata fourteen standard hours ago; it would be ten or twelve hours more before the long-range scanners picked up the first contacts, when the Isselan fleet made lightskip.

Buhlig rolled before them, tugging at its elliptical orbit like a rotund pet on a leash. The light of its star turned its atmosphere of methane and ammonia to amber and gave its windswept cloud cover the appearance of long, soft fur.

But it wouldn't provide a gentle landing for Isselan ships emerging from lightskip. They would have to use the planet's gravity and rotation for propulsion into their next 'skip, and that flight path had already been calculated. Sostish minelayers plied that corridor now, seeding it with langrage the size of skimcraft. There were no explosives; mass and timing were all that were necessary. In a few standard days, Buhlig's gravity would clear the mines, drawing them to itself in decaying orbits.

Meanwhile, the Spherzah fleet could only wait.

Allowing himself a sigh, Lujan turned toward the lift. As the door slid closed behind him, he heard the OOD announce, "Admiral off the bridge."

He took the long way up to the flag quarters, crossing through the hangar decks but staying well back to watch the deckcrews at work so they wouldn't glimpse him and call the area to attention.

Destrier had four hangar decks, each supporting a squadron of twenty fighters with its own maintenance crews and equipment, its own launch and recovery ramps. *Destrier*'s fighter complement was almost twice that of the *Venture*'s—the carrier from which Lujan had flown against Dominion Station—but the feeling was the same. He read it in the faces of the deckcrews and in the fighters poised in their bays.

Except for the pilots on cockpit alert, standing by to relieve the ones flying combat space patrols, there were no spacecrews in the hangars. They were on crew rest, supposed to be sleeping. Lujan knew better. They might be in their berths, might be lying with closed eyes, but unless they had taken patches they wouldn't be asleep. Every nerve, every muscle, would be taut, anticipating the klaxon that would call them to their cockpits.

Lujan wouldn't be flying in this battle, but he felt the same tension in his own body.

The flag quarters were dark when he stepped inside. Almost. Starlight poured through the three observation panes, each nearly the height and width of a man, and spilled over the carpet.

Lujan crossed to the nearest pane. He stood there for a long while, looking out on the silent stars, the spinning planet.

In another few hours the space surrounding that planet would be littered with the debris of battle: the battered hulks of ships, the frozen fragments of human bodies. He set his jaw, remembering the aftermaths of the battles he'd fought during the War of Resistance.

But he also knew what the cost would be to Sostis if the price were not paid here at Buhlig. He had also seen what the Dominion had once done to Issel.

The weight of it made his shoulders sag. He stepped back, still facing the starfield, and knelt, resting his hands on wide-planted knees and bowing his head.

He had no idea how long he'd been praying there when the intercom on the bulkhead buzzed. He raised his head, turned slightly. "Open."

The officer of the deck appeared in its screen; he looked instantly apologetic. "Excuse me, sir—"

Lujan reassured him with a motion of one hand and rose to his feet. "What is it?"

"Sir, scan has reported a contact, bearing zero-four-three, declination two-seven, range ten thousand kilometers. Speed is undetermined; it appears to be decelerating from lightskip reentry."

Lujan glanced at the timepanel. Twenty-five standard hours since the Isselan fleet had departed Ogata. The timing was right. He said, "Only one contact?"

"Two now, sir—no, three. Captain Horsch is ordering the ship to general quarters."

"Good," Lujan said. "Tell him I'll be in the Combat Information Center."

As the stateroom door slid shut behind him, the address system filled the passages with the alert horn and the deck officer's voice: "General quarters, general quarters! All personnel man your battle stations!"

In moments the slam of hatches and shield doors sealing echoed through the bulkheads: insurance for the carrier's integrity under attack. Lujan strode along the passage with one shoulder to the bulkhead as the spacers pressed past him to their posts. Some wore the pressure suits and oxygen packs of Damage Control, others the helmets and heat vests of gunners. Recognizing him, they nodded acknowledgment and quickened their pace.

The fleet looked like a new constellation, thought Mebius: stars winking into existence in the shadow of Buhlig.

—Until one of them exploded.

It didn't happen all at once. Secondary detonations ripped along its hull in what seemed to be a chain reaction, rolling it over and over and leaving it to burn until its internal atmosphere was finally exhausted.

"We've lost the carrier *Accolade!*" said the communications officer.

Mebius spun about in his chair. "What—? Scan!"

The scan operator bent over his console, brow creasing. "Asteroids," he said after a minute. "We've come out in an asteroid field!"

"Shields full-front!" said Mebius. "All ships, fire braking thrusters! Reduce speed to—"

"All ships have not cleared lightskip, sir!"

Another ship broke clear as he watched, and smashed, still scan-blind, into an asteroid. It blossomed like a supernova, just port of the *s'Adou The'n*, lighting up space with a moment's fireball and hurling debris through the fleet like shrapnel.

"Lost radio contact with the destroyer *s'Ahbad!*" said the comms officer.

"Sir—" The scan officer almost choked. "We have numerous contacts, bearing three-one-seven, declination three-three-three! Estimate sixty contacts, range eight-niner-five-two kilometers."

"On screen!" said Mebius.

Beyond the asteroid field, the blips came up like a three-dimensional wall across space.

Mebius sank back in his command chair and cursed. "These aren't asteroids," he said. "They're space mines."

The masuk personnel on the bridge looked puzzled; k'Agaba Id Qum, the officer who stood at Mebius's right, growled, "What is this?"

"An ambush." Mebius straightened, in control once more. "All ships, battle stations! Accelerate to launch speed and prepare all fighters for takeoff."

* * *

The last "manned and ready" calls were coming in as Lujan
entered the Combat Information Center. He looked at the
operations officer.

"All stations report manned and ready, Condition Zed
set throughout the ship, sir," Ops reported, and turned to
the three-dimensional display glowing over the projection
table. "We had forty-two contacts, lost two in the minefield.
Range is eight-three-four-four kilometers, speed point-
eight-three kilometers per second."

Lujan absorbed the display with a look: forty points of
red light sliding into battle positions against his fleet of
sixty, marked in green. "Fighter status?" he asked.

"Three squadrons launched, sir. The fourth is standing
by."

"Get them off. And the other carriers?"

"The same, sir."

"Let's go," said Lujan.

The ops officer keyed his pickup. "Charger Fleet, this is
Charger Base. Launch all remaining fighters; I say again,
launch all remaining fighters. Execute!"

Lujan saw the hangar decks through the vision of memory. Pilots sealing their helmets and canopies and firing up
engines until their scream drowned the orders ringing
through the address system. Deck crewmen in tethered
pressure suits pulling power cables, guiding the fighters
into the ramps, setting the catapults.

"Charger Group, this is Charger Base," Ops said into his
microphone. "We've got multiple contacts bearing zero-
four-three, declin two-seven, holding positions at range
seven-niner-two-zero. Acknowledge."

"Charger Base, Charger Lead. Contacts at zero-four-
three and two-seven, roger." The lead pilot's voice was a
crackle over the bulkhead speaker. "Request release to vec-
tor for intercept with weapons free."

Ops glanced back.

"Given," said Lujan.

"Release is given," Ops said into his pickup. "Bag us some hairballs, Charger Group!"

Lujan studied the display over the ops officer's shoulder, watching the points of light which were the fighters forming up: one squadron taking defense stations around the carrier, the others arcing away to the attack.

"Sir, we have numerous incoming small craft!" said the scan officer. "Coming in from bearing three-five-zero, declination three-three-three, range four-eight-niner-three."

Mebius leaned forward in his command chair. "All ships, Warning Red! Weapon systems to active mode! All carriers, launch your fighters."

In a few moments they were visible on the forward screen: points of light that shattered into whole squadrons of attacking craft as they drew near enough for scan to distinguish them. Mebius's hands turned hard on the arms of his chair. On either side of him, masuk eyes were narrowed to slits and masuk teeth were bared.

"Charger Base, this is Charger Lead." The pilot's voice rattled through the Combat Information Center. "I'm picking up numerous weapons signals but only from half the fleet. My scope says the rest of 'em are—transports."

Ops exchanged a glance with Lujan. "Are you sure of that, Charger Lead?"

"Dead sure, sir."

"First wave, target only the combatants," Lujan said quietly, "but stay sharp; it looks suspicious. If they are transports, the third wave can take them."

"Roger, Base," said Charger Lead. And then, "Charger Group, form into first, second, and third attack waves according to squadron. Each wave make your run from a different angle and heading to throw off their trackers. Acknowledge."

"Lead," another flyer broke in, "I'm painting multiple bogies, bearing zero-one-zero, declin five-four, range one-three-niner-eight."

"I've got 'em, too," Lead said after a moment. "Heads up, Group; they sent out a welcoming committee!"

Lujan studied the tactical display. The enemy fighters weren't visible in it yet but it'd be too late by the time they were. He saw how the Spherzah battle cruisers and destroyers held their battle spread formation, loose enough to prevent the enemy from shooting into a crowd, close enough to provide mutual cover. "Request all ships to upload missiles and put fire-control on standby," he said.

Ops relayed the order.

Pilot chatter filled the speakers:

"Tally two, tally two! Coming in at zero-one-four!"

"Got 'em noses-on, inside one thousand kilometers!"

"Plasma cannon armed. Centering the box. . . ."

Green lights converged on red, too far away to follow the attack with any visual detail. But the audio painted a clear scenario.

". . . heavy fire from the destroyers. Lost Devin and Raphel!"

"Closing on the frigate. . . . It's a kill, it's a kill!"

. . . And then, "I'm hit! I'm hit!" The cry burst through the static of distance, rang over the rest of the chatter. "Ordnance launch and targeting systems are disabled. . . . Aborting the mission."

"Alert the deckcrews," said Lujan.

The system-failure lights warned that her starboard engine was gone, too. Gryfiss shut it down, pulled the T-handle to cut off fuel, toggled the switches of the starboard directional thrusters; they'd have to substitute for the main thrust to get her home.

As she left the destroyers' rockets and the fighters' searing ribbons of plasma cannon–fire behind, her breathing began to steady under her oxygen mask. But her mouth was dry. Her voice was a rasp when she said, "Base, this is Charger Eight. I'm coming in with my starboard engine blown. This'll be an emergency egress."

"Roger that," said the controller. "You're cleared for ramp one, Charger Eight. Emergency personnel are standing by."

Approaching the carrier, Gryfiss concentrated on the emergency landing and egress lists: check pressure-suit integrity, initiate cockpit depressurization, release canopy locks for nonejection egress, check landing gear, fuel lines, electrical systems . . .

She had to bring the craft around twice, leaning hard on the thruster switches to make a tight enough bank before the AG lights showed green. Ramp one loomed up like a square mouth. She fired braking thrusters, extended landing gear and hooks, and locked her cockpit harness against the impact with the arresting net.

Emergency personnel in pressure suits dashed out from equipment bays, surrounding her craft even before the ramp doors slammed closed. Gryfiss didn't notice. Both hands flew over switches and knobs, shutting down the remaining engines, fuel lines, electrical systems. Sweat streamed off her forehead under her helmet. She yanked the canopy trigger, popping it open.

"Engine's in bad shape," she heard in her earphones, "but it doesn't look like there's much risk of fire. Go ahead and pressurize." It was her crew chief, standing under the damaged engine and gesturing at an unseen ramp operator.

A noise like a wind filled the bay. The influx of oxygen snatched flames from the stricken engine, sweeping them up at the cockpit.

Gryfiss dived headlong over the port wing, knocking over two crewmen who reached up to break her fall. Personnel with extinguisher packs shot gray foam at the engine, sending it spattering off the wing and across the canopy before the crew chief confirmed the fire was out. Then he sent a couple of deckies up to pin the ejection seat and plasma-cannon studs, and to secure the tow bar that swung down from its overhead track.

Gryfiss followed her craft down the ramp, through four sets of shield doors that opened before them and closed behind, into the heart of the hangar deck. She loosened her helmet seals as she walked, and pulled off its rounded weight.

"You did everything right, Lieutenant," said the crew chief, clapping her on the shoulder. "Emergency procedures, safety checks, everything by the book. We'll replace that engine and have your bird turned around in forty-five minutes."

Gryfiss only nodded, watching men and mechanicals maneuver her fighter into its bay, running her hand through sweaty hair. She was still watching, working off her gloves, when the fighter exploded.

TWENTY-THREE

The concussion hurled Lujan over the projection table in the Combat Information Center, two levels above the hangar bays. He struck the deck hard on his right shoulder as all the displays in the Center blacked out.

He knew what it meant: the ship's computer had cut power to threatened areas. The Combat Information Center would be sealed off, with only emergency lighting and communications and minimal ventilation, until the fire danger was under control.

He pushed himself up, teeth locked. He had to use his left arm to do it; the right one wouldn't bear his weight, and pain lanced through his shoulder.

He was reaching out for the table, to pull himself to his feet, when someone on the deck nearby groaned. It was too dim to see who it was or even where he was at first, but Lujan recognized the Ops officer's voice. "Robard," he said, turning toward the sound. "What's wrong?"

"My back—"

"Don't move. I'll try to contact the bridge."

Lujan winced, gaining his feet—staggered under a moment's dizziness—and leaned on the intercom button. "Serege to bridge, come in!" The words came as if he'd been running.

There was no visual, and the audio was half lost in static, but he knew it was the captain who replied. "Admiral, are you all right?"

"We're intact, Ben, but—" Lujan glanced around the CIC, at the shadows that were scan operators slumped over blank consoles, and Robard on the deck. "—there're some injuries. What happened?"

"Explosion in hangar deck one, sir. Cause unknown at this time," said Horsch. "It started fires in hangar two and the pilots' quarters up one deck as well. Damage Control is on the way."

Lujan nodded. "How many casualties?"

"Thirty-nine presumed dead, sir. Sixty-seven reported injuries so far, some serious."

"There's at least one serious injury down here," Lujan said, glancing around at Robard, "and there may be more."

His own knees felt as if they might give out; the pain in his shoulder was increasing, and the CIC was already stuffy and too warm. But he said, "Our intership comms and tracking displays are down, Ben. Is Communications still functioning?"

"Yes, sir."

"Patch through to the carrier *Ouray* and request them to keep us informed until we're back on-line."

"Aye, aye, sir," he heard. And then remotely, "Admiral? Are you still there?"

Someone was moving him, turning him. A stab through his shoulder shocked him back to awareness, made his breath catch. He opened his eyes.

A firefighter and a med tech, both with sweaty faces and smoke masks dangling, bent over him in the dim red of emergency lighting. He was sweating, too. "Help Robard first," he said, motioning toward the Ops officer.

"Relax, sir," the fireman said. "They're with him already."

"The crew at the consoles—"

"Mostly just cuts and bruises, sir. They're okay. Take it easy."

The med tech ripped his uniform from his shoulder with one practiced yank, baring massive bruises down his right side and the old scars that twisted around his upper arm. His shoulder was misshapen and already discolored. He grimaced. "Is it broken?"

"Dislocated, sir," said the med tech, probing the joint. "It's swollen some but it doesn't look too bad. More painful than anything else." She shifted back and offered a hand to help him sit up. He clenched his teeth at the pain that came with the movement—passed his good hand over his face when his vision momentarily tunneled.

"Take it easy, sir," the medic said. She took the canteen from her web belt, twisted off its cap, offered it to him. "If you'll come back to sick bay with us, we can run a holoscan and reposition your shoulder."

Lujan took a couple of swallows from the canteen and said, "There'll be time for that when the battle's over. Just wrap it up so it's not in the way. I'll come in later." He surveyed the Combat Information Center, saw medics strapping Robard onto a med sled, and shaken scan operators being ushered away from dead consoles. "Right now I have to get back to the bridge," he said.

"Admiral on the bridge!" someone shouted when the doors slid open to admit him.

Lujan said, "Carry on," and crossed to the communications station, where he steadied himself against its rail. But for the medic's blanket thrown around his shoulders he was naked to the waist, his right arm braced and bound against his chest.

"Admiral—" said Captain Horsch.

"I'll live," Lujan said through clenched teeth. "What's the battle status?"

"We're recovering the first wave of fighters now, sir," said the officer of the deck. "The second wave is over the target area. We've taken some losses but we've inflicted worse." He indicated the forward screen, where green lights and red, transmitted from the *Ouray*'s Combat Information Center, diagrammed the battle. Only two enemy carriers, two destroyers, and five planetary attack frigates remained of the combatants, and their flashing markers indicated damage.

"The first wave got a visual confirmation on the troop transports," the OOD continued, "and the third wave is forming up for a run on them."

"Are the transports armed?" Lujan asked.

"Minimal weapons, sir," the OOD said. "They're dependent on the combatants for defense."

"Then they're not to be destroyed," Lujan said. "Relay orders that only weapons and propulsion will be disabled. If life-support systems are left intact, the transports will suffice as POW facilities until we can remove the personnel—"

"Sir!" The communications officer pivoted around in her chair. "Sir, we've lost comms with the carrier *Ichorek!*" She pressed her earphones hard to her head, straining to hear. "Two internal explosions, seconds apart. . . . Both hulls have been breached!"

"On screen," said Horsch.

Across the distance, *Ichorek* looked like a broken, burning toy ship in the moment before another blast tore it to spinning fragments.

There was silence on the bridge for a full minute. Then Horsch said, "Where did the initial explosions occur?"

"In hangar deck two, sir," said the comms officer. "One of the forward launch areas. They had just recovered a couple of damaged fighters."

Lujan stiffened. "Where was Gryfiss's fighter recovered?"

"Deck one, sir."

"That's what I thought." Lujan said, "Alert the deck-crews on all carriers to inspect incoming fighters for any-thing abnormal and to take appropriate action. These explosions are not coincidences."

"Charger Fourteen, you're cleared for ramp three," said the controller.

"Ramp three, roger." Lieutenant Marney checked off his landing list and banked into final approach. The AG lights came into line. He reached out to extend landing gear—

—and a system-failure light blinked on: his port gear hadn't come down.

"Base, this is Charger Fourteen on the go," Marney said. "My gear's stuck. I'm giving it another try."

He went around three times, toggling the switch, tug-ging at the manual lever. The light stayed on.

"Base," he said, "I'll have to make a gear-up landing, arresting hooks only."

"Roger that," the controller said. "Emergency fill and arresting nets are in place, and artificial grav level is being reduced to point-five."

There was no shower of sparks, no shrieking noise in the ramp's vacuum when Marney's craft struck the emergency fill. It bounced, then fishtailed as it snagged the arresting net. When it skidded to a halt, he popped the canopy and leaped clear, and his deckcrew moved in from all sides.

In another moment, one of the deckies gulped, "Holy Dzhou!" and scrambled out from under the fighter. "Clear the area! There's an unexploded ordnance the size of a pulpfruit jammed up against the landing-gear cover!"

"Bridge, hangar three." The speaker sounded like he'd been holding his breath. "I think we've isolated the threat, sir."

Horsch pressed the intercom button to reply. "What is it?"

"A high explosive, sir, in a casing with suction surfaces," the crew chief said. "It came in attached to Lieutenant Marney's fighter. The EOD mechies took it apart and found an ambient pressure-timer detonator set to blow ten minutes after the pressure registers one atmosphere—just long enough to get a bird down into the hangar bays after pressurization."

Horsch glanced up at Lujan. "Limpets. Devious," he said. "How difficult are they to detect?"

"Not very, sir, now that we know what we're looking for," the crew chief answered.

"Then don't your lower guard," Horsch said. "There may be something else as well. No fighter will enter the pressurized hangar areas without a thorough inspection."

The crew chief said, "Aye, aye, sir."

And Lujan said, "Make that a general order to all carriers."

As the comms officer spoke into her pickup, Horsch returned his attention to the forward screen, his brow furrowed. "Battle status?" he said after a moment.

"The third wave has just cleared the target area, sir," said the comms officer. She listened briefly to the dialogue in her headset. "*Ouray* reports three transports destroyed and the rest disabled. According to Charger Lead, all enemy vessels are dead in space and some are still visibly burning."

Horsch acknowledged with a nod. "Open hailing frequencies to the Isselan flagship," he said.

"Aye, aye, sir." The comms officer worked briefly over her console keyboard, toggled a row of switches. In a few moments she said, "Sir, the carrier *s'Adou The'n* is responding."

The *s'Adou The'n*.

Lujan felt his heart contract, his stomach knot up. Darcie had been taken aboard the *s'Adou The'n*!

"Admiral," said Captain Horsch, and deferred the communication to him.

Lujan made himself draw a deep breath, straighten. Made himself loosen his sudden grip on the comms station railing. "Put them on-screen," he said. If Darcie were still on board, he would know soon enough.

He noted the mix of human and masuk officers in the bridge crew when the flagship came on-screen, and remembered the hologram of Darcie that Kapolas had delivered.

He recognized the ship's captain. Knew him, via intelligence briefings and news media, to be Edouard Mebius, one of Issel's foremost space-fleet commanders. Lujan fixed his vision on him. "In the name of the World Government of Sostis and the Unified Worlds," he said, "I order you to surrender your fleet."

"There is no honor in surrender!"

It was one of the masuki, the equivalent of a space-fleet captain by the shoulder clasp of his cloak. He said it with his teeth bared.

Lujan studied him as he said, "You don't have an alternative, Captain."

But if they were holding Darcie they would try to offer him one.

They didn't.

"We will die before we will surrender," said the masuk officer. "We will be worthless to you, Admiral Serege. And the most worthless one among us will die first!"

He half turned, snapped words that sounded like a snarl, and reached for the knife that rode bare-bladed in the sash of his tunic.

Two masuk subordinates flanking Mebius's command chair seized him by the arms, dragging him to his feet and forward before their superior. Mebius had no chance to struggle. He started to shout, "No—!" but one masuk twisted a hand into his hair and jerked his head back, stifling him.

"It is a worthless commander," said the masuk captain as he placed the point of his blade at the base of Mebius's neck, "who leads his force into an ambush. We will all die, Captain, but because it is by your mistake, you will die first."

With a motion surprisingly deft for thick masuk fingers, he flicked the blade up on its edge—

"Screen off!" said Horsch.

The faces of the bridge crew were pale, grim when Lujan glanced around. They knew what was happening on the bridge of the s'Adou The'n; they also knew what would be left when it was over.

Lujan forced it from his own mind. He watched Horsch press the intercom button, listened as he said, "Damage Control, report. What's our condition?"

The OIC who answered said, "Fires are out, Captain, but hangar deck one's been gutted and deck two's got fire damage as well."

"Ouray will have to recover some of our fighters, sir," said the officer of the deck.

Horsch nodded agreement. "See to it, Mr. Dowlen. I'm going below to check on the damage."

Standing in the blackened cavern that had been hangar deck one, Horsch and Lujan studied the scattered wreckage of Gryfiss's fighter. Flying fragments had touched off the fuel network and severed power cables. The Damage Control officer pointed out evidence of secondary blasts, the source of the fires.

Horsch asked, "How extensive is the structural damage?"

"Severe enough that we're not lightskip-capable, sir," said the DC officer. He indicated support beams across the overhead, which were bent like sportsmen's bows from the explosions. "Those would never withstand the stress of making 'skip, sir. They'd buckle and we'd have a chain reaction that would end with an implosion."

"Can the necessary work be done under way?"

The other studied the sundered overhead for a few moments and let out his breath in a whistle. "Yes, sir, it's possible," he said at last, and returned his attention to his captain. "But it'll take time."

"How much time?" Lujan asked.

"At least a full day, Admiral."

Lujan glanced at his timepiece. There was no alternative, he knew. But there were only forty-six standard hours until the rendezvous at Saede.

TWENTY-FOUR

"How's he doing?" Chesney asked.

"Physically," said Brandt, "he's doing okay. His vital signs are back to normal, the remaining kidney is functioning, and he's starting to get some strength back. But he still has no appetite and he's not sleeping well—he has a lot of nightmares. He's really touchy about his back and ribs, too. Looks like post-trauma stress."

Chesney glanced through the doorway into the cubicle. The boy lay on his belly with his face turned toward the bulkhead, and the bedsheet didn't cover the livid welts across his shoulders. She grimaced. "He's probably got enough reason for that."

"More than enough." Brandt sighed. "I've tried to persuade him to talk about it, but I haven't had any success. I thought that giving him some time alone with his friend might help, so yesterday I took him next door"—he jerked a thumb toward the neighboring cubicle—"where we're storing the body. He stood by the stasis capsule for a couple of hours, stroking the alien's hair, but that was all. He just seemed numb, even after I brought him back here." Brandt shook his head. "If he doesn't externalize it, he's going to end up with some real problems."

"So you want me to give it a shot?" asked Chesney.

Brandt nodded. "He seems more responsive to you, ma'am. It's worth a try."

Tristan didn't seem to be aware of her until she stood beside his berth and quietly spoke his name. Then he jumped. He turned his head as if it were too heavy and questioned her with eyes that betrayed his inner ache.

"Sorry, hotshot," she said. "I didn't mean to startle you. Feeling any better?"

"No," Tristan said. His eyes kept asking why she was there.

Chesney unfolded the seat attached to the bulkhead and sat down. "I thought you might want somebody to talk to."

"Why?"

She shrugged. "It helps more over the long haul than drinking does. Besides, your father would probably deep-space me if I got you blitzed."

There was a brief silence, and then, "I can't talk about it," the boy said.

Leave it alone for now, Chesney counseled herself. She leaned back on the narrow seat, stretched out her legs, and crossed her ankles. "You're quite a pilot," she said. "Even delirious. I didn't have to watch you handle that boat for very long to know it was Jink's kid at the controls."

"Jink?" said Tristan. He wrinkled his nose in evident puzzlement.

"Your father's nickname from pilot training," said Chesney. "It ended up becoming his running name. . . . He'd really be proud of you."

The boy looked away from her. "No, he wouldn't," he said.

She wasn't expecting that. She softened her tone. "Care to tell me why you think that, Tris?"

He shrugged, as well as he could lying down, and kept his face toward the bulkhead. "I don't know what to think about my father anymore," he said. "All that stuff about betraying people, and being an assassin, and—"

"*What?*" Chesney straightened abruptly on the folddown seat. "Who told you *that*?"

Tristan's vision jerked back to her. He swallowed hard. "Governor Renier," he said.

Chesney rolled her eyes. "He would," she said, and leaned forward. "Tristan, your father never betrayed anybody. He just did his duty—and it was probably one of the hardest duties he's ever had to carry out." She shook her head again. "We'd probably all be eating live dirvilice with pointed sticks and chanting prayers to some despot at the galactic center about now if he hadn't."

Tristan didn't make any reply to that, so she asked, "Does that clear up a few things?"

He only shrugged again.

"Feel any better now?"

He shook his head.

She studied him for a long while before she reached out to brush his hair away from his eyes. He started at her touch, locked his teeth on his lip, watched her warily.

"You're sure you don't want to tell me what's hurting you?" she said.

He only shuddered.

"Does it have to do with your father?" she persisted.

His features were taut, strained; he shook his head again. "I can't tell you!" he said.

"Even if it'd release all that pressure inside you?" she asked. "Even if it'd let you sleep without nightmares?"

"I *can't!*" he said again, and his breath caught, and he choked.

For an instant Chesney thought he might break down, spill it out that way and free himself; but he didn't. He just turned his face away and wouldn't look at her anymore.

"I'm sorry," she said at last, and drew the sheet up over his shoulders and left the cubicle.

On her way back to her quarters, she wondered what it would take, outside of Jonican whiskey.

She didn't have time to think about it when she arrived; a message line flashed on her desk terminal. She sat down with a sigh and keyed in her code. The text rolled down the monitor.

She scanned it quickly first, then leaned forward in her chair and read it through again:

IMMEDIATE
131638L 2 3308SY
TO COMMODORE C CHESNEY, ABOARD UWS SENTINEL
FM ADMIRAL L SEREGE, ABOARD UWS DESTRIER
S E C R E T
1. CONTACTED ENEMY ON SCHEDULE. IMMED THREAT TO SOSTIS CONTAINED AT COST OF ICHOREK AND BD TO DESTRIER.
2. ATTK ON SAEDE STILL ON SCHEDULE UNDER CMD OF CAPT RASSAT NIGHIA OF OURAY DUE TO BD TO DE-STRIER. YOU HAVE YOUR ORDERS. WILL JOIN YOU WHEN ABLE.
3. DARCIE CONFIRMED NOT ABOARD S'ADOU THE'N; POSSIBILITY SHE IS AT UNKAI UGF ON SAEDE.
4. MASUK MORALE APPEARS SERIOUSLY DEGRADED. EXPECT SUICIDAL TACTICS AND DESPERATE ACTIONS.
E N D   O F   M E S S A G E

Chesney cleared the terminal's memory, but one paragraph of the message kept repeating itself in her mind.

Maybe it wouldn't take Jonican whiskey after all, she thought.

She returned to sick bay when Evening Watch began and the ship's lighting dimmed to simulate nighttime. She paused in the doorway of Tristan's cubicle.

The boy didn't appear to have stirred since she'd left. "You awake, Tris?" she said quietly.

He didn't answer at once, and when he did the single word was half-muffled by his pillow. He didn't move at all.

She went in and unfolded the seat and sat down again. She didn't say anything at first, just reached out to run her hand up and down his bare arm where it lay on the bed.

After a while she said, "You're blaming yourself for whatever happened, aren't you?"

He turned his head to look at her then, and the agony in his eyes was undiminished. "They were trying to help *me*. It should have been *me* that died! I never should have—"

"Tris, don't." Chesney placed her hand over his. "This is war. Nemec was a soldier—a Spherzah. He knew the risks when he accepted the Issel assignment. The medic and— your friend—probably knew, too. They *chose* to do what they did for you."

The boy lowered his gaze. "For me," he whispered. "It's not fair. Why would they do that for me?"

"Probably," said Chesney, "for the same reasons you chose to risk your life for your mother."

His vision shot up to meet hers. "My mother is dying! All I wanted was to help her—"

Chesney tightened her hold on his hand and leaned closer to him. "When I left here this morning," she said, "there was a message waiting for me. She's still alive, hot-shot, but this little crisis is far from over."

She saw how his face changed at that, how his jaw tightened and the pain in his eyes retreated before an edge of anger. "She's at Issel!" he said. "They brought her to Issel!"

"She's not there now," Chesney said. "The night you were flogged, they took her aboard another ship and left the system."

Tristan pushed himself up on his elbows. "For where?"

"We believe for Saede," she said, "and we're going after them."

"I'm going with you!" Tristan turned over and sat up fully.

"Wait, wait, throttle back a minute!" Chesney said. "You're getting the wrong message, hotshot. You've been through more than your share already—you just had major surgery three days ago!"

"I have to go," said Tristan, suddenly solemn. "I have to keep my *jwa'lai.*"

"Your what?" Chesney wrinkled her brow.

"My duty—my promise—to my mother."

Chesney shook her head. "Tris," she said, "you've already done your part. I think your mother will forgive you if you leave this one to the trained troops. Your duty right now is to get yourself well, got that?"

He didn't answer.

When Schey brought him dinner a short time after Chesney left, Tristan asked, "How long until we get to Saede?"

"About a standard day and a half," the med tech told him. "We'll make our last lightskip tomorrow morning."

Tristan grimaced.

"You can take a patch," said Schey. "You got through yesterday's 'skip okay."

Tristan didn't say anything; he just eyed the dinner tray.

He made himself eat everything on it, though most of the food was almost flavorless.

"It's good to see you getting your appetite back," Schey said when he came back to collect the tray. "You've lost a lot of weight in this ordeal."

Tristan only shrugged.

"Do you want a patch to help you sleep?" the medic asked.

"No," Tristan said. "It won't stop the dreams."

He resisted sleep as long as he could. It wasn't difficult

at first, even in the darkness. His mind was full of his mother and his *jwa'lai*.

But then he was running through the blue caverns again. It was always the same: the shield door that cut off Nemec's escape, the bright bolt of energy that slammed Weil to the wall.

He woke, sweating, at the sound of his own outcry and a hand shaking him by the shoulder.

"Are you sure you don't want a patch?" Schey asked, offering him a glass of water.

"Yes," Tristan said. "It won't help."

The next time he dreamed, it was of Pulou sagging in his acceleration harness and bleeding from invisible wounds, and his mother's body on a funeral pyre, enveloped by flames.

He was still awake after that one, staring hard at the bulkhead to keep from sleeping again, when Brandt came in. "You need to take a patch now."

"No!" Tristan said. "I don't want one!"

"We make lightskip in less than an hour," the surgeon said.

He didn't argue further. But he closed his eyes and gritted his teeth when Brandt pressed the patch to his temple.

When he woke it was mid-morning and Kerin was placing his hand on the vital-signs sensor. She said, "Hello, Tristan. Don't move for a minute. Are you ready for breakfast?"

"I want to get dressed," he said when she let him take his hand from the sensor plate and sit up.

She looked a little surprised, but she said, "I don't see why not. Go ahead and eat while I see what I can get for you."

She came back with a battle dress uniform in shades of streaky green and brown. "The stores officer doesn't have any shipboard uniforms," she said, "just a lot of these. It may be too big but at least it won't irritate your back."

The trousers were loose enough not to pinch or chafe,

and the tunic allowed him to move his arms freely. Satisfied, he picked up one of the boots. He examined it, turned it in his hands—then put it aside, wrinkling his nose.

"What's wrong?" Kerin asked, watching him.

"I can't walk in those."

She looked amused. "How far were you planning on going?"

"As far from this box as I can!" Tristan said, and indicated the cubicle with a motion. "I'm tired of being in here."

She raised an eyebrow. "What brought this on? Yesterday we could hardly pry you out even to go to the head."

He ducked his head and wouldn't look at her. "It hurts too much to think. I need to do something else."

"Yes, you do." Kerin's teasing subsided. "You haven't even seen the ship yet, have you? Maybe we can find someone who can give you a tour."

She was gone for a long time. He'd almost given up on it when there was a step at the doorway and Kerin said, "Tristan, you have a visitor."

He sat up on the bed when a young man came in: a trooper from *Sentinel*'s surface assault force who was only a few years older than himself.

"Tristan Serege?" he said. "I'm Eddie Yedropolappano, Petty Officer Second Class, Unified Worlds Spherzah."

"Yed-what?" said Tristan.

The other laughed. "Never mind; nobody else can say it, either. I go by Yeddy. How are you doing? They said you were hurt pretty bad when you escaped."

"I'm all right," Tristan said. "I'm just tired of sitting in here."

"Well, let's go have a look at the ship, then," Yeddy said, "and I'll introduce you to some of the others."

Walking up the passage beyond sick bay's doors, Yeddy glanced sideways at him and asked, "What's it like to have the Old Man for your father?"

"The old man?" Tristan cocked his head.

"That's what we all call him," Yeddy said. "It's sort of a—title of respect."

Tristan glimpsed unabashed admiration in the other's eyes. He puzzled over that for a moment. "I don't know what it's like," he said at last. "I don't remember."

They went forward from sick bay, crossing the recovery bay where Tristan's shuttle had been taken aboard, and climbed a ladder up one level to the troop quarters. Coming into the first bunking area, Yeddy said, "Be glad you have a room to yourself. There're twenty-four of us in here, and seven more areas just like this one."

Yeddy didn't take Tristan through all of them; half of the combat company was on its sleep shift. But he seemed to know everyone he met, and he introduced them to Tristan by name. The troops gathered around, asking questions and wanting to talk, until the faces lost their individuality and melded into a crowd. Then Tristan shot a desperate look across at his guide.

"That's enough, people," Yeddy said. "Give him some space."

Beyond the bunking area, the passage opened into a small dayroom furnished with holovids and cabinets full of chip texts. It was occupied by several more troops.

"We spend our off-duty time in here and working out in the rec deck," said Yeddy.

Tristan scarcely heard him. The far bulkhead was mostly viewpane and in the center of it drifted a teal-green globe. Tristan crossed to it, Yeddy still at his shoulder, and touched the pane. "Is this a holograph screen?"

"No," Yeddy said. "That's really Saede out there. That's where we're going."

"Why does it look so blurry?" Tristan asked.

"Because we're under cloaking," said Yeddy. "Do you know anything about jamming?"

"A little," Tristan said.

"That's kind of how it works," Yeddy said. "It makes us invisible to Saede's detection systems until we're close enough to launch the landing craft. The rest of the attack force is probably out there by now but they're under cloaking, too."

Tristan acknowledged with only a nod, his vision narrowed on the planet. "They've got my mother there," he said.

"They won't after tomorrow." Yeddy shot him a tight smile. "We're going hunting for hairballs in the morning."

"Hairballs?" Tristan furrowed his brow.

"You know—masuki. We call 'em that because they're all hairy." Yeddy's smile broadened a little, turned mischievous. "That's *not* a title of respect!"

Tristan recognized the expression in the other's eyes. He studied Yeddy for a moment. Then he said abruptly, "You said there were landing craft. Where are they?"

"Right under us, forward of the recovery bay," said Yeddy. "I should've shown you on the way up. You'll be able to hear the klaxon in sick bay. . . . You'll probably hear all of us running down there, too."

Tristan turned back to the viewpane and lowered his head. "Probably," he said.

He felt Yeddy watching him. "You want to go with us, don't you?" the other said.

"I have to go," said Tristan.

Yeddy hesitated. "We'll get your mother out," he said. "I promise."

Tristan glanced back at him, then out at Saede. His right side had begun a dull throbbing with all of the walking. He rubbed at it for a few moments. And he suddenly realized how weak he was, how worn he felt. "I need to go back to my room," he said.

He didn't speak, climbing the ladder back down to the

recovery bay and crossing its ringing expanse. He kept his teeth locked against the ache and his vision fixed mostly on the deck. Yeddy didn't say much either, until they stood at the doorway of his cubicle, and then he said again, "We'll get your mother out. You just take it easy and don't worry."

Tristan didn't answer.

Alone, he undressed and dimmed the lighting in his cubicle and lay staring at the bulkhead. Thinking. Planning. Reviewing in his mind what Yeddy had showed him about the layout of the ship. . . .

He was still there when Brandt came in on his evening rounds. He barely glanced up when the surgeon put the sensor plate on the bed beside him and reached for his hand.

"Your blood pressure's up a little," Brandt said a few moments later. "Did you wear yourself out, touring the ship today?"

"Yes," Tristan said.

"Well, maybe that'll help you sleep better tonight." Brandt put the sensor plate away. "I'll send someone in with your dinner in a few minutes."

Tristan ate everything on the tray again—found that he was hungrier tonight and it wasn't so much of an effort, although it didn't taste any better.

He got up after Schey came to take the tray and put on his battle uniform again. Then he lay back down to wait.

He hadn't slept before the klaxon sounded.

TWENTY-FIVE

Tristan jumped at its sudden scream and sat up, staring around the cubicle. His heart slammed hard and fast against his ribs, making him gulp for breath. Shoving himself out of the berth, he almost stepped on the discarded boots. He hesitated, then left them where they lay.

There was dim lighting in the corridor beyond the cubicle. Quiet on bare feet, Tristan made his way down it. The klaxon's repeated blasts covered the sound of the automatic door opening to let him through and then closing behind him.

The horns were louder outside sick bay but they didn't drown the sudden noise of bootfalls from the deck above. Tristan jogged across the recovery bay, pressing a hand to his right side when the motion sent little jabs through it.

The bulkhead that separated the recovery bay from the launch bay was designed to retract, to allow movement of craft from one to the other on rails and tracks. It could be opened only by a controller in a booth tucked up next to the overhead. But there were utility doors marked MAINTENANCE PERSONNEL ONLY in the forward corners, which were secured with manual bolts. Tristan tugged at the lever of the nearest one.

It grated partway down and stuck fast.

Beyond the bulkhead, the clatter of bootfalls crescendoed. There were voices, too, shouting orders, but he couldn't make out the words.

"Open up!" Tristan gasped. "Come on, open up!" He shifted his grip on the lever and threw his whole weight against it.

The effort shot lightning through his right side, despite the nerve clips blocking his healing ribs. His vision tunneled; he sagged against the door. But the lever had fallen; the door swung inward.

Panting, he slipped through and shoved the utility door closed behind him.

The clatter of boots turned to thunder. He looked up. The troops came down catwalks on either side of the launch bay in close file, double-time, to board the landing shuttles. They wore helmets and half-armor over their battle uniforms and carried energy rifles on their shoulders.

Tristan fell in at the rear of one column and followed it up the boarding ramp into the closest shuttle.

In its dimness, the troops strapped themselves into web seats that ran the length of the shuttle's hold. Tristan glanced around at them as he fastened his own straps. Their jaws were tight, their eyes narrowed behind camouflage paint. He didn't recognize any of them but he lowered his head, not wanting to be noticed.

When the ramp folded up at the rear of the craft, clanked into place and sealed, and the roar of engines shook the hull, he braced himself for the crush of acceleration.

The message from k'Agaba Id Qum was transmitted in masuk and b'Anar Id Pa'an knew that by the time he received it Qum and his crew, both masuk and human, were no more. He felt no grief, no loss: Qum had failed, and failure had exacted its price.

Pa'an had put the base on Warning Yellow status and hadn't left the command post since. It had been almost forty-eight hours. When the Unified forces struck Saede, *he* would not fail.

He straightened in the commander's chair when a light began to blink on the console before him. He looked at one of the human officers, who pushed its button and said, "Command Post, Colonel Pryce."

"We've got contacts, sir." It was another human, in the scan station. "Multiple tracks, range one-two-two-zero kilometers, speed one-zero-five kilometers per minute, bearing three-five-four. They just appeared out of the ether, sir, inside the orbital detection platforms."

Pa'an saw shock on the faces of the humans. "*Inside* the detection systems?" said one. "Have you got an identification, Lieutenant?"

"Not yet, sir," came the reply.

They exchanged glances, and the human with the greatest rank said, "Recommend we go to Warning Red, sir, with air defense weapons in passive tracking mode for the moment."

Pa'an considered, inclined his head slightly. "So be it," he said.

"Listen up, troops!"

It was Chesney's voice, and Tristan started, wrenching around to look.

She wasn't there; her voice came through speakers in the overhead. "The attack's under way," she said. "The carriers' birds are going in after the air defense systems and we'll be coming in right behind them. ETA is fifty-two minutes."

Tristan released his breath in a rush.

He knew when the craft entered the atmosphere. Weightlessness gave way to a sense of descent, and turbulence took the craft in its fist and shook it and roared at it. Tristan put his head back against the webbing, closed his eyes, drew in each breath through his mouth. It quelled the discomfort in his stomach but his hands still felt clammy. He rubbed them on his trouser legs.

The thunder of landing rockets swelled, then subsided, and the shuttle hovered on its thrusters. Around him, the troops scrambled free of their seat straps, adjusted battle harnesses, retrieved rifles from bulkhead racks. Then the aft hatch grated open, admitting a wave of wet heat and moonlight mottled with smoke, and the platoon leader shouted from the forward section, "Move out, double-time!"

Tristan shoved himself out of the web seat and moved, and the others came close behind.

Several shadows stood clear of the ramp and the thruster wash: platoon leaders, company commanders, and Chesney. Armored and armed like her troops, she was pointing, gesturing, giving orders.

Tristan tried to lose himself in a knot of soldiers, but Chesney had already spotted him. She caught him by the shoulder, and he cringed, half expecting for a moment that she would shake him, as gan mothers did to discipline their young. But she only said, "Have you lost your stabilizers, Tristan? What in great space do you think you're doing?"

"This is *my* battle!" he said. He had to shout it over the roar of thrusters as the empty shuttle lifted from the landing site.

"Like crikey it is!" Chesney's vision followed the shuttle, too, banking away over the tops of the trees. "Blast it!" she said. "Now I can't even send you back to the ship! Those crates aren't coming back until we've cleaned up this hole."

When she returned her attention to him, her face was stern. "I don't have any choice now but to take you along, so you listen to me, hotshot, and you listen good. If you so much as try to get out of my reach, I'll have you put under guard in restraints like a prisoner of war! You got that?"

The expression in her eyes left no doubt that she'd do it. Tristan said, "Yes'm."

She watched the troops form into platoons and move out in different directions. "Come on then," she said, and her voice had softened slightly. She started to turn away—but then she stopped short. "You don't even have any boots!"

"I can't walk in them," Tristan said.

She rolled her eyes. "Well, don't expect me to carry you when you step on a burr beetle!"

"No response from air defense batteries thirty-nine and forty-eight!" a human voice said over the speakers. "Several hits were registered in those sectors. Scan shows multiple light craft on approach to . . ."

Pa'an paused in his pacing to study the tracks on the holotank map through narrowed eyes, and his lips curled back from his teeth.

"Sir!" It was the human at the communications console. "Message coming in from the Issel system."

Pa'an turned around. "Put it on the holotank."

The holographic map and tracks vanished; another human face, larger than lifesize, replaced it: one of Governor Renier's chief generals at the Isselan Command Post.

Pa'an was weary of human faces, hairless and tuskless and impotent as a whelp's, but he said, "What is it?"

"Word from Yan, sir." The general appeared apprehensive at facing him even across light-years of space. "Our task force there was outnumbered and overwhelmed; the survivors were forced to retreat. It's absolutely imperative that you hold Assak Base on Saede."

Lips drew back from fangs again. "I will not fail," Pa'an said.

* * *

The night air was a vapor rising from soil and foliage, laden
with the scents of vegetation and decay. Its heat plastered
clothing to skin with sweat and made every breath an effort.
It was like traveling through Issel's blue caves again, Tristan thought, except for the scream and flash of fighters
overhead and the shock of explosions that shook the
ground underfoot. One step ahead of Chesney, two behind
the platoon leader, Tristan pressed a hand to his side and
forced himself to keep up.

The stench of decay persisted over the biting scent of
smoke as they went farther. When a fitful wind struck him
full in the face, Tristan gagged. He and Pulou had once
come upon a peimu carcass, dead for three or four days and
only half-eaten; it had smelled like that.

There was a shout from up front in the loose formation
and several members of the platoon drew up around the
bole of a tree.

"Umedo," said Chesney when two or three soldiers
played their palm lights over it. "At least, it was. Looks like
a masuk execution."

The corpse was vaguely humanoid but its face looked
unfinished to Tristan: mere slits where its nose should have
been, tympanic membranes in the place of ears. Its eyes
seemed to bulge from their sockets, its mouth was con-
torted in a silent scream, and all were thick with insects.

It had been tied to the tree trunk and laid open with a
knife stroke from gullet to groin; carrion eaters had mostly
disposed of its entrails.

Grimacing at the odor of rot, Chesney pulled a knife
from the back of her web belt and severed the cord that held
the umedo's hands. It fell forward into bloodied under-
growth, and the flies rose up in a cloud.

Chesney sheathed her knife and motioned at the platoon
leader, and he said, "Move out."

Resuming their positions, the troops moved easily through the trees, probing the dark on all sides through nightvision helmet visors.

Several minutes later, the soldier in the point position raised his hand in a signal to halt, dropped to his belly, and crawled forward. Only a ripple of fern fronds showed where he had disappeared.

The platoon leader touched his headset and turned to glance at Chesney. "He says the trees end about five meters beyond him and there's a clearing in front of the tunnel entrance. Says the ground's been torn up by tracked vehicles but there's no sign of personnel outside the entrance or in the vicinity."

Chesney nodded. "Tell your troops to take their positions, and have the other platoons report when they're in position, too."

In another few meters, Chesney and the platoon leader went to their bellies as well, and Chesney pulled Tristan to the ground, too. "Keep your head and your rear down."

"I know how to do it!" Tristan said. He was panting. "I hunted peimus this way on Ganwold."

It had been easier then. His shoulders and legs hadn't ached from disuse; his back and side hadn't throbbed from the pull at recent wounds. He locked his teeth and pushed himself forward.

Concealed behind the trunk of a fallen tree, the lieutenant pulled his voice pickup away from his mouth enough to say, "All platoons are in place, ma'am."

Chesney nodded. "So now the waiting begins." She passed her electrobinoculars to Tristan.

He scanned the clearing beyond, focusing on the tunnel entrance. It looked like a yawning mouth at the base of the mountain. They lay far to its left but the view of the entrance was unobstructed. Through the binoculars it seemed they were almost inside it, though it was probably fifteen meters away.

"They've got my mother in there," he said.

"Yes," said Chesney, "along with a few other people we'd like to take alive."

"What are we going to do?"

"Wait." Chesney looked across at him. "A couple of Spherzah were dropped on the mountain about the time we landed. They're going to penetrate the complex and open up that main entrance from the inside. And when they do, we're going in."

"But, my mother—"

"My people know she's in there," said Chesney. "They'll get her out."

Tristan glowered. Restless, impatient, he fidgeted with the damp soil under his hands, took up a handful and curled his fingers around it, hard.

Chesney was watching him. "Look, hotshot," she said, "this isn't a game and I didn't just send you to the bench. It's a dirty business and it costs lives. Too many of 'em. Your mother's going to be rescued. That's what counts, isn't it? A moment of glory isn't worth dying for."

Tristan looked over at her, teeth clenched. She met his look and held it, the way Pulou would have.

T'saa'chi is serious thing. Always, someone dies.

Pulou.

And Weil and Nemec.

And Larielle.

Tristan's hand curled more tightly around the ball of soil.

Is anger important enough to die for?

A sudden siren blasted through the command post and everyone stiffened. A light had begun to flash on the security monitor and the sergeant at its console spun around in his chair, his face pale in the half-light. "The controls to the main shield door are malfunctioning!" he said. "It's opening up!"

"Override!" shouted an officer, leaping toward the console. "Enter the code for override!"

The young man did. A system-failure light flashed on the console.

Thunder swelled in the passage beyond, the heavy boot-falls of masuk security troops running toward the main loading area.

Pa'an rose from the command chair, gesturing at a masuk subordinate. "Bring the woman to me," he said, and reached for the naked knife in his belt. "It is time to learn how much she is worth as a hostage."

"This is it, ma'am." The platoon leader glanced over at Chesney, touching his earphone, and gathered himself into a crouch. "Our men report deactivation of all the shield-door controls; the main entrance is opening up!"

Chesney spoke into her helmet's pickup. "Company commanders, the barricade is going down. Move in on my order, weapons set to fire. Expect return fire." She glanced at Tristan. "And you stay behind me and stay low, got that?"

He only nodded. His mouth was dry.

He could hear the scraping shriek of the shield doors retracting. The noise of it echoed between the mountain and the forest.

"Move!" Chesney said sharply, and sprang from her concealment.

Tristan cleared the log close behind her, winced at the impact of landing, and clamped a hand to his side.

Two hundred shadows emerged from the trees as if from a different dimension and swept across the clearing like tsigis in a swarm.

Chesney's platoon was the first through the tunnel entrance. Bright energy screamed at them across the dark of the loading area and soldiers on either side of Tristan went down.

The troops hit the deck, rolling for cover. Their infrared rifle sights picked out the snipers, masuk security forces crouching in the corners. Spherzah rifle fire riddled their concealment, and the platoon leaders signaled their troops to advance.

But there was movement at the tunnel's rear doors, and Chesney suddenly shouted, "Hold your fire!"

Two figures came out to the center of the loading area.

One was small, wrapped in a pale robe, fragile in the limited light and her captor's hold. The other was as dark as the cavern in which he stood, and his bared tusks gleamed like the blade that he held to his hostage's throat.

Tristan's heart contracted at the sight of his mother in the masuk's grip. "Pa'an!" he said. He turned the name into a hiss through his teeth.

Jwa'lai was important enough to die for.

TWENTY-SIX

Tristan jerked the knife from the back of Chesney's web belt and sprang past her. "Pa'an, you jou!" His voice rang across the loading area. "Let go of her!"

Pa'an's blade flicked toward the sound of the shout. "Whelp!" he said. Snarled it, and tightened his grip on Darcie.

"Let her go!" Tristan said it through locked teeth, like a gan in *tsaa'chi*. He advanced in a crouch, ready to spring.

Behind him, Chesney's marksmen raised their rifles, waiting for a clear shot.

But Pa'an took a combat stance, holding Darcie hard to himself and shifting the knife in his hand.

Destrier cleared lightskip near enough Saede for the gravity well to pull it into braking orbit. With the planet turning from lighted side to night in the forward screen, Horsch said, "Open communications with *Ouray*."

"Aye, aye, sir." The comms officer worked over her console.

In a few minutes she said, "*Ouray* reports that the attack is under way, sir. The air defense systems are down and our ground troops have penetrated the subterranean base."

"Tell them reinforcements are on the way." Lujan turned toward the lift doors off the bridge and said, "Call my landing force to the aft shuttle bay."

Tristan leaped headlong at the masuk.

Pa'an shoved Darcie away, planting his feet wide, his knife poised to impale.

Tristan shunted it aside with his own. His momentum flung them both to the floor; he turned the fall into a roll and came up on his feet. He staggered at the shock through his body and steadied himself.

They circled for a moment, testing each other with thrusts and feints. Tristan felt a rush of heat through his blood, felt his muscles loosening up. The giddiness, the shakiness passed. Baring his own teeth, he lunged at the masuk's midsection.

Pa'an pushed his blade away and snarled at him.

She had no strength left. When the masuk pushed her away, Darcie crumpled to the floor and lay still. She couldn't lift her head; she could barely breathe.

Somewhere someone shouted, "I'll watch out for this one. The rest of you, secure the base. Move it!"

Bootfalls rang up the length of the tunnel, echoed beyond the opening through which the masuk had dragged her. She heard a scuffed footstep close beside her, and firm hands raised her up. Her head sagged back, but it let air into her starving lungs. She gulped at it and gasped out, "Tristan?"

"No, Darcie." It was a woman's voice. "He's—doing all right. Lie still."

Her eyes flickered open. It was a few moments before she recognized Chesney, wearing commodore's crests. Chesney had been only a lieutenant when Darcie had seen her last.

A flash caught Darcie's focusing vision. She turned her head.

Edged steel drove at Tristan's chest. He dodged sideways, dove in under Pa'an's guard. His knife point caught in a tunic fold. The masuk roared at the slice—and smashed his arm down across Tristan's.

Fire shot through bone and nerve, convulsing Tristan's knife hand. He fumbled for his weapon, dropped to one knee to save it. And Pa'an brought his knee up sharply under Tristan's jaw.

The blow snapped him backward, sending a shock through his ribs and right side, sending his knife spinning across stone.

Pa'an planted a boot on its blade and bared his canines. "Foolish whelp!"

Stunned, Tristan stared up at a silver glint over his head. His lip streamed blood.

Pa'an's knife came down in a flashing arc.

Tristan rolled clear. Fingers scrabbled on stone, closed about the hilt of his knife. Coming to his feet, he took the masuk in a flying tackle.

Pa'an went down on his side with Tristan on top and they grappled, lethal steel gleaming centimeters from both throats.

In another moment, Tristan found himself flung onto his back with a force that winded him. Cold lightning whistled across his vision. He jerked his head away—and the dagger clinked into stone, close to his ear.

He twisted, using one leg for leverage to wrench himself over. The movement pulled at some laceration along his ribs. He ignored it. Seized Pa'an's right wrist with his left hand. . . .

Landing lights pierced the jungle like alien eyes, uncovering the landing pad concealed beneath the foliage. The shuttle hovered over it for a moment and then settled on pillars of thruster fire.

Lujan scanned the steaming growth beyond the landing circle as the hatch opened. The sky was turning pale to the east. He switched on the headset in his helmet and narrowed his eyes at what he heard.

"This way," he said, and motioned his troops to follow. "Move out."

He swung the energy rifle off his shoulder, disregarding the twinge there. The bindings were gone. The analgesic patch and regen infusion had done their work; only a little soreness remained, as if he had overworked his arm.

He moved out with the ground-consuming stride of a warrior accustomed to the forced march. Around him, the troops spread out in patrol formation and found themselves hard-pressed to keep up.

They pushed apart, came to their feet together.

Panting, trembling, Tristan locked his left hand over his right side and adjusted his grip on his knife. Sweat plastered his uniform to his flesh, smarted in myriad raw spots across his back. He circled Pa'an, watching his eyes, watching his blade.

The masuk lashed out.

The knife point caught Tristan's sleeve, ripping it to the elbow. Cold steel grazed his skin.

He staggered back, stalling for time to catch his breath, to gather a little strength.

The battle had taken them to the far end of the main cavern, and the thin, shifting veil of dust they had stirred up separated him from his mother and Chesney.

Pa'an jabbed at him; a couple of rapid feints, and Tristan dropped back, barely managing to parry.

The passage from which Pa'an had come, through which the troops had gone, loomed behind him. Pa'an was deliberately driving him toward it. Tristan tried to circle around, to maneuver away from it, to hold his ground. But the masuk countered him, lunged, and there was only one way he could evade.

In the moment that he retreated into the passage, shadows fell across the tunnel entrance.

Lujan glimpsed only Chesney at first, kneeling in the middle of the loading area and supporting someone on her arm. One of the casualties, probably; the shapes crumpled on the floor and the stench of blood and burned flesh confirmed that there were several. "Secure the area and get the medics in here," he ordered the platoon leader at his shoulder, and crossed to Chesney at once.

It wasn't a dying soldier that she held.

He sank to his knees. "Darcie."

The word was only a whisper but she lifted her gaze to his. "Lujan?" She sat up, weak but without assistance, and stretched out a hand to touch his cheek, his jaw, as if she didn't trust her eyes alone.

He couldn't speak. He cradled her face in his hands and pressed his mouth to hers.

But her eyes were clouded with fear when he drew back. "Tristan!" she whispered.

Lujan looked at Chesney.

"He went after the hairball that had her," Chesney said. "They went through the rear doors."

His jaw tightened. His eyes met Darcie's again; his fingers stroked reassurance along her face as he rose.

Tristan put out a cautious hand and touched stone: the passage turned. He shot a glance over his shoulder—caught a shadow's flicker against the dim emergency light a few meters behind him. And then nothing. Soundless on bare feet, he slipped around the corner, keeping his back to the wall, and stood still, listening.

Waiting.

In those few moments he felt how every muscle in his body ached, how his back burned, how his right side throbbed. His legs shook, supporting his weight. He slid down against the wall, into a crouch, and closed his eyes.

Then he heard the scuff of a boot upon stone. He looked up. His eyes had adjusted to the darkness; he could make out the masuk's shadow on the wall facing the turn.

He clamped his mouth closed so that Pa'an wouldn't hear the sound of his panting.

Gathered himself, as if he were stalking a peimu.

Turned the knife hilt in his hand.

Pa'an strode around the corner with his knife extended—

—and Tristan lunged up, putting all his remaining strength behind his blade.

He felt it go in upward, under the breastbone. Felt the masuk stiffen, roaring with shock and fury as he staggered back against the wall. His knife grazed Tristan's shoulder as it fell from rigid fingers.

Tristan jerked his knife from Pa'an's body. Blood spilled over his hand and spattered his uniform. His breath caught like a sob. He raised the knife—

"Tristan!"

The voice stayed his blade as abruptly as a hand on his wrist. He paused, panting hard. Lifted the knife again—

"Tristan, it's over!"

He straightened a little, shaking. Swayed on his feet. He tried to turn around—and buckled, the knife still in his grip.

Hands caught him by the shoulders, kept him from falling. The blade clattered harmless to the floor.

"It's over, son," Lujan said, quietly this time, and drew Tristan to himself with both arms.

EPILOGUE

URGENT URGENT URGENT
151809L 2 3308SY
TO CP ISSEL II
FM ASSAK SHP DEPOT, UNKAI, SAEDE
UNIFIED WORLDS FORCES HAVE ENTERED UGF. TWO
EXPLOSIONS, SEVERAL FIRES, SYSTEMS FAILING, HEAVY
CASUALTIES. SECURITY FORCES NOT SUFFICIENT. CANNOT
HOLD BASE MUCH LON S Y S T E M   F A I L U R E
S Y S T E M   F A I L U R E

Sector General Renier let the dispatch fall to the desktop. He didn't look at the messenger. Didn't speak. He just stared out through the command booth's panes at the tracking screens.

They had blacked out two hours earlier.

After several minutes he rose, slowly, stiffly, and left the command post.

He entered his office alone and closed its doors before he crossed to his desk.

There was a sidearm in one compartment. He took it out and adjusted its setting with hands that shook. It would be swifter than death at the hands of the masuki.

He was the only one who heard its single shot.

ABOUT THE AUTHOR

Originally from Smithfield, Utah, Diann Thornley now lives in Ohio, where she was stationed during her active-duty career in the U.S. Air Force. She has also lived in Texas and the Republic of Korea, courtesy of the Air Force. Now a member of the Air Force Reserves, she is still fascinated with high-performance aircraft (both U.S. and foreign) and anything related to medicine. She has completed her second and third novels, for Tor Books, and is currently working on a fourth, also set in the Unified Worlds universe. Her short fiction has been published in *The Leading Edge* magazine and in a 1993 anthology entitled *Washed by a Wave of Wind*.